WITCH'S PYRE

THE
WORLDWALKER
TRILOGY

TRIAL BY FIRE

FIREWALKER

WITCH'S PYRE

BOOK THREE OF THE
WORLDWALKER TRILOGY

WITCH'S PYRE

JOSEPHINE ANGELINI

FEIWEL AND FRIENDS
NEW YORK

A Feiwel and Friends Book
An Imprint of Macmillan

Our books may be purchased in bulk for promotional, educational, or business use.
Please contact your local bookseller or the Macmillan Corporate and Premium Sales
Department at (800) 221-7945 ext. 5442 or by e-mail at
MacmillanSpecialMarkets@macmillan.com.

Library of Congress Cataloging-in-Publication Data is available.

ISBN 978-1-250-05091-5 (hardcover) / ISBN 978-1-250-10531-8 (ebook)

Necklace design © 2015 by Mandy Pursley with Forever Faire Designs

Feiwel and Friends logo designed by Filomena Tuosto

First Edition—2016

1   3   5   7   9   10   8   6   4   2

fiercereads.com

To my husband, my newborn,
and Nespresso . . .
Thank you.

CHAPTER
1

LILY PROCTOR WAS NOT ASLEEP. SHE WASN'T UNCONSCIOUS or dreaming, nor had she accidentally slipped into another universe. She was here, she was alive, and for good or for bad, she was in charge. She had to keep telling herself that or she knew she'd fall apart completely. To stay calm, Lily quickly listed off the things she knew to be true.

The last thing she remembered was fighting the Hive somewhere in the center of the North American continent. In her version of the world, that meant somewhere out on the prairies of Kansas. But in this world, the center of the continent was an uncharted area, long abandoned to a little-known and nearly mythical subspecies of the Woven called the Hive.

Lily and her small band of braves had lost the battle; nearly all of those who had followed Lily west had lost their lives. The few that had survived had been anesthetized by the Hive, rather than killed, and brought to an enormous field that lay outside the gates of a city, all the way across the continent on the western coastline. Above the main gate was a large inscription, declaring that this place was Bower City. It was a city that Lily knew shouldn't exist.

Lily also knew that Tristan, *her* Tristan, was dead. He had died fighting the Hive. She got stuck inside that thought, unable to go forward or backward. All she could do was stare at the city walls in front of her and repeat it in her head. *Tristan is dead. And he's dead because of me.*

"Lily?"

Lily turned around at the sound of her name and tried to discern who had spoken to her. Standing in a vast field of flowers that surrounded Bower City for miles were Juliet, Caleb, Breakfast, Una, and the other Tristan. They were all she had left. Everyone else had either abandoned her or died on the Trail of Tears. Even Rowan had betrayed her and left her to starve in a cage. A cage that Tristan—Lily's Tristan—had somehow broken. Tristan had saved her from Rowan. He'd saved her and now he was dead.

"Lily?" the other, and now only, Tristan repeated.

His clothes were in tatters, and his eyes were wet with tears and rimmed with red. He felt the loss of his other self deeply, but he didn't feel it the same way that Lily did. He wasn't responsible for it the way Lily was.

"What do you want to do?" Tristan asked as she stared at him blankly.

The place high up inside her chest, just below the U-shaped divot at the bottom of her throat, was rubbed raw with held-back sobs. She couldn't give in to her grief, not now, so she floated above it, her sadness burrowing deeper and deeper inside like a swallowed splinter.

Lily looked down at the bees flitting around the flowers at her feet, trying to reattach herself to the moment. Her ears buzzed and she couldn't tell if the sound came from outside her head or inside it. She stared at the bees, wondering whether they were natural or the

Worker members of the Hive. Workers looked the same as regular bees, and there was something about that—their seemingly innocuous appearance—that made them more disturbing than if they were monstrous.

"They didn't kill us," Lily said, not answering Tristan's question. "The Hive."

"It's been said the Warrior Sisters sometimes carry people off," Caleb said, referring to the terrifying half-human, half-bee members of the Hive. Warrior Sisters were over seven feet tall, covered in a plated exoskeleton hard as armor, and they fought with barb-tipped whips that they coated with powerful venom milked from their own stingers. "Maybe this is where they take their captives," Caleb finished in a hushed tone, as if simply mentioning the Warrior Sisters could conjure them.

"We must have been unconscious for days," Una added, scanning the skies. "There's no way they could have flown us from where we were to the West Coast in less time than that."

Lily nodded vaguely at Una's logic. Her mouth was dry and coated with the bitter residue of a drug-sleep. She focused her witch's sense on traces of the chemical cocktail still left in her bloodstream from the Hive's stings and decided that it could have kept them unconscious for days. It was an ingenious substance, and Lily's wandering mind wondered whether something so elegant could have evolved naturally. She also wondered at the intelligence of a creature that could choose to kill some and kidnap others, and supply the proper venom to do either as it saw fit.

"Where are you going?" Juliet called out in a shrill voice. She raced to catch up with Lily and took her sister by the arm. Stopped short, Lily realized she had been staggering toward the city gate.

"In there, I guess," Lily replied, shrugging. "It's not like we have many options."

Juliet looked over Lily's shoulder at Caleb. "She's in shock," she told him.

"I think we all are," Breakfast added quietly. "Let's take a second and think this through before we go marching into some strange place."

Lily felt Juliet lead her back to the group. Her hands stung at Juliet's touch and she shied away. Lily's palms were only half healed from gripping the burning ground. She licked her cracked lips and imagined she could still taste the smoke and dirt of the prairie as the wildfire blazed around her. She recalled digging her fingers into the ground to anchor herself against the witch wind and dragging herself forward as the fire line moved, one agonizing fistful of burning ground at time.

"Here," Tristan said, reaching into the mechanic's pack that was still strapped across his back. "I have salve. I think I do, anyway."

Lily couldn't look him in the eye. As he cupped her hands in his and dabbed at her red and broken skin she fought the urge to pull away from him. *He's not my Tristan,* she reminded herself.

They all took a moment to tend to their injuries with Tristan's salve, although everyone seemed to be on the mend already.

"Whatever the Hive injected into us must have had an antibiotic in it," Tristan said. He paused to look at his own arms and hands, which were only slightly burned, his face twisting with puzzlement. "But even still. Considering we were fighting *inside* the fire, you'd think our injuries would be much worse."

"I thought we were dead when Lily's wildfire caught up with us," Caleb added. "But it only killed the Hive. Not us. How'd that happen?"

"I did something to you," Lily admitted. "Directed the energy. I don't really know what I did."

"Could you do it again?" Una asked, dabbing at herself with salve.

"Because it came in handy. Killed a ton of the Workers and left us barely singed."

Lily tried to recall exactly what she'd done, but all she knew for certain was that she had broken her promise. She'd possessed her mechanics and had become something different. An Us or a We. And when members of the We had died, a part of her had died with them. Lily felt the holes in her still, like the bleeding gaps left by knocked-out teeth that she couldn't stop probing with her tongue. The biggest and most painful was Tristan-shaped.

He should be getting ready to go to Harvard right now. But instead he's dead.

"I don't know. I don't know exactly what I did," Lily mumbled, not wanting to examine the episode anymore. Luckily, they either hadn't felt her possess them in the chaos of the fight, or they hadn't figured it out yet. Lily hoped they never did.

Lily looked at Juliet, who was regarding her with a furrowed brow. "What?" Lily asked defensively.

"I've spent my whole life around witches and I've never heard of anyone doing that before," Juliet replied. "You said you were directing the energy inside of them, not just giving it to them. It's as if you could control—" Juliet broke off with a frown and didn't continue.

"Control what?" Lily asked, but Juliet shook her head, dismissing the thought. Lily let it go because she didn't want Juliet, or any of them, to think about it too deeply. Caleb, especially. Lily knew he, out of all of them, would never forgive her for possessing him if he ever figured it out, and she couldn't lose him, too. She couldn't bear to lose anyone else. A desperate, clawing panic started to rise up in Lily's chest. She cast her eyes up and tried to breathe.

How could I have done this? How could I have put them all in so much danger?

You had no choice, came the answer. Lillian was there with Lily, sharing the echoing loneliness of her head.

Help me. I feel like I'm drowning, Lily replied. She looked around her, stiff as a statue. *How long have you been with me?*

Since you woke. You were reaching out, Lillian told her. Lily could feel Lillian's shock at the view they were sharing. *What are you going to do?*

Lily turned toward the city. "We only have two choices," she said. "Go into the city, or not. I have no idea what to do."

Her coven shot one another looks, obviously exchanging mindspeak.

"You're not yourself," Caleb said gently. "Each of us has tried to connect with you in mindspeak and it's like hitting a brick wall. You've totally shut us out."

As she considered it, Lily realized that she had been feeling her claimed brushing up against her mind, asking for entry, but she'd been blocking them out subconsciously. She didn't want anyone inside her mind, no one but someone who was as culpable as she was. The enormity of what Lily had done hung like a sword over her head, and only Lillian knew what that was like. Only Lillian had sent people she'd loved to their deaths.

How do you keep it from eating you up?

You don't, Lillian replied. *Let it eat you, and be grateful for the pain. If it goes away, then you know you're dead inside.*

Lily didn't feel pain. She didn't feel anything. She was numb, her head full of white noise to drown out the shouting inside. As soon as she named the numbness it went away, and hatred bubbled in her throat. Hatred for herself so thick and dark it was like drinking tar.

I can't do this.

Yes, you can. You can because you must, Lillian replied. *I'm here. I understand what it's like to wake up changed.*

"Lily?" Juliet said, moving toward her with an outstretched hand. "Say something."

Every choice I make gets someone killed. I don't want to make any more, Lily thought. *I'm stuck.*

Doing nothing isn't an option, Lillian said. *You had to be ruthless when the Hive came for you, even with Tristan. He died to protect you and the rest of the coven.*

No. He died because he wasn't ready for the burden I put on him. He never should have been in this world.

You're past that. What's done is done. All that matters is the task at hand, the city in front of you, and what you're going to do about it. Don't waste Tristan's sacrifice. Swallow your guilt and get moving.

"Eyes up. Someone's coming," Una said sharply.

The coven turned and saw a small party approaching from the direction of the city gates.

"Do we have any weapons?" Caleb asked, his hand going to the empty sheath hanging from his belt. Tristan's arm flexed to look for his knife as well, and he shook his head at Caleb, his eyes anxious.

"Easy, boys. We've still got our witch," Una said after coming up empty for weapons herself. She turned to Lily. "How much juice you got left?"

Lily grimaced. "Nothing," she replied. "I need salt."

"They might be peaceful," Juliet said optimistically. Everyone looked at Juliet sideways.

"Because peace is something we've had so much of since coming to this world," Breakfast groused.

"There's no reason to go on the defensive. It's not like they're charging toward us with weapons drawn," Juliet persisted, squinting in the direction of the approaching group.

Juliet. Always making the best of a terrible situation, Lillian whispered to Lily.

Yes, Lily agreed, feeling something beginning to thaw inside her as she watched this other version of her sister.

Juliet smoothed her charred linen shirt, tucking its tattered hem into her dusty wearhyde riding pants. She squared her narrow shoulders, making Lily smile. Juliet never looked more delicate than when she was trying to look tough. "Let me handle this," Juliet said confidently.

Caleb looked like he wanted to argue, and Lily realized that if she was going to lead this coven, she had to start taking control—first and foremost, of herself.

Lillian. I need to allow my coven in, so you must leave me now or they may sense you in my mind. I'll reach out to you again when I can.

Yes, Lillian agreed. *We both have a lot of work to do.*

Lily caught the edge of Lillian's cold determination as they stared at the emissaries from the foreign city before Lillian severed contact. Lily turned her attention to her coven and reached out to Caleb in mindspeak.

Let Juliet speak to them, Caleb. She's a lot less threatening than you.

She's a lot less threatening than a kitten. And I wouldn't send either to meet a bunch of strangers.

Caleb shot Lily a half smile, and she felt him relax some.

As the foreigners approached, it was clear that they were not hostile. The two women and two men who approached were unarmed. They were dressed in flowing kimonos or tunics and adorned with jewelry. They joined Lily's coven with concerned looks on their faces.

"Do any of you need medical attention?" asked the handsome woman who seemed to lead the party.

She's an Outlander, Caleb whispered in Lily's head. *But her paint is from no tribe I know.*

The woman's face, hands, and bare shoulders were decorated

8

with painted stripes and dots. She was in her late twenties and had the kind of cut-glass features that would only look more attractive as she aged. Strands of her silky black hair were braided with multicolored thread and eagle feathers, and her arms jingled with gold bangles. Lily noticed that the brief kimono she wore was made of silk. She couldn't recall seeing anyone else in this world wearing silk before. Lily's eyes went to the smoke-colored willstone around the woman's neck and stayed there. It was not as large as Lily's smoke stone, but it was onyx black. She felt Tristan brush against her mind and allowed him entry.

That's the darkest willstone I've ever seen, Lily. It's even darker than Una's. Warrior black.

What do you mean, warrior black?

Just keep your guard up, Tristan, because trust me—this witch can fight.

Lily had a theory about willstones that wasn't common knowledge, not even among highly trained mechanics like Tristan. Having three willstones, one of every color, had given Lily a unique understanding of how they worked and she'd noticed that each of her willstones seemed to be better suited to different types of magic. Her medium-size pink stone seemed to glow brightest when she performed healer magic. The small golden stone excelled at kitchen magic. It was Lily's smoke stone, the largest and most powerful of her willstones, that came to life when she performed warrior magic. Lily quickly hid her pink and golden stones but allowed her larger, if not quite as dark, smoke-colored willstone to show on her breastbone.

"None of us are seriously hurt," Juliet said cordially in reply to the strange witch's question. Juliet's eyes narrowed at the woman's stone as she noticed it, and she smiled broadly to cover her hesitation. "But we need water . . . and salt for our witch."

Juliet stepped aside to give the strangers a clear view of Lily, flanked on either side by Una, Breakfast, and Tristan, with giant Caleb looming behind her.

Nice one, Juliet.

Just a little reminder that we aren't completely helpless, Lily. I hope you don't mind.

Of course not.

"Certainly," the foreign witch replied unflinchingly. Her eyes skipped to Lily's willstone and away again as if the huge jewel were of little notice. She waved a hand and the three people accompanying her stepped forward with brightly glazed ceramic jugs of water. "My name is Grace Bendingtree. I'm the governor of Bower City. Welcome."

"Thank you, Governor Bendingtree," Juliet replied in a voice that even the smoothest politician would envy. "We're honored to meet you."

"Please, call me Grace. We don't stand on ceremony here," she said with a wide smile as she watched Lily's party drink thirstily.

"I'm Juliet Proctor. This is my sister, Lily, and her mechanics— Caleb, Tristan, Una, and Stuart."

They tipped their heads in greeting as their names were spoken and Grace faced each in turn, meeting their eyes with an open and accepting gaze.

"Welcome," Grace repeated warmly. "You look like you could all use some food and a lot of rest."

"Thank you," Juliet said, accepting the governor's invitation. For just a moment, Juliet's brow creased, and if Lily didn't know her every expression so well she would have missed the apprehension she saw there. "Is it the custom here for the governor to risk coming outside the walls to welcome everyone into the city?"

"When they arrive as you did, definitely," Grace said with laugh. Her three attendants nodded hesitantly. Their confused faces made it apparent that this must have been such an unusual situation that they barely knew how to react.

"It's so rare that the Hive brings anyone anymore, and even rarer that those people survive," Grace continued sadly. "You must be very strong." She addressed them all, but her dark eyes lingered the longest on Lily, and softened as if she knew that Lily was suffering. "And as for the risk of coming out from behind the walls—you'll see for yourself that things are quite different here from what you're used to."

Grace gestured for Lily to walk beside her, but Lily deferred and urged Juliet to take the lead. Lily wanted to observe without having to think of something to say.

"Are these your mechanics?" Juliet asked politely, tipping her chin in the direction of Grace's silent attendants.

Grace frowned. "We don't have mechanics here," she said, her tone chilly.

"Pardon me," Juliet apologized, taken aback. "Have I offended you in some way?"

Grace's smile was brittle. "I know that you are from the east and that you do things differently there, but we don't claim people in Bower City." Grace cast her eyes back at Lily's mechanics, looking as if she pitied them. "And it might be better not to talk too much about your . . . situation . . . with others while you are here."

Lily and Una exchanged a look.

"We'll be discreet, if that's your wish," Juliet said. "But may I ask why it's such an issue?"

"I guess there's no way to be delicate about this," Grace said plainly. "We consider claiming mechanics a form of slavery, and owning another person is a crime here."

Lily opened her mouth to argue, but Juliet waved her protestations away. This was not the time to get into an argument about whether or not claiming someone was the same as ownership.

"But how do witches perform magic without mechanics?" Caleb asked.

Grace stopped and turned to face him. "Witches, crucibles—and yes, even mechanics—can heal, create energy to power a city, and make products that the people need without anyone having to claim anyone else. There's only one form of magic a witch truly needs a vessel for. Warrior magic. And we don't think people should die because witches can't control their lust for battle."

"That's very noble," Tristan said with a raised eyebrow, "but how to do you defend yourselves without warriors?"

"We don't," Grace said simply. "Something else does that for us."

They had come close enough to the city to see through the main gate. Grace turned to it now, directing their attention to the city beyond. Before Lily could get a clear look, Tristan's arm shot out, barring Lily from going any farther. As he pulled her up into his arms and turned to bolt, she could feel fear and confusion ringing through Una, Caleb, and Breakfast, their mindspeak coming at her in a jumble.

Run!

It doesn't make any sense . . .

Get her out of here, Tristan!

Over Tristan's shoulder, Lily was just able to make out Warrior Sisters hovering around the entrance, their whips hanging ready by their sides.

CHAPTER
2

HER VIEW OF SKY AND FLOWERS JOSTLED CHAOTICALLY AS Tristan thundered toward what looked like a stand of trees rimming the horizon, but no matter how hard Tristan ran, the trees didn't seem to come any closer.

"It's too far!" she yelled. Tristan only dropped his head and ran harder.

Lily looked over his shoulder and saw one of the emissaries catching up to Tristan. He was waving his arms over his head and shouting, "Wait!"

Tristan wasn't waiting. But there was something about the emissary that made Lily beat against Tristan's chest, some combination of surprise and openness that made her believe that there was more to this situation than peril.

"Tristan, stop," she yelled. "Let's talk to them, at least."

Tristan finally slowed to a stop. Lily slid out of his arms, avoiding his eyes. She watched the emissary instead.

He was about Tristan's height, but his build was less bulky and his bone structure much lighter. He had black hair and eyes, and Asian features, although Lily couldn't quite place his heritage. She guessed he was only a few years older than they were. The emissary wisely came to a halt several paces away from Tristan.

"I know it's a shock, but please come back and let us explain about the Hive," he said in a thoroughly rational tone. "I promise no harm will come to you."

Tristan hesitated, but Lily stepped forward, avoiding contact with him. "Let's at least hear them out," she said, still not looking at him. "Not like we've got any other choice."

They followed the emissary back to the group and Grace explained the strange arrangement between the people of Bower City and the Hive. For over a hundred years the Hive had been "choosing" people, flying them to the coast as they had with Lily and her mechanics, and leaving them there. The Hive had allowed those chosen humans to build a city and go about their lives as long as they did so in a diligent and orderly fashion. "That's all they want?" Caleb asked, sneering his disbelief. "Order?"

"I swear it," Grace replied. She gestured down to the bright blossoms at her feet. "They don't even demand that we maintain these fields of flowers to provide them with food. We do it voluntarily. It's our gift to them for giving us so much."

Lily looked around at her coven, silently asking them what they thought.

"They're right there," Una said, gesturing toward the Warrior Sisters hovering around the gate. "They could have killed us at any time."

"She's right," Breakfast said, backing her up.

Tristan nodded reluctantly, but Caleb was the hardest to convince. Lily could feel his hatred for the Hive, and for all Woven, like a hard lump inside of him—an infection that had calcified. She couldn't blame him. The Woven had killed most of the people he'd ever known.

Where else are we going to go? Lily asked him in mindspeak.

I don't like it. There's something off about all of this, Caleb replied.

I don't like it either, Lily replied. Then she shrugged a defeated shoulder and followed Grace, who was leading the rest of her coven toward the walled city.

Skittish as a herd of spooked horses, Lily and her coven had to pass under an arch of hovering Warrior Sisters in order to enter Bower City. The hum of their wings puckered her skin and sent bolts of static down her legs. Lily looked up. The Sisters' black-faceted eyes glinted with oil-slick rainbows and their bulbous heads twitched lightning fast atop their long stalk necks. They looked back down at her, and Lily couldn't tell what they thought or felt—or if they thought or felt anything at all.

"It's okay. Really," Grace soothed. "The Hive craves order above all things and, if you behave peacefully, they won't bother you. All we need to live in harmony with them is to live in harmony with one another."

Caleb didn't argue entering the city, but as they walked through the gates, he couldn't help but comment. "Harmony," he whispered as he ducked under the dangling tips of a Warrior Sister's cat-o'-nine-tails whip. "You sure they're not tone-deaf?"

Lily curled up a cheek in a wry half smile, thinking that Caleb had struck on what was bothering her about them. The Sisters may have some of the physical attributes of people, but there was something distinctly alien about them. Lily couldn't read emotion in them, nor could she imagine them understanding and enjoying something as fundamentally human as music.

When Lily got her first good look at the inside of Bower City, she had the nagging feeling she'd been there before. The brightly painted buildings were topped with terra-cotta roofs, and every windowsill and trellis spilled over with flowers. Blossoms dripped from every gable, and the pristine streets were edged not with grass, but with carpets of wildflowers. Even the trees that lined the street—each housed in its own enormous pot—were of the flowering kind, and the air tasted bittersweet with pollen.

"Do you like our city?" Grace asked after an appropriately long pause.

"It's so"—Una looked around, her face puckered with confusion—"clean," she finished.

Grace laughed—a throaty, warm sound—and flashed her straight white teeth. "I told you. Order. Symmetry. Peace. The Hive is diligent about keeping things neat, to the benefit of all who live under them."

Looking down at cobbled streets that were so spotless she reckoned she could eat off of them, Lily couldn't find one thing that was out of place. Not a hinge on the cheerful shutters leaked a red stain of rust. No flaking paint or loose tiles on any of the vaguely Italian-villa-style houses. Everything was picture perfect.

"Like Disneyland," Breakfast muttered.

"Exactly," Lily agreed, nodding. That explained her déjà vu. She stifled a memory of singing animatronic dolls before she got that saccharine tune stuck in her head. She hated Disneyland.

"Except with a vaguely Mediterranean flair instead of storybook-Swiss-chalet," Breakfast added.

"I wonder where we are, exactly."

Breakfast shrugged. "Somewhere between San Francisco and LA, I'm guessing. Where all the farms and vineyards are."

Tristan gave Lily and Breakfast a puzzled look, and Lily averted her eyes and shook her head as if to say that it didn't matter. He seemed entranced with Bower City, and Lily had to agree it was a beautiful place. Even the sunshine seemed, well, *shinier* than it did back east.

As they threaded their way through the grid system of the streets, Lily saw open-air trolleys gliding soundlessly up and down the center of the road. People wearing brightly dyed tunics and kimonos hopped on and off the rail system with ease, the men's voluminous capes and women's silk ribbons trailing behind them. If the beautifully attired and heavily perfumed citizens thought anything was odd about the bedraggled appearance of Lily's coven, they hid it well.

Questioning glances were quickly followed by averted eyes as the busy people went about their day. Occasionally, Lily would catch a glimpse of a Warrior Sister perched high on top of a building, but they seemed to stay away from street level. They were there, though. Lily could feel their presence echoing down the scrubbed streets, like the mounting pressure of a storm that had yet to break.

Lily wondered how large the city was. She glanced up the street, but couldn't see an edge to it. She noticed that the grid system curved ever so gently in a pleasing fashion, rather than adhering to boxy ninety-degree angles. It struck Lily as being a more organic, although still highly structured, way of building a city. Rather like a honeycomb.

"Is anyone tired? Do you need to rest?" Grace asked.

Lily shook her head. She just wanted them to get wherever it was they were going so she could be alone for a few moments. Her frustration passed to Juliet.

I think she's taking us the scenic route, Juliet said in mindspeak.

I have a feeling this whole city is the scenic route, Lily replied.

After a few more minutes of striding by manicured buildings and down immaculate streets, they came to a large plaza with a huge fountain in the center. Skirting around the plaza were a number of gracefully columned buildings, the largest of which had a sprawling staircase. Many groups of people stood on the steps, talking in clusters.

"This is our Forum," Grace told them. "Where we make government policy. Or try to, at any rate. Mostly we just argue."

All eyes seemed to turn toward them and conversations stopped as they entered the plaza. Grace led the newcomers up the grand staircase, and as they passed, the chatter struck up again in urgent undertones. Lily nodded to herself, finally understanding why Grace had chosen to walk a bunch of battle-weary, shocked, and grieving people through the city. She and her coven were on parade. This wasn't about them. It was for the people of Bower City.

Lily glanced up and tried to make eye contact with the members of the closest cluster, but they all looked away nervously. They were playacting. Pretending that this was just another day, but their forced nonchalance carried more tension than if they had gathered around, pointing and staring.

Grace and her attendants brought the coven through a forest of marble columns, and into a huge domed room. It was a colossal building, something that belonged on top of a hill in Italy or Greece.

Lily craned her neck to look up at the oculus in the center of the dome, which flooded the room with air and sunlight. Something large flew past, sending a swift shadow across the gleaming marble floor. The faintest hum followed, tickling the back of Lily's neck.

They're watching us, Una said in mindspeak.

Lily nodded, and glanced at Caleb, who was eyeing the oculus warily.

"This is the Governor's Hearing Hall," Grace told them.

"Nice office, Gracie," Breakfast muttered under his breath. The acoustics of the room amplified his voice, and his mutter came out loud and clear to everyone in the room. Breakfast cringed.

"And we call it the Hearing Hall because you can hear even the slightest whisper," she continued, smiling at him. "So even the smallest voice matters."

They crossed the circular expanse of the Hearing Hall and went through one of three doors that were evenly spaced along the curved back wall. They walked down a long hallway, through another door, and into a private home.

Finally, Juliet said. The rest of the coven echoed her relief.

"You're welcome to stay with me for as long as you like," Grace said as she led them into a palatial living space. "I'll give you a chance to clean up and rest, and we'll speak later."

"Thank you," Lily replied, finally stepping forward to stand next to her sister.

"My pleasure," Grace said, and left them with one of her emissaries.

It was the same young man who had chased after her and Tristan. He stepped forward and smiled at her. Now that they were no longer running for their lives, Lily couldn't help but notice that he was extremely attractive.

"We have two rooms ready for you upstairs, if you'll follow me," he said in a pleasing voice.

"I didn't catch your name," Lily said, looking at his willstone. It was a deep rose color—almost burgundy. *He's a healer,* she thought. *A powerful one.*

"My name is Toshi Konishi," he replied. "And I'm up here," he said, pointing to his face. Lily tore her gaze off his willstone and met his amused eyes, her face flushing.

"Sorry," she stammered, "I'm just surprised by the color of your willstone. Is it common here for a rose stone to be so pigmented?"

"No," Toshi replied. A slow smile crept up his face as he held Lily's eyes. "Bedrooms," he said, turning suddenly, "are this way. We've readied one apartment for the men and one for the women, but you're welcome to make your own adjustments to the sleeping arrangement as you like."

Toshi pushed the doors open to the first suite of rooms and revealed a common area with deep-seated leather club chairs and furniture made of dark, glossy wood.

Lily and her coven looked at the wealth and comfort around them blankly.

"The two sitting rooms are connected," Toshi said, leading the girls through the man cave and opening up a set of double doors.

The girls' sitting room had a large white couch and a velvet settee, and it was made bright and airy by a large balcony and many fresh flower arrangements.

"Your rooms are on the other side," Toshi told them. A worried frown creased his forehead as he registered the listless expressions around him. "Is this arrangement not to your liking? If you don't find the rooms suitable, just let me know what you require."

"They're lovely. We've been traveling for a long time," Lily said in explanation. "And we've lost . . . a lot."

"I'm sorry," Toshi replied, his concern deepening. "I'm sure you need your rest. What you've done—just getting here—it's amazing."

Lily's head filled with the mountains they'd climbed, the rivers they'd crossed, and the lives that she had lost along the way. She smiled at Toshi uncomfortably and went out onto the balcony as her coven broke away from one another silently and went off to be by themselves. Lily took a deep breath. A wisteria vine framed the wrought-iron casement and spilled over the railing like lavender locks of hair tumbling down a woman's shoulder.

She felt Toshi join her on the veranda. "I mean it," he said softly. "What you've accomplished is nothing short of a miracle. Those you've lost would be proud to see that at least you made it."

Lily didn't turn to look at him. She thought of Tristan's body lying somewhere in a burnt-out field, probably already rotting in the sun, and wanted to say that pride had nothing to do with it. *I did that,* she thought.

Lily trained her dry, staring eyes on the city that rolled out in front of her. Like a patchwork quilt, interlocking blocks of color were saved from looking too busy by the orderliness of the pattern, and beyond the bright blanket that was Bower City, Lily saw a ribbon of sparkling blue.

"The ocean," she whispered.

"I can take you there if you'd like," he offered carefully.

Lily kept her attention on the view, neither accepting nor declining his offer. "Are those *ships*?" she asked, squinting into the distance.

"Yes."

Lily turned to face him. "From where?"

"All over," he said, shrugging. He suddenly understood. "The east is cut off from the rest of the world because of the Woven plague. No other countries will risk contamination through contact with you, but there's no chance of that with Bower City." His brow creased with a thought. "There are restrictions, of course, and immigration is carefully watched, but we trade with the rest of the world."

"Carefully watched by who?" Lily could feel heat rising to her cheeks. She gritted her teeth, resisting the urge to scream.

"The Hive," he said. "The Hive watches over everything in Bower City." Toshi's worried frown was back. "I should warn you to watch you temper. They react strongly to anger."

Lily looked down at the purple blossoms surrounding her. The bees buzzing in and out of them began turning their attention from the flowers to Lily. More came. Toshi didn't notice, but one had landed on his sleeve. Lily pointed at it.

"Careful," she warned.

Toshi didn't even look. "You don't have to fear being stung

accidentally. As long as you don't attack them, they'll leave you alone. But you must try and maintain a calm demeanor here in Bower City."

Lily moved her elbows away from the wisteria. "And if you step on one?"

"They're smarter than that," he assured her. "I've lived here my whole life and they've never stung me."

Lily relaxed a little, and then considered that maybe she shouldn't. Watching the Worker go back to picking her way through the petals was not reassuring. They were always there. Always watching. No matter how much she wanted to find a room, lock the door, and start crying and throwing things at the wall, she couldn't. She had to remain "calm."

For all the fresh air, this place is more suffocating than the oubliette, she said in mindspeak to Lillian.

When she looked up again, Lily noticed that Toshi was standing very close to her. He seemed to notice it, too, and jerked away from her, embarrassed.

"Well, I'm sure you're tired," he said, taking his leave. "Would you like me to send up some food now?"

"Yes. Please," Lily said, following him back inside. "And thank you, Toshi."

He opened the door and paused before going through it. When he looked back at Lily he seemed surprised. "It was my pleasure," he said, and then left.

Lily stayed at the closed door, replaying the conversation in her head.

"Thinking of adding him to your collection?" Tristan asked. His hair was still wet from a shower and he was dressed in one of the silk tunics the men here wore, the laces at his wrists still undone. He looked furious.

"No! I was—he was—" Lily stammered. "It's not my fault."

"Forget it," he said, turning away in a huff and going back to his room.

"And I don't have a collection!" Lily called after him.

She heard him shout, "I said forget it!" from deep within the other apartment and sighed.

Caleb came through the adjoining doors, cringing at Tristan's wake. "That could have gone better," he said.

"It's not my fault," Lily repeated.

"It's a weird witch-mechanic thing. I know that," Caleb replied. "Tristan does, too. He's just angry that the line to you got longer."

"There's no line," Lily argued, but Caleb continued as if he didn't hear her.

"Don't worry about Tristan. He's just mad at you because it's a convenient distraction. It's easier to be angry at you than to be sad about, well, everything."

"Not here it isn't," Lily said, noticing that more Workers were coming in through the window. She pointed it out to Caleb and told him how the Hive had reacted when she'd started to feel anger.

They can feel our emotions? Caleb looked disturbed.

I doubt that, but they can certainly sense them somehow, she replied. *And they don't allow anger. Tristan's blocking me. Tell him to calm down and show him why.*

Caleb took a moment to converse with Tristan in mindspeak, and then turned back to her. *I really hate this place.*

Get ready to hate it some more.

Lily brought Caleb out onto the balcony and showed him the ships in the harbor. She told him they were from all around world and watched as he stared at them, his breath stalled in his chest and his jaw lax with surprise. His eyes flew out over the water as he imagined other countries, other continents—all of them Woven-free.

"How does Bower City keep the Woven from contaminating

other countries?" he asked. "Because all you need is one to climb inside a crate that gets loaded on a ship——"

"The Hive," Lily replied. "I'm pretty sure that, apart from them, there are no Woven out west. I don't think they let anything past them, maybe as far to the east as where they picked us up. That's about halfway."

"No Woven over half of the continent," he whispered. It was almost too much for him to accept. "How could we not know that?"

The Workers had settled down after Tristan's outburst. They went back to gathering nectar, buzzing in and out of the wisteria, their brightly striped bodies weighing down the blossoms.

Toshi mentioned "restrictions" on immigration, Lily told him in mindspeak. *If the Hive only allows a few people to come to the city, I doubt it lets many out.*

Caleb's eyes angled up the edge of their roof as a Sister escaped out of his line of sight. *Many——or any?* he asked.

We'll see.

A porter arrived with a rolling cart piled high with food, drawing Lily and Caleb back inside. The smell of hot food drew the rest of the coven out of their beds and baths and into Lily's sitting room. While they passed plates around, Lily shared in mindspeak what she had learned from Toshi.

Una eyed the nearest flower arrangement warily and saw a Worker waddle out of the wide throat of a bloom. She elbowed Lily and tipped her chin at it.

Lily gave a faint nod and stood. They'd been sitting there silently for too long. "I think I'm the only one who hasn't had a bath yet," she said.

Converse out loud, but be careful, she told her coven in mindspeak. *I don't know how much the Workers can or can't understand and I don't want the Hive to know anything private about us——especially not about where*

24

Breakfast, Una, and I come from. As far as anyone in Bower City is concerned, we come from this *world.*

Does that include Toshi? Tristan asked in mindspeak.

Lily didn't bother to respond. She knew he was fishing for something to feel other than sad, and he needed someone to blame. It wasn't helping matters that Lily couldn't look him in the eye. Not yet. Not so soon after.

She went through to the bedrooms and found that Juliet and Una had left her the largest room, and understood why when she studied the flower arrangements. The bouquets were made up exclusively of every different kind of lily that Lily could recognize. Her smile at Una's and Juliet's sweet gesture to leave this room for her turned hesitant as she considered whether or not their host's flower choice had been intentional or coincidental. Lilies are commonly used in arrangements, so it wouldn't be a stretch of the imagination to think that this was just a happy accident. More to the point, there was no way anyone in Bower City could have known Lily's name ahead of time. Still, it nagged at her.

Lily undressed self-consciously while she filled the generous soaking tub. One of the casement windows had been left slightly ajar and a tall glass vase held a bunch of enormous, long-stemmed tiger lilies by the full-length mirror. Lily couldn't see them, but she knew the Workers were there, free to come and go out the open window.

The bath soap she drizzled into the water was so heavily perfumed it made Lily sneeze. The scent was lovely, but so concentrated she knew that her skin would smell like it for the rest of the day.

Either the Workers liked it, or it made the people easier for the Hive to track. Either way, Lily found herself unable to enjoy it knowing that it was, somehow, for the Hive.

As she soaked, Lily watched as the last of the burns on her hands faded away. She looked more carefully at the decanter of soap, and saw that it contained a strange chemical that was almost like the burn salve, but that she had never encountered before. The water grew cold as she tried to pick its composition apart with what she had learned of medicines. The most she could discern was that it had regenerative properties. She was so engrossed in trying to figure it out she nearly called out for Rowan to come and take a look. The thought of him stopped her breath, and she dropped the image of him as if it had stung her.

He betrayed me.

Lillian was listening. The memory of Rowan taking her willstones and locking her in a cage flew from Lily's mind to Lillian's.

He didn't want you to turn into me, Lillian replied. *After what I did to him, can you blame him?*

Lillian shared a memory of her own . . .

. . . I can hear Rowan coming down the hallway. Gavin is trying to stop him, but it's like a sparrow trying to distract a bull. I'm aching to see him, and I dread it. All I want is to be held and comforted, healed and cared for by Rowan. But he can never touch me again or he'll see. He already knows something's wrong because he keeps reaching out to me and I won't let him in my mind. If I let him touch me, he'll see the illness I brought back from the cinder world, and there's no way I'll be able to keep the whole story from him. No way I'll be able to hide what happened in the barn.

He bursts through the door, his riding clothes still travel stained from the Outlands. He's been looking for me since I disappeared three weeks ago and his eyes are tired and his skin is pale with worry. He's gorgeous. My throat closes and I swallow the urge to say his name. I want to beg for him to come to me and make it all better, but I'm not a little girl anymore, and no one can make it all better ever again.

The only thing I can do is take steps to make sure that my world doesn't become one of the millions of cinder worlds I see closing in around us. I've seen that the number of cinder worlds is growing as versions of Alaric detonate their thirteen bombs inside the Thirteen Cities. It's only a matter of time before that happens here. Unless I am ruthless.

"Where have you been?" Rowan asks. His voice is shaking. He knows something is terribly wrong. He knows that we, and everything we ever were to each other, are over. He just doesn't know he knows it yet.

"I can't tell you," I reply.

He laughs, like the thought of one of us not being able to tell the other anything is ridiculous. I stare at him until his face changes. "You're serious," he says, still not really believing it.

He enters the room and tries to come to me. I do something I haven't done since I was eight and he was ten. I possess his body and stop him in his tracks.

"That's far enough," I whisper. When I let him go he draws a panicked breath, not because he's winded, but to reassure himself that he can breathe again on his own.

"What's going on?" He's terrified. Now he knows. I'm going to break his heart, and he has no idea why. It's like watching someone fall—his panicked face slipping farther and farther away as he tries to hold on to nothing. I'm thin air, less than smoke, and he slides right through me.

If I love him more than I love myself, he'll never know. Not even when he finds out that I've arrested his father and sent the order to hang him at dawn . . .

That's enough, Lily said, ending the memory. *I don't want to think about him.* She pushed the image of Rowan's face forcibly out of her mind.

You never want to think about him anymore.

No. I don't.

Lily had shelved all thought of him since he betrayed her. The entire trip cross-country she'd skirted around the mountain of emotion any thought of Rowan entailed, and she still didn't have the strength to climb.

Lily got out of her bath and wrapped a thick towel around her. She opened the closet and found three light kimono-style dresses for her to choose from. As she slid her fingers across the buff-colored silk of one of them she imagined how perfectly this particular shade suited her redheaded complexion. A sapphire-blue kimono, and one more in jade green, hung next to it. She took the green one off the hanger, slipped in on, and stood in front of the mirror to tie the darker emerald obi around her waist. It matched her eyes perfectly.

She rubbed some conditioning cream into her curls and wound them up into a twist. She stabbed the twist with one of the many ornate pins, combs, and clips that were in a tray by the sink. *A strange thing to offer,* she thought. *Unless you knew your guest had a lot of unruly hair.*

Lily took one last look at herself, resisting the urge to sneer at the pampered woman reflected back at her. The way she looked couldn't have been more at odds with what she felt, and the disconnect disgusted her. She wanted to look as warped as she felt.

Hide two of your willstones, Lillian reminded her.

Lily tucked her pink and golden stones into a fold of her obi and adjusted her smoke stone so it lay prominently on her breastbone.

On her way out of her room, Lily passed by the bed with its crisp linen sheets and wondered why she wasn't tired. Instead of resting, she went back out to the sitting area and found her coven fed, bathed, and dressed in their hosts' colorful clothes. Toshi had rejoined them, and he must have just said something funny because everyone was laughing. Even Tristan, she noticed. Laughter didn't feel right, and Lily stepped into the room irritated by the sound.

"Lily," Toshi said. He stood and smiled, his eyes washing up and down her. "That color looks lovely on you."

"I was just thinking that it's a tricky color, jade green. You almost have to be a redhead to pull it off." She watched Toshi carefully. "Are there many redheads in Bower City?"

"No," he said. "There are some fairer people of Russian descent, but mostly we have darker complexions."

"What an amazing coincidence, then," Lily remarked.

"I guess so," he replied. There wasn't even a flicker of discomfort in him and Lily wondered if maybe that's all it was. Coincidence. "I was just telling your coven that I'd be happy to show you some of the city," Toshi continued when it became clear that Lily was not going to comment further. "You seemed interested in the docks."

"I'd like to see them," Juliet said.

Lily looked around at her coven and saw that they were curious about the city. They should have been tired, but no one was. She gestured for Toshi to lead the way. He brought them down the grand staircase they had come up, but then took them in the opposite direction across the high-ceilinged entry room and out through a different door rather than going through the Hearing Hall. It let out onto a wide boulevard. Across the street was a well-manicured park, surrounded by stately villas.

"So is this the nice part of town, or the nicer part of town?" Una asked.

"Nice-*er*, I'm guessing," Breakfast said. He waved the air toward his face and inhaled. "I smell money."

"Right?" Toshi flashed his ready smile, his eyes crinkling around the sides. "This area is where most of the legislators have their homes because it's close to the Forum," Toshi told them. "But where I grew up, we called it Bullshit Row."

He won a chuckle from Una and Breakfast.

"Where'd you grow up?" Lily asked, purposely interrupting the light moment. The sound of laughter grated on her.

"I'm bringing you near there, actually," he said, his eyes drifting down. "We have to catch a trolley, though. It's a long way away."

At the end of the block they crossed a street busy with foot traffic and waited at the curb. Lily studied the tracks that ran parallel to the sidewalk, but couldn't find a third rail. There were no wires overhead, either.

"What fuels the trains?" she asked.

"They're electric," Toshi answered. "Rechargeable power packs on the bottom allow for about twelve hours of use before they need to visit an energy depot."

"And what powers the energy depots?" she asked.

"Electricity from crucibles and witches, just like in your city," he answered with a shrug.

"And mechanics?"

"Since we can't transmute, we aid them by monitoring their bodies while they work, but mostly mechanics focus on creating new materials, medicines, and other things the city needs. We may not be claimed, but we contribute."

"Like the bath soap," Lily said.

"Interesting stuff," Tristan agreed, his eyes hooded in thought.

"That formula was created by a mechanic. Many years ago," Toshi said. He watched the street as he spoke, his expression neutral—even disinterested.

Lily smiled at the trick. The quickest way to make something seem boring is to act bored by it.

"What else does it do?" she persisted. "Besides heal and energize?"

"Slows aging. Helps the body fight off sickness . . ." He trailed off. "It's something all citizens have in our baths."

A trolley swung into view and Toshi turned to it and pointed. "They only stop completely every fifteen blocks, but they slow enough for people to hop on and off if they see you waiting. Is everyone okay to jump on?"

They all nodded their assent. As the trolley neared, it slowed just enough for their party to step up into it. Lily felt Toshi take her elbow as she hopped aboard.

"Take the rail," he said, guiding her hand to the brass rail that stood out at about head level.

"What about old people, or the handicapped?" Juliet asked. "How do they get off and on?"

"See the inside track?" Toshi pointed to a rail line that ran down the middle of the street. Awnings with benches under them were provided every few blocks and Lily saw a woman with a baby and an armload of packages waiting at one of them. "That one stops completely every five blocks. It goes much slower so it can be accessed by people who are less mobile. But we don't really have that many people who need to use it because of an infirmity. Our medicine is quite advanced here."

"You got that soap," Una said.

"We got that soap," he agreed, chuckling.

Lily's eyes fell down to his dark garnet-colored stone and guessed that he must have been part of some of the medical advances here. There was so much potential in his stone she could see it glimmering inside the facets of his willstone, like whispers shushing down a dark hallway. The train slowed for more pedestrians to jump aboard, making them sway where they stood. The motion tipped her closer to Toshi, and jarred her out of staring at his stone. She looked up to meet his eyes and saw a slow smile spreading on his lips.

Caught, she looked away quickly and busied herself by searching the crowds for anyone that could be considered less mobile. She saw older people, but no one seemed infirm. Even the most silver-haired among the citizens had straight backs, robust complexions, and the vigorous strides of much younger people.

So this is what you can accomplish when several generations of mechanics are free to focus on healing rather than fighting, Lillian said. *Rowan would love it here.*

Lillian shared another memory of Rowan before Lily could block her out . . .

. . . I sneak up behind Rowan. The room is darkened. His shoulders are set with concentration, and the magelight coming from his willstone is a deep red. He's casting a complicated spell that has all of him ensorcelled. I hate that something other than me has so much of his breathtaking focus. I admit it. I'm jealous of anything that takes his eyes off me, and I'm going to punish him for it.

I still the air around me. I place my feet delicately. I quiet my breathing, ready to pounce—

"I know you're there, Lillian," he drawls without even turning around from his workbench.

"How do you *do* that?" I huff. I've never once been able to surprise him.

"You're louder than a herd of buffalo," he teases, spinning around on his stool to face me. I launch myself at him anyway. He catches me, already protesting as I pepper his face with kisses.

"Come on, Lillian," he groans. "I have so much work to do."

"It's so late, though. Come to bed," I reply, pouting as he pulls away.

"I don't have time to work on this during the day," he says, hassled. "We've been so focused on keeping the other Covens in line. I've had to officiate *three* duels in the past *two* days."

"Exeter and Richmond are at it again," I say, sighing. "It's lucky for us they're content with singular duels instead of demanding to send their mechanics against each other in full skirmishes."

"I don't think that's far off," he says, a troubled frown creasing his brow. He rolls his eyes. "Witches. Always looking for an excuse to fuel your mechanics."

"We do like to fight," I admit with a shrug. The beakers in front of him catch my eye. "What are you working on, anyway?"

"Well, I don't know yet," he says, smiling sheepishly. "I've isolated an interesting compound from a squid—"

"A squid?" I interrupt scathingly. "You're throwing me over for a squid?"

He chuckles, shaking his head. "I can't win with you."

"Of course you can," I say, pulling on one of his hands and tugging him along with me toward our bedroom. My smile is a promise. "I'll let you win right now."

His laugh is a purr in his throat. He stops short and pulls me back to him, wrapping me up against his chest. "You always get your way," he whispers as he lowers his mouth to mine. . . .

Lily snapped back to the here and now, a flush staining her cheeks. *Enough, Lillian. Why show me that?*

To remind you how much you miss him. You should forgive him.

Lily blocked her other self out.

Rowan. He had been younger in Lillian's memory. There was so much they had shared that Lily didn't know about. They'd essentially run a country together. Lily felt herself choking on the wild, sick feeling that thought gave her. She didn't know if it was jealousy or longing or the shock of feeling physically close to Rowan again, but it threw her and left her feeling bare and off balance. She looked up to see Toshi watching her, the barest hint of a smile on his lips. Lily looked away uncomfortably and trained her eyes on the scenery scrawling past.

They rode the trolley for over twenty minutes, passing through different neighborhoods. The style of the buildings changed from Italian villa to downtown loft to Japanese wooden temples, complete with rock gardens and sliding screens rather than walls. There was even a Chinatown, teeming with people. All of the neighborhoods were orderly, perfectly maintained, and immaculate. Flowers were everywhere, spilling from windows and rooftops and lining the streets. There were many parks, and Lily noticed that in each of the parks were four towers, one in the vicinity of each corner. The towers were taller than any building, but still shorter than the green-towers in the east, and they weren't covered in vegetation. They were thin structures, barely noticeable, with a flat surface on top.

"What are those?" Lily asked Toshi, pointing to one of the spindly towers.

"Oh, those are for the Hive," he said, unconcerned. "The Sisters rarely come down to street level." He turned toward the ocean. "Just a few more blocks."

The light was lying long across the city by the time they arrived at the docks. Ships of all shapes and sizes crowded into port, some of them so gigantic that they rose up from the water like windowless skyscrapers, hemming in the horizon. Cranes unloading shipping containers, and warehouses to store goods stretched past Lily's field of view. From every high vantage point a cluster of Sisters hovered, barely visible, their whips ready at their sides.

Caleb and Tristan took in the enormous scope of the port with a mixture of awe and anger.

"So, is every other country in the world in on this?" Tristan asked, his bitterness strangling him.

"Most of our trade is with China, Russia, and Japan, but yes," Toshi answered. He was sensitive to their charged emotions, but not pitying. "The whole world knows about Bower City, and they know about the thirteen 'untouchable' cities in the east. They also know about Outlanders, and how you live out in the wilds with the Woven. You're legendary, actually. There's a lot of respect for your people around the world."

"But no help," Caleb said. His mouth twisted into a sneer. "Not one country has ever thought to try to lend us a hand? My people are *dying* out there."

Toshi didn't try to make excuses. "Everyone knows," he repeated gently.

Caleb made a sound between a laugh and a sob and turned away. Breakfast started to go after him, but Una's hand shot out to stop him.

"Let him be," she said aloud. Lily could tell by the jumble of emotions that played across their faces that Una and Breakfast were sharing mindspeak, but they didn't include her.

Tristan was staring at Toshi, his anger at the world distilling into one person.

Come on, Tristan. It isn't Toshi's fault, Lily said in mindspeak. Tristan didn't answer. He broke away from the group and wandered, still reeling, down to the water's edge. Juliet, who was hiding her shock with silence, followed him. Una and Breakfast slowly peeled off to go their own way. Lily found Toshi watching her as they walked to a more open-looking part of the wharf that had smaller ships that didn't loom over them and block out the sky. Lily looked down at a few bobbing docks that were unoccupied by vessels but teeming with sea lions. They barked at the humans and flapped their flippers.

"I have a feeling a lot just happened between all of you," he said. "Especially Caleb and Tristan."

"Somehow it was easier to think the rest of the world had disappeared, or that they didn't know, rather than own up to the fact that they'd abandoned us to genocide." She gestured to the huge ships, the signs of progress. "We all suspected that the world was still turning, but it's hard to swallow when you see just how much."

35

Toshi nodded, his lips pursed. "And you can feel what your coven feels right now?"

"Some of it."

"What's that *like*?" He was trying not to seem too eager, but his eyes were hungry. Lights danced inside his willstone like a tingle. Lily looked away at the tidy dock and the scrubbed hulls of the ships. Even the sea lions looked well groomed.

"It's annoying," she snapped, her tone intentionally harsh. "Are we done here?"

"Sure," Toshi said, his face falling. She remembered, too late, that he had said he was going to show them where he grew up.

"You were raised down by the docks?" she asked, trying to salvage the situation. "That must have been——"

He shook his head once. "Some other time." He flashed one of his dazzling smiles and Lily wondered if he'd been insulted at all. He started leading her back up to the street. "We should get going, anyway. We have other plans for you tonight."

"We do?"

"New arrivals, chosen by the Hive? The whole city wants to meet you. Unfortunately, you only get to meet the boring half tonight."

"Ah. Bullshit Row?" she guessed.

"Exactly. Important people first, I guess."

"I thought *everyone* was important in Bower City." She was baiting him, hoping to find a crack in the high-gloss shellac that coated everything here. "What did Grace say when she paraded us through the Hearing Hall? It was built like that 'so even the smallest voice can be heard.'"

"Oh, the smallest voices are the most important," he said impishly. "Especially mine." Lily couldn't hold back a laugh. Pleased that he'd gotten what he wanted, Toshi started looking down the street for a trolley. "So, do we call for your coven, or . . . how does this work?"

"I already did. They're coming."

He looked away. The hungry shine was back. "Convenient."

"For some things." Lily sought out the hole that had been Tristan, worrying it like a hangnail. "Most of the time it just hurts."

CHAPTER
3

"I T'S LIKE BODY ORIGAMI," LILY SAID.

Juliet made an exasperated sound, looked down at the instructions, and then back up at Lily's obi. The kimonos they'd been loaned for that afternoon's outing to the docks were point-and-click, but the fancy dress kimonos for that evening's ball were an entirely different matter.

"No—you have to fold *that* down twice, and then twist it. Can that be right?" Juliet studied the obi. "Yeah. That's it. Down twice, then twist, then tie." She did it for Lily. "There."

Lily looked at herself in the mirror. She looked glorious in the petal-pink, crimson-red, and soft-cream kimono with a cherry blossom pattern. Her hair was swept up in lacquered combs and her face was subtly painted. The more layers of luxury this place seemed to pile on top of her, the more smothered she felt. She didn't want to look beautiful. She resisted the perverse urge to spit at the liar in the mirror.

"I'm hot," she said.

"You'll live," Juliet replied unforgivingly and then switched to mindspeak. *You were quiet today.*

So were you.

I had nothing to add, Juliet replied. Then, she suddenly changed her mind. *Why the perimeter wall? Why is this city walled off like Salem if they're not afraid of the Woven?*

I don't know, Juliet. There must be something they're not telling us.

Una barged into Lily's bathroom—yards of icy-blue silk in an ocean-wave pattern hanging off her—looking like a kid in her mother's date-night robe. "I've had it with this thing," she said flatly.

"Juliet, you do hers and I'll do yours."

They formed a train. Lily helped her sister wrap, tie, and rewrap her yellow kimono with a sunset pattern fairly easily, but Una was in worse shape. She had to strip down to the bottom layer and start over.

"No wonder the Japanese are so smart," Una muttered. "You need a frigging PhD to get into their dang clothes."

Careful, Una. You don't know if they have PhD's here, Lily reminded her in mindspeak. She couldn't see it, but she knew at least one Worker was inside the trumpet of an enormous tiger lily blossom in her bathroom.

That was careless of me, but this place is so nerve-racking, Una replied. *And all the perfume is giving me a headache.*

You don't trust perfect, Lily said in mindspeak.

My mom liked to pretend that things were perfect. That we were perfect. I pretended along with her for longer than I should have.

Lily glanced down at the rows of thin white scars on inside of Una's forearm. They were hidden hatch marks that she'd given herself with a razor blade when she was a little girl—one for every time her mother's boyfriend had touched her. Una knew she was looking at them.

"I'd like a drink," Una announced.

"The boys have already started," Lily told her, needlessly, though. Una and Breakfast were in near-constant contact, always sharing whispers of their thoughts. Lily had that once. It hurt to see it, so Lily made herself stare as they entered the sitting area and Breakfast held up a glass, already poured for Una. Lily didn't need a razor blade to cut herself.

She caught Juliet watching her watching them, and the sisters shared a sad smile. Neither of them commented. They both knew what the other had given up.

At least I have her, Lily thought to Lillian. She felt her there, distracted, half listening, but not engaged.

Lily's mechanics were impeccably dressed in the tunic-style of clothes that the men wore in Bower City, and although she was no expert on fashion here, even she could tell that the tailoring and the materials were a cut above what she'd seen so far in the city. The shoulders had crisp lines, the trousers were the perfect combination of structured and snug, and their shoes had the buttery look of the best Italian leather.

Tristan grinned at Lily when he saw her. "That took you half of forever," he said, gesturing to her kimono.

She shrugged and tried to move away, but Tristan caught her elbow and made her stay with him.

"It was worth it, though," he whispered. "You look stunning."

He was too close—too close to her, and too close to being who she needed him to be—but not close enough. She couldn't look him in the eye. She looked at his hands instead and noticed that his glass was full, and rightly guessed that he was already on his second drink.

"What is that stuff?" she said, pointing to the crystal tumbler in his hand.

"Whatever it is, it's amazing," Caleb said.

The lights in Lily's willstone twisted as she looked into the amber liquid and the perfect sphere of ice that rolled in it as if oiled.

"May I pour you one?" Toshi asked.

Lily turned to find him rejoining the group with another bottle. He was wearing a midnight-blue tunic that made him look longer and leaner. She looked away. "I don't drink," she said.

"Ever?"

"Once. That was enough."

Toshi didn't press her. "I don't blame you. This stuff will teach you a lesson." He filled a glass for Juliet. "The first time I had it was at a spring solstice party on the other side of town—a good twenty minutes on the trolley. The party was on the top floor of some rich guy's apartment, and he'd had the whole floor carpeted with grass for people to sit on like they're back in nature." He paused to fill Caleb's glass. "I take off my shoes like everyone else to feel the grass between my toes and have a few of these drinks. And then a few more. And then I *think* there were fireworks—either that or somebody hit me." Tristan chuckled despite himself. "About then I realize it's probably time to go, so I stagger out onto the street to wait for a trolley. Couldn't find a trolley if it ran over me. So I walked home." He refilled Una's glass, taking another well-timed pause. "I wake up the next day and my feet are just killing me." His sparkling eyes lifted to meet Lily's. "I'd left my shoes. I was so stinking drunk I hadn't noticed I'd walked halfway across the city barefoot."

Everyone laughed, tipping into a huddle. Everyone except Lily. Toshi didn't ruin his good story by stopping to bask in his own cleverness. Before the laughter had a chance to get stale, he put down the bottle, his demeanor turning crisp.

"Drink up, everyone," he said. "Grace will kill me if I get you there *too* late."

They finished up their drinks and he swept them downstairs,

across the foyer, and through a side door that let out into an atrium. The fountain in the center was large enough to swim in and it was lit so invitingly Lily had an urge to do just that.

The thought of throwing off her clothes and wading into the water pestered her. Lily's lips twitched as she stifled an upwelling of mirth. So many inappropriate impulses were fighting to come out of her. She wanted to tear off her clothes, break every mirror she walked by, and tell everyone in the world to go to hell.

I think I'm going crazy, Lily said, reaching out for Lillian.

You're not, Lillian answered. *That would be easier, though.*

You've felt like this?

Sure. Dozens of times, but most acutely when I took the crown.

What crown?

It would be quicker to show you . . .

. . . Rowan raises the crown over my head, and for the first time I get a good look at it in the mirror. The crown of the Salem Witch is made of burnt iron and diamonds. It's a cruel-looking thing, barbed and jagged, frosted with icy jewels. It's a thing of gothic beauty, born of fire and pressure. Like the Salem Witch herself.

That's me now. I'm the Salem Witch. At thirteen that makes me the youngest in history. As Rowan places it on my head all I can think is *finally*, as if I've waited centuries.

"Proud of yourself?" Rowan teases.

"Let's go," I say, rolling my eyes and trying not to blush.

"Are you sure you don't want those?" Rowan gestures down into the black silk for the rest of the Salem Witch's crown jewels. I balk. I don't even want to look at them.

"I'm not going to the pyre this instant," I say, rubbing my wrists absently. "It's overkill."

Rowan nods and covers them so I don't have to see them. I've heard that the blood of other Salem Witches is scored into the metal, baked there by such high heat that nothing could ever really scour them clean. I'm not ready for the shackles of my new position. Not yet. Tonight I just want the crown.

We go downstairs and all eyes land on me. Councilmen smear on their smarmiest congratulations. The heads of the other twelve Covens narrow their eyes in dislike while they congratulate me, their smiles wide and frozen.

Laughter froths inside me. I try to stamp it down, but the more solemn I try to behave, the more I find myself fighting the urge to bray like a donkey. I'm a liar. I've somehow convinced this pack of fools that I'm good enough for this, but I know I'm not, and soon they're all going to figure out what a fraud I am.

I want to laugh in everyone's face, I say to Rowan.

Don't, Rowan warns. *They already hate you.*

If they already hate me, then why bother?

Lillian—

But it's too late. I'm already laughing, laughing, laughing in their stupid faces . . .

Lillian breezed out of Lily's mind again, called away by something urgent. Lily wondered what it was that kept diverting Lillian's attention, but she supposed that being the Salem Witch would keep one busy. Lily had never filled that role personally or experienced much of it through Lillian's or Rowan's memories.

It seemed like every memory of Lillian's had Rowan in it. Lily was beginning to wonder whether there was any part of Lillian's life that didn't include him. At least, any part she cared to remember.

Lily, are you okay? It was Juliet. Lily looked at her and shook her head.

I feel like I'm losing it. What are we doing here, Jules?

Juliet shook her head and shrugged, wearing a helpless grin. As Lily smiled back she realized that she'd called this Juliet Jules—that was the nickname she had only ever used for her actual sister. She didn't regret it, though, or wish she could take it back. It comforted her too much.

Toshi brought the coven across the atrium and to another wing of Grace's enormous mansion, where the ball was already in progress.

A slim Indian woman in her mid-twenties met them before they could slip in through one of the sets of French doors that opened into the atrium from the ballroom.

"Toshi. Grace is waiting," she said. Her voice was tight and her sharp smile didn't make it up to her eyes. She wore a smoke-colored willstone. It wasn't as dark or as large as Grace's, but it was still impressive. Lily belatedly recognized her as one of the attendants who came with Grace and Toshi to the field of flowers earlier that day.

"We've met, but we haven't been introduced," Lily said, putting herself forward. The woman recoiled slightly, as if Lily were some blundering hick.

"I'm sorry," Toshi apologized, making it seem as if the breach in etiquette was his fault. "Lily Proctor, this is Mala Nehru—Lieutenant Governor of Bower City."

"You look much better," Mala said, her lips smiling but her eyes narrowed.

"Feeling great," Lily said. Her return smile was made through gritted teeth.

"Good. All these people are here to see you, after all. We wouldn't want you to be feeling poorly." Mala stepped uncomfortably close. Lily felt her mechanics stiffen and silently told them to keep back. For a moment she thought Mala was going to try to uncover the other two willstones she'd hidden inside her obi, but instead Mala untied the outer sash and retied it while she spoke. "You knot once, twist—like this—and then tuck the edges."

"Thank you," Lily said, meeting and holding Mala's eyes. They were standing close enough to kiss. Lily didn't back away.

"Anything I can do to help," Mala answered before turning and leading them into the ballroom.

That was creepy, Breakfast said to the coven in mindspeak. *Do we have to follow her?*

The coven laughed under their breath to relieve some of the tension. Toshi watched their changing demeanor like a kid pressed against a candy shop window.

She's just trying to throw you off balance, Juliet said to Lily in mindspeak. *It's such an obvious power play it makes her look weak.*

Juliet had a knowing smirk on her face as her eyes followed Mala into the ballroom. This Juliet, the one who'd been raised alongside Lillian, knew how to navigate a nest of vipers.

Keep telling me things like that, Lily replied, and stepped between the billowing curtains that framed the French doors.

Inside, the chandeliers overhead filled the room with a bubbly golden light, as if the air had been infused with champagne. Gilded walls and sparkling glass doors bounced that light around until it fell in soft focus upon the jewel-like people. The style of dress seemed to favor kimonos, but there were also some saris and a few dresses that appeared to be from the Georgian era in England. Some of the men and women wore war paint, but it was placed to please rather than intimidate. Everyone looked slim, healthy, and relatively young.

Flowers exploded from vases. Flowers were pinned up in ladies' hair. Flowers decorated the buttonholes of men's jackets. Flowers adorned every table, and Lily knew that in some of those flowers a Worker was picking its way through the petals on needle-like toes.

As Lily entered the ballroom, heads turned. Drinks were halted halfway to mouths. Eyes stared, unblinking. Lily resisted the urge to look at the floor, and instead met some of the stares. No one held her gaze or tried to engage her attention.

If they're all here to meet me, she asked Juliet, *why are they avoiding me?*

They're here to see you, not meet you.

I feel like an idiot.

Keep your chin up, Juliet encouraged. Lily felt her sister briefly squeeze her hand before letting it go.

Mala melted into the crowd, abandoning Lily without making one introduction. As jostling bodies swallowed Mala's lithe figure, a man's thick shoulders replaced hers. He was making his way toward them, lifting a hand to hail them. He was tall, well over six feet, and he had thinning blond hair and blue eyes that reminded Lily of sky rather than ice. His features were thick, his cheeks were ruddy, and his chin was dimpled by a deep cleft. Physically, he looked about thirty, but he might have been nearer to fifty for all the cares he seemed to carry. Around his neck he wore the largest golden willstone Lily had ever seen.

For kitchen magic—simple but tiring stuff to make, like cleansing mists and water purifiers. Useful guy, Lily thought, and wondered whether Lillian was listening. She could feel Lillian in the back of her head, but she wasn't actively engaged. Lily could sense that Lillian was occupied with something that was taking her whole attention again.

"Ah, Toshi," he said, approaching them with a distracted look. He pulled Toshi aside to tell him something in private and then turned his attention to Lily's coven. "So, we're all here, then?" he said, smiling broadly.

He looks like a retired boxer, Breakfast whispered in Lily's mind. His description was so dead-on that Lily had to stifle a snicker.

"Good to see you again," Juliet said, recognizing him as the final member of the trio of attendants that came with Grace to welcome them into the city.

"And you," he said. "You were all a bit too tired for introductions when we first met. I'm Ivan Volkov. Head Mechanic of Bower City."

Lily's coven greeted the Head Mechanic. She noticed Ivan marking Caleb's golden willstone, and the two of them sharing an exchange of understanding. Golden stones weren't given as much glory as smoke or rose stones, and because of that their bearers tended to be overlooked. Ivan's position as Head Mechanic was exceptional—something that Lily couldn't imagine happening back east.

"I'm sure we'll speak more later," Ivan said with an apologetic smile. He was a busy man, apparently, and left them, saying, "Ah, Simon," in the same tone he'd used to greet Toshi.

"That's Ivan," Toshi said, smiling after him warmly. They continued on toward the far side of the room.

"You're fond of him," Lily remarked.

"He's my mentor. Not that Ivan picks favorites," he amended quickly. "That's why we all respect him so much. He gives each of us an equal chance to advance."

"He's from Russia?" Una guessed.

"His family was, like my family was from Japan. But it's been so long since the Hive has allowed anyone new to immigrate to the city no one here is really *from* anyplace else anymore." He lifted his eyebrows. "Why do you think we're throwing you this party?"

"You know, I'm not really sure." Lily looked up at Toshi, testing him. She spread her hands to indicate the glittering room. "It's a bit much."

"Being chosen is a big deal," he assured her. "It hasn't happened in almost twenty years. If you're here, it's for a reason."

"So the Hive kidnaps people and flies them to a strange city to fulfill some kind of purpose?" Caleb asked. "What could a bunch of insects want from humans?"

Toshi turned to him, his face taut. "The Hive *selects* people. And all it wants is a well-run society."

"Oh, great," Breakfast said wryly. "Because perfect societies never have a downside."

Toshi laughed, dispelling the tension. "No one ever claimed Bower City was perfect," he said. "But it is well run."

They arrived at a large table, where Grace was half listening to Mala say something in her ear. Grace saw Lily arrive and stood before Mala had finished.

"Lily. Thank you for coming," she said, looking pleased. She was wearing a buckskin suede dress decorated with turquoise beads and an impressive feathered headdress. Tribal paint streaked her face and dotted her shoulders and thick silver bracelets were clipped over her wrists like gauntlets.

Lily didn't have a response, so she just smiled. Grace invited Lily to sit next to her. Mala was obliged to move down a chair, which she did with pursed lips. Toshi and the rest of Lily's coven seated themselves around the table. Ivan circled back to place his drink down between Tristan and Caleb before he darted off again. Once everyone had claimed a seat, there was still an extra place setting.

"Did you enjoy your visit to the docks?" Grace asked.

Lily pulled her gaze away from the empty seat. "Some of us more than others," she replied.

"Oh? Was there a problem?" Grace directed her question at Toshi.

"Just culture shock," Toshi assured her.

"Yes," Grace said. "I suppose it would be hard to take in, wouldn't it?" Caleb made a disgusted sound. "Speak your mind," Grace urged. "You didn't like it?"

"Oh, the ships, the trade, that's all great," Caleb said, a knife-edge gleam in his eyes. "For *you*."

"Go on," Grace said, knowing there was more.

"You're wearing a sachem's headdress, but you've left your people to die."

"Bower City is where my people are," Grace replied gently. Caleb shook his head, rejecting her answer.

"You could send out scouts right now and tell the Outlanders that there are no Woven in the west," he persisted. "They don't need your charity if you're worried about refugees, and they wouldn't have to come here to the city. They could build one of their own. There's plenty of room."

"Okay, say I do send out scouts," Grace said hypothetically. "For those who manage to get past the Pride and the Pack, what happens to the ones the Hive doesn't accept?"

"Thousands would die," Mala answered, on cue.

"Thousands *are* dying," Caleb shot back.

Mala opened her mouth to say something, but Grace raised a hand to silence her. "Caleb, do you know what the Hive wants? What guides its choices? Or why it kills some and accepts others?" she asked. Grace leaned in, holding his eyes. "What if the Hive decides it's done accepting people altogether and it kills *everyone* who tries to make the crossing? I'm sure you've heard the stories of whole tribes being wiped out."

Caleb looked away.

"So we can't tell anyone," Tristan said. He raised an eyebrow. "And I'm sure if we promise not to say anything, you'll let us leave and go back home."

"Go north, go south—there isn't anything out there, but you're welcome to look," Grace said. "I'm afraid the Hive will stop you if you try to go east, though."

"Why? What do they care which way we go?" Lily asked, her

frustration evident. Again, she found herself encountering a strange "rule" that the Woven followed for no apparent reason. No one hazarded an answer.

"I'm sorry to be the one tell you this, but the Hive won't let you go east," Grace said. "You're welcome to stay here, at least."

White-gloved porters filled all the water glasses. Lily stared at the one waiting in front of the empty chair, sitting there like an unanswered question.

"What's the rest of the world like?" Juliet asked, breaking the long silence. "Are there witches and mechanics in other countries?"

"Not like here," Grace said. "There are people with talent all over the world, but they lack the means to harness it."

"Harness?" Juliet repeated vaguely, and then understanding dawned on her. "Willstones. You've kept the secret."

"We have," Grace said.

"In our history books back east it says that before the Woven Outbreak—which threw everything into chaos—the process for growing willstones was the most carefully guarded secret that the covens had," Juliet said, as if to edify the westerners about eastern ways, but really it was to catch Una, Breakfast, and Lily up on the history of this world before they misspoke. "Even still, growing willstones is the last thing that only the most advanced mechanics learn in their training."

"We do things differently here," Ivan said delicately.

"Only the Bower Witch and two mechanics are trusted with the formula at any given time," Mala continued for him.

"When either the Head Mechanic or his second dies, another is supposed to be chosen immediately so that the formula isn't lost," Toshi said, finishing the explanation. He looked at Ivan, and many chapters of their story together passed silently between them.

"So, only three people grow willstones for everyone in Bower City?" Una asked.

"The mechanics handle the growing, and they only do that for people who have *talent*," Mala corrected. "We don't give willstones to just anyone, like you do in the east."

"I'm guessing you also don't give willstones to people in other countries," Lily said.

"Not unless they're selected for immigration and come to live in Bower City," Grace replied.

"But crucibles and mechanics in other countries can't get willstones from the east because it's closed," Breakfast said, confused.

"Which means Bower City has a monopoly on magic *itself* and all the medicines, products, and power that you can create with it," Juliet said, leaning back in her chair. She shot Grace one of her disappointed looks that Lily knew too well, pursing her lips and gently shaking her head.

"All over the world," Tristan muttered, impressed. "They have to come to you. No wonder your docks are so busy."

Grace tipped her head in assent. She could see that the easterners disapproved. "Greece kept the secret for Greek fire so well the knowledge of its making went extinct with their culture. China managed to keep the secret of making silk from the rest of the world for hundreds of years," she said unapologetically. "Bower City keeps the secret of willstones."

"And you've profited from it greatly," Juliet said, her frown deepening.

"Yes. Our city is rich and our people want for nothing," Grace said. "Tell me, on your trip down to the docks, or earlier when you came through the Forum, did you see any slums? Or people begging on the street?"

"No. Because you don't have anything like that in Bower City, do you, Grace?" Lily said.

"We don't," she replied, smiling. "Isn't it incredible? We've eradicated poverty."

Caleb made the same disgusted sound he'd made at the beginning of the conversation. "For *you*," he said again.

Lily thought of all the crucibles and mechanics around the world whose talent had been stunted because the Hive hadn't selected them for immigration. She remembered her life before she came to this world—the migraines, the fevers, and the seizures that nearly killed her. She pushed her chair back from the table with a scraping sound.

"You know what? I don't think I'm hungry," she said.

"I'd really like for you to stay," Grace said. "There's someone else about to join us."

Lily stood, ignoring the shocked faces of her coven and how their eyes kept darting over her shoulder. "Really. I think I'm done here."

"Lily," said a voice behind her.

It was a low voice. A voice she hadn't heard in months, but that she *thought* she heard at the edge of sleep nearly every night. Lily forced herself to turn and face him slowly.

"Rowan."

Lily didn't feel the chair under her, but she did feel her spine jolt as she landed on it. Tristan, Caleb, and Una stood up as Lily sank, their shock quickly turning to anger. Silly questions, like "How'd you get here?" were asked, and needless statements like "We left you with Alaric" were made.

Obviously, the Hive selected him and brought him to Bower City, she said to Lillian. And, *He must not have stayed with Alaric. He must have been following us the whole time. For months. He followed us right into Hive territory and the Hive took him like they took us.*

Either Caleb or Tristan wanted to hit him. Maybe it was both of them, but Lily couldn't tell because she could feel that both of them also wanted to embrace him as well. Voices were raised. A pinprick of annoyed heat grew into a dime-size dot that throbbed behind her left eye. Tempers flared higher. Soon her entire head was hot and buzzing until she couldn't stand it anymore.

"Enough," Lily said.

She'd barely whispered it, but a ripple of energy had traveled out of her with the single word, like a stone dropped into a pond. Her claimed gripped at their heads as if a piercing noise was deafening them. Every person in the ballroom was buffeted away from Lily, knocked back with the surge. Glass tinkled as it broke.

Dark streaks fell to the ground outside. The frames of the now-shattered glass doors burst open, and Warrior Sisters scudded in on their long ostrich-like legs. Their exo-armor glinted black over their tiger-striped skin, and their whips quivered in their human hands.

Lily's witch wind moaned as it raced to her. Her mechanics drew in a united breath at the precipice of the Gift. She felt Rowan's mind click into place inside hers, diamond bright and strong. Need almost overwhelmed her.

"Lily, don't!" Toshi called out, rushing to her side. A swarm of Workers flew in around their Sisters, blackening the air like a flurry of soot. "They're reacting to your aggression. You have to stop!"

Lily felt her coven pulling at her, all of them ready to receive her power. Out of the corner of her eye, she caught a glimpse of Grace's scowling face and the words "warmonger witch" ran through her head.

She pulled back, releasing her mechanics, and hoped it wasn't too late. She felt a jumble of mindspeak hit her at once as they argued with her.

What are you doing?

We're defenseless . . .

They're going to attack.

We've already lost.

"Just wait," Lily said aloud. The last mindspeech had definitely come from Rowan, and he was right. Her coven was dusted with Workers. Without a pyre she'd never be able to give them enough strength to survive the stings.

Lily felt a Worker crawl across her bare throat. She looked at the nearest Sister, trying to pierce through the rainbow sheen covering her bulbous black eyes, and trained every nerve in her body to fight the urge to slap the Worker away. The Sister flicked her whip and shivered her wings in agitation, but she made no move forward.

"I've stopped," Lily said to her.

The Sister's monstrous head swiveled lightning fast atop her stalk neck, but her tense posture didn't change. Lily had no idea if she understood or not, or even if this particular Sister was their leader. There was no distinction among them that Lily could see. Lily had chosen her simply because she was closest.

Everyone stay still. Lily—you can't just behave as if you're calm. You have to be *calm,* Rowan said in mindspeak.

She brushed his presence from her mind, annoyed that he felt like he had the right to advise her. She grudgingly followed his instruction nonetheless because she knew he was right. As Lily relaxed, so did the Hive. The Workers lifted off the coven's skin and the Warrior Sisters moved back, their wings still.

With one more lightning-fast twitch of her head, the closest Warrior Sister leapt into the air. The rest of the Hive followed her, vacating the ballroom as swiftly as they had entered it.

Lily looked around the ballroom. Chairs and tables were knocked down in a blast pattern that formed a circle around Lily. All the guests were on the floor, too terrified to move or make a sound.

"You'll have to get ahold of your temper." Grace's voice was raspy as it broke the stunned silence. "The Hive won't allow that a second time."

Lily found Grace watching her, a mixture of understanding and reproof in her look.

"I didn't mean to—" Lily stopped and looked around. There was broken glass everywhere, and some people were bleeding from superficial cuts. She felt hot with embarrassment. "I apologize."

"So do I," Grace replied thoughtfully. She spread her hands between Rowan and Lily. "I thought that you'd been separated, and that this would be a happy reunion."

Rowan furrowed his brow at Grace, but he held his tongue. The guests started to rise up off the floor and assess their injuries. Lily and her coven offered their assistance, but Ivan declined.

"It's fine, really," he said. "There are a quite a few people here who can heal, and it'd probably be better if you left. Toshi?" Ivan craned his head until he found his student. "Why don't you take Lily and her coven back to their apartments?"

Toshi nodded and turned to Lily. He gestured with his head at Rowan. "Is he coming with you?"

Lily turned to Caleb. "Is he?" she asked him.

I don't like it, but right now the more protection you have the better, Caleb answered in mindspeak.

Everyone in this room looks like they want to take a piece out of you, Una said in mindspeak, by way of agreement. Tristan, Breakfast, and Juliet gave their grudging assent.

"He can come," she said, avoiding Rowan's eyes.

As they passed on their way out, Mala hawked Lily's every step.

. . . and the piece she'd like to take is your head, Una added.

Toshi came alongside Lily while they crossed the courtyard. "I could find another place for him," he said quietly, gesturing to Rowan, who was lagging behind the rest of the coven.

"It's okay," Lily said. "Distance doesn't make a difference." She smiled ruefully. "I put a whole continent between us and that still didn't help."

Toshi frowned. "Is that why you came west? To get away from an ex?"

"Not exclusively." Lily looked up at him. "And how do you know he's my ex?"

"Experience, unfortunately." Toshi looked sheepish. "I've made one or two girls angry enough to throw things at me. Never had a girl try to throw a whole *ballroom* at me before, though."

Lily's shoulders shook with a silent laugh, and Toshi watched her with an indecipherable look. "What?" she asked.

"I like making you laugh," he said, surprised. His face suddenly clouded over. "Grace wasn't kidding about the Hive not allowing another show of aggression from you."

"I know," Lily replied.

"But will you be alright with him?"

"I'll be fine. I can control myself," she said. She hoped. She gave him a weak smile. "I fought the Hive once, and I'm in no hurry to do it again."

Toshi stared at her for a moment. "Incredible. No one fights the Hive," he whispered under his breath, and then left her at the door to the guest suite.

Lily and her coven went straight to the men's sitting room to have it out. She could feel them already arguing in mindspeak, although they hadn't included her yet. The silence was like a scream.

Lily sat, waiting for someone to engage her while she stared at anything but Rowan. Someone had brought fresh flowers into the rooms while they'd been away.

She reached out to Lillian again, craving some kind of counsel. *Rowan's back*, she said.

Good. You need him, Lillian finally replied. *Forgive him and count yourself lucky that you have him back.*

I don't have him. He left me, remember?

He'll always be yours—and you his. Stop wasting time. Lily sensed sweeping, jaw-grinding pain before Lillian quickly severed contact.

"Lily!" Tristan said sharply.

"What?" she replied, snapping back to the here and now.

"You've been blocking us all out again," he said, his eyes narrowed.

"Oh." Lily hadn't been aware. That was the second time she'd barricaded them out of her head without realizing it.

"Who were you mindspeaking with?" Rowan asked with narrowed eyes. Lily didn't respond.

"Do you want to chime in here, Lil?" Breakfast asked. "There's a lot going on."

She kept her face neutral, which wasn't hard to do. Now that the excitement had passed she felt exhausted. "There isn't much for me to say, is there? Rowan followed us, probably on Alaric's orders, and he got taken by the Hive just like we did. That's the *why* of him being here settled. Now, as to *what* he intends to do, it doesn't really matter, does it? He's too far to contact Alaric through mindspeak and I have no intention of allowing him close enough to me to be a threat." She stood and smoothed her kimono, not looking at him. "If he tries to get too close, I'll make him suffer. What was that he told me about Scot and Gideon? Claim your enemies. Well, I've already claimed him, and he may have surprised me once, but it won't happen again. So that's settled. Am I missing anything?"

"You don't want to say anything to him or ask him any questions?" Juliet asked. Her big eyes were round with worry and a whispered name ghosted across her mind. *Like Lillian.*

Lily turned to her. "No. I really don't. I'm going to bed."

She felt the pull of him as she walked away—a heavy bending of space around his body that threatened to drag her to him. But every step got easier, and by the time she reached her room she didn't feel Rowan's weight at all.

Carrick waited patiently for someone to come to him. He'd been here for a day and a half and so far he'd only met lackeys. Lackeys never knew what to do with him. Whenever Carrick had visited the fancy homes of the powerful people who needed his talents, like Gideon and his father, the lackeys could never figure out if they should treat him as a guest because their masters needed him, or like scum because that's what their masters thought of him.

The woman who came to get him that morning, Mala, was no different. She wasn't stupid. She could sense what Carrick was, and she had no idea why her master—an Outlander named Governor Grace Bendingtree—would want to house a killer.

"Big party last night," Carrick said. "I couldn't see from my window, but I could hear it. There was a fight. Breaking glass and a witch wind."

"Yes," Mala replied. She kept her body angled slightly away from Carrick, like half of her was about to run away. "You're not one of them, are you?"

"I know who they are. I know the witch, Lily. And she knows me," he replied.

Mala swallowed, unnerved by the way he said Lily's name. "Grace said you were following her."

Carrick stared at Mala. There was something she wanted, but she was too afraid to ask. He started with the obvious. "You don't seem to like Lily too much."

Mala's mouth trembled with all she wanted to say. "Do *you* like her?"

Carrick shrugged, noncommittal. "The things I do don't leave much room for liking."

"What things? Following people?"

"Sure," he said. If she wanted to pretend that's all he did, he'd let her. She knew better, though. But let her pretend for now.

"She's staying in another wing of this building. Would you follow her for me?"

Carrick tipped his chin at the door. "There are no locks on the doors."

Mala didn't understand. "And?"

Carrick sighed. Maybe she wasn't as smart as he'd thought, and if she wasn't smart, maybe she wasn't all that powerful. He didn't care if she was dumber than a pickax. All he needed from Mala was someone influential enough to make sure he could come and go as he pleased, do as he pleased, and that was it. If she could handle that, then they had a deal.

"No one leaves *me* in a room without a lock on the door, unless they got something better to watch me," he said.

"We don't need locks here," Mala said. "The Hive prevents violence."

Carrick stood. Mala didn't shrink from him. That was a good sign. She had some backbone. "Then if you want me to do what you can't, you're going to have to figure out how to keep the Hive away from me, aren't you?" She nodded slowly, finally understanding him. "Until then, I'll just follow."

CHAPTER
4

DAPPLED LIGHT BRIGHTENED THE OTHER SIDE OF LILY'S eyelids, and for a moment the whole world was warm and rosy red. The swaying of the trolley passed her head back and forth between invisible hands, lifting her up and out of her body. Warmth cooled, and the rosy light darkened to gunmetal gray. An old friend met her in the Mist. Someone sad and lonely. Someone lost.

She was in pain.

Lily saw an army sprawled out before her. She saw banners snapping in the wind and the acrid taste of struck iron made saliva gush under her tongue.

"Lily?" Toshi's voice startled her from her near sleep. "Sorry," he said, grimacing at her stricken expression. "But we have to hop off in another few blocks."

Lily looked around, reorienting herself in the spangled sunshine of Bower City. *Lillian?* She called to her in mindspeak, and got no answer.

"Are you okay?" Toshi asked.

Lily nodded. "Strange dream," she said, shifting the packages on her lap.

They'd been shopping half the day and stopping at cafés for cool drinks and tapas. Now, nearing the end of the day, Lily found herself alone with Toshi. Una was getting the pedicure she'd been longing for, Juliet a massage, and the guys sat for proper haircuts that were done with scissors instead of belt knives.

Rowan wasn't with them. He'd said he'd had a witch shower him with gifts before and that it hadn't ended well. Then he wandered off on his own, leaving the rest of them to take a little less pleasure from the pampering.

Lily looked down at her packages with an odd detachment. After months on the road, saying no to new clothes was not practical. It felt wrong to be out shopping, but if the clothes were a little less fine, or the surroundings a little less opulent, it wouldn't make the dead come back to life. Lily looked out the window at the sparkling day. It was easy to forget about death here. Bower City didn't do gloomy or rainy or sad. It didn't dirty its head with the ashes of mourning. It had one bright cheery note, and everyone was forced to sing it.

Toshi and Lily stepped off the trolley and he led her into a scent bar. Lily figured if she was expected to wear perfume, she might as well pick out something she liked enough to wear every day. An elegant woman, dark skinned and dressed in a sari, stood behind the bar waiting to be of assistance but too refined to inject herself into their browsing.

"Do you have those a lot?" Toshi asked as he slid a glass rod out of a crystal bottle filled with a honey-colored liquid.

"A lot of what?" Lily asked.

"Strange dreams." He dabbed one drop of the liquid onto a strip of paper, let it dry, and waved it under Lily's nose. She breathed in bergamot and blood orange.

"All the time." She shook her head at the scent. "Too sweet." Toshi moved down the bar and lifted a glass rod from another jar.

"After what you've been through—" He broke off. "I can't imagine it. To go out among the Woven, into the unknown. No map. No idea of what's out there—mountains, deserts, uncrossable rivers." He waved the strip under Lily's nose. Lemon and verbena quickened her thoughts.

Ah, actually, we sort of knew how to get to California. I'm not exactly Sacajawea, she thought, suppressing a grin. But there was no one to tell that joke to. Tristan would have gotten it.

"You're sad again," Toshi noticed.

Lily didn't reply and moved down the row. She lifted the next rod for herself. It was a powdery grandma smell. She dropped it immediately and decided to follow Toshi's cues instead.

"Have you always been adventurous?" he asked, dabbing another strip of paper with scent.

"Not at all! In fact most of my life I couldn't go anywhere. The most exciting thing that happened to me was a trip to the hospital." Lily breathed in Christmas. Gingersnap and snow. "I like this one," she said about the scent, "but it's not for me."

"What's for you?" he said musingly. "You're a woman who goes from happy to sad in a second. A woman who claims to be unadventurous, who's just had the adventure of a lifetime. You're a powerful woman who I could toss into the air with one hand." He shifted closer, his face dipping toward hers. "What's for you?"

Lily looked down and shook her head. "I'm not who you think I am, Toshi."

"No one's who we think they are," he said, waving a dismissive hand in the air.

He drew a rod out of a tiny glass jar that had only a few drops of a dark and unctuous liquor. The sales woman stiffened, about to say something, but Toshi smiled and nodded at her.

He didn't waste any of the precious liquid on a strip of paper, but waved the rod under Lily's nose. Smoke and spice. Bruised-to-sweetness sap bled from a young tree. Salt. And something underneath it all—something animal and almost revolting that she couldn't place and couldn't stop smelling. She inhaled it over and over, unable to pull herself away.

"Now tell me why you're sad."

Lily opened her eyes and saw Toshi watching her with concern. She swallowed. "I lost someone." The grief and guilt trembled right behind the words, which she spoke as plainly as possible to keep herself from bursting into tears. "He died to protect me."

"Did you love him?" Toshi whispered.

"Of course."

"Then lucky him." He tore his gaze away from Lily and looked up at the saleswoman. "We'll take a twenty-fourth of this," he said crisply.

Lily cocked her head at him. "You do that a lot," she remarked.

"Do what?"

"End the moment before it gets old. Or out of your control."

Toshi nodded pensively. "I've learned not to wait for applause. For anything."

"*You've* got a story," Lily said, half smiling.

"Some other time," he replied, his expression darkening.

"Oh, great. You're soulful." Lily said, rolling her eyes.

He looked hurt. "You don't give anyone a break, do you?"

Lily made an effort to soften her tone. "No, I don't," she admitted. "But I actually like soulful. It was a compliment."

He dropped his eyes so Lily couldn't read him. The saleswoman came to his rescue, returning with a tiny vial that she placed carefully inside a tissue-paper-lined bag. She looked anxious.

"It's okay," Toshi reassured her again as he took the bag. "Thank you."

Lily waited until they were outside to speak. "I'm guessing I picked the scent that costs a fortune?"

"Yes, but money's not the issue," Toshi said. "Only one other person in the entire city wears that scent."

A chuff of a laugh escaped Lily. She knew who it had to be. "Grace."

"Yup."

"Interesting," Lily said. "I know why I like it," she added, thinking of the smoke, the tree sap, and the salty animal smell of her own sweat sizzling in the pyre—thinking of the power and the rush of pouring herself into another person. "But why would *she* if she doesn't have mechanics?" Lily stopped and turned deliberately to Toshi. "Are you her claimed?"

"No," Toshi said, genuinely shocked.

"Look, I'm not the smartest person in the world, but I know one thing." She jabbed a finger at the little bag in his hand. "*That* scent is something a witch only becomes acquainted with by firewalking, and it's a scent she learns to crave only by giving the Gift. You know, there's been a lot of talk about how claiming is slavery, but I don't buy it." She smirked at him. "Don't tell me the people of Bower City are so pure that they're not tempted to claim."

"They're more than tempted," Toshi said hotly. "It happens—of course it happens. And when it does, it's a huge scandal and there's always a public trial. It's very, very messy. Claiming is the only crime that gets committed here, and it's punishable by banishment."

Lily stuck out a hand to stop him. "Wait, did you just say that it's the only crime in Bower City?"

"Yes."

She looked at him, perplexed. "But you have laws against murder and rape and all that stuff?"

"Of course. But those things don't happen here."

Lily started laughing. Toshi didn't join her. Her laugh died. "You're serious?"

"Lily, listen very carefully. There's no crime in Bower City. No murder, no rape, no arson, no theft, no domestic abuse, no kidnapping, no assault, no *crime*. Except claiming."

"That's impossible," she said.

Toshi reached out and led a Worker from the sleeve of Lily's kimono onto his thumbnail. She sucked in a surprised breath. She hadn't even realized it was there.

"Who knows how much the Workers understand of what we say?" he said pensively. "The Warrior Sisters can understand some, but from what Grace has said, they understand differently. Whatever that means. What we do know is that the Hive senses what we can't. They recognize hostility, fear, and aggression of every stripe. Last night, you saw for yourself how quick they are to intervene. They don't let violent crimes happen. For nonviolent crimes, like theft—well, the Hive is everywhere. They see it happen even if they don't know what it is. You only have to report something stolen for it to be found and the perpetrators brought to justice. There is no 'getting away with it' in Bower City. But claiming is the only crime the Hive can't understand because it's not like the others."

"It's consensual," Lily said, finally believing.

"Even pleasurable, I hear," Toshi said softly. "We're all tempted to do it. But since it's the one and only committable crime in Bower City, there's nothing else for us humans to put our energy into ferreting out. That's why I can say with some certainty that Grace doesn't have any claimed. Least of all me."

There was regret in his voice. Lily understood why the people here stared at her and her coven, and why they kept their distance with such dislike, even distaste. What would she feel if she had been tempted with something her whole life and denied it, only to see a group of people flaunting the freedom she wished she had? A freedom that they *should* have. Her brow furrowed.

"Why is it illegal?" she asked.

"Huh?" Toshi said, distracted. He was looking up the street for a trolley.

"Claiming is consensual," she said, thinking aloud. "A witch can't force herself on another. The willstone would shatter if she tried to break the will of the bearer. So why is it illegal?"

"There are other forms of coercion," Toshi reminded her. "Ways to make people give their consent."

"Then *that* should be illegal—coerced claiming—but not claiming itself," Lily argued. "What do the lawmakers care if people choose to give themselves to each other? It's none of their business, really." He didn't reply. "What about becoming stone kin?" she persisted. "There can't be any objection to that."

"Illegal," Toshi said curtly.

"Why?" Lily exclaimed.

"It fosters secrecy and obsession, and it's another form of intimacy that can be coerced. All individual mindspace should be autonomous, and that autonomy is protected by the city," Toshi repeated, as if by rote.

"That's utterly ridiculous," Lily retorted. "You can't tell people they're autonomous, and in the same breath deny them the right to choose."

The trolley pulled near at that moment, and he urged her onto it. Lily wondered whether he'd heard her, but decided not to press him. If he did hear her, he obviously didn't want to talk about it.

They met the rest of her coven back at the guest suite and spent a few minutes showing one another what they'd purchased. Rowan slipped in a few minutes after Lily and Toshi arrived. He'd been gone longer than any of them, but he was carrying no packages. He didn't greet anyone. He sat apart from the rest while Una, Juliet, and Tristan looked through every bag to see what the coven had acquired.

"How long were you on the trail?" Toshi asked, picking up a garment that had slid to the floor and folding it.

"Was it three months or four?" Tristan asked, casting his eyes back to Caleb.

"Nearly four," Caleb answered.

Toshi was impressed. "Did your tribe migrate a lot?" he asked Caleb.

"Some," Caleb answered. "But I'd never been out in the wild for that long before."

"Are things getting bad back east? Is that why you risked the trip?" Toshi asked.

"Define 'bad,'" Tristan said, still digging through tunics.

"I don't know. I have no idea what it's like to live in the wild," Toshi admitted. "But I'd imagine something huge must have happened to make you all risk going west. Did you think there might be something out here, or did you just go blindly?"

"You're very curious," Rowan said. His tone was not approving.

"Who wouldn't be?" Toshi said, shrugging. "It's got to be one hell of a story. Did you think there was a settlement or some kind of fort that you were heading for?"

"No one back east has any idea that there's anything out here—and certainly not a city," Tristan said.

He's pumping us for information. Don't say another word, Rowan said to all of them in mindspeak.

He's just curious, Breakfast countered. *It's totally natural.*

He's a spy, Rowan insisted.

Takes one to know one, I guess, Caleb said. Lily felt how Caleb's words stung Rowan.

"Are we going to see Grace today?" Lily asked, changing both the spoken and non-spoken conversations.

"Dinner. Tonight," Toshi said cheerfully. "She's sorry she can't spend more time with you."

"We're sure she's a busy woman," Juliet said.

"Is she going to explain what she really wants from Lily yet, or is this dinner still part of her charm offensive?" Rowan drawled.

Toshi froze for a moment before recovering. "I'm sure Grace and Lily will have a lot to talk about. But about what, I couldn't guess."

"Thank you, Toshi," Lily said. "If you see Grace, tell her I'm looking forward to speaking with her, too."

Lily waited for Toshi to leave before turning to Rowan. "Not very friendly," she said.

"Oh, so you're looking at me again?" he replied. "Nice to know Toshi's dimples haven't completely blinded you."

"He doesn't have—" Lily started to argue and stopped. She turned away.

"No, you started this. Now finish it," Rowan said, standing and crossing to Lily.

"That's close enough," she said, halting his stride for him. Rowan came up short like he'd run into a brick wall, one foot still raised.

Possessing him was a mistake—Lily knew it as soon as she did it. Not just because it was wrong, but because of what it did to her.

She saw the edge of his skin before she dove into it. The perfect, golden-smooth dewiness of it over stripped sinew and muscle—the sun-soaked softness over strength that was Rowan. She'd forgotten how strong he was. How perfectly his body responded to her desires and carried them out for her. Every dream of grace in motion she'd ever had he could give her. If she wanted to jump off a cliff into wild waves, or run up thin air to the very stars, his body was the vessel for that dream.

And if his body was her wonderland, his bright mind surpassed it. Only Rowan could corral her harrowed thoughts. Only he had a many-roomed mansion of ideas for her to barrel through, manic and crazed, to pick over feverishly as was her fashion, and pull snapshot memories from the walls. Only Rowan could let her run free inside him with no need to worry if she'd do damage.

He let her take all of him because he was the only one strong enough to survive her rough use.

Only Rowan. And he knew it. He knew how desperately she needed a place to put her frantic, frenetic energy, and he knew he was the only one who could survive her. He welcomed it.

Their eyes met, and Rowan won. She wanted him more. More than anything or anyone. All it took was a moment inside of him to make her feel like she'd be lost in his labyrinth forever.

She released him, letting go like she'd grasped the biting edge of a hot knife, and he put his foot down hard. He was panting from shock. He didn't think she'd actually possess him, and from the stunned looks on the rest of her coven's faces, Lily could see that none of them thought she would do it, either.

Stupid, she thought. Maybe Lillian heard her.

"You made your point, Lily," he said in a raspy voice. "Don't worry. I won't come near you again."

The finality of it stung enough to bring her back to herself. There was no apology in her when she addressed them all in mindspeak.

Call Toshi a spy if you want, but the truth is, we're the strangers. We're the threat. Grace wants to know more about us, and she's using Toshi to get that information for her. I would do the same. I haven't told him anything, and neither should you, but I have learned a lot from him.

Lily replayed the memory of her conversation with Toshi in the scent bar so they could all see for themselves how he reacted to her questions about the law against claiming.

Now, can we all move past the idea that I'm naive enough to spill my guts to a pretty boy and start dealing with the fact that we're in a city that's being controlled by the Woven?

You think he's scared to talk about it because of the Hive, Tristan said in mindspeak.

She looked at him and smiled. Now that he knew she wasn't smitten with Toshi he was on her side again. *What other reason can there be? They're everywhere and they're always listening*, she replied.

But can they understand us? Caleb was looking at the floor, thinking deeply, as he asked this question. *At the ball, the Warrior Sisters didn't stand down until they sensed that Lily was calm. Saying it wasn't enough.*

The Sisters didn't look like they understood anything Lily was saying, Una added, agreeing with Caleb.

We don't know what they understand. We need more information, Juliet said. *Toshi could have a dozen reasons for not wanting to talk about the laws here. We're just assuming that it's because of the Hive.*

What do we do, then? Try to strike up a conversation with one of the Workers? Breakfast smirked as he asked this in mindspeak. The thought was ridiculous enough to get a smile out of all of them—except Rowan.

What I want to know is where they come from, he said. Everyone looked at Rowan. *They're called the Hive, but has anyone seen an actual beehive anywhere?*

No one had.

I looked all over today for some place big enough for a large number of Warrior Sisters to congregate, but apart from those lookout towers, there isn't any. The towers only fit a dozen or so Sisters at a time, Rowan continued. *So, where's their hive?*

Out in the fields? Tristan guessed.

Rowan shrugged. Lily could sense that the rest of her coven felt a bit embarrassed, especially Caleb. While they were getting their hair done, Rowan had been trying to gather information about their Woven hosts. Lily looked at Rowan.

What do you suggest we do?

She didn't like asking Rowan for direction. She liked it less that for the first time she had to really look at him. He was thinner. His skin was sallow, his eyes more sunken, and his hair was long enough to brush his shoulders. He looked haunted and hungry. Like looking across a burning desert, Lily could only suffer the glaring beauty of him in small bursts. She looked away.

Keep Toshi busy tomorrow. I'll look around some more and try to see which way they come and go, he answered.

I'll go with you, Caleb offered.

Rowan shook his head.

We'll both go, Tristan said.

No. Stay close to our witch, Rowan said. His hot, dark eyes came up to meet Lily's cold, light ones. *She's in more danger around Toshi than she thinks. She has no idea how far an orphaned mechanic would go for her.*

Lily wore her new scent to dinner that night. She realized when she put it on that one of the compounds in it was designed to soak into the skin, pleasantly altering the wearer's mood. She could see it tracing around her veins, lighting her up inside. She wondered whether this agent—whatever it was—occurred naturally in the scent components, or if it had been added for her benefit. She liked it. Maybe too much. When she stepped out of her bath and joined everyone else in the ladies' sitting room, she felt a bit reckless.

Lily crossed to a pitcher of chilled water that was resting on a silver tray by the open balcony doors. The night jasmine on the veranda had bloomed and several Workers were combing through the velvety petals. She took a drink, feeling the coolness of the water wash down her throat while she watched the Workers shiver through the flowers, seemingly oblivious to anything but the task of gathering nectar.

When she turned, everyone was staring at her. Her gaze sought out Rowan and stuck there. *He was meant to wear black*, she thought to Lillian, and wondered whether, in some part of the back of her busy mind, her other self was listening. *He's like a dark flame burning out a slender slice of nothing between all the others.*

Rowan's eyes narrowed at Lily as she stared, a bemused smile threatening to break through his glower. The smoke willstone at his throat swirled with shadow and light and for a moment Lily couldn't imagine why they were fighting.

Then she remembered the cage. *He would have let me die*, she said to Lillian, although she could tell that Lillian was deeply occupied with something else. Another thought occurred to Lily, one that bit deep. *Does he still want me dead?*

"Lily," Rowan said, his forehead pinched with confusion. "Who are you mindspeaking with?"

Lily looked away. *Why does he always know what I'm up to?* she complained to Lillian. "Are we waiting on anyone?" she asked aloud, ignoring Rowan's question.

"Just you," Toshi answered. He paused to sniff the air. "You're wearing it."

They shared conspirators' grins. "I wonder if Grace will notice."

"Oh, she'll notice," he replied, stepping forward to take Lily's arm. "Even if she doesn't say anything."

"Did you tell her I got it?"

Toshi gave her an offended look. "I don't tell Grace *everything*."

Lily curled her hand over his bicep as she studied him, wondering whether that was true.

He led them downstairs and into yet another wing of Grace's impressive residence. Lily wondered if the Governor's Villa was like the White House, with a new tenant every four or eight years.

"How often do you have elections here?" Lily asked Toshi.

"Five years for parliamentary positions, ten years for service positions," Toshi answered.

Lily nodded at that. "What about the governor's position, or Ivan's place as head mechanic?"

"Head mechanic is different," Toshi said. "It's based on talent, and Ivan is the most talented mechanic in the city."

Lily eyes shot down to Toshi's deep rose stone and wondered whether he was being loyal to his mentor, or whether he truly believed Ivan was the best.

"What about Grace?" Breakfast asked. "Does the governor need to be a witch for some reason?"

"Grace was chosen by the Hive to mediate between them and the humans long ago. She's the only one they'll communicate with," Toshi said, turning his head to include the rest of the coven in the conversation. "She brings proposed laws to the Hive, and then comes back to Parliament with what they will and will not accept."

Lily could feel Caleb bristle. *Asking the Woven what they'd accept . . . ,* he fumed in mindspeak.

"The job is for life then?" Lily guessed. "The governor's position?"

"Yes," Toshi answered. "So is head mechanic."

"Cushy," Breakfast said, just loud enough to hear.

Lily chuckled to herself and began to take in her surroundings. The Governor's Villa sprawled out much farther than its street profile would suggest. Lily found herself counting hallways and trying to peek down stairwells as Toshi led them through the maze. They changed levels without taking stairs enough times to make Lily suspect that the villa had more floors than it seemed when looking at the edifice, but before Lily could ask, they arrived at the formal dining room that was already alive with guests. Mala greeted them outside the large double doors with a tight smile that wanted to grow up to be a snarl.

"Lily," she said through bared teeth. "Fashionably late again, I see."

"Is that a problem?" Lily asked, but Mala had already whirled around and left. Lily turned to Toshi. "Is there any particular reason she hates me, or is she like this with everyone?"

"She's threatened by you," he answered. "She's poised to take over someday, but all of a sudden, Grace seems very interested in you."

Lily thought about it and shrugged. There was a time in her life when petty jealousy and competition from other women had dominated her life.

Being madly in love with Tristan didn't help, she thought to Lillian. *Every other girl was a threat to me because he seemed determined to sleep with every other girl in the world* but *me. It's so strange how far away that all seems now.*

"I said—Mala isn't a joke."

Lily looked up at Toshi and realized that he was considering her strangely. He'd had to repeat himself.

"I know," Lily said quickly. She could feel Rowan watching her carefully and she wondered how long she'd absented herself from the conversation. "But I'm not a threat, and I'm sure she'll realize that soon."

Toshi narrowed his eyes at her. "How old do you think I am?" he asked.

"Ah—" Lily fumbled. "Nineteen? Twenty?"

"I'm sixty-four years old."

"Shut up," Una said, the words flying out of her.

"How old do you think Grace is?" he continued without missing a beat.

Lily stared at him, gobsmacked. He wasn't kidding. "I don't know," she said, not willing to guess.

"Neither do I. Grace has been governor of Bower City since before it *was* Bower City, back when this place was just a few tepees and a campfire. I don't even know what year that was because there are few records of the early days, and Grace doesn't talk about it," Toshi said. He leaned close to Lily. "Mala has already been waiting a *long* time. Be careful around her."

Toshi crossed the last few steps into the dining room and joined the dinner party. Lily put out a hand and stopped her coven from following so they could calm down and regroup.

"This place just got a whole lot more interesting," Tristan said. "I wonder how long Grace has been in power."

"Long enough for all of us to be scared of her," Juliet said. "Power does funny things to a person's head and the longer you have it, the more twisted you get. What I want to know is what she wants from Lily."

Lily felt a protective surge of emotion from her sister and smiled at her, but Juliet was too worried to be mollified. A fretful frown stamped a crease between her big brown eyes and it would not go away.

It's okay, Juliet. I'm not afraid of Grace.

You should be, Juliet replied in mindspeak. She sighed and rolled her eyes. *But I know you won't be. So I'll just have to be afraid for you.*

On that note they entered the dining room to find a small group of people waiting for Lily's coven to join them.

"Lily," Grace said, her ageless face spreading into a wide smile.

"Come and meet the minister of trade. I've just been telling him how you've been to the docks already."

Waiters circled with brightly colored drinks in strangely shaped glasses. Appetizers whisked by. Grace introduced Lily to several people with the title minister or chief or head in rapid succession. They all studied her like the newest wondrous beast in a menagerie. They gawked at her enormous willstone and tiptoed around the sticky subject of her claimed without ever really confronting the subject head on, or completely letting it drop, either. The women were less tactful about Lily's coven than the men. They made not-so-veiled comments about how many strapping young mechanics Lily had acquired.

"But you can't tell me that witches back east don't tend to lean toward claiming attractive mechanics for themselves when they can," said the minister of architecture. "Look at this little coven, for example."

"I'm not *for* Lily. I like men," Caleb replied bluntly.

"And I'm with her," Breakfast added, pointing at Una. "The scary one."

Lily nodded. "It's true. She is scary."

"You're a little too wholesome for me," Breakfast said to Lily. "No offense."

"None taken."

"And you're a little too female for me," Caleb said, grinning.

"It's a fact. I am female," Lily said with an apologetic shrug. She turned to the minister. "So, no. Witches don't pick hot mechanics to surround themselves with potential partners. We pick them based on trust." Her eyes found Rowan, who was speaking to someone on the other side of the room. "Or lack of it."

The prurient curiosity didn't end after they'd been seated. Then, it was Mala's turn to try to make them all feel uncomfortable.

"So, Una," said Mala, already two drinks in, "what's it like being a female mechanic?"

"It works just fine for me," Una replied.

"But didn't you ever want to be a witch so you could have a herd of adoring men to call your own, like Lily?" Mala persisted.

"No," Una replied. "Tell me, do witches here firewalk?"

"There's no reason for witches to do that in Bower City," Grace interjected sternly. "Firewalking is for battle."

"Well, I've heard Lily shrieking on the pyre," Una said, pinning Mala with a look. "And I'll take being in the battle over being on the pyre any day of the week. Herd or no herd."

Get me out of here, Lily said in mindspeak to Juliet.

Stay calm, she replied, resettling her napkin in her lap primly. *They're just testing you to see if you fly off the handle again.*

Lily could sense Rowan brushing up against her mind, asking for entry. In a moment of weakness she almost let him, but thought better of it at the last moment. She didn't want his support. When the food arrived, she felt Toshi nudge her elbow with his. When she looked over at him, he gave her an encouraging smile.

"I'm sure Lily didn't claim her mechanics for ego-serving reasons," Grace said, taking Lily's side. "In the east, a witch needs mechanics or she's not safe. But claiming is unnecessary here. The Hive protects all citizens equally." Grace put down her chopsticks. "So, Lily, have you made up your mind yet?"

"My mind?" Lily asked.

"As to whether or not you'd like to stay in Bower City."

"Actually, I haven't," Lily replied honestly. She looked down the table at her coven. "*We* haven't," she amended.

"That's a shame. This city has a lot to offer someone with your skill. More than you had back east, although I'm sure you were very important," Grace said.

"Not exactly," Lily said, frowning.

"Oh?" Grace said. She cocked her head to the side.

"It's complicated."

"Lily Proctor." Grace leaned back, thumbing through her memory. "There was a John Proctor of the Salem Bay Colony in Massachusetts. He was the first mechanic and his wife, Elizabeth, was the first firewalker. Their descendants have been the on-again, off-again Salem Witches ever since. Aren't you from Salem?"

Lily saw the conversation narrow, leaving her on a tightrope. "There are a lot of people with the last name Proctor."

Grace's smile was detached from her eyes. Thoughts moved behind them like pieces on a chessboard. Silence rolled up the long table and landed in a taut bundle in front of Lily.

"No, there aren't," Grace said in a soft voice. "You are Lillian Proctor of Salem. You are the Salem Witch, and Rowan Fall is your head mechanic."

Lily felt Rowan shoving urgently at her mind. She ignored him. She could handle this on her own.

"I never said my full name was Lillian," Lily said, keeping her voice as soft and assured as Grace's. "If the Hive won't allow anyone to go east, how could you possibly know that?"

Grace didn't answer. "The thing I want to know, and that Toshi couldn't seem to find out for me, is why? Why did you leave Salem?"

Lily decided that if Grace didn't feel the need to answer her questions, there was no need for her to answer Grace's. As the tense moment grew more uncomfortable, Grace seemed to relax, even enjoy it, until finally she was laughing.

"I like you, Lily Proctor. You remind me of me." Grace tipped her head to the side, considering this. "That *might* be a good thing." She stood and Mala scrambled to stand alongside her. "As I said, the Hive has made it clear that they want you, so you and your coven are welcome here. But there's one thing. If you chose to stay in Bower City, you'll have to give up your claimed. That's the law here. They'll have to smash their willstones and start anew. Understood?" Lily nodded once. "I'll give you a few days to think it over." Grace softened, her smile a surprisingly sad one. "They'll only hurt you, anyway. One by one, no matter how well you think you know your coven, they'll all turn on you eventually." Her gaze strayed pointedly to Rowan before she left the dinner party with Mala trailing behind.

Lily could feel the weight of everyone's stares. She turned back to her plate. "Ivan? Would you pass the salt, please?" she asked with forced civility.

Lily didn't hear a word that was said for the rest of dinner, but running and hiding in her room wasn't an option. Toshi kept trying to explain himself, but Lily brushed him off. Mindspeak among her coven kept her distracted while she chewed and swallowed and thought.

Does she really think we'd all just smash our willstones? Tristan asked.

I think it's either that or try to make it alone in the wilderness. The Hive won't let us go back, Caleb replied.

So Grace says, Breakfast said. *But she could be lying.*

How did she know Lily's name? Una asked.

And how does she know who the current Salem Witch is if it's been decades since the Hive brought anyone new? Rowan added.

Toshi must have been lying about that, Breakfast said. *They're all lying.*

I don't think so, Rowan said. *I think there's something else going on that we're not getting.*

When dessert was finally over, Lily stood and thanked Ivan. Her coven rose with her and they left the dining room without a sound. As soon as they went through the doors, Lily could hear the rest of the dinner guests burst into shocked whispers.

"Worst party ever," Breakfast said, breaking the tension.

"Remember when I had the seizure at Scot's?" Lily reminded him.

"Oh yeah," Breakfast said, grinning. "Okay, second worst for you."

"Lily, wait," Toshi said, rushing to catch up with them. He took her elbow, and her coven fanned out around her defensively. Toshi wisely removed his hand. "I wanted to say that I'm sorry."

"For what?" Lily asked.

"Ah—fishing for information and being disingenuous about my reasons?" he hazarded. He made a face. "Actually, right now I'm not sure why I'm apologizing because you don't look angry."

"I'm not. You were only doing what you had to," she said. "Come back to our room with us. I want to talk with you."

They settled into the men's sitting room and shut the doors behind them. Lily turned to Toshi.

"Grace says that the Hive won't let us go east, but what if my coven and I decided to immigrate to Japan or Russia or China? Would Grace allow it?" she asked.

"It's not Grace." Toshi looked around the room and sighed heavily. "How many of you know how to make willstones?"

"We can't answer that," Rowan said. He looked at Lily. "Don't answer him," he pleaded. Lily nodded and looked down.

"I'm sorry, Toshi," she said. "I wish I could trust you, I really do."

"No, I don't blame you," he replied sadly. "Look, if there are any among you who don't know how to make willstones, and you could prove it to Parliament, they'd have no legal reason to keep you. But you understand what's at stake here, right?"

"We do," Juliet said.

"Do you?" Toshi asked, frowning. "Coming from the east, can you really have any idea the influence Bower City has over the rest of the world?" He genuinely didn't know the answer to that question.

Lily looked at Toshi. *He's sixty-four*, she said to Lillian. *He looks barely out of his teens. I wonder if they've cured cancer here yet. He could help you. Maybe save you . . . I bet he's an even stronger healer than Rowan, and with Toshi you wouldn't have to worry. The secret of River Fall will stay hidden from Rowan.*

"Lily?" Rowan said, startling her. Her thoughts had wandered off again. She really needed to get ahold of that.

"We understand," she said, answering Toshi's question. He didn't look satisfied with Lily's answer.

"There's more to it than just the issue of making willstones. *They want you.*" Toshi let the words hang there while Lily watched a Worker crawl over his shoulder.

Now we know what the walls around the city are for, Juliet said to the coven in mindspeak. *To keep the people in.*

"We understand," Lily said.

"I should go," Toshi said. "I've already been here too long."

He took his leave, mouthing the words *be careful* to all of them before he shut the door behind him.

Lily opened up her mind to her coven. *Thoughts? Comments?*

I don't trust him, Rowan said.

I don't trust you. That hasn't stopped me from working with you, Lily replied. Fresh hurt chased across his face and she looked away rather than feel the hurt with him. *I don't think we have that many more days to decide. Do we stay or try to go?* Her coven didn't have an answer for her, but Tristan did have another question.

Is Bower City so bad? Everyone shot him a look. *I'm not saying it's ideal, but what place is?*

It's run by the Woven, Caleb said, disgusted.

And it looks to me like it's run pretty well, actually, Tristan argued.

Except for the tiny fact that the people seem to be incarcerated, Juliet said.

Think of Salem. Think of those walls. Were we any less incarcerated there by the Woven?

Seems like you've already made up your mind, Rowan said. *But you don't know what it's like to smash your willstone.*

You survived it. I'm not as weak as you think I am, Ro.

I've never thought you were physically weak, Tristan. But you're choosing this gilded cage the Hive has created for the humans over hardship and freedom. Try and tell me that's strength.

They could all feel how deeply Rowan's words hurt Tristan. As if against her will, Lily recalled what Grace had just said over dinner about her coven eventually breaking her heart.

We don't all have to stay, Tristan said sullenly.

You want to split up, Una said, surprised.

A long pause followed. "I think we should all decide on our own," Lily said. She looked at Rowan. "Some of us might have personal reasons for wanting to leave the coven."

Lily left them to discuss her without interfering. She was desperate to get out her kimono and wash the makeup off her face, and desperate for silence, both around her and inside her own head.

The thought of losing this Tristan to Bower City had hurt less than it should. She was almost relieved to not have to see him, to not be constantly reminded that he wasn't her Tristan, and he never could be. As she realized that, guilt folded over guilt until it was piled high on top of her head. She was at her door when she heard Rowan's voice behind her.

"Lily." He stopped several paces from her and kept his hands at his sides where she could see them. He didn't even try to initiate mindspeak. "Are you thinking of staying?"

"I'm not thinking anything yet," she replied. "What about you?" Lily hated that his answer meant so much to her.

"I'll stay if you stay, and I'll go if you go."

"Why?" Lily sighed and shook her head. "There's nothing for you here. Not with me."

"I can live on nothing," he said, and for the first time since he'd returned, Lily saw him smile.

Carrick finished his glass of wine and went back to work on the steak. They'd tried to give him some kind of raw fish and seaweed for lunch, and he hadn't touched it. He was sure in a classy place like this they had fresh fish, but even still. Didn't they know they could get worms that way? Carrick always cooked his fish through and through, even if he'd just caught it himself.

"Hungry?" Grace Bendingtree asked.

Carrick shrugged. "I've been hungrier," he answered. The tilt of his lips let her know how big an understatement that was. He'd been literally starving to death more than once in his life, but as he considered it, maybe this Governor Bendingtree had no idea what hunger was. It was difficult to tell. She lived high now, but she seemed broken in to him. Her features were worn smooth and her eyes were placid from years of weathering strife. Then again, she looked young, too. Carrick couldn't quite place it, but he'd bet she had some years on her.

"Would you care for some more wine?" she asked.

"Later," Carrick said. He sat back in his chair. The cushions were plump. Carrick disliked padding on his furniture. "Why don't you just go ahead and ask me what you came here to ask me?"

Bendingtree smiled at him, slow and knowing. She wasn't in any rush, but she still wanted something from him. Sure, he was her prisoner, and although this palace with its servants and fancy food and the tub so big he could swim in it didn't look like any of the dungeons Carrick had been in before, he knew what was going on here. Some captors torture their prisoners, and some pamper them. Carrick knew so much about this dynamic that he saw to the truth of

83

it. If he wasn't dead, she needed something from him. Strangely, that gave him all the power. He'd respect her more if she tortured him a little.

"You're an interesting man, Carrick. Do you have a last name?" Bendingtree asked as she poured him an unasked-for glass of wine.

"Bait men have no family names to give their children. They are what they do. Every Outlander knows that." He wanted it clear that even though she wore beads and feathers, Carrick knew she wasn't like him.

"So you are Carrick Son of Anoki and nothing else?"

Carrick narrowed his eyes. Not that many people knew who his father was. Had to be an Outlander who told her, but if any Outlander knew about this western city, they all would. Things like this place couldn't be kept secret no matter how much you paid someone.

"How do you keep your spies from talking about this place?" he asked.

She smiled a pretty smile that Carrick didn't particularly care for. "Why would you think I have spies?" she asked merrily.

"Don't be coy. It doesn't suit you."

"I have eyes on the situation in the east." She weighed her words before disclosing her hand. "Enough to know that there are two Lillian Proctors."

Carrick waited for her to talk some more. People loved to talk, especially when they were proving how smart and powerful they were. A big ego can make even the cleverest person careless, and Carrick had found that silence worked better than a beating with people who thought they were important. All except for Lillian. She never gave anything away unintended. Never talked about herself. Never bragged. Probably because she wasn't proud of what she did.

"I had hoped to get more information from the Lillian here, but she has proved to be exceptionally tight-lipped." Grace reconsidered. "Or maybe Toshi isn't as irresistible as I'd once thought."

Hearing that made Carrick smile. "Don't count on a pretty face charming that one into letting her guard down," he said. Rowan may have distracted Lily for a time, but she wasn't the type to get her head turned anymore. She came out of the oubliette changed. She liked suffering now; Carrick knew it. That's why she was perfect for him.

"So which one do you belong to?" she asked. "The sickly Lillian in Salem, or the healthy one? I'm guessing the sick one is your witch, and that the healthy one has no idea you're here."

Carrick couldn't figure out how she could possibly know about the two Lillians. She would have to have someone confirming Lillian's presence in Salem after Lily was found at Bower City's gates. Nobody could get from one end of the continent to the other that fast, and no one could mindspeak that far—not even Lillian. Carrick could sense that Bendingtree was powerful, but she was no Lillian. How was she getting her information? He started listing all the spies he could think of in his head, and stopped. She'd *corrected* him when he said "spies."

"Eyes, not spies," he muttered. He looked up at her. "What eyes?"

Grace sighed, disappointed. She was finally realizing that she wasn't going to get anything out of him, and maybe that she had given more than she'd gotten. She was experienced enough to see that, at least.

"I really don't see why you won't cooperate, Carrick, Son of Anoki. Your witch isn't going to last much longer."

"So sure the sick one's mine, are you?"

"The healthy one isn't desperate enough to claim the likes of you. I'd torture you for more information, but I have the disturbing feeling you'd like that." She stood, but paused at the door before leaving. "Please. Do enjoy the wine."

Lily flipped her pillow over to the cool side, only to find that it was still warm from when she had flipped it five minutes ago.

She rolled over in bed, an arm crooked over her eyes. The window was open and a salty breeze stirred the curtains, but the night was still too mild for her. Her overheated brain kept slinking back to Rowan like a kicked dog. Sleep wasn't going to happen anytime soon. On top of that, she kept thinking she heard steps above her, and she wondered how many floors this villa had. She had thought she was on the top floor.

You're thinking too loud, Juliet said in mindspeak.

Come keep me company, Lily replied, more excited than she should be that her sister had heard her. A minute later Juliet trudged in, sporting a red crease down her left cheek. "You've got pillow face," Lily told her.

"You've got pillow hair," Juliet said back.

Lily pushed a hand into the mad tangle on top of her head. "It matches what's going on under it, I guess."

"Man trouble?" Juliet flopped into bed, sprawling out wide so Lily had to move over.

"Am I being too hard on him?" Lily asked, knowing that Juliet would understand she was talking about Rowan.

"Yes and no." Juliet tipped her head from side to side, like her head was a scale for her thoughts. "No, if you consider what he put you through, and, yes, if you consider what he's been through since. We had each other on the trail. Rowan was alone."

"He shared his memories?"

"Some. Caleb and Tristan insisted." Juliet pulled a goose feather out of Lily's duvet. "He didn't sleep much. Couldn't. There was no one else to watch for Woven or help fight them off." She rolled the feather between her fingers. "He went through hell."

"Damn it." Lily let out a gusty sigh. "Did he show you why he left the tribe and followed us?"

He got into a huge fight with Alaric over the bombs. There's still two Carrick didn't get around to dismantling. Juliet looked down at the feather. Alaric's name was stuck on a loop inside her head.

"That must have been hard for you to watch. Just seeing Alaric, I mean."

"I've been thinking. I never should have run away from him," Juliet whispered. "I should have fought him harder."

"You left for me. And his choices aren't your fault."

Juliet looked up. Her big brown eyes were burning. *I know that staying here on the other side of the continent looks a lot more attractive when you think about the bombs, but we can't. We have to go back and stop him.*

Images of the Thirteen Cities flashed through Juliet's mind. Cities that Lily had never seen. Wondrous places—some built on pontoons floating over water. One was built up among the trees, like an enchanted elfin city. Juliet imagined the trees burning. People screaming. She clutched at Lily's hand, unable to bear her own thoughts.

Lillian's cinder world swam to the front of Lily's mind, and she had to switch out of mindspeak to shield her sister from seeing it. There was no point in hiding what she was about to say from the Hive anyway.

"I know. I don't know how to stop him from here—but I know." Lily breathed a bitter laugh. "I dragged you all across the country because I had some crazy idea that the solution to the Woven was out west, like *west* was some miraculous place. I thought I'd find a way for people and Woven to live together so the Outlanders wouldn't be trapped and there wouldn't have to be a war." Lily wanted to kick herself. "Well, people and Woven can live together. This wasn't what I had in mind, though."

"It's not really living together. It's more like living *under*," Juliet said, shuddering. "And I don't care if they're listening."

Lily shrugged. "We're already their prisoners." *For now*, she added in mindspeak. Lily almost didn't ask it, but she couldn't stop herself. "Nothing in Rowan's memories about me?"

"He did it to save you," Juliet said.

"Juliet," Lily said disbelievingly. "He took my willstones and put me in a cage."

"Alaric believed you had sided with Lillian. He was going to slit your throat where you stood. Rowan did the only thing he could do to keep you alive without having to slaughter his sachem and his whole tribe to protect you from them."

Lily looked away. She thought of Rowan's expression when he'd taken her willstones. There was no anger. No resentment. He didn't take her willstones because he was bitter or hateful. It was a calculated action performed without passion, like he was making a choice that had more to do with other people than with himself. If there was any feeling in him that she could detect, it was regret. What he'd done, he'd done for her, and even then he knew that the cost of saving her life would be her love.

Was she that unforgiving?

"I didn't really cry that much after it happened. I was too confused to cry because I knew Rowan would never betray me. Despite what it looked like, I knew there had to be more to it," Lily admitted.

"I can replay his memory for you. He showed us. Do you want to see it?" Juliet asked.

Lily shook her head. "Don't need to. Don't want to." She knew Juliet was telling the truth and that Rowan had probably saved hundreds of lives, including hers, but she still felt the grating edge of resentment inside her. Resentment and something else full of yearning that she couldn't quite place yet. "The cage isn't the problem between us anymore."

"What is?" Juliet prodded gently.

"What's your father like? The James of this world," Lily asked in response. "What is he like?"

Juliet smirked. "I barely know him. He wasn't really interested in us as children, and then Lillian sent him away when he became too interested in what she was doing as an adult. You know, once she was the Salem Witch."

"My father was never there," Lily whispered. Her whole chest felt sore. Juliet waited for Lily to continue, but Lily stayed silent.

"Are you ever going to forgive Rowan?" Juliet asked.

"I'm not good at forgiveness." Lily thought about how she'd refused to forgive Scot. She never really got around to forgiving her father for abandoning her or Tristan for cheating on her, either. And now they were all dead. "I never give anyone a break," she whispered, repeating Toshi's words.

"Is that the person you want to be?" Juliet asked gently.

"No. But I haven't figured out how to be anyone else yet." Lily shook herself. "Enough of this. Are you up? Like *up* up?" she asked. Juliet nodded. *I feel like snooping around*, Lily said, switching back to mindspeak. *Want to come?*

Juliet grinned. Lily took that as a yes, and the sisters slid out of the room, quiet as moonlight.

They followed their path from earlier in the evening and found their way back to one of the places Lily had noticed earlier. Lily and Juliet didn't dare allow their magelight to get too bright as they ascended a flight of dark steps.

Juliet asked in mindspeak—*Did you hear it, too?*

Footsteps above? Yes. From the veranda it doesn't look like there's another floor above us, but there must be, right?

I thought the same thing, Juliet replied. *Go this way*, she said when they reached the top of the stairs. *Our rooms will be below.*

They went down a long, narrow corridor with no windows. It was stuffy and baked dry from the daytime heat. The walls seemed to stare at them. The corridor ended at a door with a conventional lock.

There was no ward set to the door—just a simple lock. Lily shrugged at Juliet and easily knocked the tumblers into place with a nudge from one of her willstones. The door clicked open, and Lily peeked her head inside. She let her magelight glow a touch brighter and saw hulking shapes throughout the room. As her eyes adjusted, she could discern dusty crates and furniture covered with sheets.

Dead end, Lily said in mindspeak.

Not necessarily, Juliet replied. *Let's go to the back. I think I can see another door.*

They wended their way through the attic, passing crates, coatracks, broken armoires, shoe racks, a telescope, and even an old globe. Lily stopped at the globe and moved the sheet covering it. She noticed that there was no Canada or Mexico—just one big continent with the Thirteen Cities on one side and Bower City on the other. She had no idea how old the globe was, or how long Bower City had existed, but the globe looked like an antique—a hundred years or more.

They reached the door at the back of the attic and tested it. It was unlocked. Lily pushed the door open and found a room with nothing in it but a stairway set in the middle that led into the ceiling, and another door on the opposite side of the room.

This room isn't dusty, Lily noticed.

It gets used, Juliet replied. She started heading straight to the stairway.

Wait, Juliet. I want to check the other door first. Lily could feel the pull of magic around it, and as she got closer she realized that it was set with a powerful ward. She stopped, not daring to go any closer to it. This room was hidden on one side by a room full of forgotten objects, and protected on the other by powerful wards. Whatever the stairs led to must be important to merit so much protection.

Juliet asked—*Why set such a strong ward on this door but leave the door we came through unlocked?*

Maybe there was a ward set to it a long time ago, but it dissipated. The way we came looks like it's been forgotten, Lily replied. *Do you want to go up?* She could feel Juliet hesitating.

Lily, I have no magic and I'm Lillian's claimed, not yours, Juliet said.

It was strange to think it after everything they'd been through together, but this Juliet wasn't her actual sister—she was another version of her. No matter how much Lily loved her, this Juliet, and her willstone, belonged to Lillian.

If something were to go wrong, Juliet continued, *I couldn't be your vessel. Maybe we should go back and wake Rowan.*

His name had just popped into Juliet's head. She hadn't intended to name Rowan out of all of Lily's mechanics, she was just naturally gravitating to the one who could defend them the best. His name shot through Lily like a bolt, like it always did when she wasn't expecting it.

Sorry, Juliet said, grimacing.

It's okay. And I don't want to go back, Lily said, her pride making her stubborn. She pushed the trapdoor open and climbed up onto the roof of the villa.

Lily could see the whole city and beyond. The Governor's Villa was set on the highest point and they stood at the very top of it. The bright moon allowed Lily to see all the way to the ocean on one side, and over the wall and across the vast field of flowers beyond to a dark smudge on the other horizon.

Lily. Come and look at this, Juliet said.

Juliet was standing beside a large, softly glowing structure that dominated the center of the roof. As Lily approached she realized that it was a giant crystal, supported at the bottom by metal struts. The crystal was at least fifteen feet tall and five or six feet wide.

"What is it?" Lily asked aloud.

"It's a speaking stone," said a low voice behind her. Lily turned and saw Rowan ascending the stairs behind her.

"How did you—"

"Know you left?" Rowan finished for her. "I set a ward on our rooms."

"How'd you know where I went?"

"I can always find you," Rowan answered with a shrug. "Haven't you figured that out yet?"

Lily shut her mouth with a snap. He'd found her in the oubliette. He'd found her after the City Guard had raided the subway tunnels. He'd even managed to track her across the continent. Rowan *had* always found her. She'd think of him, and there he'd be. Lily considered that maybe he could always find her because some part of her was always calling to him.

"You shouldn't have come up here without a mechanic. No offense, Juliet, but you can't defend her." He was just about to get angry with Lily when he remembered that he didn't have that right anymore. She noticed that he stopped several feet away from her and didn't try to initiate mindspeak. This was their new normal. Something in her contracted to know that. She turned back to the speaking stone.

"What does it do?" she asked.

"It allows a witch to reach the minds of her claimed over long distances," he replied. "They're set up spaced apart every few hundred miles or so, and they work like a relay system. Years ago, the Salem Witch used to embed one of her claimed in the ruling Coven of each of the other Thirteen Cities to keep watch over them, and she'd stay in touch with her claimed through the speaking stones. That way, the Witch could maintain control from Exeter to Savannah without ever having to leave the safety of Salem."

"They haven't been used in years," Juliet said. "I didn't even know what they looked like."

"There's still one in Salem," Rowan said. "On top of the Citadel, over Lillian's rooms."

"Did Lillian ever use it?" Lily asked.

"I don't think so," he replied. "What's the point? She didn't have any claimed in the other Covens, where the other speaking stones were set up, and it only works between a witch and her claimed." He narrowed his eyes. "But why don't you ask her? You two talk all the time, don't you?"

"How did you know——" she began, and hastily cut off. Lily looked down at her hands. "Yes."

Something like a smile softened the corners of his mouth. Lily felt her cheeks heating up.

"Who would she contact?" Juliet asked, still staring at the speaking stone.

Lily had lost the thread of the conversation. "Who would who contact?"

"Bower City doesn't allow witches to claim," Juliet said, frowning. "I'm assuming this is Grace's. If she doesn't have any claimed, how could she use this?"

Rowan walked around it and ran his finger across the surface. "Someone's been using it. See the lights inside?"

Lily looked more closely at its center and saw the roiling play of light and dark that almost looked alive. "Is this a willstone?" Lily asked, incredulous.

"Same family, different capabilities. Speaking stones are far too large for one mind to bond with, so they can't be used for all the different kinds of things a willstone can, but what they lack in nuance they make up for in raw power," Rowan answered.

Lily stared up at the giant crystal. "Can anyone use it, or does it attune itself to one witch?" she asked aloud.

"Anyone can use it. But you can only reach *your* claimed, and another witch could only reach *her* claimed. It's not like your telephones, where anyone can call and anyone can answer."

"Ah," Lily said. She was reminded of teaching Rowan how use a telephone back in her world. He'd loved them, like he'd loved computers and most everything else that had to do with science and technology. He'd loved them because anyone could access them, not just witches and mechanics.

My world really is magical in its own way, she said to Lillian. *Look how large the speaking stone has to be, and still its range is only a few hundred miles. I wonder how many of them are set up and which direction they go? North—south? Or is there a line of them reaching all the way back east?*

"You're talking to her right now, aren't you?" Rowan asked. His brow furrowed.

"She's not really listening. She's busy," Lily replied.

"Then why are you reaching out to her?"

"Because I *want* to," Lily snapped. She turned to the speaking stone. "Is there any way to find out who is using this and who's listening?"

Rowan still looked troubled. "No," he answered distractedly, and then went back to what was really on his mind. "Lily. Have you told her about this place?"

"Of course I have," she said, throwing her hands up.

"Lily!" Juliet said, shocked.

"What?" Lily replied, starting to feel sheepish under Juliet's disapproval. "She's not against us. Not about this."

"Has Lillian told you what she's going to do about it?" Rowan asked.

"Not exactly." Lily looked down at her feet. "She's been busy, like I said."

"Doing what?" Rowan asked, crossing his arms over his chest.

Lily shrugged, feeling stupid. She'd been sharing so much with Lillian but she hadn't bothered to ask what Lillian had been up to in return. Lillian had seemed so busy, and there were times when Lily could feel that she was in pain.

"Why would you do that? Why would you tell her?" Rowan looked concerned, rather than upset.

"Because no one else gets it," Lily said, looking away. "No one else knows what it feels like."

"What *what* feels like?" he persisted.

A lump formed in her throat, and for the life of her she couldn't say the words aloud. An image of Tristan running across the burning plain to face the Hive welled up and set her eyes stinging before she could stuff it back down.

"I can't," she said in a strangled voice.

The numbness she had been forcing on herself evaporated, and anger surged through her. She was angry with herself, and Rowan. She met his eyes and he felt her wave of rage hit him, real and palpable as it had been in the ballroom. He took a stumbling step back as if she'd physically pushed him.

"We should get back inside," Juliet said urgently. She was looking at the sky.

Lily tilted her head and saw dark shapes starting to circle above.

Even from a distance, she could feel the air shivering with the hum of their wings. The Hive was coming in response to Lily's anger.

Rowan took a protective step toward her and pulled up short, remembering he wasn't to touch her. "Go," he said, motioning to the trapdoor. "And try to calm yourself."

Lily scrambled down it after Juliet, and rushed across the empty room. She felt Rowan only a few steps behind her as she threaded her way back through the dusty attic and down the stuffy corridor.

They made it back to their rooms without anyone in the villa spotting them. Lily wondered whether it mattered that the Hive had seen them on the roof or not. Was getting angry on a rooftop in the middle of the night enough to get them detained somehow? Lily couldn't imagine that was true. The Hive would constantly be over-reacting to normal things like toddler tantrums if that were the case.

Who decided what was normal around here?

Back in their rooms, Rowan and Juliet showed the rest of the coven what they had seen, but no one had any new thoughts on the speaking stones.

We'll see what we can learn tomorrow when we go looking around, Caleb said. *Lily, can you ask Toshi if he knows anything about them?*

I can try, she replied. *But he may not be able to tell me the truth. Toshi is as trapped here as we are.*

As everyone is in Bower City, Rowan added. *Do you think Toshi would let you claim him?*

They were shocked by Rowan's question, Lily most of all. *It's illegal here*, she said needlessly.

Rowan huffed with impatience. *Toshi wants to be a part of this coven, and he's powerful. If something goes wrong and they don't let us leave, we're going to need a lot more mechanics than just the six of us to have any chance of fighting our way out of here.*

Caleb and Una agreed with him.

I didn't think you'd want me to claim him, Lily said.

Why? My first responsibility is to protect you. That's all I've ever tried to do.

Lily didn't have a response. A part of her wanted him to be jealous.

There wasn't much of the night left, but the coven decided to go back to bed for the rest of it. As Lily approached her door she heard Rowan behind her. Again, he stopped a few paces away from her, and now that they were alone, only addressed her aloud.

"Have you asked her what she's going to do?" Rowan didn't have to say Lillian's name. Lily knew whom he meant.

"She's blocking me right now," Lily replied quietly. "But I will. It was stupid of me to not ask before."

"How often do you mindspeak with her?" he asked gently.

"I don't know," Lily replied. She sighed, suddenly feeling bone tired. "I don't notice I'm doing it most of the time. I just start talking."

That seemed to bother Rowan even more. He opened his mouth to say something and then shut it again.

"What do you talk about with her that you can't with your coven?" he asked. "And I don't mean me. I mean Juliet. Una. Tristan."

Lily shook her head. He didn't understand. "It's not what I tell her, it's what she already knows. What she and I share."

"Like what?"

"What it feels like to be the one who decides which of the people you love dies."

Rowan stared at her for a long time. "This is about your Tristan. That's why you're so angry with me. It's not about the cage anymore, is it?"

"I made Tristan my head mechanic when the Hive came for us. He wasn't ready," she said, her eyes dry and staring. "He wasn't you."

"I should have been there," Rowan whispered.

"Yes," Lily said, the anger returning swiftly and filling her to the brim. "You should have." Lily forced herself back to being numb so the Hive wouldn't be alerted. "Why didn't you just come with us?"

Rowan's lips pressed together. He either couldn't, or wouldn't, answer her. Her heart sinking, Lily went into her room and shut the door in Rowan's face, both of them finally realizing what it was that Lily couldn't forgive. His absence.

Carrick stood on the roof of the Governor's Villa in front of the towering crystal his half brother had called a speaking stone. Warrior Sisters landed on the roof around him, cocking their bulbous heads. Carrick paid them no mind. Act calm, and they were calm. But that was the problem with insect Woven like them. No matter how many times people had heard to stay still and not swat at them, most couldn't seem to help themselves when they heard the sound of those wings and saw the yellow and black of their bodies. Carrick wasn't like most people, though.

The Sisters kept their distance and watched him while he looked at the speaking stone. He put a hand out and touched its surface. It felt warm.

Lillian, he called in mindspeak.

Carrick, she answered. He could feel her confusion. It had been many weeks since they had been able to reach each other in mindspeak. *Where are you?*

It's been a long journey. So tiring, he said leadingly. *Can you use the speaking stone to fuel me so I may give you a full report?*

I've never heard of that being done before. I thought the speaking stones were just used for mindspeak.

Seems like an awful waste. Try it, he urged. Carrick thought that in some ways it was good that he hadn't been trained at the Citadel. He didn't know what was impossible. He smiled as he felt her feeding his willstone with strength and started his story with his abduction by the Hive.

CHAPTER
5

"You seem distracted."

"Sorry," Lily said. She brought herself back to the here and now with Toshi, which was a delightful brunch at a fancy restaurant by the ocean. She forced a smile, pretending to enjoy herself. "My coven is feeling very chatty today."

Toshi was momentarily puzzled before understanding dawned on him. His brows drew together as he looked down at the pounding surf below them. "You can hear them mindspeaking right now?" he asked. Lily nodded. "How far away are they?"

"Scattered all over, enjoying the day," Lily replied, lying with a shrug. No one in her coven was enjoying themselves. "Juliet and Tristan are near that scent bar you took me to. Caleb and Rowan are all the way east by the wall, and Una and Breakfast are having brunch at the villa."

Toshi smiled. "Does that ever get annoying? Hearing their thoughts?"

"Oh, it's annoying *most* of the time," she said, making Toshi laugh. "But we've learned to give one another space when we need it."

Reel him in, girl, Una said in mindspeak.

Didn't you just hear me talking about space? I could use a little of that right about now, Lily replied.

Her coven was in her head, but they weren't out enjoying another sun-soaked day in Bower City. They were watching the Hive while Lily was trying to woo Toshi into joining them.

This is hopeless, Lily said.

He wants to be claimed, Juliet coached. *Keep at it.*

Lily felt backed against a wall. For a moment she blocked everyone out but Juliet—the only person she felt safe enough to tell this to. *What if I don't want to claim him? What if I can't do this anymore? I don't want to be a leader anymore.*

Lily saw possibilities racing through Juliet's mind. Without more claimed, they were stuck in Bower City with no hope of escape. Juliet tried to picture what that would be like. She pictured the pretty gowns and the endless galas. It was the spitting image of a fairy ball where all the revelers were forced to dance until their feet bled. Juliet tried to imagine what it was like to never again be allowed to feel anger.

And without anger, Juliet said, *how can anyone truly grieve? We're all frozen inside, pretending we're okay because none of us can get angry, so none of us can get over Tristan's death. Least of all you. I know you doubt yourself and I know you're hurting. I'll give you ten seconds to wallow, and then you fight like hell to claim Toshi. I'm not living the rest of my life in a prison, and I'll be damned if I let you do that, either.*

Lily smiled to herself, some of the pressure she felt lifting off her as her sister took the weight. *Okay, Juliet. Consider my butt properly kicked.*

You're welcome.

"Can you see what they're seeing right now?" Toshi asked as he watched Lily's broadening smile with curiosity. "Are you everywhere they are?"

"I could be, but I try to go one at a time or it gets confusing. When more than one person is sharing memories or images with me there's a strange reverb effect."

Lily remembered Rowan teaching her how to make a mind mosaic. The stereovision had been overwhelming, exhilarating, and in Lily's opinion, morally wrong when done without her claimed knowing she was doing it.

"Re-what?" Toshi asked.

"Reverb. Short for reverberation?" It was a word from her world. Lily cringed inwardly and tried to cover for her slip. "You don't use that word out west?"

Toshi shook his head. "But I think I can picture what you're saying." He looked down at the glass of champagne in front of him. "But what do I know? It could be something completely different from what I'm imagining. I've never been in anyone else's head. The way I see blue might not even be the way you see blue."

"It is," Lily said. "Blue is blue and red is red for all of us. I've claimed thousands and it's the same." She rethought that. "Except for the color-blind."

"Thousands," he breathed. "You've claimed that many?"

The smallest smile tilted her lips while she held Toshi's eyes. "Yes," she replied.

"That's an army."

"An army I left behind." Lily tugged her lower lip through her teeth and took a chance. "Unfortunately," she whispered.

Toshi looked fearfully at the flowers on the table. "Is there a limit to how many you can claim?"

"If there is, I haven't reached mine."

Toshi swallowed. "Claiming must be boring for you at this point."

"Boring?" Lily shook her head slowly. "Never."

Toshi was leaning into the table. His willstone slipped free of his collar and swung toward Lily as if beckoned. She did want to claim him, no matter what the cost. It was a craving she would never be free of, no matter how many she lost, or how deeply she felt the loss of one in particular. This was her sickness. A never-ending hunger to claim the whole world.

A squad of Warrior Sisters is leaving the watchtowers, heading east over the wall, Rowan reported.

If we could get higher, we could see where they're going, Caleb added. He shared what he was seeing.

Lily saw Rowan trying to mount one of the few switchback staircases built into the perimeter wall. A Warrior Sister flew down and prevented him. Hovering, she flicked her whip and buzzed her wings. Her bulbous eyes shimmered rainbow-over-black—unreadable.

We'll have to try something else, but there aren't that many vantage points in the city that overtop the wall, Rowan said.

Roof of the Governor's Villa, Lily suggested. *Una and Breakfast, hurry.*

Toshi leaned back and motioned to the server for the check. "You're with them again," he said, irritated.

"I can block them out—" She could feel Una and Breakfast racing through the villa, silent and swift.

"No, don't bother." He pursed his lips. "It's better if we drop the subject, anyway."

Lily waited a few seconds before asking, "Is it?"

Toshi let loose a tense laugh. "For me? Definitely."

She and Toshi left the restaurant and started to stroll back toward the trolley line.

I see something, Una said from the top of the villa. She used her willstone to still the air around her and strengthen the tiny muscles that shaped the lenses in her eyes, improving her vision. *I think the Warrior Sisters are heading toward a forest beyond the fields of flowers.*

Show me, Rowan said. Una relayed what she was seeing to Rowan at the wall.

It's hard to tell, but I think Una's right, Rowan said. *They're headed toward that stand of enormous trees.*

Let me see, Lily said, and immediately saw what Una was looking at. *Those are redwoods. That's the redwood forest.* Lily passed a memory of a map of the California coast to her coven. In her world, there were several places where the ocean and the redwood forest nearly touched, as it seemed to be here in Bower City.

Ask if we can get out to see the redwoods, Caleb said.

"Do people ever go outside the wall?" Lily asked Toshi as they walked along.

"Of course. Lots of people even live outside the wall," Toshi replied. "There are farms, vineyards, small towns."

"I'd love to see that. Maybe you can take me to a farm, or out into nature."

"Maybe," Toshi said vaguely. "I'd have thought you'd had enough of nature on your journey."

"I guess I lived in the open for so long I miss it now."

"We'll see," was all Toshi would say.

Toshi knows Grace won't let you go, Tristan said.

I bet no one with a willstone is allowed outside the walls, Juliet said. *That's what I'd do if I were in charge and trying to guard how they were made.*

Then we have to sneak out. Tonight, Lily said.

We have to sneak out—Caleb, Tristan, and me, Rowan said, correcting her. *You're staying behind with Una, Breakfast, and Juliet to defend you.*

Like fun I am.

Lily—

"So, tell me the truth," Toshi said. "We're not really alone, are we? Your coven has been hearing everything I've been saying all morning."

Lily had the decency to be embarrassed. "They're very protective of me."

"I understand," he said. "I would be, too."

Lily smiled. "*If* you were mine."

He made a strangled sound. "Can I have half an hour alone with you?" he pleaded. "Really alone?"

Absolutely not, Rowan said.

Hey, this was your idea. He's not going to let me claim him if he can't trust me, and if he doesn't trust me I don't want him. I tried it with you, and look what happened.

Lily blocked her coven out. "Done," she said to Toshi. "You have my full attention."

"This way," he said. A mischievous mood overtook him. He grabbed her hand and pulled her into a run alongside a passing trolley. Toshi boosted Lily aboard and then swung up beside her with a wide grin on his face.

"Where are we going?" Lily asked, pink cheeked and breathless from the quick dash.

Toshi kept his eyes trained out the window, one hand on the rail and the other on the small of Lily's back as they swayed back and forth with the rocking car. "Home."

They traveled south along the water to where the trolley line ended at the far side of the wharf. The wall loomed close. The trolley came to a full stop inside a station and they had to go through a turnstile that was watched by hovering Warrior Sisters. There were no charming little restaurants by the sea here.

"What is this place?" Lily asked.

"It's a checkpoint. Technically, we're leaving the city although we're still inside the wall, and entering the restricted zone," Toshi answered. "Whatever happens, just hold still."

A Warrior Sister flew in close to Lily, her head twitching. She got near enough so that Lily could see the pincers in her mouth dart out and swipe over her face to clean it. The Sister's human hands played with the barbs at the end of her whip while her eyes seemed to zero in on Lily's willstone. The Sister's head suddenly jerked down to where Lily had her other two willstones stashed inside the bodice of her kimono. She landed on the ground almost close enough to touch. Several Workers flew from the Warrior Sister's shoulders and landed on Lily. They started to crawl over her, trying to get inside her clothes.

"Toshi," Lily said tremulously.

"Hold still," he repeated, his tone both understanding and urgent.

Lily could feel them tasting her with their tiny tongues as if they were sipping nectar off her skin. She prickled with goose bumps and forced herself not to slap at them. The Warrior Sister seemed to get what she wanted, reared back, and flew away, taking all but one of the Workers with her. The final Worker stayed on Lily's throat.

"That one will remain with you the entire time you're outside the city," Toshi told her. She noticed that he had a Worker on his neck as well.

"And it stays right here?" she said, gesturing to its perch just over her jugular.

"Yes," Toshi answered. "Don't do anything to disturb it."

Lily looked at the other people in the checkpoint. No one but her and Toshi had willstones, but they all had Workers attached to their throats, the poisonous barbs of their stingers poised right about the jugular.

"It's like walking around with a knife at your throat," Lily said. She felt the Worker's prickling feet and shivered with the knowledge that a bug was crawling on her. "Worse."

Toshi looked at her. "It's what you have to do so your children or grandchildren can have any chance of being chosen by the Hive one day. If any of them are lucky enough to be born with magical talent, that is."

"And if they aren't?"

"They wait."

Toshi and Lily emerged from the relatively empty station to join the throngs of people jostling up and down the streets of the restricted zone. The buildings were giant concrete blocks, bare and unadorned. The streets were scrubbed, but there was a gray oppressiveness to the place, and the lingering scent of harsh cleaning chemicals was almost as disheartening as filth. Every block a sentry tower rose up from the pavement, and the platforms on top buzzed with Warrior Sisters. The Workers did not fly around pollinating flowers in their cheerful, bumbling way. There were no flowers. Here, the Workers stayed anchored to an individual, constantly threatening to take the life that hosted them.

Toshi took her hand so they weren't separated in the crowd, and Lily soon found herself overwhelmed by the teeming throngs and pressed close to him. The sun was still shining, but there was a chill in the air. Even the people dressed in drab colors, wore no makeup, jewelry, or perfume, and they never seemed to look up. The solid mass of the perimeter wall, and the Warrior Sisters on top of it, seemed to hang over them.

"Families can wait generations in the restricted zone," he shouted over the din. "They work whatever jobs they can in the city or out-lying farms and hope that they have a child or a grandchild or a great-grandchild with talent. Only the magically talented get chosen by the Hive."

A raggedy old woman approached Lily, moaning in a language she didn't understand, and Toshi stepped forward quickly to inter-vene. He spoke a few words of Japanese and a few of something Lily couldn't hope to place and the woman backed off, doubling over with a racking cough as she moved away.

"I think she needs help," Lily said, looking back over her shoulder. Toshi hurried her along.

"She probably does. Everyone here needs something."

"I'm guessing they don't have miracle soap that keeps them young and healthy sitting around in their bathrooms."

"No. They don't. And the Hive won't let us give it to them, either. They won't let us help the people here in any way. Not medically or financially."

Lily saw the set of Toshi's shoulders and the grim line of his mouth. "How long was your family here before you were born?" she asked.

"Only two generations," he answered.

"What if someone comes here and already has talent?"

"They'd still have to wait. Everyone waits." Toshi's eyes were far away. "I've never heard of anyone being chosen by the Hive who was fresh off the boat, no matter how much talent they had. If the Hive wants you, Sisters go and get you. If not, you wait."

As they wove through the streets, Lily saw people from every ethnicity and every culture she could name in just a few short blocks. Toshi led Lily off the main thoroughfare and down a series of alleys. They arrived at the back door of a shop of some kind, and Toshi let himself in as if he belonged there.

"Toshi!" a woman's voice called out as he pushed his way in. Lily felt Toshi take her hand and bring her forward.

"And who is this?" asked an old Japanese man. His back was stooped and his hands were knobby. Lily could see arthritic inflammation, pulsing hot and painful, just under his skin.

"Dad, this is Lily," Toshi said, while the old man tipped forward in a bow. Lily looked from the old man to Toshi's young face, momentarily thrown, before she remembered Toshi's true age.

"It's nice to meet you," Lily said politely. She bent forward, awkwardly attempting to bow back, but it didn't come naturally to her. A middle-aged woman came forward and bowed from a place just behind Toshi's father. There were Workers on both the old man's and the woman's throats.

"You honor us, Lady Witch," the woman said.

"My sister, Hana," Toshi said.

"Toshi?" an old voice called out from another room. "Is that Toshi?"

"Yes, Mother," Toshi called back to her. He smiled at Lily. "Just give me a moment. I'll be right back, okay?" Toshi left Lily to go to his mother.

Two kids came tumbling into the room like nipping puppies. The boy was about six and the girl was younger, probably only five or so. Lily couldn't tell if they were arguing or playing, but they both stopped when they saw her, their mouths falling open as they stared at her willstone. Lily noticed Workers at their throats as well. Anger began to rise in her, which she had to quickly tamp down when she felt the Worker on her throat flutter its wings.

Hana pulled the children against her legs and shut their mouths for them with a snap. They went scampering out of the room in a flurry of excitement and delicious terror before Lily could even say hello to them.

"My grandchildren don't see many true witches," Hana said, blushing. She smiled broadly and stood aside for Lily to precede her. "But come in and sit. I've made tea."

"They're your grandchildren?" Lily repeated, still getting her head around the idea that Toshi's sibling, and probably Toshi himself, was old enough to be a grandparent.

"Yes. My daughter is working in the city. I watch them during the day. They help around the shop." Hana made a face to show that "help" was not really what they did.

Lily smiled and looked around her. She couldn't read any of the Japanese calligraphy, but the walls were lined with row after row of box-like drawers, each with its own label, and she could smell the different herbs and roots inside.

"An apothecary shop?" she guessed.

"Just so," Hana replied. "And we even have a few crucibles who come from the city to shop here," she said with pride. "Our herbs are the most potent in the restricted zone. That's why they allowed my daughter to have more than one child. That, and because of Toshi's talent."

Lily didn't know if she'd heard right. "*Allowed* you to have more than one child?"

Hana frowned. "Yes. It's the law," she said uncertainly. "One child per couple unless there is proof that there is talent in one of the families. Then you may have two."

"Lily's not from Bower City," Toshi said from the doorway as he rejoined them.

Toshi's father made a surprised sound in the back of his throat. They looked with confusion at Lily's willstone.

"Lily's from Salem," Toshi explained. "She and her coven were traveling west when they were chosen by the Hive."

They couldn't have looked more surprised if Toshi had said she was from the moon, but they were too well mannered to show it. Hana made herself busy pouring the tea.

"We'd heard an outsider had been brought to the city," Toshi's father said. "We didn't really believe it, though."

A tense silence followed. Lily thought they might ask her questions about the east, but they didn't. She didn't know if they were frightened to ask because of the Hive, or if it was simply considered rude in their culture. As she tried to decide if they were waiting for her to offer information about the east or if she should keep her mouth shut, Lily watched the old man grip his bowl of green tea with swollen fingers. Even that small movement was agony for him.

"Let me," she said, taking his hand. The rose willstone still stashed in her bodice flared, and she heard Toshi gasp.

"No, Lily!" he said, jumping forward to pull her away from his father.

Lily felt a prick at her throat. She waited to feel the whole sting, but the Worker stayed where she was, waiting to see what Lily did next.

"Easy," Toshi said, struggling to keep his voice calm. "Just put your hands at your sides and relax."

Lily did as she was told and she felt the Worker remove her stinger from the top layer of skin on Lily's throat. Toshi slowly released his grip on her as the Worker stood down. Lily's skin itched under the Worker's barbed feet as she repositioned herself, but she didn't dare scratch.

Toshi let out a long-held breath. "You can't use magic in the restricted zone. I should have been more clear."

"No, I should have understood that," Lily said, shaking her head at her own foolishness. "As if you wouldn't heal your father—and I'm guessing your mother, too—unless something much worse was threatened. With such a dark rose stone, you're probably a better healer than I am."

Toshi looked like he wanted to ask her something, but he held back. He waited until they had hastily finished their tea, said goodbye to his family, and were back out on the street. They walked along in pensive silence for a while before Lily finally spoke.

"The Hive doesn't let people in the city help the people in the restricted zone—not even family—so more aren't tempted to immigrate," Lily guessed.

Toshi nodded. "Population is a problem. They usually only allow one child per couple to keep it under control. I proved to have talent when I was seven, so my parents were allowed to have Hana. Apart from that, there are no perks for the people who come here. Just the hope that maybe your child will get out."

"You wanted to bring me here the first day."

"I wanted you to see more than the wealth and prosperity of Bower City. I wanted you to be the kind of person who cared more for people than she did for power. You haven't disappointed me." His eyes slid to the side as he looked at her and then drifted down to where her rose and golden willstones were hidden in her bodice. "You have more than one," was all he dared to say.

"You saw that, huh?"

"I felt it. Keep it hidden. It makes you vulnerable."

"I know." She thought of Carrick for the first time in weeks. She stopped and turned to Toshi, the memory of what he and Gideon had done to her reawakened. "Can I trust you?"

Toshi took her hands and drew her against him. He lowered his head as he put his arms around her to whisper in her ear. If anyone— or anything—was watching, all they would see were two people embracing in a quiet alley. She felt his warm breath on her neck as he spoke, and the shivers it sent down her back made the Worker at her throat twitch in agitation.

"I've waited a long time for you. I know what you want, and I want it, too—but not here. I'll have to make some arrangements."

They walked through the restricted zone back to the trolley station in silence. When they went through the turnstile, the Worker lifted off Lily's neck and she felt her shoulder loosen for the first time since she got there. On the trolley, Lily kept stealing glances at Toshi, reconsidering. His mother was sick, maybe dying. If Lily claimed him, and then left Bower City, he'd have to choose between his witch and his family.

Toshi got her back to her rooms at the villa before the sun went down. He brushed his lips across her cheek before he left her at her door.

"Did you have a nice afternoon?" Rowan asked as she entered the ladies' sitting room. He sounded unnaturally formal even for their currently estranged dynamic, and as she neared, she saw he wasn't alone. Ivan Volkov, Bower City's Head Mechanic, was sitting across from him. He stood when Lily joined them.

"I did," she said. "I didn't know we were having guests tonight." She switched to mindspeak with Rowan. *Where is everyone?*

Still watching the Hive, he replied. *I felt someone disturb the ward I set on our rooms and came back to find Ivan at the door. I don't know if he was just knocking or if he was trying to break in, but he didn't look suspicious.*

"Good evening, Miss Proctor. I'm so sorry to intrude," Ivan said.

"Please, call me Lily," she said, taking a seat across from Ivan. "Were you looking for Toshi? He just left."

"No, I came here to speak with you—about Toshi, as chance would have it," Ivan replied.

It was the first time Lily had the opportunity to study Ivan in detail. The straight-backed way he sat, his highly polished shoes, and the careful way he chose his words hinted at an era long past. Lily wondered how old he was and decided that if Toshi was in his sixties and looked twenty, Ivan could potentially be twice as old as Toshi.

Lily took an unasked-for cup of tea from Rowan with a small smile.

You're in a good mood, Rowan remarked in mindspeak. He didn't look at her. She could feel jealousy yawning in him like hunger, and she had to remind herself again that it was his idea that she get close to Toshi in the first place.

Toshi agreed to be claimed, she answered.

Did you claim him?

Not yet.

Why wait?

We were in the restricted zone.

So? What difference does that make?

The surveillance is so much harsher there, and I'd already caused a scene.

What kind of scene? What happened?

Lily found herself rattling off an explanation before she remembered that she didn't need to explain herself to him anymore. *I had just tried to heal his father, and the Worker attached to my throat almost stung me. Toshi guessed that I have more than one willstone and he didn't think it was safe—*

Rowan was not pleased. *What do you mean, Toshi guessed?*

I'll show you the memory later. Just let me deal with Ivan first, okay?

"Excuse us," she said to Ivan. Exchanges in mindspeak happened as fast as thought, but the rapidly changing emotions involved could still be noticeable to a sensitive onlooker. Ivan had been watching Rowan and Lily like he was at a tennis match. "You wanted to discuss Toshi?"

"Er—yes," Ivan said, his eyes still bouncing between Lily and Rowan. "I'm afraid what I'm about to say is rather frank, possibly even rude. I'm taking a big chance by coming here, but I feel I must." Lily motioned for him to continue. "Stay away from Toshi," he said. "Your affinity has been noticed. Even planned upon."

Lily nodded and smiled. "I didn't really think it was an accident Grace has been so conspicuously absent and that he was chosen to escort me around the city in her place. Was she hoping that I'd take a liking to him and speak more freely than I would to her?"

"Just so," Ivan agreed.

"What was she hoping to find out?"

"I'm not certain." Ivan frowned, his aging boxer's face creasing deeply between the brows. "Toshi has more talent than any mechanic I've ever seen, present company excluded, of course." Ivan tipped his head to Rowan, who nodded back. "But I fear he has some radical tendencies that have prevented him from advancement thus far. I have petitioned to make him my second for some months now, and as yet I have not received an answer. Make no mistake, Toshi is being tested as much as you, my dear, and I would hate for his involvement with you to—well, there's no way to put this delicately—ruin not just his chances of achieving his goal, but his life as well." Ivan leaned toward Lily. "It's possible that you're too valuable to imprison, but mechanics are not witches."

"I've been imprisoned before," Lily said quietly. "And I have no intention of repeating that experience or allowing it to happen to anyone I care about."

Her answer did not satisfy Ivan. "Toshi has been my apprentice for forty-two years. He thinks he knows how Bower City works." He looked at Lily with a mixture of fear and sadness that had been tempered by the weight of decades. "He *thinks* he understands, but I can't convey to you the extent of his miscalculation, and I'm afraid once he recognizes his error it will be too late."

Ivan looked down at the floor, momentarily lost in his own misgivings, before standing. "That is all I came to say. Both too much and too little, I expect."

Lily and Rowan stood. "It's been a pleasure," Lily said. She furrowed her brow. "I think."

Ivan smiled. "You are a dear girl," he said. As he lifted her hand to kiss the back of it, she felt him wedge something about the size and shape of a toothpick between her fingers. "I do hope the best for you," he said earnestly.

He dropped her hand and turned to Rowan, giving him a polite little bow before leaving.

He slipped me something. Why wouldn't he just give it to me?

He must be hiding whatever it is from the Hive, Rowan replied.

I have no idea how to look at it without being seen, she told him.

Rowan's eyes darted around at all the flower arrangements in the room.

There's no place to take it out here. I'll think of something, he replied. *Give it to me.*

Lily moved close to Rowan in order to hide the exchange. She put her hand into his and felt the texture of his skin on hers. He grew still as she swept her eyes over the familiar curve of his shoulder and the cut of his jaw just above her eyelashes.

She saw again his dream of California. She didn't know whether it was a memory she was replaying in her head or whether she was picking up on Rowan's thoughts, but she could smell the barbeque, see the bluer-than-blue swimming pool, and hear the comforting murmur of friends' voices laughing and chatting in the backyard like he'd imagined once. She glanced out the window. The golden California sun was lowering to meet the ocean, warm and lazy.

"We're here," she said, breathing in the scent of jasmine and taking in the magnificent view. "We made it."

"Not all of us," he replied. She looked at him and remembered. This wasn't his dream, and Tristan was dead.

Rowan let go of her hand, taking what Ivan had given her with him, and moved away from Lily. She stayed where she was, wondering if she was ever going to get used to this.

The rest of her coven arrived shortly, breaking the tension between them. They shared images of what they'd seen while they were scouting for a way to leave the city. It did not look promising. While the coven went about the outward business of pouring tea and eating fruit and cakes and acting merry like they were on holiday, they showed Lily the difficulties they'd encountered when they'd tried to find a way out of the city.

It looks like you can walk in or out whenever you want, Juliet said anxiously in mindspeak while she nibbled on a cinnamon scone, *but you can't. Tristan and I tried and we got stopped.*

And it wasn't just because it was us. We noticed that no one else was going in or out, either, Tristan added.

Lily sipped her tea and looked out the window. *Toshi took me to the restricted zone today.*

She shared the important parts of what she'd experienced that day with her coven, but stopped short of showing them when Toshi embraced her in the alley. He'd only done it to conceal the fact that they were whispering to each other—if concealment is possible with a Worker at your throat—but still, she felt strange about it. She didn't want Rowan to see it. She ended the memory right after Toshi guessed that Lily possessed more than one willstone.

Toshi is willing to let me claim him, but it's too dangerous for him, she explained. *He's been set up to get caught trying to join my coven, or at least that's what Ivan thinks.*

Rowan recounted Ivan's visit in mindspeak, but chose not to replay the memory. Lily didn't know why he avoided it, but she noticed that since he'd been back he hadn't shared any memories with her.

I'm going to inspect what Ivan gave to Lily, Rowan said. He stood up and went into his room. *I don't think there are any Workers in my bed, so I'll pretend to be taking a nap and look at it under the covers. The rest of you should go about your own business as if we're not sharing mindspeak.*

Lily took her tea out onto the veranda to watch the sun set. Juliet joined her, while Caleb, Tristan, Breakfast, and Una went into the men's sitting room to play at being relaxed by lounging in the leather chairs and pretending to read. Lily could feel the tension in them mounting as they sat too still and neglected to turn the pages of their books. She had to remind them all to breathe. It was a few minutes before Rowan contacted the coven again.

It's a map, he said. The coven could feel how perplexed he was.

He shared what he was looking at with the rest of them. *I think it's a way out of the city.*

In double vision, Lily saw both the sanguine stain of the sunset over the rim of her teacup and the micro-thin sheet pulled tight between Rowan's fingers. It took her a moment to realize that she was seeing a cross section of the city that focused mainly on what was belowground. There was one building aboveground that was used as a landmark, and what seemed to be a series of dug-out spaces below. Breakfast was the first to recognize the structure that was the point of entry aboveground.

That's Hearing Hall, he said. *It ruined my joke.*

The caverns beneath it look like the Stacks in Salem, Juliet said. *Where they grow the bio-assets.*

Lily felt a spark of recognition from Rowan. *You're right, Juliet*, he said. *These tall, narrow rooms are the perfect size and shape for skinlooms and this main cavern is perfect for womb combs. But it's huge. Much larger than what we had at Salem.*

Um . . . what's a skinloom and what's a womb comb? Because they both sound utterly nauseating, Una interjected.

Skinlooms are huge frames to grow sheets of wearhyde, Tristan replied. *Womb combs are vats that house ice lattices, which we use to grow both cultured meat and tame Woven.*

I'm having a hard time picturing it, Breakfast said.

I'll show you, Tristan said, and shared a memory of the Salem Stacks.

. . . I watch my feet go down steps carved right into the bedrock. So many steps. They don't just go down, they also go out. It's strange to think that by the time you actually reach the main cavern, you're out of the city and what's above you is the Woven Woods. I wonder what they're doing up there.

Rowan has already been down here for hours. No idea how he handles the smell. Blood, blood, and more blood. No amount of cleaning can get the scent of it out of the rock. Maybe it's because he's an Outlander. He's been covered in blood since the day he was born.

I reach the bottom of the steps and pass the rooms that house the skinlooms. I see a new apprentice mechanic—Gavin is his name, I think—pull out one of the tall, thin frames of the looms from the wall. It glides silently on its casters as Gavin stirs his brush in a bucket of culture, preparing to paint it on the frame. In two days it will be ready for harvest—a perfect sheet of wearhyde. They are what gave the Stacks their name, but I always thought that name was wrong. The skinlooms aren't stacked on top of one another; they stand upright, like books on a shelf. I don't know what you'd call that, though.

I enter the main room—a cathedral that soars up and up, the walls and ceiling lit by sconces that glow with magelight. The sconces seem to float like little bubbles of light against the rough-hewn rock. Below the ancient stone and eerie magelight are the stainless steel vats that hold ice lattices. The womb combs. Some of them are enormous, and they're the reason the cavern is so high. My teacher told me they were made to grow the greater drakes—huge and terrifying as the mythical dragon. They only grow greater drakes in New York now, and even then only rarely. It's been a long time since the Age of Strife when the Thirteen Cities warred with one another. Mechanics used to ride those things into battle. That must have been a sight to see. I've always wanted to fly.

I peer around a few of the smaller womb combs up front and spot Rowan three rows down. I go to him. He's pulled out one of the lattices so he can inspect the crop of tame Woven embryos that are growing inside the hexagonal cells. It looks like a sheet of honeycomb that he's holding up to the light. A dark speck of life is nestled in the center of each cell. I have no idea how he can do that barehanded. It's like he doesn't even mind the freezing cold of it. Inside the cell, cupped right around the embryo, heat is maintained by the crucibles who tend them. The rest is kept several degrees below zero. Less infection that way, but torture to touch, or at least I think so. Rowan sees me and gives me that lazy smile of his.

"Good morning," he says.

"Afternoon," I correct, and then catch myself when I see his smile turn into a grin. "I know I was supposed to be here at nine," I begin, already explaining myself. Why do I always feel like I have to explain myself to him?

"Don't worry about it. Come and help," he says. He's understanding and forgiving as usual. I don't know what's more annoying. That he's genuinely better at everything or that he's so damn accepting of the fact that everyone else is so flawed . . .

Sorry, Tristan said, abruptly ending the memory. *I didn't mean to go on like that. Sorry, Ro.*

It's okay, Rowan replied.

Lily could feel their friendship repairing. The frayed edges of where their personalities met up were weaving themselves back together as if neither of them could remember why they were fighting.

The sun had set and the lights from the city below were winking on, terrestrial echoes of the stars above. *Such a pretty prison*, she thought. Lily put down her teacup and went inside.

The cavern in the map definitely looks like the Stacks, only much larger, Lily said, trying to get back on subject. *But why would Ivan give this to us? Rowan—you said you thought it was a map out of the city.*

Yes. Rowan directed their attention to the far end of the cavern. There was a steady rise in the gradient and a small opening at the end. *That could be a tunnel to the surface.*

Maybe, Caleb said. *But that brings up another question. Why would Ivan want to help us get out of Bower City?*

Lily took a guess. *Ivan thinks Grace is trying to trap Toshi. If I claim*

Toshi like she's planned, he'll get caught and go to jail. I think it's because she wants to replace him with Rowan as Ivan's second. Toshi is strong, but Rowan is still stronger.

He's definitely trying to protect Toshi from something, Rowan said. *Maybe it's me. Maybe it's you.*

It was clear that between the two of those options, Rowan felt that she was the greater threat.

I'm not out to ruin anyone else's life, Lily said, stung. She thought of Toshi's parents—his father's swollen fingers and the sound of his mother's voice, sickly and weak in the next room. She let her coven view the memory with her. *Toshi has family here, and they need him. I've decided that claiming him isn't an option anymore, even if he is willing.* She started looking through her things for something suitable to wear. *There's only one way to find out why Ivan really gave us the map. We follow it, and maybe get out of here tonight.*

She let her coven go back and forth, arguing. There were a dozen reasons to wait and a dozen reasons to act immediately. None of those reasons mattered to Lily anymore. She just wanted out of Bower City.

Lily was dressed in a dark silk tunic, pants, and flat black shoes, and sitting patiently at the end of her bed with the lights off by the time they realized that she was going with or without them. She even had a bag of salt in one pocket and a small jar of the miracle soap in the other, just in case they actually made it out of the city and found themselves on the road back to Salem.

Okay. But we're going in three small groups, not as one big herd, Rowan insisted.

Lily stood and went into the bathroom. She lit all the candles she could find there and began gathering their energy slowly so as not to disturb the Hive. She didn't know if fueling her mechanics would be considered an act of aggression, and she wasn't about to take any chances alerting them. Their best bet at avoiding the Hive was to act as calmly as they could. A witch wind whistled through the window and Lily slowed her harvest until the wind lowered to a soft moan.

Caleb took command as he'd done on the trail. *Una and Tristan with Lily first*, he said. *I'll go with Juliet second. Breakfast, you and Rowan last.*

I'm going with Lily, Rowan insisted.

No you're not, Caleb ordered. *You go with Breakfast or you don't go at all.*

Lily could feel Rowan struggling with this and resisted the urge to support him. *Let's go*, she said, ending the conversation. She changed the energy she'd gathered from the candle flames into force and flooded her coven's willstones with power. She felt them all stretch and sigh as they soaked in her strength.

They waited for the sounds of the villa to die down, and then left their apartments in the groups and in the sequence that Caleb had designated. As Lily flowed through the darkness, Una and Tristan on either side sweeping her along with them, she connected her coven each to each, unifying them even though they were physically parted. Caleb's caution, Tristan's thrill, Una's prowl and pounce, were all joined into one. Rowan's unease at being away from Lily was like a twanging note in the song, out of tune with the rest.

The coven made their way through the foyer, through the side door, and down the long passageway connecting the villa to Hearing Hall. There were no locks on the doors and each group of the coven breezed through, so fast and silent with Lily's strength in them that they neared invisibility. Lily knew the Workers were there, but she doubted even their multifaceted eyes could see her preternaturally swift coven under the cover of night.

The map was in Lily's mind's eye as she glanced around Hearing Hall. The oculus let in a beam of bright moonlight onto the marble floor, but the light was lost in the silver-black shadows among the pillars. The air was heavy, and the empty space was anxious for them to make a sound for it to amplify. The weight of silence was a ringing pressure inside Lily's ears. She saw something move among the pillars, just off the edge of her vision. She snapped her head around to find it, but there was nothing there.

The other two groups joined hers shortly.

Look for the way down, Rowan said in mindspeak as he and Breakfast caught up to the rest of them.

The doors, Tristan replied, already moving to them. *One goes to the villa, but what about the other two?*

Caleb sped down one passageway, his connection to Lily getting thin as the crystals in the marble distorted his willstone's vibration. He came back shaking his head.

It leads to another government building. It looked like offices, he said.

Tristan tried the third door, and it opened into emptiness. *There are no stairs. How do they get down with no stairs?*

You'd need wings, Breakfast said, joking.

Rowan leaned through the open door and let his magelight brighten, trying to judge the distance down. His light never reached the ground. *Yes. You would*, he said in all seriousness. Then he launched himself over the edge.

Lily felt her heart fly into her throat. She pushed her way through the others and knelt at the precipice to watch Rowan's magelight descend into darkness. By the time he reached the bottom it was only a faint glimmer. Rowan's feet, then knees, and then hands met the ground as he dispersed the energy up through his body in stages, ending with the thwacking sound of his palms slapping down. Lily's skeleton jolted and her teeth clacked together along with Rowan's.

I'm all right, he said. He stayed in a crouch for moment, checking his surroundings before straightening up. *Two of you will have to make the jump carrying Juliet and Lily, but everyone else should be able to make it.*

Lily was still shaking when she felt Tristan pick her up in his arms and jump. She clutched at his neck and held her breath as she dropped down into the smothering belly of the earth. Even as she fell, Lily could feel the deadening hum of quartz in the soil around her. It was like entering a tomb.

Her whole body rattled with the impact of their landing. Tristan did his best to shield Lily from it, but even for a witch-fueled mechanic it had been a long drop. Lily felt Rowan's hands catching her and running over her lightly to scan for any damage.

I'm not injured, she told him privately in mindspeak. He removed his hands, but ignored the group order and stayed nearby as the coven began to move through the gloom.

They fanned out and let their magelight increase by degrees, but the space seemed to go on forever.

"It's three, maybe four times the size of the Salem Stacks," Juliet said. The sound of her voice made Lily jump, but then she realized there was no reason to continue in mindspeak. There were no Workers down here. Nothing living at all, except her coven.

"But the same layout," Tristan added. "Look. Here are the rooms for the skin looms."

They passed by a series of tall, skinny passageways. Breakfast pulled one of the looms out of the wall. It was three times his height, but it rolled out easily enough on casters that were set into tracks on the floor.

"Empty," Breakfast said. "Guess they don't have much use for wearhyde here."

"Why would they?" Una said. "They can get fine Italian leather if they want. They can afford it, too."

Lily nodded and started to move toward the hulking shapes occupying the main cavern. As she approached the first of many rows of womb combs, she could tell it was old. She put her hand on one of the stainless steel sides and imagined it full of ice lattices, each little cell housing a Woven embryo.

So many Woven, Lily thought. She brightened her magelight as much as she could without blinding herself, but she couldn't find an end to the procession.

"I've never seen so many," Rowan said, echoing Lily's thought. "Not even in New York."

"Is the New York Stack large?" Una asked.

"The largest of the Thirteen Cities," he answered. "Growing tame Woven is their main industry. Most of the city is underground on what you know of as Long Island. But this is even bigger."

"We should try to find the back wall. That's where those stairs are on Ivan's map," Caleb said.

They started to work their way down the rows of womb combs, every step bringing them deeper into the disorienting vastness of the space. Support pillars sprouted out of the floor and started to divide up the main area into smaller sections, confounding their sense of direction. Soon it was difficult to tell which of the sections led left, right, or straight on to the back.

"We'll split into our groups again," Caleb said. "Everyone stay in contact through Lily."

Her coven reached for her mind. Lily built a web of rapport that spun out as her coven dispersed in search of the back wall. The rows skewed on a diagonal as the size and shape of the womb combs changed.

Different Woven, Rowan thought. He was whispering to himself in his head, but Lily was in such close contact with him, and he was keeping so close to her physically, that she overheard.

Greater drakes, most likely, based on the size, he continued. Lily got an image of a dragon creature with iridescent skin, giant talons, and stunning wings. It was so large several people could easily ride it.

By the tanks for the greater drakes is where they made the mascots.

The image that flitted through his mind looked like an enormous dragonfly-serpent hybrid, clinging to the mast of a tall ship. It seemed to scan the sky, looking for danger, and its double-decker wings filled the sails with wind while it wrapped its long, scaly tail protectively around the rigging of the ship. Lily assumed that had to be a mascot.

Back there, the medium-size womb combs must have been where they made the guardians and other mammalian mixes. Lily got a glimpse of one of the guardians that they chained to the bottom of the greentowers.

So what are these smaller vats for? They aren't really womb combs. There are more of these than any other, but I can't think what would grow in them. Fast germinating Woven—the kind that hatches from an egg, mostly likely. Rowan pictured something that looked like wild Woven to Lily. They were mostly insect, but also part reptile or mammal, and none of them were the same. *Who would want to grow so many, and why?*

The vats stood like sentinels, lined up in perfect formation in the long-forgotten dark.

"It's an army," Lily whispered. A chill ran down her spine as she said it, and she knew she was right.

Rowan turned to her, discarding the notion out of hand. "No, this type of Woven serves no purpose. They're made from the leftover genetic material of the useful Woven, like the guardians, drakes, mascots, and cleaners—cleaners are mostly insectoid," he explained, seeing her confused look. "After you make a few batches of useful Woven you just throw whatever remains into one of these vats and see if anything good comes out of the mix. You have to destroy ninety-nine out of a hundred because all that most of them can do is eat and fight and . . ." He trailed off, a stricken look on his face.

"Pretty accurate description of the wild Woven around the Thirteen Cities, isn't it?" Lily said.

"No, because wild Woven reproduce like crazy." Rowan shook his head, unable to accept what was staring him in the face. "We make sure they're sterile—all of the Woven that we make in the womb combs are sterile. They can't reproduce."

"So how did the wild Woven start reproducing?" Lily asked gently.

"It was almost two hundred years ago. An accident—"

"Really?" Lily took a deep breath. "What if it wasn't?"

His eyes looked inward, and Lily could feel the skin on the back of his neck begin to crawl. "There are so many vats," he said, starting to think the unthinkable.

"Enough to flood the continent with wild Woven," she said. "And if you make it so they can reproduce, you'd only need to use the vats once."

Lily ran a finger through the film of ancient dust that lay on the otherwise-pristine vats. The questions that she'd been asking for months and the answers she'd been given that didn't sit right with her started to come together into one terrible truth.

"What if the wild Woven were *designed* to reproduce like crazy, *designed* to be poisonous so humans couldn't survive by eating them, *designed* to attack humans even if they weren't provoked? There are too many things about them that don't make sense, too many rules, unless you start thinking that they weren't an accident." She tapped the side of the vat. "*These* certainly weren't made on accident."

Rowan sat down hard on the dusty ground. He was looking into the empty palms of his hands, but he wasn't seeing anything. Lily sat down next to him and leaned her back against the steel. She could feel a thousand thoughts running through his head, like clouds racing across a wind-blown sky, and she waited. The thought clouds in his mind turned dark and crackled with lightning. Finally, he looked up at her.

"We need to find out why. I need to *know* what happened, not just guess," he said. "Ivan knows. That's why he sent us down here." He laughed bitterly. "A parting gift before we walked out the door."

Lily nodded. She could feel a yawning pain building in him at the thought of all the people he'd lost to the Woven. Of the childhood that was stolen from him by violence and hunger. She wrapped her arms around him and let him squeeze her tightly to the ache in his chest. No matter how many times Lily tried to push him out, Rowan managed to dig down deeper into her. He was fitted inside her so tightly now that no blame or bitterness between them could keep her from wanting to protect him from this terrible lie he'd lived with all his life.

Lily. Come quick. You have to see this.

Rowan and Lily jumped to their feet, both of them feeling the urgency in Tristan's call in mindspeak, and hurried in his direction. Lily noticed that the floor had begun to slope upward, when she slipped on something. Rowan's hand shot out and steadied her before she fell to her knees. She looked down.

"What is that?" she asked. She and Rowan inspected the coating on the floor. Rowan crouched down and touched the slippery substance, rubbing fingers and thumb together.

"I think it's wax," he said.

They kept moving forward and noticed that the wax also covered a pillar they passed. The rows of womb combs and vats ended, and the coating grew thicker until their feet were sinking into it.

"I see the rest of the coven's tracks," Rowan said. They continued on, careful of their footing, as they went down a series of ever-shrinking tunnels.

The passageway continued to narrow until they were walking down a thin tube. Hexagons rose out of the surface. Lily could smell something sweet in the air. She saw Rowan breathe it in.

"Honey," he said. He looked around. "We're in an old honeycomb."

They reached a bottleneck and had to squeeze through. The cavern they entered was stuffy, and it smelled of musk and honey. Lily saw her coven's backs. They were facing something. She felt their shock as they parted and let her through.

Sunk deep into the wax was a giant throne. On the throne, propped up by many velvet pillows, reclined the satin-clad torso of a woman. Trailing off to the side where her legs should have been was a pale, distended abdomen that ballooned up and out of the throne room into titanic proportions. Atop the human torso were the ovoid head and bulbous eyes of an insect, and around the Queen's neck hung a golden willstone.

CHAPTER
6

CARRICK COULDN'T SEE LILY AND HER COVEN LEAVE—they were moving much too fast for his eyes to follow—but he could feel that one moment there were people in Lily's suite of rooms, and the next it was empty.

He cursed silently to himself. Lillian could have used those speaking stones to send him enough power to follow them had he thought to ask, but he'd been banking on Lily's coven staying one more night. They'd cased the city all day, and then there was that long silence this evening—which he was sure was them plotting to make a break for it—but Carrick had his little brother pegged as too cautious to leave right away with no supplies and no horses. Someone else must be calling the shots. Maybe even Lily herself. She was rash enough.

Didn't matter. They had vanished and now Carrick had no excuse to give Lillian. Mala didn't concern him. She wanted Lily gone one way or another, so she wouldn't care much that they had fled the city. Mala had served her purpose by giving him enough cover to get him out of his plush jail cell. Lillian, however, would demand to know where Lily went. He was supposed to be watching her and filling in the gaps of information that Lily wasn't sharing with Lillian in mind-speak, like the existence of the speaking stones and Grace's fixation on solving the riddle of the two Lillians. Lily had been very forthcoming with Lillian, but that didn't mean she was sharing everything, and Lillian wanted to know *everything* about Bower City before she attacked.

Carrick scanned the smooth floor. He didn't think he'd be able to track Lily and her coven across marble, but he had to at least try. Still angry with himself for his miscalculation, he started down the main stair and through the foyer. Something told him that the coven had headed toward the government buildings. Maybe it was Lily's power he was sensing, or his brother's ever-lingering sadness, but he followed his hunch all the way to a door into nothing.

He had no choice but to call to Lillian and explain what had transpired. She was tired when he contacted her. Her sickness was unraveling her at the very moment she most needed to be whole. Carrick didn't doubt that she would live to see her plans through, though. And if she didn't, there was always Lily.

Lillian looked through Carrick's eyes at the door into nothing. *I think they went down there,* he told her. *I can't make the jump without your strength, My Lady.*

I can fuel you, but once you go down there I won't be able to reach you to give you more, Lillian replied.

Then I'll have to be careful with what you give me, Carrick said.

Very well.

Carrick was so consumed with receiving Lillian's strength, so focused on the fearlessness he felt as he plummeted into the darkness, that he didn't notice the Warrior Sisters following him.

Lily staggered closer to the Queen, staring at her. Workers were shuttling up and down the Queen's body, some of them cleaning her, while others marched to her mouthparts and away again, delivering a steady supply of royal jelly. Her gargantuan abdomen heaved, and the Queen's human hands, claw-like with tension, gripped at the velvet pillows.

"What are you *doing?*" Una hissed when she saw Lily move closer.

"She's in pain," Lily said.

There was no way to read the Queen's face. Her black faceted eyes held no emotion, and her mouth—a wet, tubular proboscis and waving mandibles—was downright nauseating, but still Lily could tell she was suffering. She stepped forward and took one of the Queen's human hands as her pale abdomen heaved again.

Lily wanted to comfort her, but she didn't think spoken words could be heard or understood. She tried to reach out to her in mindspeak and felt a distinct vibration clashing with hers. It was a harsh sensation that made Lily draw back immediately, like ice-cold water washing across a sore tooth. Lily knew what it meant, even if she'd never experienced it before. She looked at her coven, truly afraid.

"She's someone else's claimed," Lily said. "A witch controls the Queen."

"Grace," Juliet said, needing to voice it aloud to make it real.

"If Grace controls the Queen, does that mean she controls the whole Hive?" Una asked.

"That's a good bet," Breakfast said, grabbing Una and pushing her back toward the bottleneck. "We need to get out of here. Now."

Lily saw Caleb pull a pilfered steak knife out of his boot. She put out a hand to stop him. "No, don't! If you kill her, the entire Hive will be alerted. We'll never get out of here alive," she said.

"Oh, we're getting out," Rowan said. He snatched Lily up into his arms before anyone could tell him not to and started kicking at the wax around the Queen's belly to get into the room beyond.

"Rowan! Where are you going?" Tristan snarled.

"We'll never be able to jump up that long drop. We have to go this way," he snarled back.

The Queen's belly spasmed next to Rowan's head. Lily laid a hand on the swollen skin as she suffered through another contraction.

"Poor thing," she whispered, torn for a moment and wanting to help.

She saw the look of distaste on Rowan's face as he went back to kicking his way through to the next room. The rest of the coven seemed to collect themselves from their initial shock and joined him. The wax was thick and soft, and it absorbed their blows rather than shattering, making it difficult to move aside.

Lily thought for a moment that the Workers covering the Queen would attack them, but they didn't. In fact they hardly took any notice at all, and continued on as if blinded by their single task of tending the Queen.

We may not be so lucky with the Sisters, Rowan said in mindspeak, picking up on Lily's thoughts.

He broke through the wall of wax and put Lily down. *Protect Juliet*, Lily told them in mindspeak. *She's the only one besides me who can't fight.*

Breakfast, Caleb, and Una formed a circle, keeping her and Juliet in the center as they moved out. The rest of the Queen's abdomen lay alongside them as they moved forward.

Careful, Tristan warned them all in mindspeak.

There were lines of little Workers scuttling to and from the body of the Queen on the floor and the coven had to tread gently not to step on them. The Queen's body was at least thirty feet long and ten feet high and supported by wax buttresses that obscured the end of it.

Stop, Rowan said, raising a hand. There was movement up ahead. Rowan looked at Caleb and tilted his head. Caleb slid forward silently at Rowan's command and melted in the shadows. A few moments passed.

I think it's safe, Caleb said. *Just move slowly.*

They came forward and saw Warrior Sisters lined up at the end of the Queen's abdomen. Lily stopped short when she saw them, and then noticed that these Sisters looked different. They had lighter bodies, wore no armor, and they didn't carry whips; nor did they seem to see anything but the task before them. With each spasm of the Queen's abdomen, a translucent white egg the size of a backpack dropped from her tail into the waiting arms of a Sister. After the large egg was birthed, the Sister waited with her other hand held aloft for a drizzle of tiny Worker eggs that she caught and cupped protectively to her chest before hurrying off with the whole clutch.

I think I'm going to be sick, Una said.

Steady, Rowan replied. *Everyone stay calm. Act like you belong here and they probably won't even notice us.*

Rowan led them past the docile line of Sisters to one of the less-used hexagonal tunnels that led upward. The passage let out into a storage chamber that had two dozen wax sarcophaguses. As they weaved their way through them, Lily saw male bodies squirming inside. Their pale and heavily muscled limbs were twisted up with black veined wings. She was glad they all had their faces turned away.

Drones, Tristan said. *Keep moving, Ro.*

The next ramp opened into a huge cavern. Towers of wax held six-sided cells, each with the dark shape of a growing Sister just behind a protective film. Along one wall Sisters were bringing the newly laid eggs to empty cells. Next to them, Sisters were bricking up the cells with wax from their mandibles. Rowan led them away from the action.

They made their way up a series of ramps and tunnels, and the smell of pollen and honey grew stronger. Workers by the millions buzzed in and out like a black fog. She was scared to inhale and possibly swallow one of them. The walls dripped with honey and Lily could taste pollen dust, bittersweet and chalky, in the back of her throat.

These Workers are coming back to the Hive from the outside, Caleb said. *Where are they coming in?*

Breakfast spotted it first—a black haze of bee bodies that obscured what was probably the exit. The coven made its way there slowly. True Warrior Sisters, the big-bodied, thick-armored, whip-carrying kind, hovered around the exit. They perched on the dripping walls and licked the honey with their long, tubular tongues. Their heads twitched lightning fast, constantly on alert, but their senses were directed out into the world beyond, not back inside the hive.

This is insane, Breakfast said in mindspeak. Lily felt his heartbeat quicken.

A Warrior Sister detached from the wall and landed in front of the coven with a smacking sound. Her human hand reached back to milk her stinger for venom as she tasted the air, uncertain and trying to decide if there was a threat. She paused, transfixed on Rowan, who stood point. His chest was pumping with blood and breath.

Lily could feel fear rising in her coven like a swelling tidewater that lifted them, weightless and kicking, off the safety of the shore. The rolling draft from a million shivering wings spun the scent of panic throughout the hive in an instant. The rest of the Warrior Sisters by the entrance turned as one.

Rowan was the first to empty his heart of fear and goad the rest of the frozen coven into action.

Move.

Lily felt herself gathered up against Rowan's chest before the coven swept forward with preternatural speed that blinded her.

They made it outside the hive and into a dark forest before they were caught by dozens of armored bodies. Lily had the chance to catch half a thought going through Rowan's head.

They're moving too fast . . . before she felt herself ripped from his arms.

"Lily—no!" he screamed, his hands grasping at her forearms, her wrists, and then sliding to the tips of her fingers and releasing with a snap as they were separated. Lily saw a bright spot at the base of the Warrior Sisters' throats and knew that under their skin they must have willstones, and that a witch must be fueling them.

Rowan reared up from under a cluster of shiny black armor and yellow-and-black tiger-striped skin, wrenching heads from necks and tearing off wings and limbs in a blur of fury and desperation. No matter how many he killed, more Warrior Sisters came at him. Lily felt a barbed hand grabbing the back of her neck and slamming her down to her knees. The ground was dry and prickly with fallen needles. She looked up and saw her coven fighting among the trunks of colossal redwood trees. Her coven had formed a circle around Juliet to protect her, but their strength was failing.

Lily. Save us, Una pleaded in mindspeak. She was covered in Workers, each of them poised and ready to sting. They were holding back, waiting for the order from their witch.

Lily took a breath and the wind followed, spinning and scream-ing as it fell toward her. Digging deep, she searched for anything left inside to give her coven.

Lily, don't, Rowan said. *You'll be using what you need to stay func-tioning. Your body will shut down and you'll die.*

The Warrior Sisters looked at her. The air stopped dead, debris hanging suspended in the air, as Lily prepared to drain herself dry and transmute the last of her strength.

"You can't win, Lily Proctor," said a familiar voice. "You'll only get your coven killed if you keep fighting."

Lily raised her eyes and saw Grace being held aloft by a host of Warrior Sisters. Her black willstone was surrounded by a halo of eerie purple-green light as it transmuted the energy she was feeding her claimed. The Sisters brought Grace to the forest floor. She stepped down from their inter-clasped hands with such practiced ease it was clear she'd done it an uncountable number of times before.

"You have no pyre and nothing left to give your already-overtaxed coven, while my claimed are fresh for a fight," Grace continued, stepping forward smoothly.

"Your claimed," Lily snarled. "I thought you didn't do that here."

"I said we don't claim *people* here. The Woven are not people," Grace said. "Tell your mechanics to stop struggling. You're vastly out-numbered and out of options."

Lily sagged between the two Warrior Sisters holding her by the arms. She reabsorbed the dregs of her strength and the witch wind let go of its half-drawn breath, allowing the floating debris to fall back to earth. Lily's heart continued to beat, her nerves kept firing, but every muscle went lax with exhaustion.

Rowan bucked against the hands restraining him. Grace nodded once and he was released. Stumbling with fatigue, Rowan pitched himself forward and fell to his knees in front of Lily, trying to pull her away from her captors and into his arms. Another nod from Grace, and the Warrior Sisters backed off and let him. He ran his hands lightly over Lily, scanning her.

"You see, Toshi, as touching as Rowan's display may seem, he's actually her slave," Grace said.

Lily's head snapped around and she saw Toshi being brought to the ground by the Warrior Sisters. His uneasy look and stumbling steps made it clear he'd never traveled by Hive before.

"It isn't *love*. If she dies, he's left without his addiction," Grace continued, acting the part of benevolent teacher. "I spared you a life-time of dependency and servitude."

Toshi nodded and put on a studious face. "I see. Yes. Of course you're right, Grace."

Lily gave him a sad smile. He looked shell-shocked and sorry. Ivan had been right. Toshi hadn't known how Bower City worked, and now that he did it was too late. The Hive ran Bower City, but Grace controlled the Hive.

Lily had to look away, and as she did she saw a flash of white and a long, pale tail disappearing behind one of the towering redwoods. Lily shook her head, knowing she must be delirious. That couldn't be who she thought it was.

They're trying to separate us, Caleb said.

Lily looked and saw Juliet being pulled out of Caleb's protective grip. Lily started to panic. Out of all of them, Juliet was the most vulnerable. The Hive could sense that, and she knew they were going to exploit it. But Juliet was not the type to shut her mouth and go quietly.

"You're not saving Toshi, you're saving yourself," Juliet said bitterly to Grace as she struggled against the Sister's grip. "Your law against claiming is to keep another witch from gathering together a coven powerful enough to challenge you."

"There is no coven powerful enough to challenge me," Grace said, her eyes blazing. "My coven is the Woven. I *own* this continent."

Lily felt a collective moment of understanding dawn on her coven. Finally, all the pieces fit together.

"You use the speaking stones to communicate with them—no. To control them," Lily said, trying to keep Grace talking and draw it out as long as she could. "That's why the Woven don't go underground. Going underground would cut them off from your orders to keep every other witch behind her walls. Your orders to kill, kill, kill."

Grace caught a whiff of Lily's mockery and sneered. "Well, they are simple things," she replied. "Best to give them simple orders."

"Simple minds are probably easier to claim, too. You don't even have to touch their willstones, do you?"

"The lower species have a less defined sense of self. The Hive doesn't even see themselves as individuals, and neither do the wild Woven. They don't have will, not the way we know it. They wouldn't be much good to me if they did."

Lily forced herself to sound admiring. "Creating Woven so they grow willstones inside their bodies was sheer genius. But I bet remote claiming through the speaking stones has some flaws. Some of the higher Woven have will, and you couldn't fully claim them, not without their consent, and not without touching their willstones. They've resisted and broken free from you, haven't they?"

Grace smiled slowly. "There have been a few breeds that were useful at the start and then harder to control after a few generations."

"The Pack. The Pride. The Coyotes—I bet the Coyotes were the first to break free. The Pack and the Pride would have stronger instincts to follow because they already follow an alpha," Lily said. "That's why you eventually switched back to insects with the Hive. They don't even have a concept for disobedience, do they?"

"Enough about my coven," Grace said, growing impatient. She snapped her fingers at a tight cluster of Warrior Sisters, and they parted to reveal another passenger among them. "Let's discuss yours."

Carrick stepped forward. His shoulders were hunched and his head was cocked like a crow's. Lily went stock-still. Just seeing Carrick was enough to steal the heat from her blood.

"He's not mine," Lily rasped, her disgust at the thought evident.

"I know," Grace replied. "Which brings us to the reason I've kept you alive this long. Why I had my Hive retrieve you instead of kill you to begin with." Grace folded her hands neatly. "Explain to me how there can be one Lillian Proctor here in front of me, and another in Salem. I tried to play nice, but Toshi couldn't seem to charm the information out of you. Carrick wouldn't tell me, and I suspect his witch—the other Lillian—wouldn't mind killing him if he tried. I think I've played nice long enough. Explain how there can be two of you, and I'll let *this* one live."

Grace tilted her head and two of the Warrior Sisters hauled Juliet away from the group and pushed her down on her knees in front of Lily.

"No—she's not mine, either. She's not my claimed," Lily stammered. The panic she felt grew wings and flapped around in her chest like a broken bird. "You don't need to hurt her. Please."

Grace waved Lily's pleading away, her frustration mounting. "I know she's not yours. You've had your true mechanics carrying her about, so I can see that you are unable to fuel her. But you still love her like a sister, don't you?"

Lily nodded numbly, her eyes locked with Juliet's.

Juliet gave Lily a sad smile, her breath fluttering on the edge of a sob. She looked younger, like when they were little kids. Her skin was so pale her wide eyes look bruised. Lily had seen that stricken, terrified look on her sister's face many times, but always when it was Lily who was close to death, and not herself. Lily would give anything for that to be the case right now. A thousand times over she'd rather be the one to be in danger. Not Juliet. Lily scrounged through her head for something—anything. She looked at Rowan, but he shook his head at her, his eyes as desperate as hers. He had nothing left. The rest of her coven had nothing left. There was only one person Lily could ask for help, and Lily couldn't believe it had taken this long to think of her.

Lillian. They have Juliet.

She felt Lillian's drowsy mind rousing itself from sleep. Lily felt Lillian's pain wash over her like lava, before Lillian shielded her from it.

"I'm waiting," Grace said through clenched teeth.

"Okay. Yes. There are two of us. Two Lillians," Lily said, ready to tell her everything to buy time. "More than two. There are an infinite number of mes, of yous—of everyone—in other universes."

"You sound like a shaman," Grace said, laughing. Then her brow furrowed, half believing.

Lily, I'm lighting a fire. Hold on, Lillian said in mindspeak. *Carrick will assist you.*

Carrick started to ease himself away from the Warrior Sisters around him. Lily felt Rowan stiffen as if he were listening to someone else's mindspeak.

Carrick has flint and steel, Rowan told Lily. *We need to make a distraction so he has enough time to scrape off a spark.*

"Yes, a shaman. A shaman taught me," Lily blurted out. She cast around for something to cause a distraction.

"A shaman taught you *what*? How to farsee? Spirit walk? How can either of those things explain the fact that there are two Lillians?" Grace asked. "I've been alive for a very long time, but I've never seen this before."

A flash of white slid around the back of a redwood. Lily was desperate enough to try something that was still just an inkling, rather than an idea. She reached out to the confluence of scents, and the sharp but strange sensations she'd experienced many months ago when she found a willstone buried under the pale coyote's skin. It was the thing that had put the idea of going west into her head in the first place—a connection that she hadn't imagined possible. It had taken her this long to understand.

Pale One. Help me.

"I really hate waiting," Grace said sadly.

Lily knew that there was a universe where everything worked out perfectly. Somewhere in the worldfoam a version of her had realized that the pale coyote was one of her claimed earlier. Somewhere in the worldfoam a version of Lillian had been awake, with a fire already going, and she'd been able to intervene sooner. But this was neither of those worlds. And Lily ran out of time. The sisters shared a last desperate look.

"It's okay," Juliet whispered, her huge eyes full of forgiveness that Lily would never believe she'd deserved.

Grace didn't even flinch when the Warrior Sister broke Juliet's neck with one sharp tug. Lily watched the light go out of her sister's brown eyes. From life to death in a moment, and it was as if the body that fell to the ground wasn't even her sister. Couldn't be her sister. No. Her sister was a joyful spirit, full of warmth and hope, not a blank rag doll lying small and broken on a bed of dry redwood needles.

"Juliet?" Lily whispered. She'd get up. She wasn't dead. "Juliet!" she shouted, as if to wake her.

"Toshi. Get her largest willstone," Grace said. "Leave her the other two so she's conscious enough to feel what I'm going to do to her."

Lily didn't know if it was her scream or Lillian's scream or if both of them were screaming at the same time, but the sound was inside her and outside her and everywhere in a moment. Everything seemed to slow down. Everything went red with rage.

The pale coyote leapt over Lily's head and attacked Grace. The Hive turned as one to their fallen witch, and as they did, Carrick brought his hands together and cast a spark at Lily's feet. The resinous needles that lay around her erupted into flame and Lily stood up, planting her feet in the fire and drawing the heat into her willstone. A Warrior Sister backhanded Carrick. He fell to the ground and lay still.

Lily's witch wind boomed. The redwoods creaked in the sudden gust. Grace looked up at Lily with fear in her eyes.

Gift me, Rowan begged. *I'll tear her apart.*

No. The Hive is too strong. I can't lose you, too.

"This isn't over," Lily promised Grace. She drew as much heat into her as she could, summoned her covens' willstones, and catapulted them all across the worldfoam and back to her universe.

CHAPTER
7

LILY WAS NOT ASLEEP. SHE WAS NOT UNCONSCIOUS OR dreaming. This was happening. It was real, and it was not going to disappear no matter how much she wanted it to.

Juliet was dead. Maybe not *her* Juliet, not the version she'd been raised with, but still her sister. Lily was not going to let it go or move past it or forgive like sweet Juliet had done. She was going to go back to Bower City, but this time, she was going with an army. Hatred filled her mouth, wet and sour. She was going to go back and, when she did, she was going to kill every last one of them.

Lily looked up from the forest floor. She was standing with her coven around her. Dawn was starting to filter through the redwoods that reached above her like thick arms holding heaven over the earth. She felt shrunk down in comparison—an ant in a giant's farm. In another universe, a dying version of her was weeping. Lily wasn't. She could feel Lillian's sobs, and she had to let those tears be enough. One of them to cry, one of them to stay grounded, and maybe together they could survive this. She called out to her other self.

Lillian. You need to calm down.

My sister is dead. I can't calm down.

We have work to do. Gather your army.

I started gathering my army when you first contacted me. We're already on the move.

Is that why you were always so occupied?

Yes. Grace has to die, Lily.

There was a time Lily would have quibbled about the morality of something like that, but now everything had changed. Tristan was dead. Juliet was dead. Lily looked at Una, Caleb, the other Tristan, Breakfast, and Rowan and knew that if she wanted to keep them alive she was going to have to get comfortable with crossing lines, just as Lillian had.

Yes. She does, Lily agreed.

Finally, you've joined me, Lillian replied, and for a moment, Lily shared Lillian's view on the world.

She saw the army that Lillian had assembled. Men, women, and a menagerie of tame Woven were already on the move, and they were moving fast. Lillian climbed on the back of a greater drake and vaulted into the air. Lily could see its iridescent wings churning the wind and its talons raking the sky. She was like a warmonger witch from a bygone era, and she was going not to fight, but to completely eradicate her enemy. Lillian didn't say it, but Lily got the sense that she considered all of the people of Bower City the enemy. Lily was suddenly afraid for Toshi, his sister, his aging father, and his sick mother. Lily thought of the two children who'd stared at her with their mouths open.

Lillian, I'm going to exterminate the Hive, but the people of Bower City have no knowledge of Grace's control over them and over all the wild Woven. They're innocent.

Lily waited, but Lillian had blocked her out.

"Lily? Are you okay?" Rowan asked.

She startled and looked down at herself, but saw no burns. She was unscathed by the fire. Rowan saw what Lily was doing and shook his head.

"I'm not talking about your body," he said.

Lily looked at him. The only Rowan. He had no copy. If he died, that was it. She'd never seen him as fragile before, and the thought that anyone could go from life to death with one sharp tug made her desperate. It could happen to him.

Did you do that on purpose? she asked Lillian. *Make it so I only had one of him?* But she didn't get an answer. She didn't need one. There had only ever been one Rowan for both of them.

"Lillian is marching her army to Bower City," Lily told him. "She's emptied Walltop, the city guard, and claimed tens of thousands more from the other Thirteen Cities. She means to take the west."

Rowan nodded like he'd expected as much. "Alaric will see her army on the move. If he finds out about Bower City he'll want to take it for himself."

"He probably already knows," Caleb said. "You can't keep a secret like that once you've mustered an army. Lillian's not marching west to fight nothing."

"What about the other Covens?" Tristan asked. "Richmond, Exeter, New York . . . they'll all want a piece of what the west has got."

"The other Covens will wait and see what happens to Lillian," Rowan said. "If she kills herself and her army trying to get there, they'll set their sights on Salem. Nina, who's Lillian's second right now, won't be able to hold as Salem Witch. She isn't a firewalker."

"I remember Nina," Lily said, her eyes narrowing. Nina had strad-dled Rowan in the nightclub where Elias had died. Lily had wanted to punch her then, and as she recalled Nina throwing a leg over

Rowan's lap and rubbing her hands all over his chest, she still wanted to punch her now.

Rowan turned to Lily, unaware of her flare of jealousy. "Does Lillian know that Grace controls the Woven?"

"She knows everything that we know," Lily said. "She's going west to end the Woven, once and for all."

And she means to kill Grace, no matter how many have to die in the process, she added in mindspeak for only Rowan to hear.

Rowan nodded. *I don't blame her. Juliet was all she had left.*

Lily winced at Juliet's name, and quickly stuffed down her anguish. *Later*, she told herself. *I'll cry later.*

"Even with all her claimed, Lillian can't stand against the Hive," Rowan said aloud.

Caleb nodded in agreement. "The Hive is a million strong," he said soberly.

"Would she tell the other Covens about Grace and the Woven? Maybe get them to help?" Breakfast asked.

"I don't know," Lily said. "I don't know if they'd be willing to take the risk like Lillian would. They're pretty safe where they are."

"Yeah," Caleb chuffed. "Witches have no reason to want to get rid of the Woven. They do just fine ruling their cities behind their walls."

"Can Alaric help Lillian?" Una asked. Caleb, Tristan, and Rowan stared at her disbelievingly. "No, seriously, guys. Lillian has her personal crusade against the Woven—fine—but the people who really need to get rid of the Woven are the Outlanders. If Alaric knew that Grace made them, and still controls them, why wouldn't he want to fight her?" Una's voice flared with indignation. "She's an Outlander who's been killing Outlanders for almost two centuries. Alaric should want to kick the ever-loving piss out of her when he finds out."

"It's not Alaric's decision," Lily said coldly. "It's mine. That's my army he's pretending to lead. They're *my* claimed." Everyone went silent. Lily scrubbed her hands over her face and sat down on the ground. "And they're on the other side of the continent."

"And in another world," Breakfast reminded her.

"Oh, the worldjumping bit is easy for Lily now," Una said. "Look at her."

Lily was so spent her muscles were twitching, but she wasn't on the verge of death. "I wouldn't say easy," Lily grumbled.

"Why can't you worldjump us back east?" Tristan asked.

"Because it's . . . well, it's not the same thing," she said, trying to picture how she would do something like that. "That's teleporting, not worldjumping."

"You'd think it'd be easier," Breakfast said. "I mean, a universe is farther away than Salem, right?"

Lily looked up at him, so tired she couldn't see straight. "No, actually it isn't. Every universe is only a vibration away."

Breakfast shrugged. "Maybe Salem is, too."

Lily squinted at Breakfast, trying to order her thoughts enough to explain why he was wrong. If she'd taught him to spirit walk, like she'd intended to months ago, he'd know the difference. Or maybe he wouldn't. The shaman had only taught her to spirit walk into other universes, because his reason for teaching her was to restore the balance. He'd only taught her enough to get her back to her world, but now that she thought about it, there had to be a way to spirit walk and stay in one universe. She'd just never learned how.

Those first few times she'd spirit walked, before she really knew what she was doing, she remembered rising up and looking around. Her spirit was still in the same world that her body was in, but everything had looked gray. What had the shaman called that gray spirit world she'd walked in? The overworld? Lily couldn't be sure he'd ever said that, but she *felt* like that was its name. It was like the Mist. It dawned on Lily that maybe they were the same thing. She rubbed her forehead, confused.

"He said that I had to be close to death to spirit walk—starved, dehydrated—and every time I met Lillian in the Mist we were both near death or in pain. I think the Mist, or overworld, or whatever you want to call it, could be a path. A bridge across *this* world, not just into another one," Lily mumbled.

"Who's he?" Rowan asked cautiously.

"The shaman," Lily replied, distracted. An idea was building in her and she wanted to follow her train of thought. "If I could spirit walk to Salem and find the vibration, maybe I could world-jump us there physically. But do places have vibrations, or is it just universes?"

"The shaman?" Tristan asked carefully.

"Yeah. You see, the shaman had his own agenda," she continued, thinking out loud. "He wanted me out of his world, not able to jump to any part of it I wanted. Maybe it was the same with Lillian. He never taught her about the overworld or how to travel across it, so she made up her own name for it. The Mist."

Lily glanced up and saw that her coven was looking back at her with wide, worried eyes.

"The *dead* shaman," Breakfast said, as if to clarify.

Her coven thought that the shaman had been long dead when she was put in the oubliette.

"Do you get it? The worldfoam is the bridge to other universes, but the overworld—or the Mist, or whatever you want to call it—is the bridge across one world. It's how Lillian and I were able to meet face to face on the raft," Lily announced.

"Raft?" Una asked dubiously. "You met Lillian on a raft?"

Lily gave a frustrated growl. "It makes sense! The shaman hid the overworld from me so I'd have no choice but to leave his world or die. If I could just use the overworld to teleport myself out of the oubliette, he wouldn't have gotten rid of me like he wanted."

"I think Lily's had enough," Rowan said. "Let's deal with getting back to Salem after some rest."

"You think I'm crazy," she said to her coven. "I'm telling you. The shaman was there in the oubliette with me."

"Okay, Lily," Una said, placating her. "I believe you. But right now you need to rest."

The coven settled down in a far-flung circle. They all needed a moment to grieve for Juliet, and this was one of those times when the deep bond between them only intensified their emotions rather than helped alleviate them. Lily wished she could hole up behind the thick walls of a citadel so she wouldn't feel what the others were feeling. She wandered among the trees until she couldn't take another step and sat down inside the living cathedral, staring up at dawn's paint on the ceiling.

She reached out to Juliet, hoping some part of her was still in the overworld. She stretched and strained, pressing her will into a tight ball that she sent up and out of her like a prayer. There was no answer. Just silence and mist.

Finally, Lily let herself cry. She cried until she choked and her stomach was sour from swallowing tears. She cried until her sides ached no matter how tightly she squeezed them. Rowan lay down on the ground behind her and put his arms around her. It felt like her ribs were cracking and she'd come apart if he didn't hold her together. He didn't say a word. She didn't push him away.

Lily dreamed about the Queen. She was drowning in honey, reaching out to Lily in a wordless plea. Her insect head had Juliet's eyes. Lily woke with a start. Rowan was asleep next to her. He was still thin and bronzed from the trail. His grown-out hair fell over his sharp features, giving him a lean and wild look that made her ache. Rowan felt her staring at him and opened his eyes, his head pillowed on his bicep.

I left Juliet's body behind, she said in mindspeak.

You had to. It was that, or we all would have died with her, he replied.

What do you think the Hive will do with it?

Don't think about that. Please, Lily. Don't try to picture it.

I left Tristan's body behind, too. I can't even bury the people who die for me.

Lily could feel how deeply he wanted to reach out and pull her down onto his chest, and for a moment, Lily didn't know what she was going to do. The most natural thing in the world would be to kiss him and love him, but she couldn't. Not with an image of her Tristan's rotting body in her thoughts. Rowan caught a glimpse of what she was thinking and he let his eyes drift away from hers. The moment passed. Lily hauled herself up to standing.

She found the rest of the coven already regrouping a few hundred yards away. Tristan watched Lily as she came out from between the trees. His gaze lingered on her puffy face and her red eyes.

"Where's Rowan?" he asked.

Lily shrugged. "Back there," she said, her indifference making it clear that the rift between them had not been repaired. Tristan looked troubled by this, so she changed the subject. "Anyone have any food?"

"We were just discussing that," Caleb said. He looked hassled. "Is anyone familiar with this Monterey area?"

"I've never been, but I've seen pictures," Lily offered lamely.

"Anyone who's seen a car commercial has seen pictures of Monterey," Una said. Tristan and Caleb had matching expressions of confusion. She shook her head. "Wow. That's right. Neither of you have been to this world."

"Do we need papers to get into the city?" Caleb asked.

Rowan emerged from the brush and joined them. "No. And you can relax, Caleb. There are no Woven in these woods."

Lily noticed Caleb's shoulders drop and realized that he had been on alert. "There might be a mountain lion or a bear here or there, but it's safe," Lily added. "And we can walk into town without having to show any identification."

Caleb and Tristan shared a look and possibly some mindspeak. They both seemed uneasy with how easy things were here.

"But we do need money," Breakfast said. He stood up and brushed the redwood needles off his legs. He studied his clothes, which were from Bower City. "This kit either makes me look like the coolest guy ever, or a giant tool. I can't decide which."

Una chuckled. "Do you really want me to answer that?"

"We're in California," Lily said before they could start their back-and-forth teasing. "I think they have a broad definition of normal here. We should blend in just fine."

"California," Rowan said under his breath, a bittersweet smile on his lips. He looked up at the redwood canopy and took a deep breath, letting the dappled light play on his face. "Feel that?"

"What?" Tristan asked.

"Nothing to fear."

As they set out, Lily could feel Lillian brushing against her mind, asking where they were going. Lily blocked her out. She had to start thinking strategically again, and not run to Lillian for comfort every time she lost her nerve.

Lily still hadn't decided how to get Lillian and Alaric to work together, but she knew that she had to do it face-to-face and not give Lillian the chance to come up with a counterplan. Lily's only shot at uniting all of the armies was to confront them and force them to work together somehow, although she still had no idea how she was going to do that. Until she came up with a plan, she needed to keep Lillian in the dark about what she hoped to do or she ran the risk of being outmaneuvered by her other self. And Lily had the uneasy feeling that being outmaneuvered could mean the deaths of many innocent people. Lillian wouldn't hesitate to lose every last one of her claimed if it meant killing Grace.

They walked for hours before reaching anything close to a road. They didn't go completely hungry, though. Every few steps Rowan or Caleb would spot something edible and pick it or dig it up for the group to share.

"It's like a market day," Caleb said, his face grim.

"Pretty much everything grows out here," Breakfast said. "Farming is one of the main industries of California."

That only made Caleb angrier. "And Grace kept it all for herself," he said, fuming.

Breakfast and Una shared a worried look with Lily. The more time Caleb had to digest just how deeply wronged his people had been by Grace, the deeper his resentment went. She looked at Rowan, expecting some of that anger to be in him, too, but all she saw in him was a wistful sadness. He took in the majesty of the redwood forest as if it was the first time he'd ever been able to enjoy the woods, rather than just survive them.

The coastal road was no less stunning. A strip of concrete wound along cliffs that hung, green and misty, over the edge of dark blue water that was churned into pearly foam around the rocks.

"Surfers," Rowan said, pointing down at the bobbing figures in slick-black wetsuits. Big surf had come in with the setting sun, and they rode the frigid water with the mellow golden light behind them.

Caleb and Tristan stared down at the surfers like they'd never seen anything so outrageous.

"Those rocks," Tristan said, grimacing. "That guy is going to get himself killed."

"No. They don't let amateurs surf this break. He knows what he's doing," Rowan mumbled, focused on watching one of them paddle out and drop into a set. The wave broke sloppy, and the surfer wiped out. "Ah!" Rowan exclaimed, wincing. He turned to the group, pointing, and realized that they weren't as engrossed as he was.

"You know, it kind of fits," Breakfast said, studying Rowan.

"Yeah. Rowan the surfer dude," Una agreed.

Rowan blushed and looked down. "Hardly," he said, his enjoyment vanishing. "I would have liked to have tried it, though."

They followed the road into town, but didn't have to walk the entire way. One of the surfers leaving the break let them pile into the back of his pickup truck and he took them the rest of the way into town.

"Are you guys going to be okay?" the surfer asked as they got out.

"We're meeting friends," Breakfast lied.

"Well, if your friends bail on you, there's a party," he said. "I'm Miller."

"Hey, Miller. I'm Breakfast. This is my lady, Una. Tristan, Caleb, Rowan, Lily. Rowan wants to surf."

"Yeah? Nice," Miller said, smiling broadly.

And just like that, Breakfast had made another friend. Miller took them to the party where there were tons of salty chips and guacamole for Lily, enough for her to refuel the rest of them. The coven took turns washing up in the bathroom as discreetly as they could. Not that it mattered. Half the people at the party had spent the day in the ocean and were just as disheveled and windblown as they were.

"Is everyone in this world so generous?" Caleb asked disbelievingly.

"Not *everyone*," Breakfast answered. "But I guess that's surfers for you."

Tristan looked around. Several cute girls looked back. "I like California," he decided.

Lily and Rowan shared a knowing grin and then caught

themselves. It was easy to forget that they didn't belong among these carefree people—that they didn't belong together anymore.

"So I asked my friend, and he said you can all crash here tonight," Miller told them as he rejoined the group.

"We really appreciate that," Breakfast said. "I've got to hit an ATM at some point, though, and pitch in for the drinks."

"Don't worry about it. Just tell me where you all got those necklaces." Miller couldn't take his eyes off Lily's willstones. "What kind of crystals are those?"

"I grow them," Rowan said. *He's got talent*, he added in mindspeak for the coven. *He's drawn to Lily.*

That's probably why he stopped to pick us up, Una added.

"You grow crystals? No way," Miller said, looking admiringly at Rowan. "You know, we should go surfing in the morning. I'll take you to our break."

Rowan looked pained. "I'd love to, but I don't have a board," he said.

Miller shrugged. "You can use one of mine. I have extra wetsuits, too. You can't go in the water up here without one."

"Miller, do you have a landline?" Lily asked, saving Rowan from having to decline. "I need to check in with my sister back in Massachusetts. Let her know I got in okay. I'll call collect."

"No you won't," Miller said, shaking his head. He put down his beer and gestured for Lily to follow him. "The guy who owns this place is a trust fund baby. He won't even notice."

Miller took Lily into the kitchen. There were a bunch of people attacking a fondue set on the center island, laughing, making a mess. They looked so happy. So free. Lily watched them with a smile, imagining Juliet's bright laugh chiming out of the mix. Miller got the landline receiver out of a drawer and pulled open a sliding glass door that led to a wraparound patio.

"It's quieter out here," he told her, handing her the phone.

"Thanks, Miller. I won't be long."

He stayed with one hand on the open door. "So, you and Rowan——" he began leadingly. "Are you two, like, together?"

"Yes," Lily answered, just to make things easier. It didn't even feel like a lie, and she had to remind herself that it was.

"Cool," Miller said, backing off. He stumbled a little, his feet suddenly awkward.

Lily closed the glass door behind her and saw Miller lingering on the other side of it for a moment, reluctant to leave her. He finally stalked off, frowning to himself like he wished he could go back and do that whole conversation over again.

Lily's hands shook while she dialed her home phone number. As usual, Juliet sensed that Lily was going to call and picked up before the end of the first ring.

"Lily?" Juliet said.

"Jules——" Lily's voice broke and more tears came.

"Are you hurt? What happened?" Juliet asked, her voice high and breathy with worry. Lily tried to say something and failed. "You shouldn't have called——"

"Juliet. I need money. A lot of it," Lily managed to choke out.

"I'll wire it," Juliet said. "Can you just *think* where really hard and not say it?"

Months had passed since Lily and her coven had left Scot's body in the snow, but she should have guessed that no amount of time would make the FBI agent assigned to her case back off.

"Simms," Lily said, naming the Rottweiler of a special agent.

Lily looked through the glass and watched Miller pacing back and forth on the edge of the kitchen like a caged cat, and it clicked in her head. Simms would never let Lily's case go. She probably didn't even understand why she chased after Lily the way she did, but Lily understood. Simms was either a latent mechanic or a crucible.

"It's far, Jules." Lily pictured what she'd seen that day. She spent a long time concentrating on the different images and all the associations that she could make for this place. Several minutes passed before Juliet responded.

"Got it," she said. "Aw, I always wanted to go there."

Lily laughed and sniffled at the same time. "I really miss you."

"I miss you, too, but you need to go. The cash will be at the Walmart," Juliet said. "Be safe."

Lily hung up and stared out at the varying shades of darkness that still couldn't quite smother the beauty of the view. The house was built on the edge of the bluff, and the surf brushed and sucked at the rough rocks below, filling the air with a muffled shushing. Midnight water winked back at the moon. Lily could smell the redwoods seasoned with salt from the ocean. She didn't know what to do.

The sliding glass door opened behind her. Lily turned, expecting to see Miller there, but it was Tristan. She smiled at him. "Shouldn't you be in there breaking hearts?" she teased.

Tristan smiled back at her joke, but looked away. "I think I've gotten tired of all that," he said, sitting down on the edge of the deck next to Lily. "It's one thing to know that you run around with a lot of girls, and another thing to actually meet yourself and *see* you doing it."

Lily nodded. "When I first met Lillian, and I'm talking about that first second I laid eyes on her, I hated her. Probably because I saw in her all the things that I disliked in myself. I've never hated anyone that much."

Tristan looked at her sharply. "You've never talked with me about meeting her."

"I've never talked with anyone about it," Lily said. "It's almost embarrassing to see yourself so clearly. To know—not just think—but to *know* that you aren't as great as you thought or maybe just hoped you were."

"That's it," Tristan said, nodding. "I always hoped I'd be a better person than I am, but after meeting the other Tristan, and sharing his memories . . . well. I know how flawed I am. More flawed than anyone knows. Even you."

Tristan took a breath as if he was about to tell Lily something, but a sharp sound from around the corner of the wraparound deck made Tristan jump. As he stared into the dark, trying to find the source of the sound, the sliding door behind them opened.

"Did you talk to her?" Una asked. Caleb was right behind her, and they stepped outside to join Lily and Tristan.

"Yeah," Lily said, her mind back on Juliet. "Money's on its way. Someone's waiting for us back there, though." Lily sent them all an image of Simms.

"We can't fly, then," Una said. "She'll be all over us as soon as we try to board a plane."

"We can take a bus. Or rent a car under a fake name," Lily suggested.

"I like the rental car idea better. It's more private," Una replied.

"See what Breakfast can get out of Miller. Maybe say one of us needs a fake ID to buy alcohol or something," Lily said.

"That's shouldn't be too hard," Una said, a wry smile dimpling her cheek. "He's practically got Miller asking him to marry him." Her eyes unfocused as she passed Lily's request to Breakfast in mindspeak.

"I think Miller's more interested in Lily," Caleb said.

Lily nodded pensively, recognizing too much of Scot in Miller. "We should leave as soon as we can."

"How long will it take us to get back to the East Coast?" Caleb asked.

"If we drive in shifts? I've heard of people doing it in three days," Lily replied.

"Unbelievable," Tristan said under his breath. "How long did it take us just to get across the mountains, Caleb?"

"Weeks," Caleb replied, not in the mood to reminisce. He frowned deeply. "Three days to get back. Worldjump. Then we still have to find Alaric . . ."

"Who said we're going to Alaric?" Lily asked.

Caleb looked shocked. "You don't mean to join Lillian, do you?" he asked.

She met his eyes. When she claimed him, she promised him that she was going to fight Lillian—not the Woven, not some unknown witch three thousand miles away, not evil incarnate. *Lillian.* His eyes wouldn't give her an inch. She should have known he would hold her to it someday.

Lily sighed and looked out at the night. Little lights sparkled here and there up the coast. She could stand up right now and walk all the way to those lights and not one bad thing would happen to her. No monsters would loom up and tear her apart. No sadistic witches would kill her loved ones if she left them behind. She could climb down to the ocean, throw off her clothes, and swim in the cold, briny water until dawn if she chose. But she couldn't choose that. The time when she could have stayed in her own world had passed. Lillian had won, and whether she went back and joined Lillian's army or not didn't matter. Ultimately, they were fighting for the same thing.

"I don't know what I'm going to do," she said. "I have no reason to trust either Alaric or Lillian, but we're going to need *both* of them or we don't stand a chance against the Hive."

Even that might not be enough, Rowan said to Lily in mindspeak. He came around the deck from the other side.

"Getting Alaric and Lillian to work together might not be possible," Rowan said quietly. "It's not just them. The people who follow them hate one another."

Lily set her jaw. "Then what's the point of going back? Why even try to save them if they're too stupid to save themselves?" She looked out at the moon-clad water. "Alaric calls Lillian the enemy. Lillian calls Alaric the enemy—but we've seen the real enemy of that world. Now we have to make them see it, too. If we can't do that, what the hell good are we?"

Rowan nodded once. "Okay. Who should we go after first? Alaric or Lillian?"

"You're not serious?" Caleb said, scowling at Rowan. "You actually want to go and try and talk to Lillian?"

"That's what our witch is asking of us, Caleb," Rowan replied reproachfully. "And is it any more than asking Lily to go to Alaric after what he did to her?"

"Alaric isn't half as bad as Lillian," Caleb argued.

"Are we talking about the same guy?" Una snapped. "Alaric. He's the nut with the nukes, remember? That guy is about to bomb the whole eastern seaboard and you think he's more trustworthy?"

Caleb looked down. A silence followed while they all tried to picture how a confrontation with either Lillian or Alaric would play out.

"So, we're really going to try to fight the Hive?" Tristan said, his voice husky with fear.

They sat with that thought, each recalling his or her focus of dread. For Lily it was the sound—the buzzing that made her skin pucker and her insides watery. She heard the door slide open behind her as she suppressed a shiver.

"Fake ID guy is lined up for tomorrow morning," Breakfast said, joining them. "He isn't cheap, though." He looked around, noticing the ashen faces and the tight mouths, and realized he'd blundered into a delicate moment. He sat down tentatively next to Una. "Are we remembering Juliet?" he asked.

"Well, *now* we are," Una said, rolling her eyes. She stood up and went back to the party.

"What?" he asked as the rest of the coven followed Una inside.

The party never really ended; the coven just crept off into quiet corners to try to get some sleep. When morning came, Lily woke to find Rowan in the kitchen, making omelets for Tristan, Caleb, and Una.

"Breakfast is off with Miller," Rowan told her as she shuffled in.

"He'll be back with the rental in a few hours," Una said in between forkfuls of egg.

"But I haven't picked up the money yet," Lily said.

"Miller said he'd front us," Caleb said, eyes narrowed knowingly. "Generous of him."

"Huh," Lily chuffed. She really didn't like involving Miller any more than he already was.

"He insisted," Rowan said. "We'll pay him back and be out of here by tonight."

She went to the glass door again, pulled it open, and looked out at the shoreline. Bower City had changed it to enlarge the port in a place that had only a small natural cove, but she recognized some of the features. Using the perfect recall that her willstone afforded her, she laid one view on top of the other, making a palimpsest of the two shorelines in her mind. They were hauntingly similar, yet each one was unique.

"Lily? Oatmeal or pancakes?" Rowan asked. "You need to eat."

Lily startled and turned to see Rowan standing close to her. "Do you think a place can create a unique vibration? Something no other place in no other universe quite matches?"

Rowan breathed in, smelling the clear air blowing in through the open door, and shut his eyes. Lily saw his willstone flicker as thought ran through the crystal and became energy. She followed those fairy lights, weaving closer to him until she could feel the heat of his skin and smell the spice of his body. He opened his eyes and Lily leaned back. His face softened.

"When I first met you I kept scanning you over and over. Everything was the same. Every cell in your body was Lillian's, but you weren't her." Rowan frowned. "In the cabin, right before you claimed me, I wondered if by letting you claim me, would Lillian be claiming me through you? But no, it hasn't been that way. Maybe every person has their own vibration, regardless of how many versions of us there are, and if every person does, maybe every place does, too." His brow furrowed. "Because you can feel it. You can feel that this place is different from any other, and it's not just the way it looks or smells. It just *is* different somehow. Like you were different somehow."

Lily looked out at the water and felt the pulse of the ocean as it battered the shore. She felt the heat of the sun hitting the earth and radiating back in waves. She felt the wind press and push, lift and swirl, random and rhythmic all at once.

"I can't find it," she said.

"You will," Rowan replied confidently. "Now, oatmeal or pancakes?"

Lily smiled at him. "Pancakes. Please."

Rowan moved away from her to go back to the stove, and Lily found herself following as if every step he took tugged her along behind him.

A few more people stopped in while the coven waited for Breakfast and Miller to return, and Rowan fed them, too. One of the guys might have even been the owner of the house, but he didn't seem too concerned that a stranger had commandeered his kitchen. He wandered in, ate, and wandered out saying, "Thanks, Robert. Excellent hollandaise, by the way," to Rowan, as if he was accustomed to having someone else prepare his meals.

"Yeah, thanks, *Robert*," Una said, snickering.

"Should we tip you?" Tristan asked, stretching out the joke.

Rowan grinned and took his ribbing happily. Slowly, in increments, they were accepting him back.

Breakfast and Miller returned with the rental car before noon. Breakfast rolled up, arm hanging out of the driver's side window and bass thumping from the tinny speakers of the doublewide soccer-mom minivan.

"Hey, fancy lady. Want a ride in my precision automobile?" Breakfast catcalled to Una.

"How can I resist," she deadpanned. "The color tan gets me all worked up."

Breakfast parked and jumped out of the car, chasing Una around lecherously. Miller got out of his truck and came over while the rest of the coven checked out the rental.

"Seating for seven," Caleb said, and then checked himself. They were only six now.

Lily felt heat race through her—the ear-burning, voice-thickening kind that comes before tears. She cleared her throat and smiled for no reason.

"I go to Yosemite all the time," Miller said, looking disturbingly hopeful at Caleb's mention of an extra seat. "There are so many hidden spots I could show you. Really special stuff."

It took a second for Lily to catch up, but she assumed that Breakfast had told Miller that they were going to Yosemite as a cover story.

"Well, unfortunately we have to leave today," Lily said. "Now, actually."

"I could leave today," Miller said, his optimism increasing. "I could have a bag packed in ten minutes."

Damn it, Lily said to her coven in mindspeak. *Doesn't anyone have a real job in this state? Someone help me get rid of this guy.*

"Look, Mills. My man," Breakfast said, putting a hand on Miller's shoulder and pulling him aside, "this is a hard time for us. A friend died. It's sort of a memorial trip, you know?"

While Breakfast let Miller down easy, Lily took the keys to the car. "I'll be back with the cash," she said.

Rowan got in the passenger side and buckled himself in before anyone could tell him not to, and they drove to the Walmart off Route 1. Lily waited in a short line at the money center. She did not tilt her eyes up at the surveillance camera behind the counter, but as she picked up the cash Juliet had wired to the money center, she knew. They were on borrowed time now. She and Rowan took to the aisles to shop as quickly as they could without seeming suspicious.

"This will fit Caleb," Rowan said, holding up a pair of jeans.

"*These* will fit," Lily said, correcting him. "Jeans are plural."

"I always wondered why," Rowan replied, a quizzical smile on his face. "It's one article of clothing."

"Yeah, but there are two leg holes."

"Nope," Rowan said, shaking his head. "That doesn't make any sense."

"You know what? It doesn't," Lily said, a smile dawning on her. "It really doesn't make any sense at all. We should just start calling them jean."

Rowan cocked his head, letting the sound of the word marinate, and pulled a face. "That doesn't sound right."

"It sounds awful."

"Jeans it is."

They went back to shopping, both of them smiling to themselves. Rowan had pretty much kept to the rule of staying several feet away from her unless he was saving her from imminent danger, but now Lily found herself edging closer to him. After catching her doing it a few times as they walked side by side down the aisles, Rowan didn't move away. They filled the cart, each item they placed in it giving them the chance to be in the other's personal space and, occasionally, even touch.

They selected nondescript clothes with no labels or bright colors, black backpacks, and hoodies. They loaded up on snacks and water for the drive, stopped at a gas station, and then went back to the house to pick up the rest of the coven.

Rowan and Lily followed the sound of laughter. The other end of the wraparound deck had an infinity pool where the coven was enjoying the summer sun. Past the pool, a grill stood off to the side by a fire pit that was surrounded by several teak deck chairs. A brick-red umbrella mushroomed cheerfully over the outdoor eating area, framing the scene, and drawing the eye out into the endless blue where sky met water.

"All that's missing is the dog," Lily said, recalling Rowan's dream of California.

Rowan's head snapped around. His smile was sad as he shook his head. "That's not the only thing that's missing."

He left her with Juliet and Tristan hanging between them, their ghosts pushing Lily and Rowan apart with invisible hands.

"Tell me you bought me something cooler than this," Una said as she held up a cardigan.

Rowan laughed under his breath. *Sorry, Una, but even you have to blend in while we travel. This is a big risk we're taking*, he said in mindspeak.

But less risky than trying to travel in your world, Lily added, in case Rowan was gearing up to say it was too dangerous. He didn't, though. Nor did he grumble about Lily taking risks that he didn't want her to take. There were no safe options anymore, and no conscionable way to stay on the sidelines.

"We'd better get our stuff together and go," Rowan said.

"Don't you want to take a quick swim?" Tristan asked him as he paddled around.

Rowan looked at the pool, and then out at the ocean and horizon that blended seamlessly with its edge—aqua to azure to sapphire to the clouds. "No," he said, his deep voice rumbling in his chest.

The coven took turns cleaning up and changing into their new clothes. Caleb checked and double-checked the car and the supplies.

"You know, if we're missing anything we can stop pretty much anywhere and get it," Breakfast told him.

"I'm just looking," Caleb said defensively. "I want to know what we have and don't have."

"Forget it, Breakfast," Tristan said, smiling. "Caleb lives to worry about supplies."

"You know, there are so many great trails in Yosemite," Miller said, joining them. "It'd be a shame for you to miss out on them." He was trying to sound casual, but the attempt only made him sound more desperate.

He looks strung out, Una said in mindspeak. *I feel bad for the guy.*

Don't, Lily told her. *He's much better off without us.*

Miller was still waiting for some kind of acknowledgment of his offer, but no one spoke up. There was no delicate way left for any of them to say that he wasn't invited, so they just ignored him and kept packing.

"Thanks so much for all your help," Lily said to Miller as they were preparing to leave. "Tell the guy"—she gestured to the house, indicating its owner—"that we said thank you."

"Sure," Miller said. His face was tight with bitterness.

As Breakfast pulled the mom van out of the driveway, Lily waved good-bye to him in a friendly way. He didn't wave back.

Carrick finally found the house they were staying at in time to watch the coven pack up their vehicle and drive off, leaving a forlorn young man in their wake.

Carrick turned to his side and retched into the bushes. His vision was blurry and his head throbbed with every pulse of his heart. The blow he'd suffered from the Warrior Sister had left him unconscious for half a day. The Hive had left him for dead, and he might have slipped into the unwakeable sleep but for Lillian's constant calling and prodding inside his mind.

She would not let him die. Not while she needed him. She reminded him over and over that he was hers to kill, and no other's.

Carrick had pulled himself up, the ground tilting and reeling, to find that Lillian had worldjumped him to Lily's universe to follow and to watch. The glade around him bore the signs of the coven's overnight stay and it showed him their path as easily as if it had been illuminated, but once the coven had reached the main road they had been much harder to track.

His vision was damaged, adding annoyance to his list of problems. Carrick used all his senses when he tracked and didn't rely solely on his vision, but it certainly helped. Unable to focus his eyes, Carrick had started to wander in the dark last night, perilously close to the edge of the cliffs. The throbbing in his head was so bad it had tempted him to give up, lie down, and die, but again Lillian would not allow it.

She and Lily had finally come to an agreement about some things, but Lily was still too idealistic for Lillian's peace of mind. Lily didn't want innocents to die. How quaint. Lillian sent Carrick along behind them to make sure that if there was something distasteful that Lillian wanted done, she need not negotiate with Lily. Carrick would do the dirty work, if there was any to be found. And there was always dirty work.

Her insistence that he continue on after the coven was an exquisite torture. Never had he been so called to sleep and so unable to attain it. When he tried to let himself slip off into the roaring dark, she had taken possession of his body, forcing it to stand, and denying him his release. Never had he been so cruelly driven. He had learned to love his witch for that, and could only hope Lily would be just as harsh with him as Lillian had been after she died.

That time was approaching fast. The loss of Juliet had made Lillian's inner fire burn twice as bright with vengeance. But twice as bright meant twice as fast, and soon, Carrick knew, she would be burnt out. He just hoped he was far away from her when she went. A witch that strong always took out others with her when she died, especially if she died in the middle of a battle, and Carrick couldn't imagine his witch dying any other way.

Carrick watched the large, tan-colored vehicle carry the coven away toward the main road and sank down on his knees next to his puddle of sick. He'd lost them again. For now. The numbers on the plate were sealed in his memory. The throbbing in his head turned to blackness.

Carrick. Wake up. Carrick . . .

Lillian roused his mind back to pain. He focused on the dull agony and took a long breath to savor it before opening his eyes.

It was night. Blue and red lights flashed in the driveway and on the street surrounding the house where Lily's coven had stayed. Men and women in uniforms paced about the grounds, searching. He saw a woman get out of a plain black car. Her boxy body and wiry, graying hair were familiar. It was the agent who had hounded Lily and her family on Lily's last sojourn in this world. Simms.

Find out what that woman knows, Lillian ordered.

Carrick stumbled through the dark to fulfill her wish, but his body was weak. Lillian sent her strength to revive him. The throbbing was still there—Lillian hadn't eased that—but now that it was mixed with power, the pain morphed into pleasure for him. His witch understood him so well.

Carrick vaulted up the side of the house, a mere blur to the eye, and opened a window on the second floor. He crept through the house until he could position himself best to hear the agent's voice. She was questioning the tenant.

"No, I already told you," said a hassled man. "I didn't know any of them. One of them cooked me breakfast. I assumed he was a chef. Roger? Ronald? I can't remember his name. I don't interview the people who come to my parties, you know." The man sounded like he was used to talking down to people. "There were two hot girls with them. That's all I know."

"They just showed up and you let them in?" Simms asked, sounding skeptical. "All someone needs are two hot girls to get into your house?"

"I brought them," said another male voice. "I brought all of them."

"Mister . . ." There was a pause as Simms flipped through a small notepad. "Miller. How did you know the suspects?"

"I didn't," he said. His voice sounded small and hollow. "I saw them walking down Route One and I picked them up."

"Are you accustomed to picking up hitchhikers and letting them into your friends' houses?" Simms asked.

"No. No, I never pick up people."

"So why did you?"

Carrick heard him take a long, drawn-in breath. "It was *her*. Lily. She looked at me and I just stopped my truck. I don't know why I did it. They didn't even try to wave me down or anything. I just wanted to . . ." His voice trailed off. "Are you going after her?"

"They told you they were going to Yosemite?" Simms asked, ignoring his question.

"Yes. That's all I know."

"Yosemite is a big place. Were they specific about any particular site? Were they meeting someone? Did they have camping gear with them?" Simms's questions came fast.

"No. No camping gear," Miller said, growing more agitated. "They mentioned friends, but I think that was a lie. Agent Simms, are you going after her?"

There was a long pause. "Yes," she answered.

"Take me with you." It wasn't a request. Miller sounded desperate. "I can help you. She trusts me."

"Special Agent? We have one more for you," said another voice.

Carrick heard a young man's voice protesting as he was brought into the room. "I told you, I don't know where they're keeping the bomb," he said. "All I know is that they said that some guy had nukes."

"What's this?" Simms said harshly.

"I told them already, like, seven times," the young man said, his voice growing desperate. "I was outside. It was dark. The whole group was on the patio, talking, and one of them said something about a nuke and bombing the whole eastern seaboard. Then they went back inside. I thought they couldn't be serious until you guys showed up looking for them, then I thought maybe it's true. They didn't sound like they were joking at the time, but it's crazy. Right?" The young man sounded like he really wanted someone to tell him it was.

"Have you checked this yet?" Simms said as an aside to one of her subordinates.

"We're on it," the subordinate replied. He raised his voice to a shout as Simms ran from the room. "We haven't verified it yet!"

"Call everyone," Simms ordered in return. "I'm not waiting around for a terrorist attack."

"Agent, take me with you," Miller shouted. "I can help!"

There was no answer. Simms left the room. Carrick eased himself back into the shadows.

Shall I follow her, My Lady?

No. We both know Lily isn't going to this Yosemite place. She's going home, Carrick, Lillian replied.

I'm to go to Salem, then?

No. Stay with Simms.

And if she gets too close to Lily, what shall I do?

What you must.

CHAPTER
8

LILY'S EYES UNFOCUSED FOR A MOMENT, THE PAVEMENT still scrawling beneath her while the desert and mountains in front of her hung forever far away, like a movie backdrop. Lillian was reaching out to her. After a moment's hesitation Lily let her make contact.

Simms is coming, Lillian told her. *She got information from the people at the house on the bluff.*

Is she going to Yosemite or Salem?

She just arrived in Yosemite. She will know soon that you aren't there. She tracks you with more than the pictures from the Walmart and the witnesses from the party. She tracks you with her yearning. Stay off the main roads.

I will.

Are you coming back to my world?

Yes. Once I get far enough east in this world I'm going to worldjump my coven back to yours, Lily told her. There was no point in trying to hide her plans from Lillian anymore.

It will do you no good to try and talk me off the path of war, Lillian warned.

I wouldn't dream of it. I'm coming back to exterminate the Hive.

Finally, we agree. My army marches. Gather yours and join me.

Lily breathed an ironic laugh at the thought of joining forces with Lillian, and then the laugh turned to a chill as she considered another enemy-ally. *How do you know about Simms, Lillian?*

Lillian did not answer. Lily's skin started to crawl.

Did you worldjump Carrick? Where is he?

Lily felt the connection end and brought herself back to the present. She glanced up at the rearview mirror and saw Rowan sitting in the back, looking at her.

"Lillian?" he guessed. Lily nodded, still not completely sure how he always seemed to know who she was mindspeaking with. "Is she still planning to attack Bower City alone?" he asked.

Lily smirked at him. "She asked me to join her, but she isn't waiting around for my answer. She isn't going to like what I have to say about teaming up with Alaric, no matter how much sense it makes." A thought occurred to her. "There's only one person she ever listened to, and it certainly isn't me. Someone we're going to need to pull this off." Rowan narrowed his eyes in question. "Forget it," Lily said. "Just strategizing."

Rowan nodded and let his gaze drift out the window, a vague smile on his lips. The rest of the coven was sleeping, but Rowan didn't seem to want to miss one second of the scenery.

"Where is she?" he asked after a long silence.

Lily let her senses drift out to join her other self for a moment. She saw columns of men and women on the move. Loaded wagons, horses, and pack animals hastened with unnatural speed through the heat and haze of a humid forest. Around the army prowled guardians, and above the trees circled greater and lesser drakes to spot wild Woven, flush them out, and kill them before they could threaten human lives. Tame Woven hunting wild Woven. Not even Lillian could avoid using the Woven in some way, no matter how much she hated them.

Lily thought of Pale One, her claimed, and reached out to her. It was far, but Lily could feel the sensory tangle of her mind, a chaotic swirl of scent and information, and she could feel the keen edge of her devotion. Pale One had managed to slip away in the confusion after she had knocked down Grace. Clever little creature. Compared to her, Lillian's gigantic drakes were mere pets—impressive attack dogs, not true claimed. Unlike Pale One, the tame Woven created by the eastern Covens didn't have willstones and couldn't be claimed by a witch. Lillian saw her Woven as animals and nothing more. Lily knew in her heart that was a mistake.

"Lily?" Rowan prompted.

"They haven't crossed the Appalachians yet," she answered, shaking herself back to this world. "Lillian's giving her army strength and speed, but it's wearing on her."

Lily glanced up at the mirror and saw Rowan's worried expression. "Do you want me to drive?" he asked.

"Yeah," Lily said gratefully.

She pulled over and they both got out, taking a moment to stretch their stiff limbs and wipe the cobwebs from their eyes. They'd been driving nonstop in shifts for sixteen hours. There was a chill in the early morning air and Lily heard Rowan suck in a shivering breath while he looked at the desert around them and the mountains beyond.

Sand dunes rolled on either side of the black stretch of asphalt—a vast golden ocean, its heaving tides held in a moment. Sharp, young mountains spiked the clear sky behind them.

"I don't know which place is more lovely," Rowan said. "The ocean or the desert."

Lily nodded her agreement, feeling the dry breeze brush back her hair and trace across her neck. "I think we're about to enter a national park. The dunes or something."

A jeep came up behind them and they got back in the van and shut the doors.

"Start the engine," she told him.

The jeep slowed enough for the driver to peek in their window. A young man wearing a wide-brimmed hat sat behind the wheel.

"Park ranger," she told Rowan. "Put your directional on." She waved at the ranger to indicate that they were fine, and he drove on while they pulled back out onto the road. "Make a U turn. Don't follow him."

Rowan did as she instructed. "Where to?"

"We'll have to backtrack a little and go around the park." Lily pulled out the map and tried to find an alternate route. She saw in the rearview mirror that the ranger had stopped his jeep. "Go faster," she told Rowan.

"I think it's too late," he said.

"I know," she replied with a sinking feeling in her gut.

She looked at the impassable dunes around them. They had to get off the road, but their van was no match for that kind of terrain. The rest of the coven felt Rowan's and Lily's anxiety and woke. A moment of viewing Rowan's replay of the events, and they all understood the situation.

"Don't speed, Ro," Breakfast said.

"They've already spotted us," Una said.

"I know. But we need to be able to see any turnoffs we could go down," Breakfast countered. "A dirt road. Something to get us off this open stretch."

"We won't outrun them," Lily said in agreement.

They all scanned the side of the road. Caleb kept craning his head to look back.

"I see them," he said grimly. "Looks like the ranger's brought all his friends."

Lily turned and looked back to see several dark specks on the road behind them.

"There!" Tristan said, pointing. "A turnoff." It was no more than a path through the dunes, but it was their only option.

Rowan cranked the wheel. Sand kicked up behind them as they turned. Lily looked back at the telltale cloud, and drew in a breath. Her willstone flared as she stole the momentum out of the particles of sand and grit, first stilling the cloud and then dropping it back to the ground, covering their tracks.

"Whatever you're doing, keep doing it, Lily," Rowan said, teeth clenched as he focused on maintaining control. Sand slipped under the wheels and the ungainly van slid as if on snow.

As Lily quieted the dust, she softened the light hitting the van as well. Without sunlight reflecting off the metal, the tan van blended seamlessly into the tan sand.

Ten minutes, fifteen, half an hour passed, and still there was no sign that they were being followed. They jolted down the path at an arduously slow rate, the axle creaking and the engine growing hotter as the sun climbed in the sky and turned its glaring gaze on the desert.

Lily put her hand on the dashboard and took as much heat from the engine as she could, but there was nothing she could do about the axle if it broke. She fed her mechanics' willstones with the harvested energy, and as the hours passed the coven grew drunk on strength. When the axle finally gave way with a screech, they were actually relieved to get out of the van and have something to do with all that energy. Lily, however, was not at all happy to have to walk.

She stepped out of the shade of the van and into the sun and felt her fair skin tighten in rebellion. Rowan opened his pack and started stuffing packets of salty chips in it for Lily.

"Keep converting as much of the sun's energy as you can," he told her. "That will help. And I have plenty of burn salve for later."

"Great," Lily mumbled. She took out a long-sleeved hoodie from her pack and put it on, opting to swelter rather than burn.

Tristan counted the remaining water bottles and glanced at the map. "It's not bad news, but it isn't great," he told Rowan. "We have enough to get us to the next gas station across the dunes, but that would be pushing it."

"We'll push it, then," Rowan said. He didn't have to remind them that they couldn't wait a few hours for the sun to set. They had to keep moving.

Rowan took one of the water bottles and shook a combination of herbs into it. "Here," he said, pulling Lily aside and giving her the spiked water. "It will give you a temporary burst of energy."

Lily drank it down and felt a jittery lightness quicken her muscles and widen her eyes. The coven set off into the dunes, gliding with unnatural speed over the sand.

Carrick heard the crackle of speech coming through the black device on Simms's hip and adjusted his uniform to cover the spot of blood on the collar. So many officers had come and gone while Simms plowed on without sleep that she hadn't noticed when Carrick "replaced" the former occupant of this particular uniform and made himself a fixture at her side.

"A group of teenagers that fit the description was just seen heading toward Great Sand Dunes National Park in Colorado," said the disembodied voice. "They had California plates."

The voice went on to recite the number and letter combination that Carrick had seen on the van. It was Lily's coven. Somehow Simms's face lit up with recognition, although she hadn't seen the plate number as Carrick had.

"That's them," she said into the device. "I want them followed, but no one is to approach until I get there." Simms turned to another officer in plainclothes. "Start the chopper," she said. Her eyes were dilated and Carrick could smell adrenaline-tinged sweat starting to seep up through her pores, but the other officer balked.

"We've gotten a dozen of these calls," he argued. "Half the high school graduates in the US are taking road trips to the national parks right now. Why don't we have the locals pull them over and send us pictures for our informant to identify?"

"Abbot, it's them," Simms said. "I know it. We're just wasting time." Her irrational vehemence only weakened her position in the other officer's eyes.

The officer sighed and pinched the bridge of his nose. "It's been a really long couple of days."

"It's them," Simms promised quietly. "Something's been wrong with this whole situation right from the start. Strange disappearances. Ritual murders. And now talk of a nuclear weapon. We need to stop them before they do something . . ." Simms trailed off, unable to pinpoint what it was she thought they might do.

"We don't *know* it's even them," he began.

Simms didn't stay to hear the rest. She stepped around the other officer and went outside to order the chopper for herself.

"Damn it," Abbot said, giving in. "Send backup to her location."

"How much?" another officer asked.

"All of it," Abbot answered, throwing up his hands.

Carrick followed Simms outside. She was shouting at the helmsman of a small aircraft that had rotary blades on top. The blades seemed to chop the air, and Carrick put two and two together.

"I am in charge here, not Abbot," Simms was yelling at the helmsman, "and I don't think I need to remind you that these are terrorists we're dealing with, and——" She noticed another figure approaching the aircraft. It was Miller, the informant. "What are you doing here?" she shouted at the desperate young man.

"I'm coming with you," he said. "It's her, we both know it." Miller shifted from foot to foot. "I have to come with you."

Simms looked at Carrick as if noticing him for the first time. "And you?"

"Chief Abbot ordered me to go with you," he lied smoothly. Carrick looked at the helmsman. "He said we'd better get moving," he said with the hint of warning that two underlings would use while dealing with petulant superiors.

The helmsman threw up his hands and starting hitting buttons. "Everyone in," he said.

Carrick jumped up into the back row of the chopper and let Simms take the place in front of him. Not that she noticed him, anyway. Both she and Miller were too intent on being near Lily's power to care about anything else. Carrick smiled slightly and stared at the back of Simms's head while the chopper took to the sky.

People always looked the wrong way when they were looking forward to something, he thought.

Lily. Simms has found you. She's in flight and approaching rapidly with many people in uniform following behind. They heard you discussing Alaric's bombs and they gave you a special name that has swelled the ranks of your opposition.

What name?

Terrorist.

Lily stopped and looked across the street at the gas station that was just a few hundred yards away, the word still whispering ominously in her head.

"What is it?" Rowan asked.

"Simms found us. She's close."

The coven looked down the narrow strip of asphalt until it shimmered in the distance. It was a back road, seldom used. The only car they'd seen on it since they'd emerged from the dunes was a big-rig truck that sped by with a roar and a gust of baked air.

"We need water," Una said.

Lily swallowed. Tristan watched her with worried eyes. She tried to smile at him, but it hurt her cracked lips. He looked up at the gas station and made a frustrated sound.

"I'm going in," he said. Rowan's hand shot out to stop him, but Tristan shook it off. "We won't make it to the next one. It's now or never, Ro," he said. Rowan gave in.

Breakfast sighed and followed Tristan. "I guess someone who's actually seen American money ought to go with him."

The rest of the coven stayed on the other side of the road with the dunes behind them. The wind whistled past, snatching moisture from their bodies. The sky was streaked with white clouds that were stretched so thin they only served to turn the blue milky. They had entered the never-ending late afternoon of a summer day—the time of antsy, exasperated waiting for sunset.

The witching hour, someone else whispered inside Lily's head.

"I swear to Christmas that if he's in there bullshitting with the cashier . . ." Una let her threat run out.

Breakfast appeared after what felt like an eternal five minutes. He was halfway across the street when Lily saw Tristan's bright smile as he emerged from the shop. Then she heard the *woof-woof-woof* of the helicopter.

"Run!" Caleb hollered.

Blue and red lights flashed to the left and the right, both lanes suddenly filled with police cars converging on their location. Breakfast bounded the last few steps across the street to grab Una's outstretched hands. A helicopter lifted up and over the phalanx of police cars to hover above the coven. The air spilled down on top of their heads like water being poured from above.

Rowan glanced at Lily, a regretful smile on his face. Just over his far shoulder, but separated by distance and bad fortune, was Tristan, stranded on the other side of the road. He knew what she was thinking before she did.

Not him too. Not both of them.

"I'll protect him. Gift me," Rowan said, his deep voice penetrating through the din.

Lily called the heat of the desert to her. There was a lifting, like gravity had given up, and for a moment the cars, the police who were running toward them, and even the rocks and dust on the ground, let go of the earth and swam up for the sky. A boom sounded across the barren land and Lily's witch wind spiraled up in a column as it threw her into the suddenly freezing-cold air. The helicopter gyrated drunkenly to the side in the updraft, and as it listed off, Lily saw the passengers inside as if in tableau.

The pilot wrestled desperately with the stick and didn't even see Lily floating level with the helicopter. Simms stared at her in a mixture of horror and triumph. Lily recognized Miller, who was utterly terrified, and couldn't imagine how he'd ended up in the mix. And behind them all was Carrick. The look of hunger he gave Lily stole the breath from her body. She watched him move easily through the cabin, never taking his eyes off her, open the door, and throw himself out of the falling aircraft with the slithering grace of a snake.

The helicopter careened to the ground, narrowly missing the gas station, while Carrick dropped lightly to his knees and rolled smoothly over a shoulder, hitching his stride and flapping the dust off his jacket as he strode forward toward the small army of police that were streaming toward Rowan.

Alone, in the middle of the road, Rowan stood waiting for them. He looked to make sure Tristan had joined the rest of the coven on the dunes, and then looked up at Lily before launching himself at the oncoming tide.

She Gifted him as he leapt into the fray, throwing back her head and shouting with mad joy. Magelight pulsed out of Rowan's willstone, phosphorus bright. It stunned the officers closest to him and dropped them to their knees as they clutched at their faces to shield their eyes. He hit the second line before they could draw their weapons and wove through their ranks so quickly his progress was only made visible by the trail of unconscious bodies left to slide to the ground behind him.

The third line had their weapons ready by the time he faced them, standing knee deep in a swath of immobile bodies. They fired as one.

The crack of gunfire halted before it could resound across the sand. Lily took the thousands of little explosions into her as jubilantly as the night sky receives fireworks. She Gifted the rest of her coven with the fresh burst of power, and they streamed down the now-frosty dunes like falling stars.

Police cars continued to arrive at both ends of the street until the road looked like a garish river of flashing lights. The gunfire came randomly now, and although Lily was stealing momentum from the bullets as fast as she could, there were some that were starting to slip past her. She couldn't risk losing any of her claimed. She needed to make them impervious as she had done against the Hive. It was a little thing. One small difference that wasn't so bad, after all—at least, not compared to death.

Rowan was the only one who felt the difference when Lily invaded his stone and took it over.

No, Lily. What are you doing?

Making you stronger by making myself stronger, she replied. He balked for just one moment more, and then relented.

Lily used their willstones to transmute energy, and with five more loci of power to add to her three, Lily drank a bigger measure of energy than she ever had before. She flooded the bodies of her claimed with so much power even Rowan forgot anything was wrong.

She became They.

They bellowed and screeched with bloodlust, vaulting over the cars in their way to get at the fresh foes behind. It didn't matter how many They faced. As one, They were unbeatable. Every line but the last fell before Them. They looked down from their throne of air, purring with pleasure, and saw one among themselves who did not belong. He was a sour note that jangled out of tune in Their symphony.

The bubble of ecstasy that surrounded her shattered, and Lily was just herself again.

Carrick was not sparing his opponents. Each officer he faced he killed. Ice flaked in Lily's blood.

Lillian, you must rein in Carrick. He is killing innocents.

He feels he must kill to protect you, Lillian answered.

He's lying. He's only doing it because he likes it.

Lily watched the back ranks of officer as they set up stronger machines of war—rocket, tanks, and high-caliber assault weapons. Carrick would kill them all, and if Lily didn't stop her coven, they would have no choice but to kill as well.

The officers were signaling to one another. They planned on unleashing all their hardware at the same time, but coordinating their attack would only make Lily stronger. The more power she gathered, the more berserk it made her and her coven.

Rowan saw the firepower arrayed against them and knew what was coming.

Lily, we have to get out of here, he said. *Hundreds will die if we don't.*

Worldjump us. We can't make the crossing east in this world with so much against us.

If we go back to your world it will take us months to travel and gather my army, and in that time Lillian's army will be wiped out by the Hive. Hundreds of thousands will die, Lily argued.

They needed to get east, and they needed to be there now. She had to at least try to jump them. She sent her spirit out to look.

High in the air, Lily could see the face of the land. She saw the sand on top of the bedrock, like wrinkled skin over bones. She sent her spirit out, and let it sink a little deeper to touch the mind behind the face. The land had a pulse—a unique identity that resolved into a low thumping vibration. There was no other place on earth with this exact rhythm, and Lily knew that if she ever wanted to return here all she had to do was replay that rhythm in her willstone to unlock the path. She called her spirit back into her body again.

Lily looked down to see Simms glaring up at her. Blood streaked down her face from a ghastly head wound, but she had not given up. Simms would never give up, no more than Lily would. Simms had said once that she had been raised just a few miles away from Lily in the town of Beverly. Maybe it was something in the land that made them as pigheaded as they were. Maybe that something was a vibration she could key into.

Lily saw the commanding officer raise an arm and scream the word *fire*. Desperate, she sent her spirit out, grateful now that the burning desert had left her so dangerously dehydrated. She quickly found the Mist, passed through it rather than coasted along it on the raft, and soared into the overworld.

She looked around at what seemed to be a slippery facsimile of the world, more spirit than location. Lily knew she could travel vast distances in a moment, or it could take an infinity for her to take one step. It was a shadowy landscape with an ever-changing map and, like the worldfoam, it was impossible to traverse without some kind of beacon to guide her spirit through it. She thought of her home. She thought of how the cantankerous water pounded ceaselessly at the stubborn rocks of the shore. She thought of the low whistle of the wind and the quiet thrum of the rocky soil. Her spirit arrived there in a single step.

In spirit, Lily could easily feel the vibration of the land. She wasn't surprised to learn that she had known it all along. It was in her blood, more than skin deep. She called her spirit back and it rejoined her suspended form in an instant.

The bright wall of fire arrived just as Lily played the vibration of her particular Salem in her willstone, and with the ocean of energy her opponent unwittingly gave her, she gathered up her coven and jumped them across the continent.

Carrick picked his head up from the carnage long enough to realize that every person in a uniform was running away. That could only mean one thing. They were going to attempt a massive salvo to end the conflict, which would make Lily stronger, but not Lillian. Lillian wasn't present to harvest the energy.

Lady, I need more strength, he called to his witch.

I can't help you anymore, Carrick, Lillian replied, exhausted. *I suggest you run.*

During the fighting, Carrick had somehow worked his way back to where he had started and found himself near the wreckage of the helicopter. He leapt behind it for some cover and felt himself being pulled down.

"Hold him," Simms barked.

Miller and the helmsman wrestled Carrick to the ground just as he felt the last of Lillian's strength bleed out of him. The helmsman pulled a pistol from a holster on his hip and pointed it at Carrick, ending the struggle. Carrick sat back and showed them his hands. They were covered in blood.

Simms stood and looked up at Lily, who was soaring above the battle, her arms flung wide and her delicate feet dangling.

"I'd duck if I were you," Carrick warned.

A second later a roar erupted from the back of the police barricade . . . and was silenced. The flash of the salvo fell back onto itself just as the sound did. Then, in the absence of noise, thunks and pings could be heard as the projectiles that had been launched at Lily simply fell out of the air—robbed of their momentum. There was a great whooshing sound, as if the wind were inhaling, and then Lily and her coven vanished.

Silence. For a moment, everyone present just stared, and then the moans of the injured and the gasps of the amazed started to swell up in a clamor. Simms turned on Carrick and crouched down in front of him. She was pale under the wash of gore down her face.

"You're going to explain this to me," she said, her voice quiet and shaking. "And after you explain, you're going to tell me where she went and how to capture her."

Carrick narrowed his eyes at her. "Tell me why I should."

Simms gestured at the helmsman, and he cocked his pistol. "You aren't going to be arrested or put on trial. There'll be no jail cells or opportunities for you to vanish into thin air like the rest of them did. You'll just die right here, right now," she promised. "Or you can explain."

Carrick smiled at her appreciatively. "This universe doesn't suit you. But I know one that does," he told her, and then began.

CHAPTER
9

L ILY FELL OUT OF THE SKY.

"Catch her!" Rowan shouted.

Caleb was closest and managed to get under Lily before she hit the ground. He made a basket out of his thick arms and Lily landed with much less of a smack than she would have without him. He went to stand her on her own two feet, but picked her back up as soon as he saw how wobbly she was.

"Tired?" Caleb guessed.

Lily nodded, and the world swayed uneasily. But at least it was *her* world.

"Where are we?" Caleb asked.

"My backyard," Lily answered. She dropped her head on his shoulder and let out a long sigh. "It worked."

"Lily?" Juliet called.

Lily picked her head up and saw her sister's anxious face poking out of an upstairs window.

"Juliet," Rowan said, cutting her off before she could ask questions. "We need to come inside."

"Yes, of course. Holy *crap*." There was a thump as Juliet bumped into something in her haste, and the window closed. Lily could hear her sister scrambling down the steps as she raced to meet them. The coven trudged to the side door. Now that Lily wasn't fueling them, the minor injuries they'd incurred and general fatigue from the fight were catching up with them.

"Get in, get in," Juliet said urgently, holding open the door and waving them through. "Are you okay? What happened? How did you get here so fast?" Juliet asked in a rush.

Lily burst into tears and wrapped her arms around her sister's neck. Juliet startled and then went with it.

"I'm guessing there's a story here," she said, smoothing Lily's hair.

They went into the kitchen and sat down. Una and Breakfast took it in turns to explain what had happened. Lily tried to calm herself down, but the tears kept silently leaking from her eyes no matter how many times she brushed them away. A half dozen times she reached out for her sister's hand and squeezed it to reassure herself.

Juliet handled the news of her death by deciding not to try to wrap her head around it just yet, and in turn brought the coven up to speed on what had been going on in this world since they had left.

"They're calling it 'The Black Magic Murders.' It's a media circus," she said bitterly. Juliet remembered something and addressed Tristan. "No matter what you hear about your parents, don't go home. They'll turn you over."

Tristan's face went blank with confusion, and then pinched with an awkward apology. "Wrong Tristan," he said.

"Where is he?" Juliet asked, looking at Lily. She pulled in a small gasp. "No. Not him, too?"

Lily nodded numbly. "He's dead," she said, just to make it real.

Juliet sat back in her chair as if she'd been slapped. She covered her mouth with a hand, her eyes far away. "I can't—oh my God," she mumbled. "I don't believe it."

"He's dead," Lily repeated, and for the first time she accepted it.

She put her head down on the table. It was the same table where she had sat down with Tristan a thousand times to eat, to play, to talk, and to argue. The memories swam up out of the wood—Tristan dealing cards, puffing on a bubble gum cigar. The two of them switching chairs to put together an impossible puzzle with a picture of a pile of red candy hearts on the front. Tristan eating a hot dog with grape jelly. Doing homework together. Doing nothing together. Lily let herself cry until she felt a hand on her back.

"It's okay, Lillian," Samantha said.

Lily raised her head and turned to bury it in her mother's stomach. "It's my fault," she sobbed. "I'm the reason he's dead. I'm the reason they're all dead."

"Oh no, sweetie," her mother said. She tilted Lily's head back and wiped away her tears. "You had no control over what happened to Tristan or your father." She tittered anxiously, and Lily saw the mad light of a million other universes burn in her eyes. "That's scarier, which is why most people choose to feel guilty rather than helpless when someone they love dies. But the truth is you had no control."

Samantha smiled at Lily like what she had just said made it all better—and Lily had stopped crying, but it wasn't because she was comforted. Far from it, actually.

Samantha pulled away and turned to Rowan. "You should tell her all of it," she said. "What happened when she was unconscious in your tent? Tell her."

"Tell me what?" Lily asked. Samantha wandered away, humming a few notes to herself. Lily turned to Rowan. "Tell me *what*?" she demanded.

Rowan's face was blank. "I don't know," he mumbled.

"She's worse," Juliet interjected. She was watching Samantha tackle the stairs with a worried frown. "The cameras, the police, the pressure to keep the story straight when she can't even remember which world she's in more often than not. It's too much."

Lily really looked at Juliet. She'd lost weight and there were dark circles under her eyes. "Are you okay?" she asked. "How's school?"

"What school? I dropped out to take care of Mom." Juliet rubbed a hand over her face. "Not that I could have stayed anyway, with reporters ambushing me outside of every class."

"I ruined your life," Lily said, shaking her head.

Juliet mustered a smile. "Didn't you hear Mom?"

"It's not my fault?" Lily guessed.

"Exactly." Juliet glanced around the table, noticing the state of everyone. "You all look like hell," she said, earning a round of rueful laughs. She turned to Breakfast, who was cradling one arm in his other hand. "What happened to you, Breakfast?"

"I got shot," he said, showing them a large red-purple-and-blue welt on his arm. "The bullet didn't go through, though. It sort of bounced off. But, you know, *hard*."

"Why didn't you get out of the way?" Una asked angrily.

Breakfast rolled his eyes. "I'm fond of the color ouch."

Tristan hiked up his shirt to show Breakfast a nasty welt on his ribs. "Mine's better," he said, and then grimaced at the pain and dropped his shirt.

"That's incredible. You're all bulletproof?" Juliet asked.

"Not usually," Rowan replied. He looked at Lily, eyes narrowed. "What did you do to us?"

Lily cupped both her hands in front of her and wiggled her fingers. "It's like a field thing, you know?"

"No," Rowan said, shaking his head.

"I mean a force field," Lily said, feeling silly.

"Like in that movie *Star Wars* you made me watch?" Rowan asked, confused.

"That's *the* Force. A force field is more *Star Trek*," Breakfast corrected. "Big difference."

"You did it to us before," Una said. "It kept the Workers from stinging us when we fought the Hive. I'd say you're getting better at it, though, Lil."

"You've never seen that done?" Lily asked lightly, like it was no big deal.

"I taught you all I know about field magic," Rowan said. "And I know it isn't strong enough to repel bullets. You did something different. I felt it for a moment."

"Well, it's not actually field magic," she said, backtracking. "Instead of just putting energy into your willstones, like making a deposit, I use them to transmute energy directly. You're enveloped in a flow of energy that's strong enough to repel bullets. For a little while, anyway."

"You're controlling our willstones?" Tristan asked uncomfortably. He shifted in his seat. "Are you controlling us when you do it?"

In the heat of battle, none of them had ever been able to tell the difference. It was such a subtle thing that Lily started to resent that line in the sand. So what if she had to possess them to do it? It had kept them alive.

"I only did it for a few moments when they were shooting at you." Lily made an exasperated sound and turned to Rowan. "It's the first thing you ever taught me. Remember how you had me heal my ankle *through* your willstone that first night I was in your world? Or when we fought the Woven in the cabin? I didn't have a willstone then so I used yours to transmute the energy we needed. That's all I'm doing." She looked around at her coven's unsettled faces, feeling defensive. "You've always known this, Rowan. When I have to, I can use any of my claimed's willstone like I would use my own. Is it such a big deal I had to possess you for one second in order to save your lives?"

Lily overheard the whisper of his thoughts. *I did this*, he said to himself. His mouth went slack and he stared at her as a memory slipped through his head, unbidden.

. . . Tristan sits across from me, jealous and angry. Lily is still in my bed, and I know he thinks something happened between us. Something *did* happen. I let her claim me, and now I've given her willstones—the tools to become a true witch. I'm such an idiot. Why don't I just start hanging people myself and get it over with?

"Whatever happened to keeping her out of your head?" Tristan asks me.

"I didn't have any other choice," I reply, glad that this conversation isn't taking place in mindspeak. I *did* have another choice. I could have run and let her die. Why can't I just let her go? "Believe me. I'm regretting it," I say.

"What even gave you the idea?" Tristan asks.

He's not angry anymore. He knows I'm sick. Afflicted. Addicted. Why is she the only woman I've ever been able to love? Something's wrong with me.

"I thought about how she'd healed her ankle," I say. "It was a long shot, but I figured she'd already transmuted energy inside herself using my stone, and it was only one step farther to then pour it back into me."

"That's one hell of a step, though." Tristan looks scared. He should be. I am. His voice drops. "Do you think she could invade a stone? Take it over without permission . . ."

The memory flash ended and Lily found herself looking at a leaner, longer-haired version of the Rowan in the memory. One thing was the same, though. He was still scared of her.

"What does that mean—*invade a stone?*" she asked him. She could feel the rest of the coven's confusion and curiosity.

"It means you don't have to touch a willstone to claim it," Rowan replied, like there was no point in trying to avoid the inevitable anymore. "You can just take any willstone you want as long as another witch hasn't already claimed it." His brow furrowed in thought as something occurred to him. "And maybe you could even steal a willstone from another witch. You'd have to fight her, but I can't imagine there are many witches who would have a shot at withstanding you."

"I can think of one," Lily murmured, remembering the sensation she'd felt when she'd tried to touch the Queen's willstone.

"Grace?" Rowan guessed.

"She's been claiming the Woven remotely through the speaking stones for decades," Lily said. "So she can invade a willstone, too. And she's strong. If Grace has physically touched a willstone to claim it, I don't think I can take it over. But if she hasn't touched it, and she's only used the speaking stones to claim, I know I can muscle her out."

"How do you know that?" Tristan asked.

"Because I've done it." Lily felt their stares, and she knew she had to tell them all of it no matter how disturbed some of them might become. "I've claimed a Woven I call Pale One. She used to belong to Grace, but I touched her willstone and now she's mine."

"The coyote Woven who attacked you outside Baltimore?" Tristan said, knowing the answer. "So that's why she followed us."

Lily nodded, an uncertain look on her face. "The other Tristan told you?"

"He showed me that time you and he were sitting up against the tree, talking about how to study the Woven. You told him to leave her be. That she wasn't going to harm us," Tristan admitted. He looked down at the table and ran his hands over it as if he recognized it. "We showed each other pretty much everything during the crossing."

Seeing the shape of his hands and the cast of his features in the familiar light of home, Lily could almost imagine that this Tristan was her Tristan, but stopped herself. If she started allowing herself to think that they were the same, and that her Tristan lived on in him, then his death would mean nothing.

"So, not only are you possessing us, you're claiming Woven on top of it?" Caleb asked, the words sticking in his throat. "Are we expected to become stone kin with Pale One? Share our memories and mindspeak? Oh, sorry—what would you call it with a coyote? Mind*barking*?" His mouth was pressed thin in disgust.

Lily looked at Rowan and saw him watching her with a guarded expression. She realized that he was trying to keep his distaste in check.

"See, this is why I didn't tell you," she said, throwing up her hands. "The Woven are intelligent—they have thoughts and feelings like we do. Did you know that Pale One saved us? She's the one who jumped on Grace, giving Carrick enough time—"

"All she has to do is jump on someone and that makes her intelligent?" Caleb fired back, rising to his feet. "I suppose we have to accept Carrick now, too, because he struck the match?"

"No, that's not . . . I didn't say that," Lily stammered, breathless. "The Woven . . . Carrick . . . they're not the same."

"Maybe not to you," Caleb said with a deep scowl twisting his face. Tristan stood and placed a hand on his shoulder. Caleb shook him off. "Don't tell me to be calm." He looked at Rowan. "You know exactly why I'm so angry."

Rowan nodded and looked down at his hands as a frustrated silence spread out between them.

"Lillian? Is everyone ready to go yet?" Samantha asked, interrupting the tension.

They turned to see Samantha, dressed in street clothes for the first time in ages and carrying a packed suitcase. A hand fluttered up nervously to her bushy hair.

"It's just that some of the other versions of us have left already, so I figured this version of us would have to go soon, too," Samantha said by way of explaining. She shifted from foot to foot like a child.

"What do you mean, Mom?" Juliet asked patiently.

"We've got to go back to that world, Juliet, because you and I are the only ones who can convince the other Lillian and that Alaric fellow to join forces with each other." Samantha turned to Lily, squaring her shoulders and looking surprisingly sane. "You've got a lot of work to do, Lillian, so we'd better light you on fire and get to it."

Stunned, the coven forgot they were fighting with one another and stared at Samantha.

"Can you, like, see the future?" Breakfast asked.

"No," Samantha said, and gave a breathy laugh. "In another universe you didn't have that argument you just had, which saved a lot of time. A few versions of us are already on to the next thing, which is Lily convincing Juliet and me to come back with you." She thought about it. "I wouldn't really call that the future. Just a slightly different time line."

The stares only lasted a moment more, and then Rowan cleared his throat. "I think we should all eat and rest first. It'll be dark soon. We'll start building the pyre then," he said.

Caleb swung out of the room, still angry. Rowan stood to go after him, but Tristan stopped him.

"I got this one," Tristan said, and followed his stone kin outside.

Una and Breakfast started pulling food and drinks out of the refrigerator. Juliet stood up from the table, looking nervous.

"You really need me to go back with you?" she asked.

"Yes," Lily replied, sorry and scared for her sister. "It's dangerous, but I wouldn't ask unless I thought you could save thousands of lives."

"How can I say no to that?" Juliet asked, sighing. "You *will* explain this to me at some point, won't you?"

"Of course." Lily and Juliet shared a smile. "And you could still say no."

"No I couldn't. I'll just assume that in another universe I heard all the reasons why and got properly convinced." Juliet sighed. "Not like my life here is going great, anyway." Juliet stood. "I'd better get a few things together."

"Pack light," Rowan said. "We don't know what kind of situation we'll be entering when we worldjump. We may have to hit the ground running."

Juliet nodded and went to Samantha. "Come on, Mom. Let's see what you put in there." She took her mother's bag and shook it. It jingled. Juliet raised an eyebrow.

"Just some toys for the cat," Samantha said sheepishly.

"We don't have a cat," Lily and Juliet said at the same time.

"Oh, good!" Samantha said, relieved. "That would have been terrible."

Lily's eyes followed her mother and Juliet as they went upstairs. "You know, in some universe we've got a cat," she said, recalling that her mother had said something similar before. "And something really bad happens."

"But to you or to the cat—that's the question," Rowan said.

Lily shrugged and looked at him. They were left relatively alone at the table while Una and Breakfast busied themselves making sandwiches for everyone at the counter.

"Tell me all of *what?*" she asked. She hadn't forgotten what her mother had said to him.

Rowan buried a regretful smile and shook his head. "I can't." He cut Lily off before she could argue and took her hand to remove some of the sting from his words. "Just leave it alone, okay?"

She watched him tentatively run his thumb around the whorls of her knuckle, up the side of her finger, and back down again. He was waiting for her to stop him, and she knew eventually she would, but for just a moment she let herself pretend she didn't understand what it meant. She heard his breath deepen and felt the air between them spark with electricity. She noticed the table again, the same table where she and Tristan had sat together so many times, and thought that if Rowan had been there when they fought the Hive, Tristan would be sitting at it right now. She took her hand from his. If he was hurt, he didn't show it. They were both starting to get used to this stumbling back and forth as they danced around what they felt and tripped over things that couldn't be undone.

"Your mother is going to need a willstone to worldjump," Rowan said.

"Right," Lily gasped, remembering. "What do we do?"

"I grew far more than we needed when we were last here, and I stored them," he said. He stood and briefly ran the back of his fingers across her cheek. "I'll take care of it." He went upstairs after Samantha and Juliet.

Lily heard the dull *thunk* of an ax hitting wood and looked out the window. It wasn't quite dark yet, but Caleb had already started cutting down a tree for Lily's pyre. Tristan came back inside, shrugging at Lily and following Rowan upstairs.

"Eat," Una said, putting a container of hummus and a bag of pita chips in front of her.

"Yeah, don't worry about Caleb," Breakfast added, sliding a jar of pickles across the table to join the hummus. "He just needs to blow off some steam."

Lily knew it was more than that. "Do you two have anything you want to say to me?" she asked as she started in on her food.

They shared a look, and Breakfast decided to go first. "It would have been nice for you to tell us what you were doing, rather than letting us find out this way," he said, keeping the reproach in his voice to a minimum.

"We understand that you did it to protect us," Una began.

"I didn't even know I was doing it against the Hive," Lily interjected. "I swear, it just sort of happened."

"And we appreciate that," Una continued, "but you still should have said something once you did know."

Lily stirred her hummus with a chip, watching the swirl pattern rather than meet their eyes. She thought of what it meant to make a mind mosaic, and how Rowan had said that witches did it all the time. "You guys are making a big deal out of nothing. It's not like I'm using you for fun, or rifling through your minds, looking for secrets," she said. "There are so many thing witches do to their claimed that are way worse than what I did to protect you."

"Yeah, but we'd never stay the claimed of that kind of witch," Breakfast said, giving her the subtlest of warnings.

"Are you saying you don't want me to do it again?" Lily said. She watched them share another look, and this one was more troubled.

"You're asking us to choose between our freedom and our safety, but there's a middle ground here," Una said. "Ask our consent first."

"I was busy saving your lives. I didn't have time to stop and ask if that was okay with you," Lily snapped acidly.

"Lily, there are a lot of things that you can justify when you say you're doing it to save lives," Breakfast replied in an uncharacteristically harsh tone. "It starts with the little stuff. Going through emails—the people don't even *notice*, right? Like we didn't notice when you possessed us. But that's the start of a long and slippery slope. Are you sure you want to go down it?"

Given a moral equivalent from her world, Lily couldn't maintain the illusion that she was right anymore. She shook her head and dropped her chip. "Do you think Caleb will forgive me?"

"I don't know," Una answered. "You haven't lost him yet, but you might if you don't knock it off. Got it?"

"I got it," Lily said.

"Good." Una relaxed and smiled at Lily. "And thanks for saving our lives."

Lily smiled back, a lump forming in her throat. "I can't lose anyone else," she said. "I can't. That's why I did it." Her voice was high and thin. "I'm sorry."

"Let us deal with Caleb," Breakfast said.

Lily agreed and finally tucked into her food. After eating she went upstairs for a long shower and a change of clothes. Her bedroom smelled like other people. The police had searched her things and most of her stuff was in boxes. Lily stood in her towel and looked around like a guest, wondering if she could sit down on the bedspread. She wasn't angry or upset that some faceless stranger had read through her eighth grade homework, or touched her collection of snipped hospital wristbands from her sickly childhood. She was too numb to be insulted and she'd been through too much to mourn any one particular loss properly. And she knew there was more loss to come.

Despite what she'd said to Una and Breakfast about not being able to lose anyone else, she knew that if she faced the Hive, the chances of them all surviving were slim. And yet she was still going back and taking them with her.

Lily opened her dresser and pulled out a stack of her T-shirts that implored anyone who crossed her path to save the children, save the whales, save the world. She used to think she was a crusader—the good guy in the white hat. She had no idea what that meant anymore. Lily put the T-shirts back and closed the drawer.

She heard someone tap lightly on her door.

"Yes?"

"Lily, do you have a second to talk?" Tristan pushed the door open and saw that she was only wearing a towel. He dropped his eyes. "Sorry, I'll come back."

"Seriously?" she said, brows raised. "You see me stark naked practically every other day for some kind of ritual. What is it?"

He wavered in the doorway, half in and half out of her room. "It's Rowan. There's something—" He broke off and turned.

"Samantha's getting anxious," Rowan said, appearing at Tristan's side. "She says you should claim her quickly so we can leave right away."

"Did she say why?" Lily asked. Rowan shook his head. He waited for Tristan to leave first, and then closed the door so Lily could get dressed.

She came downstairs in a gauzy dress that lay open at the throat to display all three of her willstones. Her mother was dithering about, wringing her hands, and unable to focus her eyes on anything for more than a moment.

"We should really go, Lillian," she said.

"Why? What's going on?" Lily asked, trying not to sound too

frustrated. Usually when her mother acted like this Lily couldn't get a decipherable answer out of her, but this time was different.

"She's coming," Samantha said. "Or is she here?"

"Who? Who's here?"

"Simms."

Rowan ran to the window and looked out. "Everyone outside," he rasped. "Quick, get Lily on the pyre!"

Lily felt Tristan's hand on the small of her back, urging her forward. "Come on, Mom!" Lily yelled, worried that she would get left behind. She saw that Juliet grabbed Samantha's hand and pulled, when something occurred to her. She hadn't claimed her mother yet.

They scrambled outside to see cars had already surrounded the house silently in the dark. Floodlights burst on, blinding them, but Lily could still hear feet pounding against the ground and the huffs and gasps of men running. Caleb made it to the pyre first and threw a lighter on it. Flames exploded up and out of the wood and the dizzy smell of gasoline hit Lily in a wave with the heat.

"Rowan!" yelled a voice that made Lily's skin crawl. She didn't mean to stop running, she just froze when she heard Carrick.

He said something to Rowan and Rowan growled something back. It was so strange to hear Rowan speaking in his native tongue that it took a moment for it to register in Lily's mind. Carrick spoke again, and Rowan attacked him.

Rowan wasn't being fueled by Lily yet, but his hands flew to the silver knives on his belt so fast it was difficult to see them. He dropped down on a knee, wove past Carrick's block, and slashed back to hamstring his half brother. Carrick did something like a handspring, narrowly avoided losing his leg, and bounded forward again with a knife in one hand and an ax in the other.

Carrick spoke again and swung at Rowan with a weaving,

flowing motion, and then they started to exchange blows in earnest. They stabbed and blocked, darting in and out, trying to get inside the other's guard.

Lily felt herself being lifted up and saw Tristan's hands circling her waist. "Get us out of here, Lily!" he screamed.

The lawn was filling with officers. Three helicopters appeared in the sky around the house, one spotlight on the pyre and another on the knife fight. Tristan threw Lily on the pyre and ran to help Rowan.

Lily tumbled inside the fire as the glowing logs slipped under her hands. She finally righted herself as the heat started to eat into her skin. She pulled herself onto her knees and threw her arms out wide while screams tore from her throat. She saw Simms's shocked, chalky face as she ran to the pyre. She saw her mother looking at her and she had no idea how to get to her. She was burning, but she wouldn't transmute the energy and worldjump her coven without her mother. She couldn't leave Samantha behind.

"Mom," Lily screamed, "you have to come to me."

Samantha startled as if waking from a dream and jogged in her loping way to the side of the fire. In agony now, Lily reached through the flames and grabbed at the willstone resting on her mother's out-stretched palm.

"I'm sorry," her mother yelled through the roar of the fire.

Lily had no idea why her mother was apologizing, but then her hand touched her mother's willstone, and she understood.

A thousand moments almost exactly like the moment she was in, but each subtly different, stretched out in Lily's mind like pearls on a string—she was touching the willstone, she was still reaching for the willstone, she had touched the willstone, she knocked the willstone to the ground accidentally, she caught the willstone before it hit the ground, she touched the willstone with her other hand—the possibilities refracted inside her mind, zipping through like cards shuffling in a never-ending deck.

"Don't try to take it all in, Lillian!" Samantha yelled. Lily realized she was making a keening sound but she didn't know how to stop. Samantha reached into the fire with her other hand and slapped Lily across the face.

A thousand variations on a slap hit her, and it took all of them to stun Lily into releasing her mother's willstone and focusing on the here and now.

Rowan's shirt was slashed and blood flowed freely down his side. Caleb and Tristan wrestled Carrick to the ground. Simms stepped up and took on Tristan. She was a good fighter—strong as an ox and twice as tenacious. Breakfast and Una were on the other side of the pyre, fending off the officers who were swarming across the lawn in riot gear. Hiding behind their shields, the officers pulled out their clubs and beat Una and Breakfast. Just behind the line of officers, Lily saw Miller's face—a desperate mask among the black helmets. He was shouting and trying to get to her.

Lillian. I need you to guide me across the worldfoam, Lily called out in mindspeak.

I'm here. Hurry. You're already badly burned.

Lily breathed in, and her witch wind screeched like a living thing. By the time she let her breath out again, she and her coven were in Lillian's world.

Lily heard someone who loved her say her name. And then the pain began.

Toshi was surprised he was still allowed to come and go in the restricted zone.

After what had happened with Lily and the Hive, he would have thought that Grace would lock him up, but she hadn't. As Toshi passed under the whips of the Warrior Sisters at the checkpoint to get back into Bower City, he understood why. By allowing him all the freedoms he'd enjoyed before, Grace was showing him not only that she wasn't afraid of him, but that he'd never been free.

Toshi eyed a Warrior Sister as she moved aside to let him pass. He still didn't know if Grace could see everything the Hive saw, or if they just filled her in on the things they considered important. Again, the strangeness of the Hive struck him. What did a Warrior Sister consider important? Did they have a language, or did they simply pass along images to Grace? And if they passed on only images without language, how effective was the Hive at spying for her?

He had been forbidden to tell anyone that Grace controlled the Hive, although when she'd come to his rooms after losing Lily in the woods, she hadn't seemed too worried that he would. She'd wanted to talk about how Lily and her coven had simply disappeared, but Toshi didn't have a clue. When she finally believed that he was ignorant, Toshi had steered the conversation back to what really concerned him.

"Why the lie, Grace? Why even bother pretending that the Hive is in control?" Toshi had asked her.

"You know what I've learned in all my years of building and growing this city?" she asked in return. Toshi shrugged, not interested in playing guessing games. "Ninety-nine percent don't care how the lights get turned on or how the water gets cleaned or how we make the streets safe—just as long as everything works." She smiled at him, almost wistfully, and Toshi was reminded of one night over thirty years ago when they'd stood and talked under the stars. He couldn't really say who had kissed whom, but he remembered being happy for a while. It hadn't lasted long. "The lie is for the other one percent who couldn't bear to live under a human dictator. It's a mercy, really." Her eyes hardened in the same way that had driven him to break things off with her all those years ago. "The lie is so I don't have to kill that one percent."

"Grace the Merciful," he said bitterly.

Half her face pinched into a condescending smile. "No one mysteriously disappears in Bower City. People aren't being bullied or silenced. They have jobs, rights, wealth, and great schooling for their kids. There's no crime, no poverty, and no sickness. No one wants that to change. They don't *want* to know the truth, and if you told them, what I'd be forced to do to quell any uprising would be your fault." She brushed his shoulder like the lover she used to be, and he recoiled. She dropped her hand. "Leave the lie alone, Toshi."

When she left she didn't even bother to close the door behind her. And why should she? Privacy was an illusion.

Toshi hadn't wanted to believe her. He thought that there had to be malcontents—people who wouldn't be bought out by the perks of perfect living. So far, he hadn't found anyone. After two days of talking in code with family and friends, he was leaving the restricted zone more frustrated than when he'd entered it. He'd thought that if ever there were a place to find rebels, it would be there. He couldn't have been more wrong.

The people in the restricted zone didn't care one way or the other if the Hive controlled the city or if Grace controlled the city by controlling the Hive. They just wanted to be a part of it.

His father's advice was given in Japanese. The closest equivalent in English was "don't rock the boat."

Toshi spent a day in his family's apothecary shop, trying to feel out customers to see who would rise up if they knew that Grace, and not the inscrutable and invincible Hive, had kept them poor and sickly. He'd asked hypothetical questions that were met with blank stares and embarrassed laughs. They lived in a world where it was acceptable, even normal, to curse the Hive, but beyond curses all anyone seemed to want was to be accepted by them—to be ushered past the checkpoints and into the shining city by the sea.

At night, Toshi sat with his dying mother. He could see the cancer in her growing by the second, thinking how easily he could pluck it from her body. Like picking spilled seeds off the floor. But he wasn't allowed to do that.

Toshi asked his mother why she didn't want change. She placed her shriveled hand next to his smooth one and smiled up into his eternally young face. "You are not sick. You will never be sick," she said.

And that was enough for her. It seemed to be enough for most in the restricted zone. As long as they had the hope that their children would live charmed lives in Bower City, they didn't want change.

Toshi jumped a trolley and hung from the bar, glaring hopelessly out the window. The clean streets glittered at him smugly and the legions of fit people mocked him with their healthy bodies and pretty, smiling faces.

Grace was right. They would probably fight him—not her—if Toshi tried to change anything. That was the genius of what Grace had done. Her victims were far away and somebody else's problem. The punishment was to be locked *out* of Bower City, and so everyone wanted in.

He got off the trolley and walked the last few blocks to the Governor's Villa. Grace hadn't even hinted that she was going to throw him out or demote him in any way. Still, Toshi was certain now that he had no hope of ever learning how to grow willstones. Grace would never trust him with that. If the formula for growing willstones was ever leaked it would end Bower City's stranglehold on magic and therefore its dominance in the world.

But, as Toshi considered it, he realized that he'd never had a chance of becoming Ivan's second. Grace had stopped trusting him enough for that when he saw the hardness in her eyes and ended their brief romance. She knew that if he didn't love her she couldn't control him, and Grace would never allow anyone she couldn't control to know the secret of willstones. He wondered what Grace had on Ivan.

Toshi went inside, but he didn't go up to his rooms. Instead, he went to find Ivan. He wove through the myriad rooms and down passageways that led to other buildings. The façades of these buildings were made to look like they were separate, but behind them, nearly all the buildings in the governing area were connected. They all led back to Grace.

Toshi found Ivan in the power relays. The windy, stadium-size room was humming with the electricity being generated by the three dozen crucibles and witches who were transmuting energy for the city. They each stood in their niche in the marble walls, suspended in a gentle column of witch wind, their faces underlit by their glowing willstones. They looked like lovely floating statues. The mechanics grouped below them and monitored their bodies, making sure they didn't transmute to the point of taxing themselves. Salt and herbs were strewn on the floor. A banquet of food was ready in a niche to refuel them when they had completed their shift. Out of respect, the food was always presented spilling out of a cornucopia.

The only things that marred the hypnotic beauty of the relays were the thick cables that carried the electricity out to the city, but since they were the whole point, the cables were regrettably unavoidable. Ivan made sure they were kept out of the way nonetheless. A serene witch was a productive witch, and it just made sense to keep the generators of the city's power happy.

Ivan was checking an output gauge when Toshi came up behind him and tapped him on the shoulder. He turned and smiled when he saw his protégé.

"I didn't see you on the schedule today," Ivan said, his smile falling as he took note of Toshi's expression.

"Can we talk?" Toshi asked.

Ivan waved someone over to take his place. They went down a corridor and through some back doors in silence until they got to Ivan's laboratory. Unlike the grand and stately space of the relays, Ivan's laboratory was a cramped, untidy room full of glass beakers and tiny crystal vials of strange potions.

There were few places in the world where Toshi felt as comfortable as he did here. It was filled with memories of his childhood. After being chosen by the Hive and the subsequent commotion of bonding with such a large and impressive willstone, Ivan's laboratory was the only place that reminded Toshi of his parents' apothecary shop. It was unheard of for Toshi to wish himself back to the restricted zone, or to even speak of it, and so Ivan's acrid-smelling, usually sticky, and occasionally explosive laboratory became the only place Toshi could go as a boy to ease the homesickness he was told he shouldn't feel.

Pickled creatures, half created before they were destroyed, yellowed in their chemical baths along one wall. Each shelf was a trial and error in a series of experiments carried out on the Woven ages ago.

Toshi had asked Ivan once what they were for, and Ivan had replied, "To remind me of what *not* to do."

"What's troubling you?" Ivan asked, bringing Toshi back to the present with a small jump. Ivan perched on the edge of his scorch-marked desk and placed his hands properly in his lap, waiting with the same kindly patience he'd always given Toshi, even when he didn't deserve it.

"Did you create the Hive for Grace?"

The question brought an end to the decades of good memories Toshi had of that room and, like a bad smell lingering close to good food, tainted all of them.

Ivan looked down and let out a long, tired breath. "How did you find out?" he asked.

"You are the master of kitchen magic. And it's the only thing I could think of that she could use to keep you silent. You would have had to have done it in order to want to keep it hidden for so long," Toshi answered. "What about the rest of the Woven?"

"I can't claim full responsibility for them, but I was a part of it." He swallowed. "A large part. I made Grace the kitchen, as it were, for her to make the Woven." He swiped his hands over his face, his eyes older in an instant. "Bower City was just an outlawed trading post, scared to death that Salem would find out we existed and kill us all. We couldn't stand against the Eastern Covens. Then Grace had this idea about the Woven. I was young and angry and, I swear to you, I never thought the wild Woven would last more than a generation or two. I certainly never considered that she would learn how to make them grow willstones inside their bodies so she could control them. That's no excuse, but it's the only one I have."

"How many other people know?" Toshi asked.

"They're all long dead," Ivan said. "Like I should be."

The irony of it was suffocating. Ivan was the one who created the soap that slowed aging to a crawl, which Toshi had improved until aging and the slow decline of the body into decrepitude were essentially stopped, but you didn't have to use that soap if you wanted to grow old and die.

"Why aren't you?" he asked, cruelty flaring inside of him.

Ivan smiled down at his folded hands, accepting Toshi's anger and feelings of betrayal. "I knew I could never make up for what I'd done, but if I helped enough people, maybe my life wouldn't be a complete travesty." Ivan laughed softly. "Why aren't I dead yet? Because I have so many sins to repent before I die, I just might have to live forever."

The two of them watched a Worker crawl across Ivan's thigh. Toshi saw the loathing in Ivan that he never dared show before, and he just *knew*.

They had worked together as teacher and student for over fifty years, so it was easy for Toshi to read the subtle shift in Ivan, a shift that signaled he wanted to get to work. Over the years they had cured the incurable, mended the irrevocably broken, and essentially ended the need for people to grow old and die. That much time working together solving the biggest biological problems gave them an advantage over the myriad eyes that watched them.

Without even changing the attitude of their bodies, Toshi and Ivan agreed to solve this together. Toshi stood up, took off his jacket, and went to get a lab coat. They were going to find a way to exterminate the Hive.

CHAPTER
10

A T SOME POINT IN THE NIGHT, LILY BECAME AWARE OF THE
fact that she was thrashing about in a big, white bed.

She felt hands soothing her and smelled the grassy scent of
Rowan's ointment cooling her charred skin. No matter how many
times Lily went to the pyre, burning on it never got easier. The trauma
was not something the body could ever allow to become common-
place, and if she couldn't—or, in this case, wouldn't—transmute the
heat fast enough, agony was the sacrifice she had to make.

When it became too much, Lily found Lillian waiting for her in
the Mist. They sat on the raft, facing each other, their feet pulled in
and their chins resting on their knees.

But you didn't go to the pyre, Lily said in confusion. *Why are you here?*

I am here every night now, Lillian replied.

Your cancer is that bad?

Lillian smiled at Lily as they bobbed on top of the dark water. *It
won't be for much longer*, she replied after a quiet spell.

Lily thought of Toshi's deep red willstone, and regretted not
claiming him, if only for Lillian's sake.

Can I help you in any way?

Yes. You can help me destroy Bower City.

Lily didn't reply. She thought of all the people in Bower City who had no idea what Grace had done. They didn't deserve to die. Lily had no idea how to keep them safe, though, once the war began in earnest. While she was thinking about this, Lillian asked her another question.

How did you get your coven from the sand dunes to Salem?

I can't tell you that yet.

Why not?

I need you to wait for me and hear what I have to say.

I can't wait. I'm dying.

Hold on, Lillian. I'm coming.

Lily woke with the sun. Her stinging eyes peeled open to see stone walls, wide windows, and on the far side of the room, a fireplace large enough for her to stand in.

She knew this room. She was in Lillian's bedroom in the Citadel.

Lily sat up and saw that she wasn't alone in the bed. Rowan lay next to her, a bare arm thrown over his eyes to block out the light. Tristan was there, too, down by her feet. Juliet, Breakfast, Una, and Samantha were draped uncomfortably over various pieces of furniture. The only person missing was Caleb.

She felt Tristan twitch as he shook himself awake. His blue eyes opened and he sighed with relief when he saw her.

Hi there, he said. *You're looking much better.*

I still feel like hammered garbage. Lily smiled at him. *Where's Caleb?*

Tristan's eyes unfocused as he searched for his stone kin. *Off somewhere with a friend. He's still angry*, Tristan answered.

Have I lost him? The thought tightened her throat.

He hasn't decided yet. He had to smash his first willstone when he was still a kid to get away from his first witch, and he has no desire to repeat the experience.

Lily remembered Caleb telling her about his brief time training at the Citadel. He's been claimed by a cruel witch who used to possess him for fun. He'd never shared any of those memories, and Lily hadn't pushed it. It occurred to her that she had done the same thing to him, although for very different reasons. She could only hope that her reasons were good enough for Caleb and that he came back to her. For now it was out of her hands.

Not sure what to do, Lily glanced around absently at the basins of bloody water, the shreds of gauze pads, and the bottles of herbs piled around her. Detritus from the battle to heal her. Her coven slept deeply and in odd positions, as if exhaustion had hit them like the tide and left them scattered like driftwood.

It was quite a night, Tristan said in mindspeak. Lily caught glimpses of it from his mind.

They'd appeared inside the courtyard of the Citadel—the geographical parallel to Lily's backyard in her version of Salem. The few guards who had been left behind to defend Walltop had believed she was Lillian, and they'd ushered the group inside without a word of protest. They'd looked in amazement at Samantha, back from the grave, but these were Walltop soldiers. They did not question their Witch. Everyone had been relieved to see Lord Fall back at the Citadel, especially with the Witch as injured as she was. Lily saw herself from Tristan's perspective—a patchwork of black soot and red blood in Rowan's arms.

She heard the words *Lord Fall* echoing in Tristan's mind and she felt the struggle between envy and respect that had always plagued him sparking afresh. The elite Walltop soldiers honored Rowan and felt safer with him in command, while Tristan was merely an afterthought to them. Tristan looked at Rowan's slack body, at the rise and fall of his chest as he breathed, and something other than rivalry began to creep in on him.

Do you still love him? Tristan looked up at Lily as he asked this.

I'll never love anyone else, she replied. *But every time I almost let myself run back to him, I remember.*

Remember what?

In order for you to understand, I'd have to let you feel something that might be too much for you.

Give it a try.

Lily nodded and allowed this Tristan to feel what it was like when she'd Gifted her Tristan right before he died fighting the Hive. She let him feel the measure of power she was able to give him. And then she allowed him to feel what it was like when she Gifted Rowan.

Tristan inhaled sharply, eyes closed, his face turning away from the enormity of it. Lily backed off when she saw sweat beading on his upper lip. She let him catch his breath before continuing.

That's just a memory of what Rowan can do. If he had been my head mechanic when we faced the Hive—

You think your Tristan would still be here. You blame Rowan. That isn't fair, Lily. Not even Rowan can defeat the Hive alone.

Lily grasped at a way to turn something that had just been a jumble of feelings for so long into one coherent thought.

It's not just about Tristan, or about me. He abandoned all of us. When Rowan stayed with Alaric and let us fend for ourselves during the crossing, so many died because he wasn't there to save them. I can't forgive him for that.

But he changed his mind and followed us, Tristan argued.

He was following *us when he should have been* leading *us. No matter what he felt about me, he never should have abandoned the coven.*

She's right, Rowan said, joining them in mindspeak.

Lily saw him lying with his arm up over his head, a sad smile on his face. She had to look away. Tristan opened his mouth to say something, but Rowan cut him off.

"No, Tristan, don't. Don't make excuses for me." He looked at Lily, thoughts running swiftly behind his eyes. "Just let it go."

The moment teetered, and when the rest of the coven stirred and woke, it landed on the side of silence.

"Is she still crispy?" Breakfast croaked, his voice rusty with sleep.

Lily looked down at the pink skin on her arms. "Nope," she answered, poking her tender skin to test it. "I think I'm good."

"You're awake," Una said, surprised.

Lily waved to her, attempting a weak smile. "I feel about as good as you look," she said.

"Funny," Una said, dragging a few fingers through the knots in her hair.

Rowan got out of bed, his demeanor turning stormy. "Don't move around too much," he cautioned. "It was easier to put you back together with my tools at hand, but you're not completely healed yet."

He pulled open a drawer and took out a white shirt, snapping it once to loosen the creases. Bare chested and completely at ease in this space, Rowan opened the door and let his voice boom down the high and wide corridor. "Gavin!" he called.

While Rowan pulled on his shirt, still stored after all this time in Lillian's personal chest of drawers, Lily could hear the fumbling steps of someone scurrying to come to the door.

"Yes, Lord Fall?" inquired a blond boy who appeared before him anxiously. Lily remembered a younger version of him from Tristan's recollection of the Stacks.

"Go down to the kitchens and order breakfast for everyone here. Then come back and clean up," he said briskly, but kindly. "When you're done with that, I want you to find some suitable traveling clothes for the Ladies Juliet and Samantha, and for the rest of the Witch's guests."

"Yes, Lord Fall," Gavin said before turning and running back the way he came.

Rowan left the door open while he took up his wristwatch from the top of Lillian's vanity table, snapped it on, and then gathered a few strangely shaped coins that he slid into his pocket.

"Where are you going?" Tristan asked.

"To get Caleb and bring him back to the coven, where he belongs," Rowan replied over his shoulder. He stopped at the door for a moment to glance meaningfully at Lily. "I can't let him make the same mistake I did, can I?"

As Rowan swept out of the room, Una and Breakfast exchanged a look.

"So that's Lord Fall," Breakfast said, his eyebrows raised.

"He's very . . . lordly," Una added. "It's kinda hot." She patted Breakfast's arm consolingly. "No offense."

"No, I'm with you," Breakfast said in agreement. "I almost saluted him."

Lily could feel Tristan watching her, but her eyes stayed fixed on the previously charged space that faded into listlessness now that Rowan had left it.

Toshi met Mala for lunch at the same seaside restaurant where he'd taken Lily. He was distracted, and annoyed that Mala was running ten minutes late.

He and Ivan had been desperately trying to come up with something to kill off the Hive. The problem was, Ivan had made them too well. They were disease resistant, able to bear high volumes of toxic chemicals, and they were immune to all of the lethal forms of fungus that can sometimes plague insects. They were running out of time, and Mala was wasting his.

She rushed into the restaurant in a self-important flurry, wearing a burgundy-and-gold sari that brought out the golden highlights in her dark skin, and a tissue-thin veil bordered by gold medallions that tinkled pleasingly when she moved her head.

The veil, Toshi thought, was a bit much. But Mala had never been one to exercise restraint.

"Grace tells me you have no idea where the Proctor witch went," Mala said, diving right in before they'd even gotten their drinks.

Toshi forced a smile through pursed lips. "*Lily* never mentioned she planned on leaving," he replied. "It was very sudden."

"And the Hive just let her go?" She pulled a face. "That's odd. But who knows why the Hive does anything?"

Toshi accepted his champagne from the server and took a sip to stall for a moment. Up until now, he couldn't be sure how much Mala knew about Grace and the Hive, but it seemed she, like the rest of Bower City, had no idea Grace controlled them.

"Grace didn't discuss Lily with you?" he asked in return.

Mala flicked her head and her veil chimed. "I honestly don't care what happened to her." She scanned the horizon, her expression a placid mask over bitterness.

"Just as long as she doesn't come back?" Toshi guessed.

Mala shook her head and leaned forward, placing her forearms against the edge of the table.

"I'm past that," she said. "It's clear to me now that I'm not Grace's first choice. And if I'm not her first, I'm just waiting around until the next Lily Proctor comes along."

Toshi wondered how blind Mala had to be to miss the fact that there were no other witches like Lily Proctor. Not that Grace intended to cede power to anyone. Mala's role as lieutenant governor was created to keep up the illusion of freedom. He watched a Worker land on the white tablecloth.

"What do you intend to do?" he asked.

Mala looked down at her hands. "I'm done waiting."

"You intend to leave Bower City?"

"I didn't say that." She leaned back again, adopting airs of confidence and relaxation he doubted she truly felt. "You're never going to be Ivan's second, you know. Grace told me months ago that she'd never let your confirmation go through."

Toshi didn't appreciate being baited. He narrowed his eyes at her. "What do you want, Mala?"

She gave him the first genuine smile he'd ever gotten from her. "We've never been friends," she said candidly. "Which is strange, because we have so much in common. For a while I thought it was because you and Grace were involved a long time ago, and there's always been an attraction between us." She waved away her own musings without bothering to check if Toshi agreed with her. "The point is that both of us have been strung along by Grace for decades," she continued. "But we're not the only people in this city who've noticed that she's been in power for too long. There's a *lot* of people who—"

Toshi straightened with a jolt. "Stop talking."

He stood up, threw some money on the table, and took her by the arm. She was so shocked that she didn't even protest while he led her out of the restaurant.

He didn't say a word as he pulled her onto a trolley, and when she tried to take her arm out of his grasp, he squeezed tighter. She grew still.

"Where are you taking me?" she asked under her breath. "To Grace?"

Workers began to gather on the railing of the trolley. They rubbed their tubular mouthparts with their forearms, tasting Mala's fear and deliberating the threat level.

Toshi put his arm around her and nuzzled past her veil until his lips touched her neck. "I'm not going to hurt you," he whispered.

She smiled and relaxed. "It took you long enough," she said, and wound her arms over his shoulders.

"Listen very carefully. You're being watched. Every move you make, maybe every word you say—I can't be sure."

Mala's chiming laughter matched the merry jingling of her veil. "Grace doesn't have spies in the city. Believe me, I would know who—"

"Not *who*," Toshi said, giving her a little shake to quiet her.

He pulled back with the lazy look of a lover and turned one of her medallions over in his long fingers. Subtly, slowly, he gestured to the Workers that were disbanding now that Mala's fear had dissipated.

It took a moment to sink in, but as Toshi watched, Mala's face transformed from disbelief, to fearful calculation, to outrage. Her breath quickened and her eyes darted around as she scrolled through a lifetime of private moments that were now violated, until finally, resentment smoldered inside her.

Toshi pulled her close and let his lips dip close to her ear, covering their conversation with her veil.

"We need allies," he whispered. "People who aren't afraid to fight."

"I'll take you to them."

Lily put her feet down and tested her legs. When they didn't show any sign of buckling, she stood and took a few steps. By the time she made it to the hope chest at the end of Lillian's bed she needed to rest, and sat down heavily.

"If Rowan catches you out of bed, he's going to freak out," Juliet said.

Lily panted and concentrated on making the room stop spinning. "I don't care what Rowan does," she said petulantly. Juliet gave her a doubtful look. "Just don't, okay?" Lily continued, "I'm not being stubborn. I have to get better fast because I have to get us to Lillian."

"It's not like she's going to make it to Bower City anytime soon," Una said over the top of the book she was reading. "What's the rush?"

Lily didn't have the energy to explain it to them, so she replayed a memory of what Lillian had shared with her just a few moments ago . . .

. . . My drake lets out a trumpeting bellow. I bank and return the way we came. I'm soaring high above the fourth battalion along the outer rim of the advancing line of my army. I have to keep shifting which battalion is on the outside to spread the risk among them equally, lest I sow dissent.

The Woven devoured fifty men last night alone. They're attacking us on every front. It's more than just coincidence. Grace Bendingtree is sending them against us, trying to pick off as many as she can. And it's working. At this rate, my army will be dead before we get there . . .

"*That's* why I'm rushing," Lily said.

Juliet nodded and stood up. She came over to Lily and helped haul her to her feet. "Let's get you closer to this food," she said, steering Lily toward the tea table. "There's a disgustingly salty vegetable broth that I'm sure you'll love."

Lily made it to a chair and flopped into it. She tore at a heel of bread and dipped the crust in her broth to soften it. "Where's Breakfast?" she asked.

"He's out running an errand," Una answered. "He said he'd be back in a few hours—which should be right around now."

"A few hours? What's he doing?" Lily asked. Una shrugged but didn't offer any more information. Lily turned to Juliet. "Where are Tristan and Mom?"

"Tristan went to check on his apartment, and Mom is going through boxes of her stuff. Or the other . . . her's stuff," Juliet answered, stumbling over the tricky grammar. "I've been told there are several rooms that belonged to the other me just a few doors down, but I don't actually know this place like Mom does."

"Or like Rowan does," Una added, watching Lily.

Lily's chewing slowed and she forced down the now-heavy mouthful. "It was hard to see him like that this morning," she admitted. "He was never that comfortable in my bedroom." She picked at the spongy center of her bread, pinching some off and rolling it into a dough marble between her fingers. "He's going to see her again soon," she said after a long pause.

"Don't start thinking crazy thoughts," Una warned.

"But they have history," Lily said.

"Yeah—the bad kind. She killed his father, remember?"

Lily smiled weakly and dropped her head. "Our history isn't so great, either." Gavin appeared in the doorway, wringing his hands. "What is it, Gavin?" Lily asked, brushing the crumbs from her fingers and sitting up straight.

"One of your guests has returned to the Citadel with a stranger, My Lady, and Lord Fall isn't here, and he told me not to let anyone disturb you, and I didn't know if this would be considered a disturbance or not—"

"It's okay," Lily said, interrupting the anxious tirade. "Let him in."

Gavin blinked his wide blue eyes. "Okay. But if he ends up disturbing you, you'll tell Lord Fall that I was against it, won't you?"

Lily suppressed a laugh. "I'll tell him." Gavin breathed in relief and rushed off.

"What did Rowan do to that poor kid?" Una asked, shaking her head.

"It's not just Gavin. Everyone here is afraid of him," Juliet said.

"It's not fear," Lily said, wishing she felt less for Rowan than she did. "It's respect."

Breakfast entered the room with a pale and grubby young man who had the lanky arms and legs of a recent growth spurt. Lily stared blankly at him until he smiled at her, and she recognized him as the boy from the Providence subway tunnels.

"Riley?" she said disbelievingly.

"Hello, Lady Witch," he said, breaking into a brazen grin. "Sorry to see you're laid up again."

"Occupational hazard," Lily mumbled and turned to Breakfast. "What the heck is going on?"

Breakfast and Riley sat down at the tea table and started digging into the cold cuts of meat and wedges of cheese that Lily had no intention of eating.

"I first got the idea when we were talking about how hard it was going to be to get Lillian and Alaric to work together," Breakfast said as he spread mustard on a piece of black bread. "I thought then we were still going to need more fighters than that. It's an all-hands-on-deck situation, right?"

"Yes, but—"

"And, let's face it, if anyone needs land and a new place to live besides the Outlanders, it's Riley's people."

"We'd be willing to fight for it," Riley said with fire in his eyes. "My dad—all the men on the ranches—they aren't afraid to fight the Woven. They live out there with them anyways, and at least if we were to go west, we might actually have a shot at having our own homes for a change."

Lily held up a hand and addressed Breakfast. "How much did you tell him?"

Riley and Breakfast shared a look. "Everyone knows that Bower City is out there already," Breakfast said.

"You can't move an army west without someone finding out why," Riley said. "Especially not someone with my connections."

Lily suppressed a smile at the young man's bluster. "Yes, but how much did you tell him about me and Lillian?" Lily asked.

"Oh, he told me there are two of you," Riley said around a mouthful of cheese and fig jam.

"And that doesn't strike you as strange?" Juliet asked.

Riley shrugged, his mouth still full. "Witches are weird," he said, like that explained everything.

But he was young. Lily didn't think that explanation would suit the hardened men on the ranches or the women Lily had met in the tunnels. Thinking of them, she sat back and shook her head, engaging Breakfast in mindspeak.

You should have asked me before you did this, she said.

I knew you'd say no if I did, he replied. *You have something against the tunnel people and the men on the ranches.*

Surprised, Lily weighed his assessment and found it to be true. She hadn't liked Mary, the leader of the tunnel people in Providence, and the memories Lillian had shared with her about the men on the ranches still haunted her. Lily switched out of mindspeak to keep the nightmarish memories of those vicious men from seeping out of her thoughts and into Breakfast's.

"It doesn't matter what I think of them," Lily said dismissively. "I can't use them because they aren't my claimed. They wouldn't stand a chance against the Hive."

"We'd let you claim us," Riley said.

"And you speak for everyone?" Lily snapped. "I'm sorry, but I don't believe you, Riley. You aren't in charge down there."

"No, but I know how my people feel. I know they want to fight," he said stubbornly. "And I can bring Mary if you'd rather talk to her."

Lily opened her mouth to decline, and Juliet spoke up. "The least you can do is meet with her," she said.

"It's a waste of time," Lily argued.

"We need all the help we can get," Una said, studying Lily carefully. Una switched to mindspeak.

What's wrong with you?

One of Lillian's memories flew from her mind to Una's.

. . . I struggle and kick, but they pin me down with the noose poles. Even from five feet away I can smell the corruption of their innards in the stink of their breath. They leer at me, trying to push the bodice of my torn dress aside to get a glimpse of my bare breasts . . .

Una recoiled, shaken by the terror and helplessness that Lillian had felt.

Those are the kind of men out there on the ranches, Una. Murderers and rapists, Lily said in mindspeak. *I have no interest in claiming them.*

They can't all be like that, Una replied, more out of optimism than true belief.

"And what if they are?" Lily asked aloud.

Una gave her a calculating look. "What are you willing to do to get rid of the Hive?" she asked flatly. "You better decide now, because I'm pretty sure Grace isn't squeamish about who she'd claim."

Lily glared at Una, and saw tough love glaring back. Una never let her get away with anything.

"Damn it," Lily breathed. She turned to Riley. "Arrange a meeting with Mary, but tell her not to come if she's just going to waste my time. I'm not doing this unless she can bring me an army."

"I'll tell her," he said with a brisk nod. His horse-trading done,

Riley looked down on the remains of her bread. "Are you going to eat that?"

Lily ended up having to order Gavin to bring more food. Riley ate with the mechanical determination of someone who had spent more days of his young life going hungry than feeling full, and he wasn't about to pass up this opportunity to gorge until he couldn't see straight. When his gargantuan appetite was finally appeased, Lily sent him back to the tunnels with a basket of food for Pip and the other children who followed him around like the Pied Piper.

It was almost evening before Rowan returned with Caleb and Tristan. At some point Tristan had joined Rowan to try to help him persuade Caleb to come back to the coven, and it was obvious by the way the three of them hung together that they had spent quite a long time hashing things out. They already had similar ways of moving and gesturing from having grown up together, but it was more pronounced when they'd spent long stretches in one another's heads. Physically, they were three very different men—Caleb dark and hulking, Tristan light-eyed and tall, and Rowan slender and as elegantly muscled as a dancer—but when they spent a lot of time together they could easily be mistaken for brothers.

Lily watched Caleb anxiously. She brushed up against his mind and gently asked for entry. He let her in, but only so far. She felt a pang of rejection and desperately hoped he wouldn't stay angry with her forever. Caleb had been her shoulder to cry on in some of her darkest times. The thought of losing that closeness was unbearable to her.

I'm sorry, she said in mindspeak. She didn't try to excuse her behavior with an explanation. It was up to him to forgive her or not.

Do better, he replied, holding back a tide of unpleasant memories from his childhood.

I will, Lily promised. She felt him relax and knew that the danger of losing him had passed. For now, anyway.

"Let me see how much of my hard work you undid today," Rowan said, and came forward to check Lily's injuries.

Rowan laid two fingers on the pulse point at Lily's wrist. She saw his willstone flare enchantingly and became aware of the featherlight presence of him inside her skin. He was barely touching her with his fingertips, but the contact was still more intimate than if he'd slipped his hands under her dress.

"Better," he said quietly.

"When will I be ready for the pyre?" she asked, keeping her hand close to his.

"You need at least another week."

"Too long," she replied with a little shake of her head. "Tomorrow, after I meet with Mary."

"Mary?" he asked, surprised. "The leader of the tunnel gang?"

Lily replayed her meeting with Riley for Rowan, Caleb, and Tristan to bring them up to speed. After she was finished, Rowan picked up his argument with her where he'd left off.

"You still need to rest for a few more days at least."

"We leave tomorrow. With or without Mary's people."

"Lily—"

"Tomorrow," she said firmly. "You have to get me ready for the pyre."

Rowan knew what was happening to Lillian's army without having to be shown. He knew every day they crept along was costing lives. Finally, he slipped his jacket off his shoulders with a sigh.

"There is something else I can do now that I have my full kit again. There's an ink I couldn't get my hands on once I left Lillian," he said reluctantly.

"Ink?" Lily asked.

"Yes. It's very rare, very old, and it's going to hurt."

Lily nodded and looked down at her hands. "Of course it will," she said, trying to laugh her way through the fear.

"Tristan. I need you," Rowan called as he headed toward what appeared to be a wall of solid rock beside the headboard of Lillian's bed.

He laid his fingers carefully against the masonry, took a deep breath, and his willstone flared. The wall gave way with a grinding sound, pushing inward and sliding to the side to reveal a set of hidden stairs. Tristan looked surprised but followed Rowan up the stairway without a word of protest.

Lily frittered the next few minutes away while her mechanics prepared. Una and Juliet gave her uneven smiles that didn't have the conviction to reach their eyes. Lily tried to comfort herself by thinking that whatever Rowan had planned couldn't be worse than the pyre, although she knew that the pain of the pyre was offset by the rush of pleasure she got from the power it gave her. Something told her that whatever Rowan had planned would have very little upside to it.

When Rowan returned for her she was trying her best to be brave. He didn't look at her when he led her up the stone stairway and through a trapdoor that led out onto the roof.

The stars were out, adorning a sickle moon that glowed gold in the warm summer sky. Beneath the horns of the moon an enormous speaking stone glimmered like an opal pillar that was subtly lit from within. Lily found herself drawn to the speaking stone, and nearly had her hands on it when she heard Rowan call her name.

"Lily. Over here," he said.

She turned and saw a familiar square of black silk spread out and waiting for her. Rowan and Tristan knelt between the runes they had drawn on the silk in salt. They had nothing else with them but a bowl, a long silver needle, and a tiny mallet.

"We'll start with you sitting up," Rowan said.

Lily sat down in front of Rowan with her legs crossed. He gestured for Tristan to sit behind her, and Lily felt his hands take her head and tilt it to expose the long stretch of skin from her ear to her collarbone.

"This will leave a mark," Rowan said.

Lily took a breath and let it out slowly to steady herself. But she didn't stop him. A haze of light expanded out from Rowan's willstone, like a bright fog that spun outward to wrap them up in glinting tendrils. He dipped the tip of the needle in the bowl, picked up the mallet, and began tapping the end in a quick staccato.

Lily felt the pricking of the tattoo behind her ear. As the ink started to sink into her skin an itch turned into a burn. The burn began to build.

"Hold her," Rowan ordered, and Tristan's hands clamped down on Lily's head.

Even when Rowan paused momentarily to dip his needle, the burning kept mounting, and soon she couldn't even feel the prick of the needle over the sting of the ink. A cold sweat broke down her back, and as Rowan tapped the tattoo farther down the side of her neck, she started to shiver. She wasn't burning. She was freezing.

Tristan had to take more of her weight as the icy acid in the ink started to leach into her blood and chill her from the inside out. Lily could feel the cold sliding down her insides as if she'd swallowed an ice cube. Her teeth began to chatter.

"Okay. Lay her back," Rowan said.

Lily felt herself being put down and opened her eyes. The stars whirled above. The steady tapping and the cold burn began again along the lower part of her right ribs. Lily tracked the paths of the stars to keep her mind off Rowan's never-ending tattoo. He worked down from her ribs and curved inside the hip bone, ending just above her bikini line.

"Last one," he said, and started on the top of her left thigh.

She was numb with cold by the time he had spiraled around the inside of her thigh and ended the third tattoo at the back of her left knee. Rowan ended the spell. The light in his willstone heaved and then went out.

In the absence of his magelight, the soft scintillation of the speaking stone caught Lily's eye again. Half in and half out of her body to hide from the pain, Lily let her other eye swim in the light of the speaking stone. She idly wondered whether she could reach Pale One and called softly to her claimed Woven.

Lily's mind seemed to jump into a fast-moving river, and the impressions of places whizzed past her. She saw hills and valleys and then mountains and vast plains. Her other eye skipped from speaking stone to speaking stone, each stone tinting the world a slightly different color, until finally her mind settled inside the claimed she'd named Pale One. Lily waded through a tangle of scents so strong and clear they glowed like colors that painted the whole world, and high-contrast images seen through eyes that were not built like her own. The mind she touched pieced information together differently than Lily's did, but after a few tries, she deciphered this . . .

Inside, follow. Unseen, but here with me, she calls. Bite itch and lick. Need to howl, but stop. Biggers are close. Smell sweet stink of Biggers' honey.

Lily asked Pale One if she could join her, and then her vision exploded with color and light. After a dizzying moment, Lily realized she was looking at a fern. She concentrated and panned out with Pale One's achingly sharp eyes to see a glade, deep in the redwood forest. The colors she saw were richer, and she could see the edges of things more distinctly.

Lily felt the earth under Pale One. She felt the old minds of the trees, their roots running deep and holding the ground to their hearts like million-fingered hands. She read the vibration of the land. It was the low, thunderous rumble of a giant lung, the trees breathing for the whole world. Lily stored the vibration in her willstone and released Pale One.

Run to the rising sun, Lily commanded. *Go east until you are safely out of Hive territory.*

She calls. I run to where the wolves tend their meat, Pale One responded.

She saw Rowan's face hovering over hers. His worried frown broke with relief. "Where did you go?" he asked softly.

Lily was about to tell him, but she thought of the expression of barely controlled disgust on his face when she told the coven about Pale One and stopped herself. Instead she just smiled and struggled to sit up.

She looked down at the two tattoos she could see, and was relieved to find out that although they were long, they were as thin as ribbons, and the ink Rowan had used was a very pale pink. She ran her finger over the tattoo on her leg and felt it more than she saw it. It looked like lace had been inserted under her skin.

"Is it going to stay raised like that?" she asked.

"Yes," Rowan replied. "The compound I tattooed under your skin will help you heal faster each time you go to the pyre. It's permanent, though."

Lily studied the delicate filigree of the design. "Does Lillian have one?"

"She has two. One running down her back, and another down the inside of her right leg. I gave you three."

Rowan's face was impassive, but Lily noticed he didn't meet her eyes. She wondered when he had given them to Lillian, and if they had been in love at the time.

"They're quite pretty," Tristan said appreciatively.

Lily smiled but didn't say anything. She touched the one behind her ear that ran in a thin line down the side of her neck. It hurt, but the pain was going away quickly, as was the lingering pain from her burns. She felt stronger, and for the first time in her memory, she actually felt cool.

"Thank you," she said.

Rowan nodded. "It's my job," he said, and then frowned uncertainly.

"It *is* your job, if that's what you're wondering," Lily said. "You're my head mechanic. If you want to be."

Tristan helped Lily stand, but she found that as soon as she was upright, she didn't need help anymore. She went to the speaking stone and stared at its milky white beauty.

"My army," she whispered, and her mind whipped through the darkness, into the forest, past hordes of swarming Woven, and into another speaking stone that tinted the world blue. There, it swung over rolling hills until, finally, it settled with the thousands of her claimed still under Alaric's rule.

Many slept, but those who were awake felt the light touch of her mind—not so much that they would be aware of it, but enough so that a brief thought of her would flutter through their minds like wind across a pond.

"He's gathered them together to march west," Lily murmured, her mind half here and half there.

"Do you know where they are?" Rowan asked. "I haven't been able to reach Alaric. He's too far."

"Outside of Richmond." She snapped out of it and gathered her robe around her against the chill. "That's our first stop."

Rowan nodded. "But first, you need to rest for one more night."

Gavin awoke Lily at dawn more anxious than usual, which pushed him well into frantic territory. She heard him pounding on the door and she stirred in Rowan's arms, not clear on how she'd gotten there.

All she remembered after getting the tattoo was having something to eat with her coven, and then she went right to bed.

Rowan took a sleepy breath and threw the covers over Lily's bare shoulders. "Come," he called to Gavin, allowing entry.

"The Citadel is surrounded!" Gavin shouted as he tumbled into Lily's room. "They came out of nowhere—just popped up from underground—the streets are full of them!"

Rowan was out of bed and sprinting up the hidden staircase with Tristan and Caleb close behind before Lily had even sat up. When she, Una, and Breakfast finally made it up there, Lily could see the tops of the Citadel bristling with the skeleton guard that Lillian had left behind to defend the city. Down below, outside the Citadel gates, the streets of Salem swarmed with people. The ragtag multitude packed every inch of street for at least a dozen blocks back, and possibly farther.

"Oh. Hi, Riley," Breakfast called down to the young man standing at the entrance to the Citadel gates. Riley saw Breakfast and waved back.

Mary stood next to Riley. When she saw Lily come forward between Rowan and Tristan, she crossed her arms.

"Is this a big enough army for you?" Mary yelled up.

Lily looked at the masses filling the streets, reckoning their numbers in the thousands, and tried to pull her flimsy nightgown more tightly over her. She felt Rowan's arm wrap around her as he tilted his bare shoulders to cover her from one too many covetous stares. The crowd below was not the most respectable-looking bunch, but there were scores of them, and they looked like they were spoiling for a fight, which was exactly what Lily needed.

"It's a good start," she yelled back. Mary actually laughed at that.

"Gavin. Arrange to have the Witch's guests meet her in the main hall," Rowan instructed.

After Gavin rushed off, Rowan led the coven back downstairs.

He started throwing open the doors to closets and pulling out clothes. He rifled through Lillian's dresses until he found the one he was looking for and passed it to Lily.

"Here, put this on," he said absently before crossing to a closet on the other side of the room. This closet was filled with his wardrobe, which he started passing out to the guys. "Una, you might like Juliet's clothes better," he suggested while he dug through his things.

"Yeah, these aren't exactly my style," Una said, laughing at Lillian's collection of tiny scraps of gauze that were barely held together by jewels.

Lily looked at what Rowan had chosen for her and decided not to argue. She understood why he wanted her to wear a proper witch's gown. If she was going to drag these people into a war, they had to see her as a leader. She had to become the Salem Witch in their eyes.

"I guess someone should explain to the new recruits where we're going and how Lily's getting us there. Make sure they're all signed on for this," Breakfast said.

"I nominate you," Una said, dropping a peck on his cheek as she passed him on her way to Juliet's room.

"Any objections?" he asked hopefully, but everyone begged off. "I'll find Riley," he said with a sigh, and went off to spread the word.

Lily freshened up in the bathroom before she slid into the black silk dress inlaid with rubies. She looked at herself in the mirror and saw her red hair, which seemed to have grown three more inches overnight, billowing down her shoulders, and her pale skin glowing even whiter against the black silk.

She came out of the bathroom and saw Rowan waiting for her, dressed all in black and looking brutally beautiful. The collar of his shirt was open to show off his huge willstone, which danced with light and power. He held something sparkly in his hand.

"Turn around," he said, his voice catching as he stared at her.

Lily felt him place something on her head. He angled her toward a mirror and she saw that it was a spiked crown of iron and diamonds. The Salem Witch's crown. Lily remembered it from Lillian's memory. It *was* a cruel-looking thing, twisted and sharp. The metal was burnt black where it wasn't shining with white diamonds. Rowan opened a case and showed her what was nestled in the velvet inside. Matching shackles. Lily smiled wryly at them, remembering Lillian and how she had balked, refusing to wear them. She wouldn't even look at them.

Rowan put the matching iron-and-diamond cuffs on her wrists and locked them shut. The cuffs came complete with rings ready to chain her to the pyre.

Lily turned her wrists over and heard the metal clink. Every gesture she made would be accompanied by the sound of iron chains. She watched a slow smile spread on Rowan's face as she realized that she was a prisoner as much as she was a queen.

"So this is what it is to be a warmonger witch," she said, breath fluttering.

"You are chained to your claimed as much as they are to you," he replied. "And if you fail, you burn."

Lily looked up at him and knew he would never let that happen. He'd pulled her from the fire before, and he'd do it again because he loved her.

Tristan appeared in the doorway, sensed that he was interrupting, and dropped his eyes. "They're ready for you, Lily," he said.

Rowan and Lily took a guilty step back from each other.

"We should go down first," Rowan said to Tristan and then turned back to Lily. "Wait five minutes and then come down."

"You're not coming with me?" she asked, her voice piping with nerves.

"This is your moment," he replied with a little shake of his head.

Instead of going to the door, Lily crossed farther inside the room.

"They're expecting you," Rowan said, not understanding what she was doing.

"I know," she replied, and went to the wall behind the bed. She started feeling around the chinks in the masonry. "I'm not going to claim them one at a time. There are too many. I have to use the speaking stone. Like Grace does."

Lily felt the catch and pressed it. The hidden doorway swung open and she gestured up the secret stair.

"Will you be able to claim them that way?" Tristan asked.

"Yes, she will, as long as they consent to it," Rowan answered for her.

They climbed up the secret staircase together, Tristan in front of her and Rowan beside her. She could feel the flurry of their mind-speak swirling about her head like a buffeting wind, but she didn't need to be a part of it.

She pulled Rowan's arm against her side and let herself feel the shape of his arm under his sleeve. She felt cold and pressed the solid-ness of him against her. He glanced down at her cautiously, like he was watching something wild and rare that would run off if he looked too closely.

She could hear the low murmur rising up from the throng of people waiting for her before she reached the edge. She placed a hand on the cold granite of her keep and leaned out so everyone could see her. Silence fell over the multitude.

The drawbridge had been lowered, and the doors of the castle had been opened onto the bailey. People filled the hall and the bailey; they streamed over the drawbridge and, for all Lily could see, they were packed several streets deep into the city. All of them waiting to be claimed. In the silence, Lily's iron shackles clanked. She looked down at her wrists already rubbed red by the rough metal and felt their eyes on her like a watchful sea. She raised her head, ready now. For a moment she saw herself as they saw her—terrible and glorious as a blizzard.

"Are you willing to be claimed?" she asked. Her voice drifted through the silence and came to each individual as if she had whispered it privately in his or her ear.

"*We are*," they answered together.

She crossed to the speaking stone and looked into its soft lights. At first she couldn't think how to connect with all the waiting willstones below her. Before, she'd always had to touch a willstone to feel its unique vibration, and then once she had the pattern of it, she could use the vibration to unlock the bearer's mind. She had to think of a way of finding the vibrations without touch, but she knew that if Grace could figure it out, so could she.

Nothing came to her. She took a step back and tried to calm down. Strangely she thought of the shaman, and of the time she spent with him in the oubliette. She wiped her mind of any expectations. This wasn't a contest between her and Grace.

She stared into the speaking stone and waited.

"Those funny little lights. Look at 'em go," she murmured to herself. She giggled under her breath at how alive they looked. Each little thread of light quivered through the lattice of the crystal in its own way. Some swam up, quivering quickly. Some swooped down slowly. Others looped sideways, making tight corkscrews. Each one moved in a unique pattern, each one an individual mind. Lily laughed aloud when she figured it out.

She realized that the speaking stone worked like a net, gathering up the vibrations of every willstone nearby and displaying each of them as a vibrating string of light. Lily worked as fast as she could, her eyes skipping through the speaking stone as she learned the thousands of different vibrations. She imprinted each inside her willstone before moving on to the next. When she had them all, she played the strings' vibrations back like many voices singing one sweeping song, and claimed them all. Lily blinked her eyes and sighed.

"It's done," she said.

Rowan and Tristan escorted her back down to the bailey where the rest of her mechanics were waiting. They stood arranged in front of her pyre, which they'd built right in the middle of the bailey. The pyre was splintered and thorny, and the stake stood tall in the center, its chains dangling. A thrill ran through her, equal parts fear and hunger.

Can you jump this many? The question came from Rowan, but she knew her whole coven was thinking it. She didn't answer because she didn't know.

Lily climbed the pyre, pulled the chains through her shackles herself, and locked them with a small *snick*. The new additions to her army watched. An anxious susurration rose from their ranks.

"Light it," she said.

CHAPTER
11

TOSHI AND IVAN WERE IN THEIR WORDLESS FLOW, silently agreeing that the latest virus they had concocted to wipe out the Hive had to be scrapped because it would most likely kill everyone in the city along with the Hive, when Grace walked into the lab.

She looked at the petri dish, took its contents apart with a glance, and then looked up at Toshi and Ivan with eyebrows raised.

"I hope that's not going around," she said, alarmed.

"It's just a sample. There's no host," Ivan replied with a small shake of his head.

"Good." Grace smiled and looked between the two of them like they were her dear friends. "You two have been busy lately, although I can't quite tell with *what*."

Toshi didn't react. He'd gotten good at burying his feelings over the past week and a half. If he felt anxious that Grace was actually here in the lab to see what they'd been up to, he quickly snuffed it. Whether she was physically in the room or not, it made no difference. She was always watching, which was why Toshi and Ivan hadn't even attempted to become stone kin. It was a good thing they knew each other well enough not to need mindspeak in order to read each other's minds. Toshi glanced at Ivan, who was even better at appearing calm. But then again, he'd had almost two hundred years of experience hiding his emotions from Grace and the Hive.

"We've been updating the inoculation roster. Would you like us to walk you through the new diseases we've identified?" Ivan asked, with an ever so slightly belabored breath to indicate how tedious that would be for all of them.

"The flu is doing something interesting," Toshi added with a listless shrug.

Grace declined their unappealing offer by wrinkling her nose. She started wandering around the lab, peering into jars and touching instruments. "It's been a while since you've been down here," she said to Toshi. When she turned to face him, she gave him a glassy-eyed smile. "I wonder what prompted you to become so hands-on again?"

Toshi knew there was no point trying to act too innocent. She knew something was going on, but had decided that finding out what they were doing was more important than stopping them. For now, anyway.

"Just looking for meaning in my life now that I've discovered everything I've ever thought to be true was built on a giant lie," he rattled off as if it were of no consequence. She laughed aloud at his audacity. "What are *you* doing down here?" he asked in return.

"Alright. No more dancing around it, then." She stopped her wandering and faced them. "I want to know if your renewed interest in the lab has anything to do with how Lily and her coven disappeared into thin air."

"You're really obsessed with that, aren't you?" Toshi asked, not having to fake his surprise.

Grace's eyes flashed with anger. "My scouts can't find her. There's no trail, no scent markers. Nothing. I've sent half the Hive clear into Pack territory, and there's no sign of her."

"I don't see what you expect us to do about that," Ivan said irritably. "We deal in real materials in the lab, not hocus-pocus. Toshi and I can't help you if she's been"—Ivan waved his hands about, searching for the appropriately derisive expression—"spirited away."

"Spirited away." Grace laughed at the foolishness of that under her breath, and then caught herself. "Spirit walking." Her smirk dissolved and her eyes moved about restlessly. "Maybe she wasn't lying about the shaman."

Toshi hadn't entirely understood what Lily was talking about when she was pleading for her sister's life in the redwood grove, but he did know that she had been about to tell Grace how she could be in two places at once. She'd talked about spirit walking and a shaman, and Grace had dismissed it out of hand. It seemed she was changing her mind about that now. Dread roiled in his stomach. The last thing Grace needed was more power.

Grace started heading for the door, already forgetting about Toshi and Ivan now that she had new quarry.

"Where are you going?" Toshi asked. "Grace!" he called out as the door shut behind her.

Lily's spirit flew up and out of her tortured flesh. Down below, she saw herself writhing in flames. Out and beyond, she saw that the overworld had taken on the shapes of vast swaths of forest and rolling hills.

Lillian was out there somewhere, waiting for her. That wasn't Lily's first stop. She had to find Alaric and her braves. She turned away from Lillian's faint call.

Lily scanned the virgin tracts of land for a beacon. As her body burned she felt it tugging on her spirit, like a child pulling on a balloon. But she was calm here. Patient. She couldn't jump without some kind of tie to the land she was going to jump to. She needed the vibration of the land in order to unlock the key to that particular place in the same way she needed the vibration of someone's mind inside their willstone in order to claim them.

She thought she'd managed it with Pale One. But Pale One was so close to the earth, so in tune with where she was that unlocking the vibration had been easy. Finding a human with that kind of awareness of the land he or she was standing on was going to be a bit harder. Until she found a suitable host to gather the vibration for the unknown place she had to jump to, all she could do was soar through the gray overworld.

Her body tugged with increasing urgency. Time was short. She looked one way and saw the silvery fog of the Mist right on the edge of the overworld. She looked the other way and saw a golden haze. She chose to let her spirit fly there. As she got closer, she understood what it was—the minds of her claimed still under Alaric's rule.

Lily hoped that what she was about to do either went unnoticed or, at the very least, didn't cause her host to feel violated. She scanned her Outlander claimed and found a girl gathering water from a stream. Her hands were in the stream and momentarily a part of it, but Lily pulled back, knowing that it wouldn't work. Rivers flow over the land. They are wanderers, and not tied to any place.

Lily left the girl and went back to scanning the huge host. They were all moving about too quickly. None of them were tied to the place they occupied, but rather focused on where they would be tomorrow or the day after.

She found one of her claimed sitting on a rock. His mind was exactly where his body was in space, but the rock was too full of quartz for Lily to get a vibration from the land under it. Time was running out. Frantic now, she pulled up and out and saw what she was looking for. One of her claimed was digging in the ground, waist deep in the earth. He could feel it all around him—the smell of it, the texture, the *thisness* of that particular spot. His whole being was tuned into that particular patch of the planet because this was the place he was going to bury his best friend. She thought of calling to him by name, but stopped. She didn't want to let him know she was there.

As she let her spirit dive into his, Lily tried to comfort him wordlessly. She was with him. The horizon pitched, there was a dizzying swirl of perception, and then it was her blistered hands on the shovel, and her heart that was aching with irreplaceable loss. She invaded his willstone with a small apology, and used it to sound out the vibration of this place. When she had the particular pattern locked, she dove out of him like a bungee jumper reaching the end of her tether and plunging upward.

As her spirit sped away from the ground and back up into the gray of the overworld, she saw him pause and clutch his chest. He glanced at the wrapped body of his dead friend and then up into the clouds above.

Lily spooled back into her body, still locked in the jaws of the fire. In agony, she let out a piercing scream that echoed around the bailey. Rowan pivoted and came charging toward the pyre, an ax already in his hands. Before he could reach her, a thunderclap tore through the sky, and with the roaring sound of air suddenly being emptied of over ten thousand bodies, Lily jumped them all hundreds of miles.

They appeared around the man burying his friend. He was still clutching his chest and staring at the sky. One moment he was alone, and the next he was surrounded by a multitude. Ten thousand men and women stood facing him in an ever-expanding circle, their staring faces manifesting out of nothing among the trees.

Lily appeared right next to him inside the half-dug grave. She made a whimpering sound and the shackles on her wrists clanked as she fell forward. He caught her burnt body in his arms.

"Thank you," she whispered. Relieved it was over, she placed her head on the man's shoulder and took a few deep breaths. She could feel Rowan's tattoo cooling her burns from the inside, and every breath she took loosened the pain a little more.

Rowan ran to the edge of the grave and knelt down. "Give her to me," he demanded, reaching with his hands to take her.

The man held Lily to his chest, his arms reluctant with shock. The man was an Outlander, so Rowan repeated his order in Cherokee. The man started nodding, but still had to be coaxed into giving Lily over. When he did, she heard him saying one phrase over and over.

"What's he saying?" she asked as Rowan carried her away from the grave.

"He said he felt you before he saw you," he replied. He lowered his voice and put some distance between them and the rest of her mechanics. "He said that you were with him, and then he pointed at his chest." Rowan's tone was tight. "What does *that* mean?"

"You know what that means."

"You possessed him."

The word hung between them while Lily tried to decide if Rowan was censuring her or not. She refused to get defensive. "I took nothing from him. I even tried to comfort him a little, which is why I think he sensed me," she said plainly. "There was no other way to jump us."

He sighed and nodded. "Let's just hope the rest of them don't find out," he said, and focused on her injuries. "These don't look too bad."

She gritted her teeth to keep the pain at bay as he peeked through one of the burn holes on her dress. "I want to speak with Alaric as soon as I can," she said.

"I'll see to it," he replied.

Carrick had been riding hard for three days. The mount Lillian had given him was a tame Woven—part horse, part something with scales. It was called a runner. Carrick had no idea what the non-horse part was, and he hadn't asked.

The runner's dagger teeth and the reptilian feel of its black hide had made him a little hesitant at first, but it rode like a regular horse and he'd gotten the hang of it soon enough. The thing hadn't needed food or water until that morning. Carrick had fed it a raccoon, which it swallowed whole, and then they'd been on their way. Efficient.

Carrick had left Lillian's army on her orders and backtracked to find Alaric's. As his silent mount picked over the trail, Carrick noticed how differently a city army traveled from an Outlander tribe. Lillian's tightly packed army had trampled everything in their path, leaving a swath of dead bodies and spoiled land in their wake. The Outlander army fanned out, traveled lighter, and killed less and died less along the way. Carrick had to really look to find them as they slipped from hollow to vale, riding spread out by day and sleeping in their camouflage tents by night. But he was an Outlander like them. He knew how to look.

Yet as observant as Carrick was, the thing he was looking for had eluded him so far. Now that Lily was back in this world and had pledged to join Lillian, Carrick had been given his old orders again. Find the last bomb and dismantle it.

There used to be two. Now there was only one. Carrick had asked about the other, but Lillian hadn't answered him.

He'd been annoyed that one of her other legmen had taken care of it, mostly because he guessed it had to be one of those pompous Walltop soldiers. Carrick was used to being looked at with distaste, whether it was for his stringy hair, his unnerving stare, or the blood under his fingernails that never seemed to entirely wash away before he found himself wrist deep in it again. But even the most squeamish sidestepping that was done to avoid crossing his path was done with a certain level of respect.

Walltop soldiers were different. They regarded all Outlanders (except maybe his half brother, the legendary Lord Fall) with a disdain that lacked the fear that Carrick was accustomed to. Unfortunately Carrick could do nothing to teach them otherwise. His Lady Witch simply wouldn't have it. She was overly fond of Walltop for reasons she would not disclose to him.

Carrick rode into a copse of trees and saw some signs of Alaric's tribe—nicked bark on the side of a hickory tree and two ruts through the maidenhair ferns where one of the heavier armored carts had passed. This particular cart had caught Carrick's attention because its drovers seemed to mostly travel at night. Carrick had a hunch it was the armored cart he was looking for, but he hadn't gotten a look at it yet.

He rode fast across the open ground and slowed when he reached the cover of a forest. He dismounted and started scanning the ground. His mount hissed softly. Carrick looked up in time to stop the first blow, but he was overpowered and knocked out before he could make contact with Lillian.

Lily floated in a wooden tub of cold spring water. Rowan had sprinkled some kind of herb in it that smelled like thyme and lemon and a few drops of something that tingled.

Her new tattoos were chilly under her skin. The blisters from the pyre had shrunk, and as Lily watched, the red welts on her wrists from the shackles were disappearing. She felt tired, but it was the pleasant feeling of drained muscles, not the pounding head and nausea that usually dogged her after going to the pyre. She tipped her head back in the tub and just let herself float.

She could hear Rowan's voice outside the tent. He was explaining the situation in Cherokee to a handful of baffled Outlanders who couldn't understand how over ten thousand tenderfooted city folk had managed to appear in the woods without making a sound. Outlanders are not used to being taken unawares. She smiled to herself as she listened to his overly patient tone. He hated repeating himself. She heard Caleb take over when Rowan had finished and then she heard the crowd outside her tent disperse. Her mechanics would stay close to her through the night to guard her, although Lily knew they didn't really need to. Almost all of these braves were her claimed, and she'd already explained her strange return to them in mindspeak, even though most of them had no concept of teleportation.

Rowan ducked into the tent with a clenched jaw. Lily laughed.

"It's not funny," he said, repressing a smile. "The Elders are angry you brought so many tunnel folk and ranch hands."

"They're collectively calling themselves 'below folk,' by the way, and I don't blame the Elders for not liking them," she said. "But at least the braves are happy I'm here." She rolled over in her cool bath, hearing laughter and the beginning of a song a few campfires away.

"Are you kidding? They're ecstatic you're here. They feel like they can actually survive this war now," Rowan said, kneeling down next to the tub. "You're not the problem, the below folk are. They hate the Outlanders for what Chenoa did to them, and there've already been a few serious fights. The Elders are worried the fighting is going to turn to killing soon."

Lily frowned, remembering. Chenoa had used the women living in the subway tunnels to smuggle the radioactive materials from her lab at Lillian's college to the Outlands, but she never explained to the women how dangerous those materials were, probably to keep their contents secret. Lily had seen the result.

"They have every right to be angry," she said quietly.

"Of course they do," Rowan replied. "That only makes it worse." He picked up a bowl and started pouring water over Lily's back. "The ranch hands are a rough bunch, and most of them have family ties to the women who died transporting Chenoa's dust."

Lily knew exactly what kind of men the ranch hands were. Some of them would have been good people if their lives hadn't been so hard, but all of them had done something to earn a place on the ranches. These weren't just petty thieves. Lily didn't trust them.

"I won't let them hurt anyone else," she promised.

"How are you going to stop them?" Rowan asked delicately, unwilling to bring up the touchy subject of possession again.

"I'll tell them right now that if there's any more violence tonight, I'll be their judge and jury in the morning. They can't lie to me, and my punishment will make whatever the crime was pale in comparison," she said. She trained her inner eye on the minds of the ranch hands and sent them her warning. "There. It's done."

The sound of the water trickling over her skin seemed to fill up the tent as she watched him. He kept his eyes on his task as the tension built.

"I thought you hated me for siding with Lillian," Lily whispered, breaking the hum of attraction between them. She thought about the moment he tore her willstones from her neck. They were in such close contact that Rowan saw it, too.

"I never hated you," he said, shaking his head. "As soon as I learned about the bombs and what they could do, I understood why Lillian started hunting scientists." He pulled his lower lip through his teeth and continued haltingly. "She worldjumped to a place where the bombs had been used, didn't she? That's where she was for those three weeks she disappeared."

"The shaman called them cinder worlds. There are a lot of them clustered around this world in the worldfoam. Similar universes are closer to one another, which mean most of the worlds like yours—where there are witches and Outlanders and Woven—have already been destroyed by someone who made the wrong decision."

Rowan considered that, his forehead knitted. "So my world is on borrowed time?"

"As long as Chenoa's bombs are out there? Yes."

"When I saw the tunnel women, I knew Lillian had the same thing they had." A look of pain crossed his face. "Will you tell me why she wouldn't let me touch her, not even to help her?"

"I can't."

"It's about my father, isn't it? She didn't want me to touch her because she was scared she couldn't keep what she'd seen there from me if she did," he said. Lily pressed her lips together and pushed away from the edge of the tub. Rowan stopped her from floating away. "Look, I've put it all together. Lillian went to a cinder world and something happened to her there, something that had to do with my father because he was the first person she hanged when she got back. Just tell me what it was. What did he do?"

Lily shook her head. "I can't." It was Rowan's turn to pull away from her. "Have you ever heard the saying 'whatever doesn't kill you makes you stronger'?" she asked. He shook his head. "Every time I had a seizure and lived through it, I believed it made me a little bit stronger. I still think that being sick so much as a kid gave me the strength to handle this." She gestured to the fading marks on her wrists. "But when I saw the cinder world, I stopped thinking that saying was true. There are lots of things that can happen to people that make them weaker. Things that break them. That's all I can say about your father."

Rowan thought about what she said carefully, but in the end he shook his head. "That's not good enough, Lily. I deserve to know why she killed him." Rowan moved to stand up, but Lily put out her hand and stopped him.

"You're going to see Lillian soon. You have to ask her yourself. But do you want my honest opinion?" He nodded slowly. "Don't," she begged. "It happened in another world. Leave it there. Lillian couldn't leave what happened to her behind in the cinder world where it belonged, and that's why she killed your father."

Rowan sat back down next to her. "That bad?" His next question hurt him to ask. "Do you think she was right to kill him?"

"No," Lily said emphatically. "Lillian thinks the only difference between the different versions of us is our experiences, and if you were to make one version of a person experience what another had, they would react the same. I don't believe that. Your father was not the River Fall of the cinder world, and I don't believe he ever would have become him, even if he went through the same thing. Just like I'll never become Lillian, no matter how many memories of hers I absorb. Lillian believes our experiences and our worlds make us. I believe our choices make our experiences and our worlds."

"So you're saying you would have chosen differently than she did?"

"Not about everything," Lily admitted, her voice catching in her throat. She reached out and brushed her thumb across his lower lip. Rowan inhaled sharply and Lily saw his eyes darken and felt his mouth soften against her fingers.

But there was a gulf between them. They couldn't even talk about it because Tristan was inside that gulf, and because of that, Lily couldn't bring herself to close it. She pulled her hand back and slid it under the water.

"I'll get you something to wear," he said hoarsely, and stood without looking her in the eye.

Rowan heard the alarm yips from the sentries before Lily did. He sprang to his knees and peeked out the entrance of the tent. Shapes and shadows sped past.

"Stay here until I send for you," he said as he pulled on a shirt and slid a knife into his belt.

Lily nodded and scrambled through the sheets to find shoes. She remembered falling asleep alone, feeling cold, and then delicious warmth wrapping around her back. She'd dreamed of turning to Rowan and kissing him. Some part of her must have known he was there. He only came to her now when she was asleep, like he couldn't stop himself. It hurt her to think that they could only be their true selves to each other in dreams.

Lily finally found her shoes and put them on as Una pulled open the flap to her tent.

"She's okay," Una said over her shoulder.

Lily heard Tristan speak to Breakfast behind Una. "Who's with my mother and sister?" she asked.

"Caleb," Tristan answered. He motioned for her to come out of the tent. "We've got to move you. I'll have Caleb bring them to you when he can," he said.

They bundled Lily out of the tent, Una on one side, Breakfast on the other, and Tristan leading the way deeper into the camp. She reached out to her claimed braves along the perimeter and asked what was going on, but she got only confused images from them.

Most of her braves weren't accustomed to mindspeak, and they had either very little or no innate magical talent. Lily had gotten so used to conversing with her mechanics that she forgot most people in her army had never heard mindspeak before, and weren't capable of forming full sentences or transmitting entire thoughts. She only got images and fragments from them. She'd have to change that if they hoped to fight as one—the way the Hive did naturally.

"I think they found a spy," she told her mechanics as they entered the center circle where the one campfire was kept burning all night.

Rowan had his back to them. He turned his head as they

approached and smiled at Lily, relieved. As he motioned for her to come and stand next to him she saw that the person he'd been having words with was Alaric. There was a slight hitch in her step when their eyes met, but she recovered quickly, squared her shoulders, and joined him at the fire.

"Good to see you again," Alaric said, watching her reaction carefully.

"Is it?" she asked. "I can't say the same."

His mouth ticked up with a wry smile as his eyes narrowed. "Well, apparently you wanted to see me because you sought me out," he reminded her.

"I came for the rest of *my* army," she replied. The fire popped between them as the silence grew heavy. Finally, Alaric nodded in concession.

"From what Rowan tells me, you can bring all of your claimed from place to place with no need to travel. They'd all survive the journey if they travel with you, and I can't promise them the same." His poker face was flawless. "But would they follow you into battle?"

"We both know their loyalty is with you," Lily replied, making a concession of her own. "So here's what I'm willing to offer you. Your voice will be heard with all things concerning the Outlander braves in my army. You'll be one of my generals and you'll report to Rowan. I offer you this under one condition. That you let me claim you."

Alaric barked with surprised laughter. When he realized Lily wasn't kidding, he looked to Rowan for someone to talk reason to her, but Rowan shook his head once in answer.

"You lost my support when I found out about the bombs," Rowan said.

Alaric smiled and nodded. "And that's what this is all about."

"It is," Lily said. "I want to know where the bombs are, and I want them dismantled and disposed of properly. They are no longer an option in this war."

"Bomb. Single. I only have one left that still works—and it *does* still work"—Alaric nodded to one of his painted braves—"even though you sent someone to try to sabotage it."

"What are you talking about?" Lily asked, not even trying to hide her confusion.

There was the sound of a tussle as someone was dragged into the light of the fire. She saw Carrick pinioned between two braves. He was bucking against their restraints with real fear in his eyes as he was dragged before Alaric.

"Lily," Carrick said, baring his teeth as he breathed her name. "At last."

Lily could feel all of her mechanics step closer to her as she shrank into Rowan's side. Rowan said something to Carrick in Cherokee, but Carrick only laughed at his half brother and shook his head.

"Don't think I don't know you and Lillian sent this *uktena* to undermine me," Alaric said as he gestured to Carrick with a foul look on his face.

"I have nothing to do with Carrick," Lily replied hotly. "Lillian and I don't agree on everything. I came here with my own plans about how to deal with you and the bombs—sorry, bomb—and it had nothing to do with *him*. And where is the second bomb? I thought there were two."

Alaric sized Lily up with a guarded look on his face. A thought occurred to him and he tipped his head to the side. "She didn't tell you that she stole the other and kept it for herself, did she?" Lily stared at Alaric, horrified. He gave a bitter laugh. "I didn't think so."

Lily shut her mouth with a snap and reached out to Lillian in mindspeak.

Lillian. Do you have a bomb?

There was no answer. She stalked over to Carrick where he was still being held by two braves and slapped him hard across the face.

"Does Lillian have a bomb?" She slapped him again before he even had a chance to answer. Carrick's face whipped to the side and came back to Lily wearing an indulgent smile. Her skin puckered as if something had slithered across it. "Answer me," she warned.

"I don't know. If she got one, it happened when I was following you," Carrick replied. "But it sounds about right. Lillian plans to raze Bower City to the ground."

I don't think he's lying, Rowan said to Lily in mindspeak.

He isn't, she replied. *Lillian told me herself that she planned on destroying the city, but I never thought she'd use one of the bombs to do it. Never. It's the* last *thing she would do.*

And Lily knew that was why Lillian was doing it. Lillian believed that in order to win, she had to cross the uncrossable line.

"You came here to gather an army and join Lillian, but the Outlanders are following Lillian to stop her," Alaric said. "We want to live in Bower City, if we can get past the Hive."

They don't know the whole story about Grace. The thought came from Caleb, who was only now joining them at the fire with Juliet and Samantha in tow. He stepped into the light and spoke aloud.

"Sachem, there is no getting past the Hive," Caleb said. "Not without Lily and Lillian and every single person they've claimed. The Hive is under the power of a witch named Grace Bendingtree. It's bewitched. I've seen it myself. We can't hope to beat her without a bewitched army of our own."

Alaric heard what Caleb said, but his eyes kept darting over Caleb's shoulder to the two women who stood behind him, his attention torn.

"Juliet?" he said, his voice softer and more plaintive than Lily had ever heard it. He stepped toward her with his halting gait and went to take her hand. She stepped back, uncertain and a little frightened by the intensity of his gaze. Alaric understood then.

"You're not my Juliet," he said. Juliet shook her head and Alaric turned his gaze to Lily. "Where is she?" he asked.

Lily pressed her lips together and swallowed, hoping to soothe the tightness that was closing off her throat. Her expression was all Alaric needed. His eyes shut for a moment and a held breath came rushing out of him.

"How? When?" he asked, suddenly looking a little smaller and a lot older.

"Grace Bendingtree. Last week," Lily answered quietly.

Alaric nodded, his eyes looking inward. Anger began to mount in him the more he tried to push it down, like a smelting fire that gains heat from pressure. "This Bendingtree has claimed the Hive?" he asked through clenched teeth.

"She made them," Rowan answered. "There's something you need to know about the Woven."

Rowan switched between English and Cherokee in order to explain everything to Alaric. When words failed him, he showed his stone kin what he had seen in mindspeak, keeping Lily in the loop as he did so.

Images of Bower City, its busy port, its wealth, and the exceedingly long and healthy lives of its citizens were passed to Alaric. Then Rowan showed him the antique womb combs and explained what they had been used for two centuries ago. Alaric didn't say a word. He just sat there, staring at the fire. When Rowan finally showed him Grace and the confrontation in the redwood grove that had ended in Juliet's death, Alaric barely moved.

"She's an Outlander," was all he said, past anger. After a few more moments of staring into the fire, Alaric stood and faced Lily. "You can take all the braves safely to Bower City, and away from it again to get them out of danger?"

"In an instant," she replied.

"Then you may dismantle my last bomb. I have no quarrel with the Thirteen Cities anymore," he said. Lily breathed a sigh of relief, but Alaric waved a hand, cutting her off. "Don't celebrate yet, because I agree with Lillian. She's still got a bomb of her own, and I don't doubt she's going to use it." He laughed mirthlessly. "Can you believe it? I nearly killed you for saying this last time we met, but I agree with Lillian," he said musingly. "Bower City should burn."

"No, wait. You don't understand. The citizens don't know what Grace has done," Lily started to argue. Alaric turned away, uncaring.

"Put Carrick Son of Anoki in the yoke," he ordered, and Carrick was dragged off.

"The people of Bower City are innocent," Lily pressed, but Alaric ignored her.

Leave him be, Rowan advised Lily in mindspeak. *Give him a chance to cool off.*

Alaric stopped in front of Juliet. "I'm sorry if I offended you earlier with my over-familiarity," he said politely.

"Not at all. I'm sorry for your loss," she replied in kind. Alaric bobbed his head in acknowledgment and limped away from the fire. Juliet's eyes followed him.

"Alaric, I still need to claim you," Lily called after him. "I can't jump you if I don't." He didn't stop. "You'll be left behind!" she hollered even though she knew it wouldn't do any good. Alaric was even more stubborn than she was.

Lily woke and found Rowan sleeping next to her again. His hair had fallen across his eyes and she resisted the urge to brush it away.

She left him in her tent and went out into the camp before dawn.

The night was mild outside of Richmond, and there was a faint layer of mist between the ferns and the sycamore trees. She touched some of the minds of her braves and asked them where *he* was. She followed the faint tugging of their minds to the other end of camp and saw him chained up next to a giant armored cart.

She thought she'd approached silently, yet he raised his head as she neared. His chains clanked and she rubbed the marks on her wrists at the sound. Carrick was locked in an oxen yoke, arms suspended alongside his head, the heavy wood of it dragging down his upper body.

She looked at the armored cart behind him. Its wheels were sunk deep into the soft earth. Lily trained her witch's eye on it and saw no radiation, but she did detect a large amount of lead.

"Lily," Carrick rasped. He said her name a lot. She didn't know if he knew how it unnerved her. "Don't worry. I already disarmed it."

"So that's the bomb?" she asked, gesturing to the armored cart.

"The only weapon more dangerous than you," he said, laughing with the effort to keep his head raised. "Maybe that's why you and Lillian are so obsessed with it. You can't bear the competition."

Lily's brow pinched at the troubling thought, and she glared at him. "The only thing I'm obsessed with is saving as many lives as I can."

"Liar. You think I don't know you?" Carrick smirked. "I know you. Better than that pretty brother of mine. Oh, he sees the magic of you, but what he misses is the blood. All you witches are magic and blood. You more than most on both counts. You like the blood as much as you like the magic, but what you don't know, that I can teach you, is you *need* the blood."

She kept her face neutral by dint of will alone. "Where's Lillian's bomb, Carrick?"

"If I told you, would you set me free?" He saw Lily's lips purse at the thought and chuckled. "No. Because you'd never set a monster like me loose in the world. So why should I tell you?"

She knew that there was no point appealing to his humanity, no point in pleading for the lives of the people of Bower City. For Toshi's life.

"You'll tell me because you need me," she said. "Lillian is dying. Who's going to claim you when she's gone?"

She saw the thought glinting in his eyes—a spark across the flat black of his inner life. "You'd claim me?" he asked, hopeful but cautious.

She nodded once. "Because I'd never set a monster like you loose in the world."

A smile crept up his face. "I don't know where Lillian's bomb is. She acquired it while I was following you in your world," he said. "But I will find it for you."

"Find it. Disable it. And when Lillian's gone, I'll claim you," Lily promised. When she saw him smile—a thin reptilian upturn of the lips—she felt a part of herself lie down and die.

Lily, what are you doing?

Lily turned to see Rowan coming toward her, shirtless, barefooted, and angry. He carried one of the silver knives from his belt in one hand and a torch in the other. It took everything in her not to run to him.

Making a bargain with the devil, she told him in mindspeak.

"Missing something, brother?" Carrick taunted.

You shouldn't be with him on your own. Carrick is dangerous, even if he is bound, Rowan told her in mindspeak.

I know. But I need him—

Rowan stiffened and his head whipped around, interrupting her thought. Both his and Carrick's eyes were already darting into the murky edge of the firelight before Lily could hear what the two of them heard——the absence of sound. The tree frogs had gone silent. Not one owl hooted.

"Let me out," Carrick said in a low, desperate voice. "Brother. You can't defend her alone."

Rowan's eyes narrowed at Carrick, and Lily got the sense that they were sharing mindspeak. Whatever Carrick said convinced Rowan. One quick tug and he pulled out the peg behind Carrick's neck. The yoke fell away with a jingle and a thump. Rowan tossed Carrick one of his blades and the two of them put Lily between their backs, both of them looking out, encircling her against the silent darkness.

Lily opened her hands to the torch, absorbing the heat of its small flame. A witch wind whipped her hair about her head, whispering ghostly, half-heard words. She filled Rowan's willstone just in time to meet the onslaught. The Woven burst through the trees in a wave of noise and motion.

"Simians!" Carrick called out.

The simian Woven hooted as they knuckled forward, their thick bodies swinging between their arms with blinding speed. Rowan ran out to meet them. They barreled into the light of the torch fire and stopped abruptly.

"Hold," Rowan ordered, pulling up short.

"They're not attacking," Carrick said, like he couldn't believe it.

The simians swung around a perimeter just far enough to show that they weren't engaging in a direct fight, but not far enough to let the humans run.

Lily felt one of them look her in the eye, assessing her. He snorted and looked away, scanning Rowan's and Carrick's faces.

"They're looking for someone," Lily said, puzzled.

"Lily!" Rowan hissed as she stepped forward. She felt Carrick snatch at her arm and she shook him off.

"I'm okay," she told them, walking to the edge of the perimeter. "Look—they're not here to kill anyone. I don't think those are their orders."

The simians retreated as she neared, rolling their lips back and baring their fangs anxiously. One of them darted in at her, bluffing to push her back. It was just what Lily was waiting for. Instead of falling back in fear, she dove forward, her hands reaching for the Woven's neck. The creature was so startled by Lily's brazen action she had time to find a small, hard lump under its skin.

Lily touched the Woven's embedded willstone and felt someone push back against her mind. A flash of fury ignited and fizzled in a moment as Lily shoved the other witch out of this Woven's willstone.

"It's okay," she murmured to the frightened creature. "I won't harm you."

It wasn't like a human mind. He had a vague sense of self, and even less of a sense of will. Lily knew she could invade his stone without cracking it as Grace had done, but she didn't want that. She didn't want to make any of the choices Grace had. Instead, Lily asked. She felt the Woven give his assent and claimed his willstone for herself.

Mine.

A barrage of images sped through Lily's mind. Swinging through treetops. A beloved grooming the scales on his blue back. Peacefully warming in the sun. Awoken and commanded to kill. Shown a face by the angry one within—a face that must be found.

"Breakfast!" Lily piped, surprised, when she saw the face. She broke off the mindspeak with her newly claimed Woven and turned. "They're looking for Breakfast—except he's an Outlander?" she finished doubtfully as she assessed the image she'd seen. It had been Breakfast, but he'd had long, braided hair and war paint on his face.

"Lily, get back," Rowan said. She felt him pulling on her arm, trying to get her to step away from the Woven who stood only inches away.

Without warning, the simians turned as one and sped back into the trees, hooting and howling as they went. All but one. Lily's claimed Woven stayed where he was while the rest of his family group sped off.

Follow them, Blueback, Lily told him. She added an image of him turning and leaving her in case he didn't understand. The Woven took her command and knuckled his way off into the darkness.

"Ro!" Caleb called.

"Here!" Rowan called back. He turned and made a disgusted sound. "He's gone." Lily looked at him, her mind still sorting out what Blueback had shown her. "Carrick is gone," Rowan clarified.

"Lily's fine," Caleb said into the darkness behind him. Tristan appeared behind him at a jog, and they joined Rowan and Lily.

She reached out to the rest of her mechanics, searching for Breakfast. She found him, still shaken, as he and Una joined them. Una was covered in Woven blood. She started wiping at it to get it off her.

"They tried to carry me off," Breakfast told them, offended. "They would have, too, if my girl hadn't stepped in."

"It wasn't me," Una said, declining to take any credit. "We were totally outnumbered, and then they just dropped him and ran off."

"They weren't looking for Breakfast," Lily replied. She grabbed Rowan's arm, her alarm growing. "The shaman Red Leaf. They came for him."

Lily could hear braves calling out in alarm. Caleb and Rowan cocked their heads, listening to the coded signal calls for a moment before sharing a dismayed look.

"They got him," Caleb said.

"Why would the Woven want the shaman?" Una asked.

"Not the Woven," Lily said, shaking her head. "Grace. Why would *Grace* want a shaman who knows how to spirit walk unless it's because of what I told her in the redwood glade?"

The coven's eyes went wide as they realized what Grace wanted.

"Let's get him back," Tristan said, already breaking away from the group. "Come on, guys, let's go."

"There are too many," Rowan said quietly.

Lily pulled heat from the torch, but it was a small flame. She gave her mechanics as much force as she could, and looked at Rowan. "She can't learn how to worldjump, Rowan. She *can't*."

He nodded, but his face was furrowed with a doubtful frown. "Breakfast, stay and guard Lily," he ordered, and then the rest of her mechanics took off so fast it was as if they'd disappeared. As soon as they were gone, the darkness seemed to grow eyes that watched her hungrily.

"Stay close to me, Breakfast," Lily said. "Carrick is out there."

"If we're lucky he'll get eaten by something ugly," Breakfast said, kneeling down on the ground to build a proper fire. "I doubt he'd risk coming back for you tonight."

Lily nodded and relaxed some. She reached out to Blueback in mindspeak. *Find the human your kind has taken*, she told him.

For a moment Lily was crashing through the underbrush and then vaulting up to the trees to careen through the branches. Blueback chased down his group by scent and sound, but when he caught up with them, none of them had Red Leaf. Blueback started to retrace his steps to find one of the other family groups that had been a part of the raid. He smelled for the human, but there were so many humans in the forest that night he couldn't be sure which was the one Lily wanted.

You may stop now, she told Blueback. *Go join your family, but watch for the stolen human.*

She reached out to Rowan, only to hear from him what she had already learned from Blueback. The Woven trails broke off into over a dozen different directions and there was no way to be sure which group had taken Red Leaf. She called her mechanics back.

We know where they're taking him, Lily told them, trying to quell her unease.

"Breakfast. Red Leaf is the other you," Lily said. "You can reach him in mindspeak."

"Ah—I'll try," he said uncertainly. His face scrunched up in confusion. "How do you contact another you?"

Lily smiled, remembering what it had felt like when she heard Lillian whispering to her across the worldfoam.

"You have to go a little crazy," she replied.

Lily had no idea how long it would take the simian Woven to get Red Leaf to the edge of the Hive's territory, and from there, how long it would take them to get all the way west to Bower City, but however long it was—days, maybe weeks—that was all the time she had to get her army assembled and ready to jump into battle. In the meantime, something had to be done about Grace's control of the wild Woven.

CHAPTER
12

G RACE WAS IN A CONSPICUOUSLY FINE MOOD THAT morning, which was terrifying.

Toshi pulled his gaze from the bow of the yacht as it dipped into the surf and looked across the brunch table at Mala, hoping she didn't crack. Grace's good humor seemed to hide a thousand threats, and the Warrior Sisters perched in the rigging didn't help. They looked down on the forced merriment, twitching their heads and shivering their wings with malice. Toshi could practically hear Mala chanting *she knows* under her breath.

Of course, it would be a miracle if Grace didn't know. Toshi and Mala had been meeting with malcontents for the past week to gather up opposition, and hopefully, some kind of fighting force. They had plenty of support from foreign sources. Every other country in the world wanted what Bower City had, and they risked little by pledging money, weapons, even soldiers. It wasn't their home that would be destroyed in a war with the Hive, or their lives that would be left in tatters afterward. Every meeting where he spoke in code and exchanged microcapsules of pre-written terms with a handshake had left Toshi feeling like a traitor. None of those foreign forces cared if Bower City fell, just as long as they were the first to get the formula for making willstones, and because of that Toshi had forgone accepting their help. So far.

The homegrown opposition that Toshi really wanted was harder to come by. The natives knew what would happen if they tried to fight the Hive. They knew the Hive wouldn't hesitate to kill them all.

"Toshi?" Grace said, as if she were repeating herself.

"Sorry," he said, shaking his head and giving her one of the more charming smiles from his repertoire. "I was miles away."

"And I can understand why. You haven't been getting much sleep lately," Grace observed casually, as if it were normal for her to know something as private as his sleep schedule. She spooned more caviar onto her crostini. "Lunch with the minister from Japan. Then drinks with the foreign trade envoy from Germany. And that was just yesterday."

A Worker ambled toward him across the tablecloth, feeling her way through the salt spray in the air with her antennae. Toshi watched her slow progress and concentrated on his breathing. She was trying to taste his sweat. If she did, all she would taste was fear.

"I'm always looking to improve our relations abroad," he replied when he knew he could do so without his voice breaking.

Grace's eyes narrowed over a brittle smile. "Are our relations in such bad shape that the two of you feel you must repair them with *every* nation?"

Mala hadn't moved a muscle in too long, which is difficult to do on the deck of a yacht. Toshi looked at her and laughed, letting the sun bounce off his upturned face to show how carefree he was. Mala joined him a beat late, but at least she broke out of her frozen posture.

"Mala and I have come to an understanding recently," he said, reaching across the table for her hand. She took his cue and looked at him with a simpering fondness that he forced himself to duplicate. If they were going to play lovers, they might as well play it to the fullest. "And we decided it was time to think about our futures. If we ever want a family, we're going to have to focus on our careers now while we can."

"Family?" Grace asked. She looked between the two of them, stricken. "I never thought of you as the type to want children."

Toshi shrugged a shoulder in a way that could be seen as apologetic, allowing her to assume that he hadn't wanted children with *her*. If they were lucky, Grace would be so derailed by the blow to her ego that she would overlook the fact that both he and Mala were sweating.

There was something about being on a boat with someone you didn't trust. It didn't make much sense, seeing as how Grace could have both of them killed anytime she wanted, but out on the open water where there were no witnesses, Toshi still felt less secure than he did on dry land. He couldn't shake the image of his body being dumped overboard, never to be found. He could tell Mala was thinking the same thing from the way she kept peering over the railing, contemplating the deep, cold waters of the bay.

"So you can see why we're eager to be indispensable to you, Grace," Toshi finished.

"Yes," Mala said, her voice gravelly with disuse. She hadn't said a word yet, and was now forcing an overly animated smile to make up for it. Clumsy. Especially considering the fact that she had nothing more than "yes" to add. Toshi poured them some more wine. Maybe if he got her drunk she'd calm down.

"So, to what do we owe this little excursion today?" Toshi said. He'd hoped to sound lighthearted, but the abrupt change in topic was as jarring as grinding gears to his ears. He winced a little at the awkwardness of it.

"I've had some good news and I was looking to spend the morning with two *indispensable* people," Grace replied.

Toshi didn't know if he should laugh at her play on his words or not, so he settled on looking inquisitive. "What news?" he asked.

"I found someone I've been looking for. I think having him as part of the team is going to open up more opportunities for all of us." Grace sipped her wine. "You two both speak your native languages, correct? Japanese and Indian?" Toshi and Mala nodded. "Good. We might be expanding soon. I'm going to need people I trust to acquaint me with the locals."

Toshi and Mala shared an uneasy look, trying to decide if she was being facetious.

"I'd be happy to show you where I'm from. But, Grace, in all the years I've known you, you've never left Bower City," Mala said.

"And I don't intend to." Grace popped a strawberry into her mouth.

"So how do you expect us to acquaint you with the locals in Japan and India?" Toshi asked. He was thoroughly sick of playing this game of cat and mouse.

Grace grinned, enjoying his frustration. "Haven't you ever heard of being in two places at once? It's a skill I'm planning on acquiring very soon."

Lily paced back and forth in front of the fire. The light had grown long and the day was nearly spent. She lifted her eyes expectantly as her sister approached. It hit her again—that happy-sad tangle of feeling every time she looked at Juliet now. A part of her was relieved to have her Juliet, and another part felt guilty for being comforted, as if the other Juliet had been nothing more than a spare. Her thoughts skipped to the surviving Tristan. She was still avoiding him, and although she recognized that fact, she couldn't seem to make herself stop.

"Any luck?" Lily prompted, dragging herself into the here and now.

Juliet joined her, shaking her head. "I don't know why you thought I would be able to convince him," she said. "The guy's as stubborn as a mule. And I'm not *his* Juliet."

"What on earth were you doing in there for four hours, then?" Lily asked, dumbfounded.

"Talking. Not about anything that I intended to talk about, though," she replied, looking confused. "Every time I specifically tried to avoid a subject I'd end up telling him all about it." Juliet sighed in exasperation. "I told him about us. About you while we were growing up—how you were sick and Mom was crazy and Dad was gone. About medical school, and how I want to heal people. All kinds of random stuff, really."

"Did me claiming him even come up by *accident?*" Lily asked petulantly.

"I did my best, okay?" She scratched at a red welt. Mosquitoes adored Juliet. Her tender skin was absolutely irresistible to them.

"We're running out of time and I need him, Jules," Lily pressed. "The braves still follow him, not me."

"But I don't *know* him," Juliet said, rolling a delicate shoulder. "I mean, sometimes he'll look at me and I feel like I know him, but I know I don't. Does that make any sense?"

"It does to me," Lily said. She knew she shouldn't take her frustration out on Juliet, especially since she was having such a rough time of it. This Juliet wasn't the version who had toughened up on the trail, and she looked a little worse for wear—still adorable with her bug bites and burgeoning freckles, but definitely like an indoor cat that had been suddenly thrust outside. "Was there any sign at all that he didn't want to be left behind, at least?"

"No." Juliet tipped her head to the side in thought and threaded a tress of hair behind an ear. "In fact, he spent nearly twenty minutes trying to convince me how foolish it was to go. He kept reminding me that in a battle no one was going to be able to do my fighting for me."

Gotcha, Lily thought. She tried not to smile. "Interesting."

"I told him I was still going, of course," Juliet said quickly. "I don't care how dangerous it is."

Lily turned away as nonchalantly as possible. "Well, you tried. We'll just have to get along without him."

"That's what I said to him," she said, her eyes flaring. "I told him that I was going no matter what, and he could stay behind for all I cared."

"Good. You don't need him," Lily said.

"Of course I don't. I don't need anyone to protect me," Juliet agreed haughtily, crossing her skinny arms over her chest. She found another mosquito bite on her wrist and scratched at it. "I can take care of myself. And that's exactly what I told Alaric."

Lily peeked around her sister's shoulder. She wasn't the least bit surprised to see Alaric striding toward them, surrounded by his painted braves. Juliet couldn't have played it better if she'd actually known what she was doing.

"You can claim me on one condition," Alaric said, fuming.

"Which is?"

"That Juliet stays in my sight at all times, and that I get first and last say about her personal safety. No arguments from either of you."

"Done," Lily said with a nod.

"Lily!" Juliet protested, smacking her sister on the arm.

"What? You said you'd help. *This* is helping." Lily rubbed her arm. "Ouch."

Juliet grabbed Lily's hand and dragged her a few feet away. "You can't just pawn me off to that . . . savage!"

"I'm not pawning you," Lily said in an injured tone. "I'm selling you at a very high price. Now get over there where your savage can see you."

"I can't believe you're doing this to me," Juliet muttered, following Lily back to Alaric.

"Personally, I don't see how it could have worked out better," Lily replied under her breath, just low enough so Juliet could pretend she didn't hear it. At least this way Lily knew that Juliet would be kept safe, no matter what happened to her.

I'm claiming Alaric, Lily told Rowan in mindspeak.

How'd you manage that? Hang on. We'll be right there, he replied from the perimeter where he and rest of the coven were on patrol duty. Rowan, Caleb, and Tristan arrived a moment later with grins on their faces.

Lily stared at Rowan, caught in one of the rare moments when she could admire him from afar. He was dressed in light wearhyde and he carried a tomahawk in an absentminded way. A feather was braided into his hair at the back and he looked wild and pure, like a piece of the forest turned human. He gave Alaric an I-told-you-so smile that stopped well short of smug, and Lily could see how easy it was for anyone to love him. He never pushed too far, especially when he was right.

Alaric faced Lily with an uncertain look on his face—something Lily had never seen before.

"It's okay," Lily said, reaching for the willstone at the base of his throat. "I won't take anything you don't give to me freely."

Lily didn't see full memories from Alaric—his internal barriers were too strong for that—but rather she saw impressions that he swept aside as quickly as they surfaced. She saw her sister—then, dreamlike,

Juliet morphed into another woman with the same sweet smile and huge doe eyes. Then the smile was blotted out by driving snow. She felt helplessness that was bigger than drowning as she watched an infant turn blue and go still. She heard weeping as if it'd come from a distant room in a labyrinthine house. She tasted nothing but ice and ash and felt nothing but a sinking anger that was almost like falling. She saw the sweet smile again as Juliet scratched at a bug bite.

The streak of impressions ended. Lily let go of Alaric's willstone and let out a shaky breath. His anger still yawned inside of her as if she stood on the edge of a great cliff. He looked so calm. Lily marveled at his ability to hold so much rage and not shake with it. She met his eyes and nodded, finally understanding him.

There aren't enough bodies in the world to fill up that hole, she told him gently in mindspeak.

He startled, and considered it. "There's only one scalp I'm after now," he replied softly. They moved away from each other, both of them needing to put a little distance between them. "What can we take with us?" Alaric asked, changing the subject.

"Unfortunately, only what each of us can carry," Rowan said. "The armored carts, horses, extra food, and weapons will have to stay behind."

"And Bower City is surrounded by walls, you said?" Rowan nodded and Alaric frowned. "That doesn't leave a lot of options if we have to lay siege."

"The land is rich there," Caleb added.

"Lots of farms," Tristan said, meeting Caleb's eyes.

"We're not thieves," Lily said warningly.

"We'll need to eat, Lily," Rowan said plainly. "Anyway, this is all *if* there is a siege. The Hive may not give us the chance for that."

They all fell quiet, thinking of the Hive.

"Don't we have to meet up with Lillian first?" Juliet asked, breaking the long silence.

"Yes," Lily replied. "That's our next stop." She looked at Rowan. He didn't meet her eyes, even though she knew he felt her stare.

"The sooner the better," Tristan mumbled. "I don't know how much longer the ceasefire between the tunnel people and the Outlanders is going to last."

Caleb snorted. "It's only going to get worse where we're going."

"What do you mean?" Lily asked.

"Lillian's army is mostly Walltop soldiers," Caleb replied with a grimace. Lily looked at him blankly. "You'll see when we get there," he assured her.

"Walltop soldiers are . . . different," Rowan said, looking at Alaric's stony expression cautiously.

"If by different you mean a bunch of unfeeling, inhuman bastards," Caleb grumbled.

"You need to rest," Rowan told Lily, changing the subject. "We'll build your pyre in the morning."

The group broke apart and started drifting in different directions. As Lily headed for her tent, followed by Rowan, Lily saw Alaric approach Juliet to speak to her privately.

"What does Alaric have against Walltop soldiers?" she asked, turning to Rowan.

"You know he had a family before?" Rowan said. Lily nodded. "Walltop soldiers refused to open the gates to Alaric and his family during a blizzard because it was after dark."

"Outlanders aren't allowed inside the cities after dark," Lily recalled aloud.

Rowan nodded. "They stood there and watched while his wife and baby girl froze to death in his arms."

Lily looked down at her feet as they walked. "Is this going to be a problem?"

"It already is one," he said through a mirthless laugh. "Walltop soldiers look at Outlanders like they're no better than rats, and Outlanders hate Walltop for watching from on high while they died."

"Let me get this right. The ranch hands and the below folk hate the Outlanders, the Outlanders hate Walltop, and Walltop look down on all of them?"

"Exactly," Rowan replied. "At least they agree on one thing, though."

"What's that?"

"No matter how much they hate each other, they hate the Woven more," he said bitterly.

"Do you?" she asked.

"Of course."

"Even still?" she asked. He nodded, his lips tight. "But it was all Grace. She was controlling them," Lily persisted.

"I know it might not make much sense to you, but telling my people it wasn't the Woven, it was Grace *using* the Woven, doesn't change much. It doesn't change what we went through."

"But they're intelligent—"

"That makes it worse, Lily. Not better," he said in a choked voice. His eyes turned inward to watch a dark memory, and Lily stifled what she was going to say next. Telling him that the Woven had suffered even more than the Outlanders wasn't what Rowan wanted to hear. He couldn't hear it, actually, no matter how loudly Lily shouted it. The Woven were his enemy. His hatred for them was in his blood. It was handed down to him from generations past and was as much a part of his makeup as his dark eyes and clever hands. Somehow, she had to find a way to get him past that, or they were going to die.

"Then let's hope the Hive will be enough to get all the different factions of my army to work together," she said.

"The Hive is more than enough." He looked hopelessly at the night sky. "More than we can handle."

They slowed to a halt. "Is it that bad?" she asked.

"It is. We don't have the numbers. We're about thirty thousand. They are millions."

"Most of them are Workers, though. I can protect you from them. I did it before——"

Rowan shook his head, cutting her off. "So instead of the odds being a hundred to one, it's still twenty Warrior Sisters to one of us," he said. "I might be able to take twenty Sisters in battle. Caleb, Tristan, and Una probably could, too, but the rest of your army can't be counted on for those kinds of numbers. The ranch hands have never been in a real battle before. A lot of them are going to desert as soon as they see the Hive rising."

"Not if I make them stay and fight," Lily said quietly.

"Possessing them would keep them in the battle, but it won't keep them alive for long," he warned. He was right, of course. Lily knew she couldn't win this war with an unwilling army.

"So what do we do?" she asked.

"I don't know," he whispered. "I've gone over it a dozen times in my head, and I can't make it work. We don't have enough fighters."

After a few pensive moments, Rowan finally shook himself. "I'll figure it out," he promised.

He left her at the entrance of her tent and went to rejoin his stone kin out on patrol. She watched him until he disappeared among the trees, hoping he would forgive her for what she knew she had to do. She went into her tent and sat down on the ground.

She hadn't had water or eaten most of the day in order to prepare. She didn't know how far she'd have to roam on this spirit walk, but she figured it was going to be a long trip. She threw some herbs that were good for relaxation on the fire and settled back, breathing in the fragrant smoke.

There was one moment where she felt like she was falling even though she was pressed to the ground. She briefly looked down and saw her body lying below her wandering spirit, and then she turned her attention out past the Mist and into the overworld.

Spirit walking isn't sequential like normal traveling. There are gaps in the journey, and vast stretches of space are covered in the blurry blink of an eye. It's easy to get lost, and hard to pick a destination and simply go there unless you have some kind of landmark or key to highlight the path. But Lily knew what she was aiming for. She'd touched it with her own hands and chased its inner light with her own eyes, and although its pattern was too big for her to ever claim for herself, she knew how the first few notes of its great song went.

Lily sent her spirit all the way back to Bower City to find the pearlescent speaking stone on top of Grace's villa. Starting there, she looked out across the overworld and saw them—bright and clear like searchlights beaming straight into the sky. She wondered how she could have ever missed them, but not knowing they were there had kept the speaking stones hidden in plain sight.

From her vantage in the overworld Lily could see that each speaking stone was unique. Each had a slightly different hue from the others, making it possible to know where your message was coming from based on the tint of the image you saw. Lily saw Grace's line of speaking stones stretching across the continent and meeting up with another line of thirteen speaking stones down the eastern seaboard, one to each of the Thirteen Cities. Now that Lily had both of the paths clear in her mind's eye she could use them when she returned to her body.

She soared back down to her body, noticing that the sky was

turning pink. Rowan was sitting on the ground cross-legged next to her still form. She entered her body and felt the chill of stiff muscles and a creaky ache in all her joints as she dragged in a rattling breath.

"There you are," Rowan said. He started chafing her cold limbs. "Where did you go?"

Lily's teeth were chattering too hard to answer right away. Rowan lifted her up and brought her closer to the coals of the fire.

"All the way across the country and back," she finally managed to croak. "I've never been this cold before."

"It's the tattoos. You'll have to be more conscious of getting cold now." Rowan sat behind her and wrapped his arms around her, holding her hands closer to the fire. "Why did you go so far?"

"I was looking for the line of speaking stones all the way across the country," she told him. "It's how Grace claims and controls the wild Woven from so far away."

"Did you find them?"

"Yes."

"Can you jump us to them?" he asked, the wheels in his head already turning.

"I can't jump anywhere unless I have the vibration of that specific location in my willstone, and I don't have any claimed near the speaking stones to gather the vibrations for me. I could send out riders, though. I know where the nearest one is."

Rowan's face lit up with hope. "All we need to do is pull down the one closest to us and Grace won't be able to reach the wild Woven in our area."

"Knock out any link in the chain and her signal would fall short. She wouldn't be able to make them attack us anymore," Lily said musingly, nodding her head. She looked at the fire, frowning. Grace wouldn't be able to use the line of speaking stones—but neither would Lily.

Rowan sat back, studying her face. "You're hesitating."

"Because I need the speaking stones to communicate with one of my claimed," she replied evasively.

"Who?" His eyes narrowed when he saw her hesitate. "Did you claim Toshi?" he asked, jealousy flushing red across his cheekbones.

"No," she said, shaking her head. "Pale One."

"The Woven?" he asked needlessly. He drew away from Lily, a thinly veiled look of disgust on his face.

"Would you rather I had no one scouting for us out west?" Lily asked, frustrated.

"Honestly? I think it's a small thing to give up to keep the Woven from attacking us," he said angrily. "What do you really want the speaking stones for?"

Lily felt Breakfast brush against her mind and she was glad for the interruption. It kept her from having to explain her real reason for needing the speaking stones intact. Her eyes unfocused as she listened to Breakfast.

I found Red Leaf, he told her.

Where is he? Lily immediately shared what she was getting from Breakfast with the rest of the coven.

He's in bad shape. A raptor has him. This is what he showed me . . .

. . . I only let my eyes crack open—barely enough to see—and hope that it doesn't notice that I'm awake. If it thinks I'm awake, it holds me tighter to keep me from struggling until I can barely breathe.

Great, leathery talons encircle my chest and my waist. Wings that are ten times the length of a man pound the clouds to either side of me. I'm so cold and the air is so thin.

There's that voice in my head again that is so like mine. Maybe I'm crazy. Maybe I'm dying. The voice inside my head asks me where I am.

I look down and see nothing below but flat green stretches.

The Ocean of Grass. A cloud hangs low on the horizon—a smudge across the otherwise blue sky. No. Not a cloud. Great Spirit, protect me. It's the Hive . . .

He's about halfway across the country, Una said in mindspeak.

The raptor has taken him to the Hive's territory, Breakfast added.

Grace will have him soon, Lily said. *We have three, maybe four days until she has him, and we still have to join up with Lillian's army.*

Lily looked at Rowan. His expression was guarded, their disagreement on pause, but not forgotten. "We can go now if you want. Your pyre is ready whenever you are," he said crisply.

Lily climbed the pyre and, with no claimed in Lillian's army for her to use, she was forced to call out to Lillian herself.

I need to use you as my lighthouse.

Where are you? Back in your world?

No. I need you to put your hand on the ground and feel the earth under you.

I'm doing it.

Now I need you to let me possess you.

Why?

It's how I'm going to get my army to yours. Hurry. The fire is rising.

Lily smelled the smoke billowing up from the bottom of the pyre and felt the heat that followed. The next moment she was out of her body and soaring across the overworld toward the beacon that was Lillian. She was easy to find, high up in the Appalachian Mountains.

She dove down and felt searing pain—Lillian's pain. Her guts rolled with nausea, and her vision tracked a few seconds behind the movement of her eyes, setting the world into a dizzying spin around her. It took her a moment to push past Lillian's sickness enough to feel the vibration of the earth under Lillian's hand, summon the willstones of her claimed, and jump them all to Lillian's position.

Lily's army appeared amid Lillian's. There was no boom or gust of wind or streak of lighting. The Outlanders, below folk, and ranch hands simply materialized among the open spaces between the Wall-top guards on the rocks and cliffs.

Lily appeared next to Lillian, inside her tent. "Tell your soldiers not to panic," Lily said.

Lillian's cracked lips were parted in surprise, but she gathered herself and closed her eyes for a moment, sending out a message in mindspeak to all of her claimed. Lily could hear the shocked murmurs coming from outside the tent, but luckily, she didn't hear the sounds of fighting.

"I probably should have given you more warning," Lily apologized. "A bunch of Outlanders and criminals appearing alongside a bunch of soldiers could have been bad. I see that now."

"I know why you didn't warn me. You couldn't give me any chance to figure out how to do this . . . feat . . . and go without you," Lillian replied. She crinkled a wan cheek into a half smile. "What would you call this in your world?"

"Teleportation," Lily answered. "But that sounds so corny I've mostly been calling it jumping." Her face pinched in sympathy. "You look terrible, Lillian."

"I told you. I'm dying," she replied with a humorless laugh.

"I'm sorry." The words didn't seem big enough.

Lillian was paper white, skeletal, and the sickly sweet smell of decay clung to her. Her head was wrapped in a strip of linen, and from the bare pink sheen of the skin high on her temples, Lily could tell it was because her hair had fallen out. Even her eyes seemed drained of color. Lily reached out and took Lillian's hand. She wanted to hug Lillian, but she knew that any contact would feel like knives sticking in her.

They heard voices outside the tent and turned in unison as Rowan, followed closely by Captain Leto, pushed into the tent. Rowan stopped abruptly and made a dismayed sound deep in his chest when he saw Lillian.

"I'm sorry, My Lady," Leto was saying as he grabbed Rowan's arm. Rowan didn't resist. He'd gone boneless as he stared at Lillian.

"It's all right, Leto," Lillian said, raising a placating hand. "Rowan is here for her."

Leto noticed Lily and dropped Rowan's arm in shock, looking back and forth between the two Lillians.

A long sigh gusted out of Rowan. "Oh, Lillian. Why didn't you let me help you?" he asked. He took a step toward her and Lillian lurched away from him, her eyes pleading.

"Don't, Rowan. There's nothing you can do to help me now," she said. She turned to Leto. "Captain, would you please escort Lord Fall out of my tent and ask him what his people need? Lily and I will be out in a moment."

Rowan allowed Leto to lead him away. Lily turned to Lillian.

"You're still not going to tell him?" she asked. Lillian shook her head. "I think you're wrong," Lily persisted. "I understand why you hid the version of River you saw in the cinder world, but Rowan's changed since you knew him. He accepted that I wasn't you. He can accept that his father wasn't that man in the barn."

Lillian looked down, wringing her hands. Lily watched her, eerily recalling how she was prone to do that when she doubted herself.

"I can't," she whispered. "What was this all for if I do?"

Lily felt truly sorry for her. "Do you want me to see if there's anything I can do? I don't know much about healing," Lily said, trailing off with a shrug. She thought of Toshi. He would know how to heal Lillian.

"I can show you," Lillian said, accepting Lily's offer.

Lily helped Lillian comb through her cells and kill off as much of the cancer as she could, but there weren't enough healthy cells left after that to keep her organs running properly. Lily might not have done much healing in her time as a witch, but she knew a failing liver when she saw one. When she had done everything she could to keep Lillian going for a few more days, she sat back on her heels.

"Your rose stone did all the work," Lillian said. She wiped away the sweat beading on her upper lip. "So it's true that the different colors are better at different kinds of magic?"

"Yes," Lily answered distractedly. She heard shouting outside the tent. "Lillian, we need to talk."

"We do. It was always my intention that you take my place when I'm gone. That's why I went to find you in the first place," Lillian said. "I'll leave instructions with Leto that you are to be treated exactly as they would treat me. Salem is yours."

"No, that's not—" Lily stammered. "It's the Hive. We can't beat them. Not with the numbers that we have right now."

"I know. That's why we need to use the bomb."

"But that's insane—you know it is," Lily said.

The shouting outside the tent grew loud enough to bring Lillian to her feet. She and Lily looked outside and saw people running past as Lily felt Rowan reaching out to her mindspeak.

Things are getting ugly out here. Come quickly.

"It's Rowan," Lily said urgently.

She and Lillian rushed out of the tent and followed the sound of a fight to a clearing among the trees, where a year-old rockslide had knocked down a swath of thick timber. Rowan was holding back someone who looked like he was trying to attack Alaric, while Caleb and Tristan restrained two screaming ranch hands. Una, Breakfast, Captain Leto, and some of his uniformed soldiers seemed to be busy with crowd control as waves of people, most of them from the ranches, shook their fists and shouted. At the center of it all was a small Out-lander woman with steel-gray hair and skin like leather. She stood stock-still with her hands crossed in front of her, her gaze elsewhere and her expression unconcerned.

"Chenoa," Lillian said, teeth bared. The name hissed out of her like a curse word.

As Lily and Lillian approached the center of the clearing together, the shouting fell to a murmur. The crowds stopped pushing against the barricade and the man in Rowan's headlock settled down enough that Rowan let him go.

Chenoa looked at the two Lillians, her mouth tilting with a knowing smile. Her eyes were like two black beads—hard and clear—and they sent a thrill down Lily's spine.

"So I suppose you'll be fixing to hang me," Chenoa said, instigating a fresh round of hateful calls.

"She *should* be hanged!" yelled the man recently released from Rowan's headlock.

"Otter—don't," Rowan growled in warning in case he decided to lunge at Chenoa again. Rowan knew this man. He spun away from Rowan and faced the bloodthirsty crowd.

"She killed my Lena and our baby," Otter said. Voices shouted out the names of more dead. "She could have told us what was in those canisters." More voices rose like "amens" in church. "She *should* have told us it was going to make them sick."

Lily looked out at the quickly turning mob, and then back at Lillian's impassive face. Lillian would let the mob hang her, and as Lily recalled the women dying horrible deaths in the tunnels, a tiny voice in her head said maybe Chenoa deserved it.

But then she noticed the Outlanders in the crowd were slowly detaching themselves, watching with their weapons ready. Lily reached out to Rowan.

Will the Outlanders fight if the ranch hands try to hang Chenoa?

Yes, Rowan replied in mindspeak. *To a lot of Outlanders she's a hero. This could get very bad, very fast. Find a fire and get ready to fuel us.*

I don't think you can stop my army from tearing itself apart, Rowan.

Neither do I. The only thing that I'm concerned with now is keeping you safe.

While Lily racked her brain for a way to defuse this powder keg, Mary stepped forward, holding up her hands for everyone's attention.

"We below folk know all about the dust sickness that Chenoa brought on us," Mary said in a commanding voice. "We've seen it with our own eyes. And if you're anything like me, you've had nightmares about it ever since." She started to pace around Chenoa, circling her like a cross-examiner. "This isn't just something she brought on the women who agreed to carry her poison dust into the Outlands. It's something that got brought *back* to those women's families. Children. Babies, even."

Chenoa grunted and smirked. Mary broke off and turned to address her.

"You think babies dying is funny?" Mary asked. Chenoa leveled her with a look. Anger seemed to gather around the old woman like a cloak. "Speak," Mary urged. "Give us some reason why you did what you did. I'm trying to give you a chance here, or would you rather I just let my people string you up?"

For a moment it seemed as if Chenoa would remain silent on her own behalf. She looked out at the mob as if it were happening to someone else, and then nodded to herself as if she already knew the ending to this story.

"I've always been good with numbers," she said in a soft, dry voice that carried. "I've always been able to look at numbers and equations and understand them. Always been able to see through the numbers to the truth hidden behind them. I don't know, maybe it's a kind of magic. How many children do you think I've had, blond city woman?" she asked.

Mary was taken aback by the question. "I don't know," she replied.

"Four. All dead in their first year." Chenoa's voice was even and empty, her words pressed flat by the weight of the grudge within her. "My first babe starved to death. Belly swollen and so weak she couldn't even cry anymore. She just made this mewing sound, like a kitten." A long silence spilled out of her and swept over the crowd. "My middle two were taken by the Woven and the pox got my youngest. You ever see a baby die of the pox, blond city woman? No, you haven't. The witches wouldn't help us Outlanders when the pox came, but the below folk, they got the medicine 'cause they're citizens." Chenoa laughed, her head settling deeper into her shoulders, like a bird's in a rainstorm. "You below folk are acting like you invented suffering, but how many of your children were lost by what I did? A few hundred? How many hundreds of thousands of our babies starved, were taken by the Woven, or died from the pox . . . or maybe you've done the math and think your pink babies are worth a thousands times more than our brown ones?" Her mouth pressed into a sneer. "Well, I've done the math, too, and I got some different numbers. One number in particular." Her eyes dropped to the ground, all the fire suddenly snuffed out of her. "Four."

When it became clear that Chenoa would say no more, the crowd began to shout their grievances at her again. There had never been anything she could say that would have persuaded them not to hang her, and the fact that they pitied her only served to anger them more. A rock was thrown. Then another.

Oh my God, they're going to stone her, Una said in mindspeak. A score of Outlander braves notched arrows into their bows.

Tristan addressed the coven in mindspeak. *Lily, can you jump us out of here?*

Jumping might be our only option, Caleb agreed.

Jumping won't stop them from killing one another, Lily argued.

We can't contain this, Rowan said.

I brought them here to fight together, not one another. I can't just let them riot.

While Lily looked around at the mounting chaos, she met Lillian's eyes. Lillian turned away from her, unyielding. She wanted Chenoa dead. Samantha dithered her way into the center and stood next to Chenoa. She looked out at the crowd, wringing her hands and trying to duck as rocks sailed by. Lillian took a step forward to stop her, but Samantha moved even closer to Chenoa.

"You can't have both, Lillian," Samantha said, suddenly calm. "You have to decide. Chenoa or Grace."

Samantha stared Lillian down. She was chillingly sane and in control of herself. She didn't back down until Lillian finally looked away. Knowing her job was done, Samantha seemed to unravel. She shuffled off into the crowd where Juliet hastily corralled her and took her away.

Lillian turned to the crowd, raising her voice so everyone could hear. "I need her," she shouted. She stepped forward, stood in front of Chenoa, and raised her hands. "Listen to me—I need her." The sound from the mob died down. "When we get to Bower City, we are going to be facing a force too large for us to conquer. That's a fact. Our only hope is to use the last remaining bomb against the Hive, and Chenoa is the only person who knows how to detonate it safely."

Surprise, confusion, even sounds of dismay arose from the mob.

"But Alaric promised the western city would be our home," shouted one of the Outlanders.

"Mary promised us the same," said a ranch hand. "What good is fighting the Hive if we're just going to blow up the city when we get there? We'll still have no place to live."

"We came out here to fight for a home," someone else added stridently, touching off an avalanche of responses.

Alaric stepped out next to Lillian and quieted the crowd. "Let us consult with the leaders from all factions before we make any decisions," he said. "Everyone make camp until we've had a chance to discuss the best plan of action."

The crowd began to disperse, but Lily could hear the grumbling and feel animosity mounting as they went.

CHAPTER
13

TOSHI WALKED CASUALLY DOWN THE HILL TOWARD THE trolley line. It wasn't easy to walk casually. In fact, just thinking of what it meant to act casual stopped him from being able to do it.

A Worker landed on his shoulder. Then another. Toshi forced himself to breathe in and out. He thought of the color green and recalled the sound of rain. When he opened his eyes again, the Workers were gone.

The Hive had been on edge for almost a week now. The Warrior Sisters had come down from the high watchtowers that had kept them out of sight, and they now hovered over the streets or clung to the rooftops and to the sides of the buildings. Workers were quick to swarm, and more than one panicky citizen had been anesthetized with a sting, collected by a Warrior Sister, and never heard from since. Any elevated emotion could call Workers to you for closer inspection. Toshi was even setting them off in his sleep now. He'd wake, drenched in sweat, to find his body completely covered in them like a living blanket.

Toshi broke into a light jog and swung himself up into a passing

trolley. He spotted his contact and shuffled through the other passengers until he stood back to back with him. It wasn't long before
he felt his contact bump into him. Toshi opened his hand and passed
his contact a small vial of antidote—or what Toshi and Ivan hoped
was an antidote—to the Workers' stings.

His contact palmed the small vial easily and then waited for the
next bend in the trolley line to disguise bumping into Toshi again.
Toshi briefly felt the man's hand tuck a note in the folds of his tunic,
and then his contact hopped off the trolley.

Toshi watched the man blend seamlessly into the garment district's
waves of humanity. He wondered whether he would be the one to test
the antidote himself, or whether the vial was going to be smuggled
out of the city to one of the farms for the rebels hidden there to test it.
Toshi knew it might be safer to get it out of the city, where the death
of a Worker might be chalked up to accident, but that would take
longer.

In the Hive, every single member was accounted for. If even one
Worker used her stinger or was killed, a Warrior Sister came to collect the tiny body and investigate the reason. Even the death of one
Worker could alert the Hive to foul play, and thus Toshi and Ivan had
been unable to test their antidote.

They still hadn't completely abandoned the idea of finding a way
to kill the Hive, but keeping what homegrown rebels they could find
alive in case of a rebellion had become a more pressing concern. Mala
had insisted. She argued that they couldn't hope to gather more support for the cause unless they could offer some kind of protection
against the instant death that was, at present, the only outcome for
defying the Hive.

For defying Grace.

Toshi stared out the window at the people on the street. Heads
that used to be held high were now bowed with fear and suspicion.

The entire city seemed to know. Maybe they had always known deep inside that Grace was behind the Hive, and it only took someone else to say it in order for them to believe it. Toshi knew he had accepted it quickly, as had Mala. And the Hive had been quick to sense the change in the populace.

He jumped off his trolley, crossed the tracks, and caught one going in the other direction back home to the government center. He felt more relaxed now that the exchange was over and opted to take a seat rather than stand. Back at the Governor's Villa, Toshi ran up the stairs to his apartments to change before meeting Ivan in the lab.

Grace was waiting for him in his sitting room, idly thumbing through some of his papers. She looked up from the formulas he'd been working on the night before and smiled.

"This is a very powerful insecticide," Grace said, eyes sparkling.

He opened his mouth and let the first lie he could think of spill out, knowing that any pause was death. "That's what we're hoping. It should sell well in France and Germany." Toshi unlocked his spine and forced himself to cross to the bar. The note he carried in his pocket weighed on him. "Would you care for a drink?" he asked, trying to think how he could destroy the note that undoubtedly had instructions for his next drop. His hands shook.

"No. And none for you, either. You're going to need to be completely sober for what's coming," she replied.

Heat began to build under his arms. Toshi felt a Worker alight on his forearm. "And what is coming, Grace?" he asked quietly.

Grace stood and crossed to the balcony. She opened up the double doors and took in a lungful of fragrant air. "Isn't it a glorious day?" she asked.

Toshi stayed just inside the doors. He could see a cluster of Warrior Sisters approaching and knew it would be pointless to run. He felt strangely calm, as if the real torture had been waiting to be found out rather than whatever it was Grace had planned for him now. He was considering whether or not he had enough time to write a letter to his family when he noticed something strange about the approaching Warrior Sisters. They were carrying someone—someone who seemed to be unconscious. They weren't coming to take him away, but rather to leave someone behind.

Toshi ran to the railing of the balcony and saw that the young man suspended between three supporting Sisters was badly injured. Fear for himself dissolved, and his medical training took over. He dashed back inside, gathered up a healer kit from his closet, and started pushing furniture out of the way just as the Warrior Sisters landed.

"Tell them to bring him in here," Toshi ordered. He kicked aside the coffee table and spread out one of the throw blankets on the ground. "Gently! It looks like his shoulder is dislocated."

"This is why I had them bring him directly to you," Grace said fondly. "You've always been the most gifted healer."

"There's a basin under the sink in my kitchen. Fill it with hot water, and set it down here," Toshi instructed. Grace didn't do it herself, of course, but after the barest of pauses one of the Warrior Sisters strode out of the room on her ostrich-like legs. "He has hyperthermia, hypoxia, broken ribs, multiple contusions." Toshi listed just a few of the injuries he recognized as his willstone flared to life. He ran a hand through his hair. "Get me more bandages. In my bathroom . . . the linen closet." Another Warrior Sister bounded out of the room. Toshi looked up at Grace as he began loosening the young man's clothes. "He's an Outlander."

"A shaman," Grace said, nodding.

He rolled the half-dead shaman over and got a better look at his face. "Breakfast," he said. He couldn't keep the dismay from his voice.

"Not exactly," Grace said, excited. She sat down on the edge of Toshi's couch as if she were at a luncheon and had juicy gossip to dish.

"I just pieced this all together. As near as I can figure, he's one of the *versions* of the individual you know as Breakfast. Isn't that fascinating?" Toshi didn't reply. "He's going to teach me how to get to those other universes."

Toshi repressed a shudder at the thought. "If he lives."

"Oh, he'd better live, Toshi," Grace said, her voice dropping dangerously low. He didn't need for her to say "or else."

Lily lay next to Lillian, her spirit hovering over their bodies.

In the overworld, Lillian's spirit was as strong as ever, but in the real world her body could barely survive the separation. Lily's spirit looked down on the two bodies below, and saw that Lillian's breath was faltering.

That's enough, Lillian, Lily told her. *Go back into your body.*

I'm almost there, her spirit called across the overworld. *I can see the redwood grove. I can feel its vibration.*

You're suffocating. Come back.

Lillian's eyes snapped open and she drew in a gasping breath. Lily's spirit rejoined her body and she sat up next to Lillian.

"I can do this," Lillian said defiantly.

"I know you can," Lily replied. "But maybe we should have Rowan monitoring us? He can take much better care of you than I can."

Lillian shook her head and sealed her lips, still unwilling to let Rowan touch her.

"I really hope I'm not as stubborn as you," Lily snapped.

Lillian laughed. "Oh, you are." She sighed in frustration as the two of them got off the ground. "I need to learn this. Now," she said.

For the past few hours the three armies had made a tenuous camp on the side of the mountain while the leaders of the factions talked to their people. Raptors were picking off pack animals from above and the Pride was taking the rear-flanking battalions, but there was no help for it. Lily had given Lillian the vibration she needed to get to the redwood grove, but she still had to learn how to jump before she could move herself and her army.

Captain Leto appeared at the entrance to Lillian's tent. Chenoa and Alaric were behind him and he escorted them inside.

"Sit," Lillian said stiffly, making it clear that although she had saved Chenoa's life, there would have been no love lost if she hadn't. She gestured to a small camp table and chairs that were set up in the middle of her quarters.

"There was one Woven attack on our eastern flank while you were occupied," Leto informed her. He helped her into her chair at the head of the table and stood behind her.

"Casualties?" she asked.

"Five killed, seventeen wounded," he replied. His lips tightened as he looked at Alaric. "And there have been several brawls that have broken out since the arrival of . . . them."

"Thank you, Captain," Lillian said.

Lily called to her coven in mindspeak. Rowan, Tristan, Caleb, Una, and Breakfast all entered the tent and arranged themselves behind Lily's chair at the other end of the table, opposite Lillian.

Chenoa narrowed her eyes at Breakfast. "I know you, boy," she said.

"No, you know Red Leaf," Lily corrected.

"Does he have the gift?" Chenoa asked. When Lily nodded, Chenoa cackled. "Watch that he doesn't go crazy."

Crusty old bat, Breakfast whispered in mindspeak.

Lily stifled a smile as Mary bustled into the tent with a grim look on her face and Riley in her wake. After Lily quickly introduced her to Lillian, Alaric, and Chenoa, Mary took the final seat at the table. Riley stood behind her as her second.

"The long and short of it is this," Mary said with no preamble. "The below folk won't go west if you're just going to blow it up."

"Many of my braves won't go either. Not unless it's for a home," Alaric said.

Captain Leto made a dismissive sound as his eyes flicked away. Alaric's nostrils flared in barely contained ire.

Lillian held up a hand to stave off an argument between them. "We can't fight the Hive soldier to soldier. We'll lose," she said.

Mary and Alaric looked to Lily. "She's right," Lily said reluctantly. "They outmatch us in numbers and in strength. We can't beat them."

"Maybe not with the kind of soldiers you've provided," Captain Leto said. "Walltop soldiers are different."

"The only way to destroy the Hive is at its source," Lillian said, defusing another argument between Leto and Alaric. "Bower City. Once we do that, the rest of the country is anyone's for the taking." She turned to Chenoa. "How much land would be lost if one of your bombs was detonated underground?" she asked.

"Depends how deep you go, what kind of bedrock we're talking about," Chenoa replied, palms up. "I could give you some estimates if you could give me some more facts about the terrain."

"Whoa, wait," Una said, waving her hands in the air. "You want to detonate underground?"

"From what Lily showed me, that's where the Queen and the actual hive is. That's where the bomb will be most useful," Lillian replied.

"But isn't Bower City, like, right above the San Andreas Fault?" Una gave a semi-hysterical laugh. "Someone please tell them why they can't do that."

"I hadn't thought of that," Lily said. She quickly explained what she knew about the unstable geology of the western seaboard and the positioning of Bower City. "Detonating aboveground or belowground is insanity. This should be a nonissue, everyone."

Chenoa made a thoughtful sound deep in her throat. "I'd have to see some data before I'd advise *against* detonating," she said.

"Earthquake zones aren't ideal, but in some cases it could be better if the contaminated land broke off and slid under the sea."

"And then it would be safe to live on the land that was left?" Mary asked. She shifted in her seat and planted one of her thick fists on a hip. "The bald truth is that if I can't tell my folk that they're going to get a piece of land out of this, they're not going to fight."

Again, Captain Leto made a disparaging sound, and this time he went so far as to turn to Lillian. "My Lady, you don't need to pander to them. Walltop's loyalty doesn't need to be bought. If you decide to bomb the city—"

"Easy to say when Walltop soldiers *have* a place to live," Alaric said scathingly.

"We can't do this," Lily pleaded. "There are over a million innocent people living in Bower City. They don't deserve to die."

"Neither do we," Alaric reminded her gently. "You've said yourself that we can't win in a straight fight."

"Not with the numbers we have," she admitted. She turned to Lillian. "You, of all people, should be against this. Please, Lillian. What you saw in the cinder world—"

"*One* bomb won't make a cinder world," Lillian said loudly, as if she were trying to drown out a conflicting voice shouting inside her own head. "One bomb, detonated all the way out there, isn't going to poison the Thirteen Cities or bring on a never-ending winter for the rest of the world. The only thing one bomb will do is destroy the Hive, end Grace's dominion over the Woven, and bring the rest of us out of the dark ages. With Grace gone, the Woven won't be driven to attack humans anymore. The whole country will be up for grabs."

"Oh, for Pete's sake," Lily said, rolling her eyes in exasperation. Instead of ending the argument, all she'd done was give Lillian a platform from which to draw more people to her side. "There's another way," Lily began.

She looked around at them and debated telling them what she had in mind, until her eyes rested on Caleb. He would smash his will-stone and leave her rather than agree, and so would thousands of others. Lily knew the only way for her idea to work was for everyone to already be on the battlefield when it was revealed. Give them no choice but accept her decision or die.

When Lily remained silent, Rowan spoke up on her behalf. "Maybe there's a way to infiltrate the Hive and kill the Queen without using a bomb," he said. "We got in there before. It was easy."

"Yeah, *too* easy. There's no way we're getting back into the Hive now," Tristan said.

"Lily could jump a small team of us in," Rowan suggested.

"I can't," Lily said, shaking her head. "The Queen is deep underground. There's tons of silicone in that land, and it blocks me as well as quartz."

"Then something else," Rowan said, frustrated.

"Are you so sure that killing the Queen is enough?" Lillian asked quietly. She didn't look at Rowan as she spoke. "That might disband the Hive, but Grace controls all the wild Woven. She's the one who has to die." She turned to Lily. "Is there any way you can jump someone into the city to assassinate her?"

"It's a big city. There's no way for me to know exactly where she's going to be at any given time," Lily answered. "And if I can't jump someone directly to her, whoever I send will most likely be chewed up by the Hive in a matter of moments. Grace has every inch of Bower City covered with Workers."

They were all silent for a moment, trying to think of some alternative.

"But I might be able to use someone already inside the city to kill Grace for us," Lily said in a small voice.

"Who?" Rowan asked.

"Toshi. I'd have to claim him first, but I know he's willing. And he's close to Grace."

"How could you claim him?" Lillian asked, narrowing her eyes at Lily. "You're here and he's there."

"Remotely. Through the speaking stones," Lily replied. She sent Lillian the memory of how she used the speaking stone above Lillian's rooms to claim the ranch hands and the below folk.

Lillian gasped. "I didn't know you could use it to claim."

"I didn't think of it. Grace did, actually. She's been using a line of speaking stones to claim each new generation of wild Woven that hatches in the east. She's been doing it for over a century now. I can use the same line to claim Toshi. But——" Lily broke off.

"But what?" Alaric asked.

"We're calling it assassination. It's just another name for murder," Lily said.

Mary humphed. "Honey, *war* is just another name for murder."

Alaric turned to Lily. "Think about it, Lily. If Toshi can get to Grace, no one else has to die."

Lily nodded, knowing this was the smartest choice. She looked up at Lillian and saw her staring back.

Think of the last line you're unwilling to cross. That's the line you must cross in order to win.

Like you and the bomb?

Exactly.

I'm not like you, Lillian. And murdering Grace is not my last line.

After the meeting, Lily made her way to the tent she had been assigned, hoping that there was something clean for her to change into. Just outside her tent, Breakfast and Una caught up with her.

"So what are we doing?" Breakfast asked, holding open the tent flap.

"What do you mean, what are we doing?" Lily asked, not getting it. She ducked inside and Una and Breakfast followed her.

"What are we going to do to stop those crazy bastards from nuking a million innocent people," Una clarified, looking a little wild around the eyes as she closed the flap behind them.

"Well, I'm going to try to claim Toshi, and once I see what's going on in Bower City . . ." Lily began. Una waved a hand in the air to cut her off.

"Uh-uh. Not good enough," she said. "Even if you do manage to assassinate Grace, the Hive will still be alive, and you know the batshit brigade is going to want to exterminate them with that bomb."

"We need to make the nuke go away," Breakfast rephrased a bit more calmly. "As long as it's out there, someone is going to be threatening to use it."

Lily sighed and rubbed her forehead. "I know," she said. "I have someone on that problem."

There was a pause while Breakfast and Una decided who would be the one to speak.

"Who?" Una asked.

Lily twisted her hands. "Carrick." They stared at her, too shocked to speak. "I know, I know," Lily continued, agonizing over her decision, "he's probably going to murder about a dozen people to fulfill my order, and those deaths are going to be on me." Lily's stomach soured and her mouth warped into a sickly smile. "But if I don't use Carrick, than I only have one other option. My last line."

Breakfast paused and then inhaled sharply through his teeth. "I'm almost too scared to ask," he said, turning to Una with a grimace.

"I'll make a mind mosaic to find the bomb, and then steal instructions for how to dismantle it from Alaric's memories," Lily said.

"Come again?" Breakfast said, confused.

"A mind mosaic is when I use my claimed like an array of cameras. I look through all of your eyes to find what I'm looking for. Sometimes I have to look through your memories, too, sort of like fast-forwarding through recordings on a surveillance camera," she explained. "You don't even know I'm there, but I'm spying through you."

Una looked horrified. "Please tell me you've never done that before," she said.

"Once. When I was learning, and only for about a second," Lily admitted. "Rowan told me that witches do it all the time," she said, becoming defensive at their accusing looks.

"But not you," Breakfast said hopefully.

"No. Not me," Lily said. "At least, not yet. But if Carrick doesn't find the bomb or doesn't dismantle it for whatever reason, I'll have to try it."

"Yes, you will," Una said, looking at the ground. Breakfast turned to argue with her but she continued before he could say anything. "She'll have to, Stuart. A million people . . ." She trailed off, the scope of it overwhelming her.

"It's wrong," he said quietly.

"I know that, Breakfast," Lily snapped. "I asked a man who tortured me—who tortured and murdered my father—for *help* in order to avoid it. Is that the right thing to do? I don't know. I'm trying to do what's right, but I don't know if there is such a thing as a right option anymore. Just different kinds of wrong."

Breakfast narrowed his eyes at her. "Don't get too comfortable with that notion."

Carrick walked back into Lillian's camp, slipping through the occupied throngs unnoticed.

People tended to ignore Carrick until they couldn't, and then afterward, they tried to forget about him as quickly as possible. Sometimes they would say or do just about anything to make him go away. That had its advantages.

Carrick passed a squirrely page boy gnawing a thumbnail down to the quick as he walked, and grabbed him.

"Lady Lillian's heaviest armored cart. Where is it?" he asked, standing a little too close.

"I don't know—the carts are that way?" the boy replied with a desultory wave of his hand. He was trying to extract himself, but Carrick just smiled, unnerving the boy even more.

"What's your name?" Carrick asked, friendly-like, sidling even closer.

"G-Gavin," the boy stammered.

"Gavin, I'm in a lot of trouble if I don't find our Witch's biggest, heaviest cart. I'm supposed to already know where it is." Carrick leaned over the boy, still smiling, and the boy leaned back, desperate now to get away.

"There is one she's kept separate. Over that ridge, out of sight," he said.

Carrick released him. "That's the one. Thank you, Gavin. If there's ever anything I can do for—"

But the boy scurried away, probably already trying to forget the encounter had ever happened.

Carrick mounted the ridge and dropped into a crouch behind a boulder. The cart that was housing the bomb would be guarded, of course. He'd have to kill the guards swiftly and without them ever really knowing what it was that was taking their lives, or Lillian would know, too. But Carrick had spent so long out in the wild with the Woven that he knew how to move like them, strike like them, and leave no trace. Except, of course, for the useless bomb he would leave behind. But no one would know about that until they tried to use it, and then it would be too late.

Carrick waited until dusk. He stayed crouched down until he was almost a part of the rock, like he was growing out of it, turning to stone. He stared at his hands. He'd just gotten them clean again.

Captain Leto strode confidently to the waiting greater drake, wear-hyde riding clothes creaking, sliver epaulets flashing, and looking very much like a grizzled old Viking stepping forward to slay a dragon.

"You want to check the cinch around the drake's neck before you climb up," he instructed. He tugged on the leather straps that encircled the drake's long, lowered neck. They didn't budge. "Nice and tight," Leto said approvingly. "Next, you see that the stirrups are the right length for you. Then, just grab hold of the pommel and swing yourself up."

Leto mounted the drake and it squawked, shifting onto its thick hind legs and grasping the air with its smaller forelegs for a moment before settling back down. Lily took a reflexive step away and bumped into Rowan, who was standing right behind her. He steadied her and gave her a little push forward.

"And you wonder why I never learned to ride one," he teased quietly in her ear.

"You never learned because you're a big baby," she whispered back. She felt him chuckle and elbowed herself away from his chest. "And since you never learned," she continued accusingly, "I have to ride to the nearest speaking stone with Leto. You should feel horrible for abandoning me like this, you know."

"Oh, I do," he replied, grinning. The drake flapped its talon-spiked wings, irritated at being penned in by the huge spruce trees. "Just horrible."

"It's perfectly safe to come forward now, Lady Lily," Captain Leto called.

"Ha," Lily retorted.

"Leto is a good man," Rowan admitted grudgingly. "He won't let anything happen to you."

Lily took a step toward it, and the drake squawked again. "It's not Leto I'm worried about," she grumbled.

"Who's the big baby now?" Rowan said.

Lily forced herself to stride confidently to the drake, even if it did look like a giant dragon with red eyes. She swung herself up behind Leto and found that although the drake's neck was wider than a horse's, the feel of it wasn't so different. The drake's hide was warm, which surprised her. She was expecting it to feel cold, like a snake's.

"Hold on tight," Leto said needlessly.

The drake lurched under her as it clawed its way up the trunks of two of the surrounding trees. She could hear the wood crack as the drake scrabbled with alarming speed up above the canopy of evergreens. Then she felt an undulation in the drake's neck and heard the billowing sound of a sheet snapping in the wind as the drake's wings made the first massive downstroke. Her stomach swooped as if she'd left it behind on the rapidly diminishing ground. The wings churned on either side of her, jolting Lily up and down and back up again. Then the pounding stopped abruptly, and they were hanging in the sky as if caught on a hook. Lily felt weightless as they began to soar.

"It's actually quite enjoyable once you get used to it," Leto yelled over the whistling wind.

Lily allowed herself to relax and watch the scenery fan out around her. After what seemed like only a few more strokes of the drake's wings, she saw the mountain peak they were headed for—Mount

Mitchell in her world, the tallest peak in the Appalachian Mountains. Somewhere on top of it rested a speaking stone.

Leto had the drake bank, and it spun delicately on a wingtip. They circled the green peak, but the dense red spruce and Fraser firs made it impossible to see the ground. As they came around the hulking shape of the mountain, they saw that the eastern slope had fallen away, leaving sheer cliffs.

"There," Lily said, pointing toward the top of the ridge. She'd seen a brief glimmer, like a mirror flashing.

The drake came in for a landing, its wings scooping backward and its talons extended to grasp the treetops. It alighted delicately, and then turned to climb down the tree trunk on all fours like a lizard. The huge spruce swayed and cracked under the drake's massive weight, but thankfully, it did not fall.

Leto dismounted first, and then helped Lily down. She went directly to the emerald-green speaking stone, already feeling the pulse and whisper of the hundreds of thousands of minds that were gathered and amplified inside it.

"Are they haunted?" Leto asked, sounding uncharacteristically unsure of himself.

"No," Lily replied. She refrained from laughing at what was, to him, a serious question. "Although I can see how calling them haunted would keep them protected from vandals," she added.

"The voices," he said, still angling his thick body away from the softly glowing stone. "They say the disgraced dead who didn't fulfill their witch's bidding are trapped inside."

"It isn't true," Lily said gently. "Speaking stones are tools for the living, not the dead." Lily thought of how she'd tried to reach out to Juliet in the overworld after she'd died. "The dead don't speak. No matter how much you beg them too," she said in a gravelly voice.

Leto nodded, accepting Lily's answer. "She doesn't deserve to die this way," he said, switching topics. Lily knew he was speaking of Lillian.

"I know," she replied. She frowned, thinking of the pain she'd felt when she'd possessed Lillian's body. "No one does."

"Can Lord Fall help her?"

"She won't let him."

"Stubborn," he said with gruff affection.

"Willful," Lily suggested instead.

Leto nodded and looked down in thought. "I guess that's why she's as good at magic as she is." He looked back up at Lily, his expression hard. "Are you going to finish what she started?"

"I am," Lily replied, surprised to be saying it. "I'm just not going to do it the same way she would."

"Fair enough." He nodded once, making a decision. "If her time comes before the battle, Walltop will answer your call."

"Thank you, Captain," she replied, sensing the gravity of his pledge. She turned to the speaking stone. "But hopefully what I'm about to do will make a battle unnecessary." *And maybe Toshi can save Lillian's life*, she added silently, keeping that thought to herself.

Lily looked into the scintillating center of the speaking stone and placed her hands on its warm surface. Her mind dove into a fast-flowing stream. It raced green over the mountains, into the valley, and across miles of verdant land. Next, a blue haze diffused across her mind's eye, and she jumped rivers and sped past plains. Yellow light pulled her up sheer, rocky heights, only to drop her down again into the red-tinged light of the baking desert and scrubland. Her mind's eye sped over chaparral-covered hills buckled by earthquakes, and finally rested inside the milky white glow of the westernmost speaking stone in the chain.

Millions of threads of light were gathered there. Grace had quite an army.

She called for Toshi, whispering his name, and found a vibration inside the milky speaking stone. It was strong and clear and free. Lily focused on it, and felt his mind push back against hers, like a hand brushing away a tickling hair in sleep. She called him again, this time speaking his name with authority, and she felt recognition douse him like cold water.

She asked: *Are you still willing to be claimed?*

She couldn't hear his mindspeak, not without claiming him, but she could feel his assent like a gift being given. She played the unique pattern of his willstone back inside her own and claimed him.

Mine.

Instead of seeing his memories, Toshi's intense focus on what he was doing brought Lily directly into the moment with him. She joined his perspective and realized that he was struggling to save a life.

Lily looked down at the hands that she now shared with Toshi. They were running over a set of smashed ribs. Blood foamed in the lung under them. Toshi looked at the face of his patient, and Lily recoiled inside his mind. She needed a moment to remind herself that she wasn't looking at Breakfast.

Red Leaf. He could teach Grace how to worldjump, she told Toshi.

He's dying, Toshi replied.

For a moment Lily felt relieved. A part of her wanted to tell Toshi to let him die, but even as the thought tiptoed across her mind she felt a surge of denial from Toshi that was akin to hitting a brick wall.

I can't kill a patient, he told her. *It's against everything I've ever believed in.*

Of course. No, you must try to save him.

You're really here with me, aren't you?

I really am, she replied. Lily could feel wonder and elation skate across Toshi's mind, but he quickly turned his focus back to his patient.

His hands leaked magic as his willstone flared with ruby light. Lily stayed present in his mind, a silent observer, while Toshi dealt with Red Leaf. Toshi scrolled through Red Leaf's many injuries. Lily deemed it hopeless, but Toshi managed to pull Red Leaf out of the danger zone in a few precious minutes.

Toshi was the best healer Lily had ever seen, maybe even better than Rowan, although Lily decided to reserve judgment on that as she was usually unconscious when Rowan was doing his best work.

"He's stable," Toshi said, slumping back in exhaustion. When he looked up, Lily could see Grace sitting on Toshi's couch with a rapt expression.

"It's such a joy to watch you work," she said. Her eyes flicked over Toshi appreciatively. "The heroic healer, fighting to save lives."

Lily felt Toshi's frustration. "He's stable, but he'll need more care," he said.

Grace flicked her head to the side and two Warrior Sisters strode forward to take Red Leaf.

"Gently," Toshi scolded, but the Sisters paid him no heed. If they understood him, they weren't about to take orders from him. "Tell them to be careful with him," Toshi said to Grace.

"Oh, I wouldn't let my prize die on me now. Not after going through so much trouble to acquire him." Grace stood and rubbed her hands together briskly. "I expect you're tired. I'll leave you to rest."

"Where are you taking him?" Toshi asked as Grace and the Warrior Sisters left his rooms. She didn't reply.

It's okay. Breakfast can contact Red Leaf in mindspeak once he's conscious, Lily told him. *I'll let you know where she takes him if you want.*

With Grace gone, Lily felt elation bubbling up in Toshi again.

Did that really happen? Did you claim me?

Yes. It was definitely one of the strangest claimings I've ever done, but you're mine.

Lily smiled to herself where she stood, thousands of miles away from him on a mountaintop. The difference between Toshi and the vast majority of soldiers she'd claimed recently was like the difference between sending someone a written note with a pencil that kept breaking and speaking to someone while you looked each other in the eye. As a mechanic, Toshi was capable of full mindspeak, and he was gifted enough that she could feel his presence in her mind as much as he felt hers. She should have been prepared for the intimacy of it, but it had been a long time since she'd claimed anyone with Toshi's level of talent. He felt it, too. Conflicting emotions spun through him, and Lily realized that he was shy.

Can you see everything in me? My memories? My desires?

I could, Lily responded, feeling a little shy as well. *But I try not to pry into the private thoughts of my mechanics. I've had a lot of practice getting out of someone's head before they think anything intimate.*

She felt a creeping fear edge in on his happiness.

There must be a reason you decided to claim me now, he guessed. *What is it?*

There was no point in delaying. *We want you to kill Grace,* she said.

Lily saw Workers land on Toshi's arms at the very thought of murder. *I can't,* he replied.

I can fuel you. I can make you as strong as a god, and as soon as it's done I could make you disappear. I'd bring you here to me, instantly. The Hive wouldn't be able to catch you.

More Workers flew in and landed on him. One took position over his jugular. *Lily, I can't. Don't you think I've considered it? Since you left, I've made contact with thousands of rebels in Bower City. We all want Grace* dead, but we can't do it. *The Hive smells aggression before we can commit any act of violence.*

Lily could feel their prickly feet scaling up and down his skin, and she shuddered for him.

Please stop thinking of it. Please calm down, she urged.

Toshi unclenched his fists and took a series of deep, calming breaths, trying to rein in the frustration that choked him.

I've thought about nonviolent ways of killing her, like poison, but the Hive tastes her food. I thought about designing a virus specifically for her, but I can't get close enough to take a sample of her DNA. Did you know that the Hive doesn't allow even one of her hairs to fall to the ground? Silly as it sounds, I've even considered leaving booby traps throughout the villa, but the Hive scours every room she's about to enter before she goes in there. Everything you can think of, I've thought of it. The Hive is everywhere and they watch for danger in everything where she's concerned.

I'm sorry, Toshi, I should have known. Lily waited until she felt Toshi relax enough for the Workers to lift off his skin. *I could still jump you out of there*, she said. *You're mine now. You don't have to stay in Bower City.*

She could feel how tempted he was. He wanted to join her so badly it hurt.

I can't leave, he said finally. *Ivan and I are working on an antidote against the Workers' stings, and some kind of pesticide to use against them. We're trying to come up with some way to fight the Hive.*

Good. We'll need a way to neutralize the Workers. I can protect my claimed from them for a while, but I've never been able to sustain it for long, she replied. *You mentioned that there were rebels in the city. How many of them do you think would be willing to become my claimed?*

She felt hope swell in Toshi at the thought of a bewitched rebel force. *Most are begging for that chance. Some might need convincing.*

Let them know that they have one day to think about it. Tomorrow I'll be back to claim as many as are willing.

They'll be ready, he promised.

And, Toshi, there's one more thing.

What is it?

Someone who needs healing. She may be past even your help, but I'd like you to try.

Have you touched her? Can you show me her sickness? he said, every inch a doctor again.

Lily passed along what she'd seen when she tried to help patch Lillian up enough to keep going.

It's bad, he said. *If I don't get to her soon, she'll die.*

But could you help her?

I could do more than help. I could cure her, but it would have to be soon.

I'll get you here, Lily promised. *Somehow, I'll get you here.*

Her heart lifting, she cut off the connection with Toshi. She turned to Leto, who was watching her from a respectful distance.

"Did it work?" he asked, trying not to sound too eager. She could feel the rest of her coven waiting for a response as well.

"Yes and no," she replied. "Assassinating Grace isn't an option, but I think I've found us a rebel army inside the city. And I think I've found a way to help Lillian." She looked at the lowering sun. More time had passed than she'd thought.

Leto mounted the drake and reached down to give Lily a boost. "That sounds like a very productive sojourn to me," he said, visibly happier. Lily could tell he cared deeply for Lillian.

She climbed up behind him, trying to hang on to what hope she could, and not think of the thousands of rebels who would most likely be the first to die when the war began.

"He's awake," Breakfast said. His eyes closed as he made contact with Red Leaf. "Grace is there with him." He frowned. "She's asking about spirit walking."

"She doesn't waste any time," Tristan grumbled. He shook a handful of nuts into his mouth.

"I didn't expect her to," Lily said, looking sternly at her bowl of lentils. She and Lillian sat side by side in Lillian's big tent. Lily's coven surrounded them, eating dinner. It had been a tense meal, shared out of necessity so Lily could spend more time training Lillian how to jump, but even still Rowan, Caleb, and Tristan stayed far away from Lillian, hardly looking at her.

"Aaand, he's out again," Breakfast said. He rubbed his eyes. "Grace is going to have Toshi work on him some more. Shouldn't be long before he's up and about."

"How long to do you think it will take Grace to figure out how to jump?" Rowan asked.

Lily shrugged. "I *thought* about it for maybe a week, but I figured it out in a split second."

"Because you had to," Lillian said, nodding. "We've always worked well under pressure. I've been trying for two days now and I haven't been able to do it."

"You almost had it the last time," Lily interjected.

"Still, I haven't been able to do it," Lillian repeated.

Because she's weak, Rowan said to Lily in mindspeak. *If she weren't so distracted by her pain she would have been able to do it by now. She hasn't eaten a thing tonight.*

I noticed, too, Lily replied, trying not to care that Rowan was obviously paying more attention to Lillian than it seemed.

"So that's good news," Una said. "It's not like the Hive is going to just appear and kick the snot out of us."

Lily saw Caleb shudder at the thought. If the Hive caught them unawares, they were all dead. Pyres take time to get burning. If they were ambushed, their armies could be wiped out by the Hive before

Lily and Lillian had a chance to bewitch them and give them enough strength to fight back.

"It might be a good idea to have two stacks of wood ready at all times," Lily suggested.

"I'll see to it," Rowan said.

"That's not going to help," Lillian countered, as frustrated with herself as she was with the situation. "We need to strike first or the Workers will kill us all. Surprise is the one advantage we have. We need to move."

"I promised Toshi the day to get the rebels together. I'll claim them in the morning. It's just a few hours away," Lily said.

"Not that they can do anything," Breakfast mumbled. Lily frowned at him. "I'm just saying—if the Hive doesn't allow them to show aggression, how can they help us?"

"It'll be different once the fight starts. The Hive will have to fight on two fronts. They'll be thrown off balance," she replied with more confidence than she felt. "And they're working on an antidote and a pesticide. If they can neutralize the Workers inside the city, all we have to do is fight the Warrior Sisters."

"That's all?" Breakfast asked. Una smacked his arm.

"Better than the alternative," Una said to him. She looked at Lily. *And better than you having to possess us so you can protect us against their stings*, she added just between them in mindspeak.

I told you, Una. I'm not going to possess you again unless I have your permission, Lily promised.

Breakfast and Una shared a look. "Are you sure he can't just—" Breakfast pantomimed sneaking up on Grace and throttling her. "We could coordinate with Red Leaf. He could tell us when she's out of her body and we could send Toshi in there."

"The Hive would sniff him out," Tristan said with certainty. "He'd have to be able to do it without any kind of emotion changing his body chemistry. Maybe he could do it while he was sleepwalking or something."

"Or possessed," Lillian said quietly. The word slithered through the tent. She looked up. "I know mechanics hate thinking about possession, but consider the alternative."

Lily could nearly hear Caleb gritting his teeth and intervened before he had a chance to say anything. "I'll ask Toshi if he wants to try it."

"But then he'll *know*," Lillian said, shaking her head. "If he knows, the Hive will be able to smell it on him."

Lily felt everyone staring at her, waiting for a response. "And what if they smell my fear on him?" she asked quietly. "If I'm in complete control of his body, would my fear make his chemistry respond?"

"Yes," Rowan answered. Lillian opened her mouth to argue with him, but he turned and looked directly at her for the first time and cut her off. "It's too risky, Lillian," he said. The way he said her name carried years of intimacy with it. Lily flushed and tried to wipe the thought of them together out of her mind.

"Why?" Lillian replied, pressing her point. "If it fails, all she has to do is jump him out of there. Even if she were too late and he were to die he would simply be the first of many in this war."

Caleb stood up. "I wonder if Grace knew the moment she became evil," he said. He looked at Lillian. "Did you know?" She didn't respond. Caleb looked at Lily. "Will you?" He smiled to himself, figuring it out. "But none of you think you're evil, do you? Not even Grace, I bet. Not even when she made the Hive. Didn't she tell us that they protect the city so humans didn't have to fight and die?" He paused, staring at Lily. "I bet she's got it all worked out in her head so that *she's* the hero."

When he left the tent, no one tried to go after him. Breakfast was the first to speak.

"Just to be clear, you're not going to possess Toshi, are you?" Breakfast asked.

"There are other options I want to try first," Lily replied.

"Like what?" Tristan asked, raising a doubtful eyebrow.

Lily didn't answer. Una eventually announced that she was tired and she and Breakfast retired, followed shortly by Tristan. Lily stood to leave when they did, but Rowan didn't move from his spot on the floor of the tent.

"Are you going to bed?" Lily asked, standing uncertainly at the exit.

Rowan didn't look at Lily. He was staring at Lillian. "Not yet," he replied quietly. "Lillian and I have some things to discuss."

Lillian had her eyes trained on her lap. Lily looked back and forth between the ex-lovers anxiously. After a few short moments her lingering presence grew painfully awkward.

"Alone, Lily," Rowan added.

Lily left them, her head strangely light and her feet heavy. She took three slow steps before she heard Rowan say, "I'm not leaving until you tell me about my father, Lillian," and she rushed back and hid by the entrance.

"There's nothing to tell," Lillian said.

"Stop it. Just stop," Rowan said tiredly.

"It's for your own good," Lillian pleaded.

Rowan laughed bitterly. "My own good, huh? You still think you have the right to decide what's good for me?"

"No," Lillian whispered.

What the hell are you doing?

Lily spun around to find Una giving her a scathing look. Lily tried to think of a lie, but there was no explanation for why she would be lurking outside Lillian's tent.

I'm eavesdropping on Rowan and Lillian, she admitted sheepishly. *I think she's going to tell him about that thing.* An image of River Fall in the barn sailed from Lily's mind to Una's. Una stifled a gasp.

Move over, she said, as she crouched down next to Lily.

"I didn't want you to change," Lillian said, stammering. "That's why I never told you."

"Lillian, I'm *changed*, and not for the better. If you think you were protecting me, you failed." His voice was bitter. Lily had never heard him speak with such rancor to anyone. "I've imagined it all, you know. Every possible evil one person can commit against another, and I've pictured my father doing it to *you*. Whatever you think you're protecting me from, it's already happened in my head. You're not saving anyone."

There was a long pause. And then, surprisingly, Lillian spoke. She told Rowan everything about the cinder world and how it poisoned her body. She told him about the men who had hunted her, caught her, and put her in the barn. She described the people in the barn, calling them lambs. And then she told him about his father and what he did to them.

Lillian spoke quickly, letting it all pour out. Rowan let her talk, never once interrupting. She ended by telling him how she'd drained the lambs of their life force to fuel her worldwalk back home.

"I swore I would never let it happen to this world," Lillian said, her pace finally slowing. "When I drained the lambs, I promised them that if there were versions of them in my world, they wouldn't end up in the barn. I'd make sure there'd never *be* a barn, or a River Fall to mutilate them, no matter what I had to do. I owed them that much."

Rowan was silent for a long time.

"Say something," Lillian begged.

"I wish you'd just told me. Right from the start," he said.

"It wasn't you I was trying to protect, you know," she said in a wavering voice. "I was trying to protect your memory of him. I thought, even if I took him away from you, I could at least leave his memory alone."

There was another long pause.

"Now *that* I can understand," he said softly. "I'm so sorry, Lillian."

Lily and Una heard weeping. Una squeezed Lily's arm and they left Lillian to take the comfort Rowan was offering her.

It was after midnight when Lily crept out of her tent.

It had taken her that long to decide. After hours of staring at the note from Carrick, trying to tell herself that she'd done the right thing, she finally accepted that she had doomed both hers and Lillian's army if she didn't act. Losing the trust of her coven didn't matter anymore.

Hours of sitting still and then, once decided, she couldn't dress fast enough. She pulled on black wearhyde pants, boots, and a jacket, threw the bloodstained note she'd found waiting on her bedroll into the fire, and stole through the thick fir trees.

She went through the kennel where the guardians were tied up. Their bear-like bodies were only hulking shapes in the dark, but she could tell they were awake. She passed the corral of runners, and even though they didn't nicker or prance, the raised hairs on Lily's arms told her that they were watching her. All of the tame Woven were uncannily still in their pens. They never wasted their energy on super-fluous movement. Lily supposed that was probably part of the reason they required less food and water. Efficient as it was, the result was quite disturbing. They regarded Lily with empty statue eyes, like snakes waiting to strike.

She went to the clearing where the greater drakes were tethered to fat spikes that were hammered into the ground. The drakes turned their wedge-shaped heads toward her as she approached, their chains clinking.

Lily smiled wryly at the sound, thinking of her diamond-and-iron cuffs, and searched for the drake she'd ridden that afternoon. She hoped it would remember her, and that it might even know the way back to the speaking stone in the dark. She'd forgotten to take the vibration of the speaking stone mountaintop, and she was kicking herself for that oversight now. Lily hadn't gotten used to taking the vibration of every new patch of land she encountered, but she knew she wouldn't make that mistake again.

When Lily found the drake it gave her no sign of recognition. She approached it slowly, dreading the moment when she had to bend her neck in front of it in order to unchain it from the stake.

"Do you know what I don't understand?" Rowan asked. Lily spun around, her hand clutching at her thumping heart, and saw him emerge from the shadows. "I don't understand why someone as intelligent as you can't seem to grasp that I always know when you're going to sneak out."

"What are you—?"

"What am *I* doing?" he interrupted indignantly. "What are *you* doing?"

"This is not what it looks like."

"So you're not going to the speaking stone?"

"I am, but . . ." Lily paused momentarily to gather her thoughts and Rowan spun away from her, growling with frustration.

"Why do we keep having this fight?" he asked the stars. He spun back around and faced her. "I know you think you're saving a lot of lives by doing this. I know that it seems like the fastest, most painless way to end this conflict—you possess Toshi, murder Grace in her sleep, and the war never even needs to happen. Hundreds of thousands of lives could be saved. I know how tempted you must be. Hell, I'm tempted to counsel you to go through with it. But just *think* about what you'd have to become in order to do that. Ask yourself if someone who could do that is someone you would want in power." Rowan paused, and a pained look crossed his face. "You're trying to protect people. So was Lillian when she hid what she saw in the cinder world about my father from me. I'm pretty sure Grace was trying to protect people, too, when she developed the Woven. But look how Lillian and Grace ended up. They're soulless."

He drew in a deep breath as if he had set down a heavy weight. "I know you believe murdering Grace will save us, but you'd have to give up too much of yourself to do it. I don't want you to end up empty like Grace and Lillian. I'd fight a hundred battles to stop that."

Lily looked at Rowan with a funny smile on her face. The smile turned into a quiet laugh. "I'm not going to end up like Lillian. And I'm not going to the speaking stone to murder Grace," she said.

"You're not?" he said uncertainly. "Then why are you sneaking around?"

"Because I know you're not going to like why I *am* going." She sighed, accepting that she got caught. "I'm going to claim the Woven."

Rowan stiffened, completely taken off guard. "The Woven?" he repeated with a blank look on his face.

"We can't win without them. I've known for a while now that it was our only option, but you and Caleb and Tristan and pretty much everyone from this world wouldn't even consider it, so I kept my mouth shut."

"But Grace controls them," he argued, still not accepting it.

"Not all of them. She doesn't control the Pride or the Pack—their will is too strong for her to claim them remotely without their consent. She admitted as much to me in the redwood grove," Lily said, shaking her head. "The Hive is hers—I know I'll never be able to take them over because she controls the Queen—but I think I have a shot of pushing her out of some of the insect Woven's willstones, at the very least. If we can get even half of the insect Woven on our side, we might win."

"The insect Woven," Rowan repeated. His face was still a blank mask.

"See? This is why I didn't tell you," Lily said accusingly. "You think I *like* keeping secrets from you? I hate it. But what choice do I have when you're so prejudiced you can't see the Woven for what they are?"

"And what are they?" he asked, crossing his arms over his chest.

"Victims." Rowan let out a surprised laugh, but Lily pressed on. "They are Grace's slaves. They're cannon fodder and they die by the thousands. Maybe I can't save them. Maybe I can't save anyone, not the Outlanders, not the kids in the subways tunnels, not even my own coven. Maybe it's some giant cosmic joke that I'm even here, and I should go home and go back to *not* being able to save my own world." She bent down and started tugging on the lock that chained the drake to the ground. "But I'm going to try first. I'm going to go to the Woven and I'm going to ask them if they want to fight with me, because if anything on this blasted continent should want to get out from under Grace's boot, it's them." She gave up on the lock and started tugging at the spike. "And if you're too pigheaded to see that they've been abused as horribly the Outlanders have, than you can just stay here."

Rowan watched her heaving ineffectually on the spike. "What are you doing?" he asked, suppressing a laugh.

"I'm trying to get this dang thing off!" Lily shouted, at her wit's end.

"Use your willstones," he said. He moved her back. "Look. It's a lattice. You just touch it and think *open*." He did it and the lock clicked.

"Oh," Lily said.

"That was one of the first things I taught you about magic. In the cabin. Remember?" he asked.

"*Now* I do." She looked at him and shifted from foot to foot uncertainly, remembering the cabin. Remembering claiming him. Every speck of her wanted to kiss him. "So . . . are you coming with me?" she asked, just short of pleading.

"Of course I am," he replied. "I may not like the thought of running into battle alongside the Woven, but it's certainly better than watching you sell your soul."

"And easier than fighting a hundred battles," Lily added cheekily.

Rowan laughed and looked down as a dark thought crossed his mind. "Yes." His voice dropped. "I think this one battle is going to be quite enough."

CHAPTER
14

LILY SAW THE MILKY-JADE GLIMMER OF THE SPEAKING stone and eased back in the stirrups to let her drake know she wanted it to slow down. It cupped its wings forward, essentially stopping in midair before the sheer cliff on the eastern side of the mountain.

Lily didn't have all the proper signals learned after her single flight with Leto, but she had noticed that drakes were much more sensitive to commands than any horse she'd ever ridden and as such only required a minimum of direction—the rest, the drake figured out on its own by reading its rider's body language. Lily touched the side of its neck with her heel and gently indicated by shifting her weight that she wanted it to land. She felt Rowan's hands on her waist tighten as the drake flew them into the treetops, but to his credit, he didn't panic when the drake clamped on to a violently swaying tree and scrambled down the trunk in a barrage of cracking timber and whipping branches.

As they dismounted, Lily realized she didn't know how to make the drake fly back to camp. She tried pointing in the direction they'd come and saying *go home* to it several times, but either it didn't understand or it didn't want to. After a few failed attempts, Lily gave up and allowed the drake to follow her and Rowan through the trees to the speaking stone. It tucked its wings back and waddled alongside her like a very large dog. Rowan eyed it skeptically a few times, uncomfortable with being accompanied by a Woven in the dark, but again he showed a commendable amount of restraint and held his tongue.

"It'll be a miracle if she's there already," Lily mumbled.

"Maybe not," Rowan replied. "The Woven are capable of incredible things."

Lily looked at him, surprised. "That almost sounded like respect," she commented.

"Don't get carried away," he said, pursing his lips around a smile. He bent down to build a small fire at Lily's feet.

She touched the speaking stone and reached out to Pale One. Her mind dove into the fast-moving river of the relay, whipping past thousands of miles of country, and finally rested inside one of the yellow-hued speaking stones on the Ocean of Grass. She called out to her claimed and felt her excitement. Pale One yipped and danced in circles.

Lily pictured the Pack. *Where are they?*

Close. Tending their meat.

Lily saw the seemingly unending herds of bison. She asked Pale One if she could join her inside her skin again. Pale One allowed it.

Lily felt the packed earth under her paws, and just below the surface she felt the gophers in their underground city. She telescoped out and felt the miles and miles of land pressed flat beneath its twin brother, the sky, and it dawned on her that once, long ago, water had covered this land as the sky now covered it. The pressure of the ancient inland sea had pushed the land down, muffling it. The Ocean of Grass still held on to that watery silence. Its vibration was a dull, sleepy thud.

She gathered the heat of a fire as fuel, called out to Rowan's will-stone, and jumped them to Pale One's location.

She heard Rowan exhale a tensely held breath as he opened his eyes. "That is still unbelievably strange," he told her, taking in their surroundings.

Pale One let out a series of whines and yelps as she came toward Lily with her head down. Rowan jerked backward, but Lily held out her hands to Pale One and she was greeted with a flurry of licks and nuzzles. Lily could feel she was hungry. She fed Pale One's willstone with energy, and while she did, Lily felt Lillian reach out to her.

I did it! Lillian told her in mindspeak. *I teleported to Salem and then I was able to bring someone back with me! I'm ready, Lily.*

Wait for me, Lily replied. *I'm gathering more forces.*

From where?

Lily hesitated. She thought of how deeply Lillian hated the Woven. *You'll see. Just trust me. Give me one more day,* she asked.

I may not have one more day, Lillian replied testily, and then cut contact.

"Lillian is ready to jump her army now," Lily told Rowan.

"She knows she needs your army or she can't win. She'll wait for us," Rowan said, but his tone was less than certain.

"She doesn't intend on winning," Lily reminded him, keeping her voice lowered. "All she needs is to get close enough to detonate. Or so she thinks."

Lily looked at Pale One. *Take us to the Pack,* she asked.

Pale One bounded forward, flooding Lily with images from her journey as she went. Her excitement was quickly curtailed as she caught a scent on the breeze. Pale One stopped right in front of Lily, blocking her way and forcing her to stop as well. She howled into the darkness and the lonely sound was answered from a source close by.

They waited, Pale One tensing into the darkness at something the humans couldn't see, until Lily felt Rowan stiffen. He unsheathed his long knife, thrust out an arm, and tried to put Lily behind him, but as he spun around in a circle she felt him deflating. They were already surrounded.

It's a trap, Rowan said in mindspeak.

Then Lily saw them—dozens of pairs of softly reflective eyes staring at her. She didn't know how far back into the gloom the Pack stretched, but Lily could feel that the darkness all around her was alive.

Not hunting you, Pale One assured Lily. *They are afraid. And angry.*

Lily wasn't sure if that was any better. *Can you tell them I mean no harm?*

Speak, and they will understand.

Lily hesitated, not sure she understood Pale One correctly. Mindspeak was one thing, where concepts were passed along as much as words. The times when Lily had doubts that her Woven claimed could understand her all she'd had to do was picture what she wanted and pass the images along, as they did with her. Speaking aloud was different. Language, and the ability to understand it, was different. She hadn't even attempted speaking aloud with Pale One yet, thinking it might be too complicated for her.

Speak with sounds, Pale One urged. *They lose trust for you.*

"I come to ask for your help," Lily said, trying to sound confident. She heard growls as a response.

"Lily, what are you doing?" Rowan asked. "They can't understand you."

"We understand the witch," said a low, raspy voice.

Rowan said something in Cherokee that was no doubt a swear

word, and then a different raspy voice said something in Cherokee back to him. Rowan went very still.

I don't believe it, he whispered inside Lily's mind.

"Have you always been able to talk?" Lily asked.

She heard something like a bark and a laugh coming from the dark. "Of course," growled another member of the Pack.

A different voice picked up the dialogue. "We have always had language and the use of tools," it said.

"Why wouldn't we?" asked a fourth voice.

"We are more like you than we are like wolves," purred a fifth.

The Pack was circling them, passing the duty of responding from one member to another as if they were one mind with many voices.

They are a coven, Rowan said, realizing it at the same time Lily did. *They're sharing mindspeak as they talk to you.*

They're toying with us, Lily replied to both Rowan and Pale One, connecting them to each other through her.

Circling closer and closer, Pale One added. Lily felt Rowan startle to hear the Woven in his mind, but he accepted it.

Pale One, watch Lily's flank, Rowan ordered, taking the defensive lead.

Next thing: one will come inside circle and snap with teeth to show they are Biggers, Pale One said as she followed Rowan's order.

They may be Biggers, but they aren't stronger, Lily replied.

"Where is your witch?" Lily demanded, suddenly sick of playing this game for dominance. "Bring me to her."

"We need no witch," hissed yet another voice from the dark. Lily felt Rowan count *six* in his mind.

Many more, Pale One said, disagreeing. *Many, many smells.*

"You have no fire, witch," sneered a seventh.

"You are meat," said yet another.

"I didn't bring fire because I didn't come here to fight you," Lily said. "I came here to ask you to join us. In three days we go to destroy the Hive."

Yips and barks burst from the Pack. There were dozens of them out there in the dark. Maybe hundreds. Lily felt Rowan slump, knowing they didn't stand a chance against so many.

"My army is thirty thousand strong," Lily said proudly, her voice ringing out in the darkness.

"The Hive are millions," said a softer voice, and all of the other Pack members fell silent at the sound of it. "Thirty thousand is not enough, not even for a witch."

Lily turned to face the soft voice. "I am not like other witches," she said.

The soft voice chuckled. "And yet you still need our help," it taunted.

"I need the Pack, the Pride, the raptors, the simians, and even the insect Woven, or I don't stand a chance," Lily admitted shamelessly. "And you need me or *you* don't stand a chance. Because if I fail, the Hive will be coming for you next."

There was a momentary silence. "The Hive can't reach this far. Their range—"

"Their range will mean nothing in a few days," Lily said, interrupting. "The witch who fuels them is going to learn how to appear anywhere she wants in the blink of eye. She'll be able to be practically everywhere at once, and when she can do that, she'll claim new Queens who will start new Hive colonies, spreading farther and farther until she's conquered the whole world. Unless we stop her."

Lily stared into the silent darkness, her heart in her throat, as the seconds ticked by. Finally, the soft voice spoke again.

"Light a fire and let the witch see us," it said.

A spark was struck and torches flared. Lily tried not to show her reaction to the half-human, half-wolf figures that came to light. Their faces were snouted and fanged, and their arms were elongated to reach the ground in a sloped-back posture that had them hunkering over their dog-like hind legs. Their hands were clawed and padded with thick calluses like a canine's, but still five fingered and mobile like a human's, and their eyes had round pupils.

"My name is Lily," she told the one who sat on his haunches across from her.

"We don't have names like your kind," he responded. "Who we are is more complicated than that."

"Who you are is a scent and a rank, both of which are always changing," Lily said. She saw surprise flash across his eyes and knew she'd guessed right from what she'd gathered from sharing mindspace with Pale One and Blueback. "You're the alpha. For now."

"You may call me Alpha." He regarded Rowan and Pale One in turn. "The western witch only claims Woven," he remarked, "but you claim all kinds."

"So you know about Grace," Rowan said.

Alpha's eyes flicked over to Rowan. "We've always known. She created us to hunt and kill your kind, and your kind hunted and killed us in return. Many of us died. She was a bad alpha." His eyes went back to Lily. "We would not be ruled by a witch. Not during my ancestors' time. Not during mine."

Lily nodded understandingly. "I have no interest in controlling you or forcing you to do anything you don't want to do."

"We don't want to go to war."

"Neither do we," Lily rebutted.

"Witches always want war," Alpha said, a faint sneer on his lips.

"Not Lily," Rowan said. He and Alpha locked eyes. "I didn't trust her at first, either, but you don't have to trust her. You just have to decide what's better—being claimed and having a chance at survival, or being free and getting wiped out by the Hive."

The Alpha stood, obviously done with this interview. Lily called after him.

"You've seen them, haven't you?" she asked, loud enough for the betas to hear. "You've seen the Hive flying through your territory, carrying humans back and forth. You've seen the Hive searching for someone. They enter your lands now without fear, and no matter how many of them you've tried to turn away at your borders, Grace sends more, doesn't she?"

The Alpha turned back around and glared at Lily. He gave one curt nod.

"She's not afraid of you," Lily said. "Grace allowed the Pack to maintain this land after you defied her because she realized it was too far from her city for her to hold on to it remotely. She let you live, as long as you kept the eastern humans in the east, because she physically couldn't be everywhere at once. That's about to change. She's coming back, and when she does it won't be to claim you. It will be to exterminate you."

Toshi ran the last few blocks back to the Governor's Villa. He tried to imagine that he was just out for a bit of healthy predawn exercise and that the adrenaline pumping through his body was from enjoyment, not fear. He envisioned a stress-reducing jog followed by a little tai chi, and gradually the Workers clinging to his arms lifted off.

After spending the night going to every restaurant, tavern, nightclub, and after-hours bar he could think of, looking for people who might want to be claimed by Lily, Toshi was running on fumes. He climbed the stairs two at a time, but stopped before he entered his apartment. He could tell that someone was in there.

He backed away from the door. It burst open and two Warrior Sisters stalked out of his rooms, their whips wrapped around their waists. They grabbed him roughly, tearing his skin with their barbed hands, and even though he struggled against the iron strength of their arms, he knew it was useless. They dragged him to a window. His gut lurched as the Warrior Sisters jumped.

This is it, he thought, and then it occurred to him. He wasn't alone anymore. *Lily! Help me!*

Toshi—what's happening?

The Warrior Sisters flew him around the building and into another set of rooms.

I need strength, he answered as they threw him roughly onto a balcony. *I think they're going to kill me.*

Toshi staggered forward and tipped onto his hands and knees. When he looked up he saw Grace lying on the floor in front of him. Next to her was the shaman. They were immobile, barely breathing, and too pale and stiff to be simply sleeping.

They're spirit walking, Lily told him. *You must stop them, Toshi. I have no fire ready—wait—*

One of the Warrior Sisters buzzed her wings in agitation and then she grabbed Toshi by the back of the head and dragged him by his hair to Grace's side. All of the Warrior Sisters in the room seemed distraught. Their heads twitched and their hands grasped at their whips, unraveling them from their waists or from across their chests and then rewrapping again to no purpose. They weren't attacking him, he realized, not intentionally.

I think they want me to help her, Toshi said.

You can't, Lily insisted. Toshi felt a swell of fear overtake Lily and he briefly caught a glimpse of an enormous creature looming over her before he felt her leave him.

Lily and Rowan left Pale One with the Pack—her new claimed—and jumped back to the speaking stone on the mountain. Pale One would be no help to them, and maybe even a hindrance, on their subsequent missions. They arrived as the sun was rising.

"I'm running out of time," Lily said. She looked around for the drake. "Here, boy," she called, feeling like an idiot. She heard Rowan's rumbling laugh.

"Tame Woven aren't boys or girls," he said.

"I can't just say 'here, *it*.' Here, Spike," she called again, figuring that was as good a name as any.

As they searched the gloom for the wayward drake, Lily felt Toshi roaring into her mind in a panic. She stuck out an arm and grabbed Rowan's hand.

"It's Toshi," she said, her eyes far away. "The Hive has him."

"What about the rebels he was supposed to gather for you to claim?" Rowan asked urgently.

"Shh—wait." She gasped. "There's Grace. And Red Leaf. She's spirit walking." Her face screwed up as she shared a rapid exchange with Toshi. "I think they want him to heal her?" she said uncertainly.

The bush in front of Lily trembled. As a member of the Pride pounced on her, she vaguely wondered how it was possible that she could have overlooked a cat the size of a rhino. She felt Rowan's weight coming down on top of her at the last moment, and then she saw the cat Woven jerk backward and lift off the ground. Behind the lion Woven's outraged roar, Lily heard a sound like the flapping of a sheet in the wind.

Rowan rolled with Lily under him. The two of them came up on their hands and knees to see Spike caging the armored cat to the ground under his talons.

"Wait, Spike," Lily shouted, holding her hands out in a stop gesture. Spike held the member of the Pride down, his eyes sliding off to the side.

"There are more hidden out there somewhere," Rowan said, watching the drake's movements.

Lily came forward and knelt down to look the member of the Pride in the eye. "I want to speak to your alpha," she said. The Woven made a growling sound in the back of her throat. "I'm not here to kill you. I'm here to help." The Woven did not respond. Lily looked up at Rowan and shrugged.

"Maybe she doesn't understand language," Rowan suggested.

Lily didn't have many options. She reached out to find the Woven's willstone, buried somewhere under the skin at her throat.

"Witch," the Pride member hissed.

"You *can* speak," Lily said, removing her hand. "I know the rest of your Pride is out there somewhere. Tell your leader to come forward."

The Woven's eyes skipped around in confusion. Rowan tried speaking to the Woven in Cherokee, but her eyes stayed clouded.

"I don't think she understands much," Rowan surmised.

"What do we do?" Lily asked. She looked up at the sun, already above the horizon, and remembered Toshi. She reached out to him.

I'm okay, Toshi replied. *The Hive is keeping me here to watch over Grace. I get the feeling that as long as she doesn't die, neither do I.*

Wake her.

I've been trying to. I'll keep at it. Aren't there a bunch of rebels you should be claiming right now?

Are they ready for me?

Ready, willing, and able. They're waiting to hear your call.

Lily smiled at Rowan. "Toshi's people are waiting for me," she said. She looked back down at the Woven. "I'm not going to hurt you." Lily petted Spike's talon. "Let her up," she said.

Spike cautiously lifted his claws. The lion was uninjured. She sat back on her haunches, glowering at Lily.

"What do I do with you?" she asked, not sure if the Woven could understand her. "You've got too much will for me to claim you without your consent, but not enough to grasp any verbal argument I could make to convince you."

The lion cocked her head. Her nearly human eyes narrowed. Maybe she understood more than she could say.

"I need your help," Lily said. She moved closer to the lion and felt Rowan's hand shoot out to pull her back. "Just let me try one thing," she said, pleading with him.

Rowan's grip on her arm relaxed but he didn't let Lily get more than an inch away as she moved in closer, holding out her hand for the lion to smell. Lily tried to ignore the fact that her hand was shaking violently as it hovered in front of the lion's saber teeth, and she kept it outstretched by force of will alone. After a moment that was filled with the sound of Lily's heart pounding in her ears, the Woven allowed Lily to touch the side of her hulking face. Lily moved her hand onto the big cat's forehead and closed her eyes, concentrating. She thought about Grace's face as hard as she could, willing the image into the Woven's brain, and whispered her name. She heard the cat growl.

"Enemy," hissed the bushes all around. The rest of the Pride glided forward, surrounding Lily, Rowan, and Spike.

"My enemy, too. Fight her," Lily replied, looking at each member of the Pride in turn.

The largest female came forward. She looked infinitely bored, like only a cat can, but her agitation was betrayed by the twitching of her tail. She sat down in front of Lily.

"My pride," she purred, as if daring Lily to take it away from her.

Lily nodded in agreement. "Yours. But I can make it stronger."

Lily fought her fatigue and filled Rowan's willstone with as much strength as she could.

Her newly claimed Pride members watched as Lily and Rowan jumped up onto Spike's back and he clambered up the trunk of a tall tree and took flight from the topmost branches.

Find more lions, Lily told her Pride. *Bring them back here.*

They rose, stretched, and rubbed their faces against one another languorously before melting into the trees.

Lily let the drake circle to find the best updrafts in the early morning chill. They soared over to the next valley and found what they were looking for. Three enormous raptors were riding the air currents, scanning the ground for something to eat.

"Get above one," Rowan said.

Lily directed Spike to fly up, and he beat his wings and stretched out his neck, climbing a ladder into the sky.

When they were high enough and the raptor was just a dark shape beneath them, Rowan put an arm around Lily and swung his legs over to one side of the drake's neck. Lily felt the hot and cold surges of terror as she took her feet out of the stirrups.

"Are you sure about this?" Rowan asked.

"No," Lily shouted over the whipping wind. Her voice came out choked as it tried to get around her stomach, which was now lodged in her throat. "But it's the only way."

Rowan looked over the side, his face serene as he timed it. Lily saw his willstone pulse as every sense in him sharpened, and he pulled her tightly against his body and launched them off the drake's neck into thin air.

Lily shrieked uncontrollably, clutching at Rowan desperately as they fell. Rowan spread his other arm out to the side like a rudder to steer them and slow them down. His willstone pulsed again as he changed the air—thickening it until it was almost as viscous as water. By the time they hit the raptor's back, Rowan had slowed their descent enough to land gently on the Woven.

Startled, the raptor tucked its wings and barrel rolled. Rowan pressed Lily flat against the Woven, holding them tightly to it. Lily scrabbled through its feathers, trying to get her hand up to its forehead, like she had with the lion.

"I can't reach," Lily yelled.

Rowan inched them around while the raptor plummeted to the ground. Lily stretched and strained, and as she neared the raptor's head she started talking, hoping that the raptor could understand.

"I need your help!" she yelled. The raptor shrieked in response. Lily grabbed handfuls of feathers and finally got close enough to lay her hands on the raptor's head. She concentrated on sending images of Grace's face, and a fantasy of Lily's army fighting the Hive.

The raptor kept diving.

"Please!" Lily screamed desperately.

The raptor cupped its wings and pulled out of the dive just in time to land softly on the ground. Lily and Rowan were thrown off the raptor's neck and tumbled across the ground under its enormous beak. Lily stood and looked into a big yellow-and-black eye that was the size of a car windshield. She stared at the Woven and threw all of her will behind showing it what she intended to do. Her willstone wove a glowing mist around her and she strained to make contact with a creature that was not her claimed. The raptor laid its wings across its flanks.

"I don't think raptors have any language at all," Rowan said.

"I'm trying to fight the witch in the west, but I need an army," Lily said. "Grace Bendingtree. Do you want to fight her?"

The Woven cocked its head to look at Rowan, and then trained its eye again on Lily. Rowan started drawing Lily back.

"This isn't going to work," he said.

The raptor fluffed the feathers on its chest. Lily saw a gently glowing chip buried in the down. She stepped forward, hoping that this was an invitation.

"I don't know if you understand, but I'm not here to make you my slave," Lily said. She reached out and touched the raptor's willstone.

The kettle of raptors that Lily had claimed flanked them as she and Rowan sailed over the Woven Woods outside Richmond astride Spike.

Fan out, she told her raptors, picturing what she needed from them. They had even less language than the Pride, and the concept of individual will was beginning to get blurry. Lily sensed that she might have been able to take their willstones without their consent, but she chose not to. She wanted her raptors to *want* to fight. The kettle broke their tight formation. They were intelligent enough to understand that she was hunting nests of insect Woven, and that they had flown this far east because she wanted the biggest nests they could find.

There were so many things about the Woven's behavior that hadn't made sense to Lily before she'd understood their origin. One of those things was how the wild Woven clustered just outside the Thirteen Cities. Unlike normal animals that avoided cities, the greatest numbers of insect Woven were always to be found right outside the city walls. Lily understood it now, of course. Grace positioned their nests outside the densest populations, like a line of pawns on a chessboard, to keep the people from ever wanting to venture out.

One of her raptors found what Lily was looking for. His keen eyes showed her a startlingly bright and clear image of a very large hill of sticks and twigs. The shape and size of it reminded Lily of an English barrow.

Keep searching. Find all of the big ones, she commanded.

Lily signaled for her drake to land and, as Spike crashed through the branches of a stately old black walnut tree, Lily could sense Rowan's hesitance.

"Whoa, boy," he said to Spike before they reached the ground.

Spike obeyed and stopped. He wrapped his tail around the central trunk, clasped the thick lower branches with the hand-like appendages that stuck out of the leading joint of his wings, and hung upside down like a bat. Lily and Rowan clambered awkwardly onto a branch to dismount the upside-down drake.

"What's the matter?" Lily asked.

"Just stay here in the tree for a second, okay?" Rowan snapped. His forehead was furrowed with worry and Lily could see the pulse in his neck throbbing fast. His willstone flared and he jumped out of the tree. He landed silently and stole away toward the nest.

Lily waited in the tree next to Spike. She reached out and petted his iridescent scales, more to soothe herself than him, until she saw Rowan reappear and signal for her to climb down.

I don't like this, he told her in mindspeak.

Lily knew why. These Woven were not like the Pride and the Pack, or even like the less-organized raptors and simians. These Woven were the most alien, both in looks and behavior. Rowan had been fighting them his whole life and he still didn't understand them. These particular Woven—the hodgepodge ones that were the odds and ends of insects and reptiles and mammals and birds all thrown together without rhyme or reason—these were the creatures that had chased him in his nightmares since he first learned what it was to fear.

I don't think you're going to be able to communicate with them at all, he said in mindspeak.

I don't think so, either, Lily admitted. *But I won't need to.* She took his hand and made him meet her eyes. *Find the one that laid the eggs. I've got a plan.*

You can't reason with these Woven, he argued.

I know. That's why I need the queen. If I claim her, I claim all of her offspring.

Rowan gave her a questioning look. *How do you know that?*

Lily thought for a moment before answering. *Grace started with wolves and apes and lions because they work in groups and they instinctively follow a leader. They aren't fully human, and they don't have self-awareness exactly like we do, so she could bend their will to hers.*

Invade a willstone without shattering it, Rowan thought.

Yes. But remote claiming forms a weaker bond, and they started breaking away from her. Even if they weren't human, these kinds of Woven still had wills of their own. Grace had to go to the insect kingdom to get what she needed.

And what's that?

Total, unquestioning obedience. Lily looked at Rowan. *Ever wonder why she doesn't have a human coven?*

Because mechanics argue too much with witches?

Lily shook her head. "Because you have minds of your own and you can leave us," she whispered.

She felt Rowan wanting to say that he would never leave her, but of course, he already had. His face fell when he realized that the complete honesty of mindspeak wouldn't allow him to make that vow.

"It's okay," she said, "I don't need you to say that. If I don't treat you right, you *should* leave me. All of you. Caleb, Una, Breakfast. Even Juliet."

Rowan dropped his gaze in thought. For a moment it looked like he was going to say something.

"What?" Lily asked. "I know there's something you've been wanting to tell me." But he shook his head, unwilling to answer.

"The queen should be close," he said. "This nest is fresh. Let's give her a reason to come back and defend it." Rowan took Lily's hand and brought her to the top of the mound. "That should get her attention."

Rowan had Lily stand tall at the very top while he lay flat against the mound and covered himself with some of the mulch. It wasn't long before Lily heard something coming through the trees, hissing.

The queen was enormous—fifteen feet tall, and twice as long. She had eight spidery legs attached to a bony body. Her head was triangular like an alligator's, but it was her mouth that terrified Lily. As she stalked forward, she hissed another sinister warning and the pincers on either side of her mouth opened to display rows of needle-like teeth as long as Lily's forearm.

Lily looked at the queen and deliberately kicked the nest.

The queen darted forward, her eight legs a blur as she mounted her nest. Lily fought the urge to run and planted her feet. When the queen was just inches from tearing Lily in half, Rowan sprang up from the mulch, jumped astride her back, and wrenched her head back, exposing the queen's neck. Lily lunged forward, her gorge rising in revulsion, as she placed her hands on the queen's pebbly skin and searched for the willstone.

As Lily claimed the queen, she saw as if through neon facets. The world had grown another color around the edges as if a new wavelength of light were now visible. Moving shapes left tracks across her eyes and chemicals lit up the air like dancing motes of information. Fear was not fear—it was extra energy to spur on action. Hate was not hate—it was nails on a chalkboard that needed to be silenced. There was no self. No conscience. No memory. There was only on or off, stop or go, attack or stay.

Lily separated herself from the exchange and looked at Rowan as he climbed down off the now-docile Woven's back. She recalled him telling her a story about a little girl from his tribe who had tried to make a pet of one of the insect Woven. A shudder went down her back at the thought of a little girl cuddling up to something like the queen.

"You were right," she said, her voice catching in her throat. "These Woven are nothing like us."

Rowan nodded, also remembering the little girl who had been eaten by her pet. "Do you control the whole nest now?"

Lily searched inside and felt the web of creatures now bound to her by chemicals and scents. There were thousands spawned by this one queen. "Yes," she said dully. It was not a pleasant feeling to share mindspace with these unfeeling creatures. "Unfortunately."

He took her hand. "Where's the next nest?" he asked gently.

Lily reached out to one of her raptors. "About twenty miles from here," she replied, her gaze far away and eagle sharp.

Lily heard Lillian calling out for her and allowed contact.

Breakfast just told us that Red Leaf is teaching Grace how to spirit walk, Lillian said in mindspeak. *Red Leaf told him that Grace is learning fast. Our time is up. We need to attack.*

Wait, Lillian. Please. We're dead if we go with as few fighters as we have now.

We can't wait. If Grace learns how to teleport the Hive, the Thirteen Cities will be destroyed in a matter of hours. It's now or never.

Don't use that bomb, Lily pleaded. *Give me more time.*

Lily felt Lillian cut her out.

"What is it?" Rowan asked. Lily shared the exchange with him and he broke into a run, pulling her along behind him.

Lily heard what sounded like the flapping of a huge sheet and the drake's talons raked the ground in front of them as it landed. Rowan pulled up short, surprised.

"I told you they were intelligent," Lily said. Rowan didn't argue as they jumped on Spike's neck and flew to the next nest.

The hour when Toshi was supposed to have met his contact had long since come and gone, and still, he was stuck tending to Grace. Now he had no way of knowing how the tests for the sting antidote had turned out. He hoped Ivan was having better luck with the pesticide.

Toshi rolled the cluster of extra serum vials in his pocket between his fingers, unable to tell if they could protect him and Red Leaf during an escape attempt or if it was suicide to try. He played a little game with himself. If more of the vials were facing up than down he would risk it. He pulled them out of his pocket and looked.

Half up, half down. He'd have to make his own luck.

"Are you ill?" Grace asked.

"Tired," he replied immediately. Respond fast and be as honest as possible.

"You've been working too hard," Grace said, almost as if she cared about him.

Toshi couldn't figure out why she was still acting like everything was normal between them. He knew what she was, and she knew he knew. There didn't seem to be any purpose to it, and then it occurred to him. Maybe this *was* normal for her.

Grace took the long silence as an invitation to bait him some more. "Or is it Mala keeping you up at night?" she asked with a tilted eyebrow.

"Mala?" Toshi repeated, and then he remembered. They were supposed to be engaged. He hadn't seen Mala in days, and he was quite sure that Grace knew that. "I wish," he said playfully. "But, no. I've just been working."

Grace studied him with hard eyes, her teeth grinding together faintly. She wanted him to confess. That's why she was playing this game. She wanted to hear from Toshi that his involvement with Mala was a lie. Red Leaf stirred and Grace turned her attention to him.

"Give him another dose," she said.

"I don't think keeping him unconscious is—"

"Give him another dose," she ordered. "I don't want him contacting anyone."

"You'll kill him," Toshi said quietly.

She huffed, as if Red Leaf's death would be nothing more than an annoying inconvenience for her. "Fine," she said. "I may as well go under again, then. I'll keep him in the overworld myself." She lay down next to Red Leaf on the floor, laughing. "I know I'm getting close because he keeps insisting that he won't show me any more," she said excitedly.

Toshi looked at Red Leaf in sympathy, wondering what kind of emotional damage Grace was doing to him in the overworld. Grace slipped into cold stillness and the Warrior Sisters guarding her grew anxious. To them it seemed as if Grace were dying, and even though Grace had explained it to them, they still got frantic when she left her body.

One of them prodded Toshi with the handle of her whip, indicating he should attend to Grace. Toshi held up his hands, signaling that there was nothing he could do. At least he hoped that's what he was signaling. He had to get out of this room. He had to get to the lab.

He stood up and crossed to the door. Two Warrior Sisters barred his exit, their wings buzzing.

"I have to go get medicine," he said, overenunciating his words. Little good it did him. He picked up an empty dose of the drug he'd been using on Red Leaf. "Medicine," he repeated, pointing to it.

One of the other Warrior Sisters picked up one of full doses that were left on the table and showed it to him as if to say *you still have more*. They weren't stupid, but what they understood and what they didn't was still a mystery to him.

He took the medicine from her and pointed at Red Leaf, nodding. Then he pointed at Grace and shook his head dramatically, still holding up the vial. "Bad for her. Need different medicine," he said.

The two Warrior Sisters by the door twitched their heads atop their stalk-like necks and stepped away from the door. Toshi made for the door as if walking on a tightrope. Three Workers attached themselves to him, one of them positioning her stinger right over his jugular. She clung to him tighter than usual, as if in warning.

As soon as he was out the door, Toshi walked to the lab. He had no idea how long Grace would remain spirit walking, and when she woke it was possible she'd decide that she'd had enough of toying with him and order the Worker to kill him. He took one of the vials out of his pocket, twisted it open, and tipped the few drops inside onto his tongue, figuring the illusion of safety was better than nothing.

As Toshi approached the lab he saw an orderly line of people snaking through the hallway. He glanced out a window and saw that the line went outside and all the way down the street. At the head of the line Mala was calmly distributing vials of the antidote.

"Where's Ivan?" Toshi asked.

"Inside. Making more," she answered. "We thought you were keeping Grace occupied." Her eyes were wide and staring with fear, but she was breathing slowly, forcing herself to keep it together. "We *need* you to keep her occupied," she stressed.

Toshi looked down the line. Tight faces looked back at him. If everyone stayed calm, the Hive would have no idea that anything was amiss, but only so long as Grace's full attention was elsewhere. As soon as she saw people lining up outside Ivan's lab through the Hive's eyes, they were caught.

"It's not me. She's still playing with her new guest," Toshi replied bitterly. "Are we sure about the formula?"

Mala's face fell. "That was your job."

"I missed meeting my contact," he said, and she glared at him as if it were his fault Grace had kept him locked in his rooms for hours. "I'd better get in there," he said, and brushed past her to join Ivan.

Inside the lab, dozens of people were very calmly, very carefully packing vials of antidote into whatever bags or satchels they happened to have handy, and leaving the lab with haste—but not too much haste. Most of the faces Toshi recognized as contacts of his, although he knew none of their names.

"For the restricted zone," Ivan said, gesturing to the people leaving with bags.

"And the pesticide?" Toshi asked.

"Over there," he replied, pointing to a line of vats against the opposite wall. "We've managed to retrofit a few crossbows to distribute it." Ivan picked up a crossbow and demonstrated. "Shoot a dart into a swarm of Workers, the dart explodes and sends out a mist of pesticide. Trouble is, there are only so many crossbows to go around—just what a few rebels here and there have managed to steal over the years."

"How do we get more?"

"All the Hive's watchtowers are stocked with crossbows."

Toshi thought of the platforms soaring high above the city streets. "But who can get to them except the Hive?" he asked. Ivan shrugged as if say he could only do so much. "Does the pesticide work at least?"

"Who knows? We can't test it without alerting the Hive," Ivan said with a fatalistic laugh. "Come. I need help."

Toshi rolled up his sleeves. "Grace could wake at any moment. I'm on borrowed time," he said.

"We all are," Ivan replied.

Toshi was just about to put on a pair of gloves, when he heard a low hum in the air and felt all three of the Workers clinging to him suddenly lift off his skin. He looked around and noticed that all the Workers in the room were leaving. He and Ivan ran out of the room, hearing startled gasps, and pushed their way past the confused masses and out onto the street.

The sky had gone dark. Toshi looked up. Every inch of airspace was covered with Warrior Sisters. They were all flying toward the perimeter wall simultaneously. Ivan ran back inside, Toshi close on his heels, both of them taking the stairs inside the villa two at a time until they reached the top floor. Ivan pushed open a door to a room that was empty except for a single staircase that led to a trapdoor in the ceiling. They emerged on the roof of the villa and looked out past the wall.

An army stood on the field of flowers, ready for battle.

CHAPTER
15

L ILY FELT JULIET CALLING TO HER AFTER SHE FINISHED claiming another queen.

Lily, Lillian has taken her army to Bower City without us. They just disappeared.

Rowan's brow furrowed in question at Lily's expression. "Lillian didn't wait for us," she told him.

I told you I was gathering more forces, Lily called out to Lillian in mindspeak.

I gave you all the time I could, Lillian replied. *Join me now or the war is lost.*

Lily turned to Rowan. "What do I do?" she asked him.

Over the course of the day they'd managed to claim almost twenty nests, but it was only a tiny fraction of what they needed. Rowan pulled his lower lip through his teeth, his eyes scrambling across the ground as he thought. Finally, he shook his head.

"We don't have a choice. Dividing our forces would be suicide," he said. "We have to go."

"But we don't have enough soldiers," Lily said, holding her hands out helplessly.

Rowan was calm. He looked at the Woven Lily had just claimed and smiled to himself. "Then I guess it will come down to which side has the strongest queen," he said. He took her hand and kissed the backs of her fingers and warmth traced up her arm. "It's time, Lily."

Lily nodded. She was exhausted. She had never felt more awake.

Rowan struck flint against steel and sent a spark into the mulch at Lily's feet. As the fire rose she closed her eyes to gather up all of her claimed.

She started with the insect Woven. Seeing through the pale lavender tinge of the speaking stone near Richmond, she summed all fifty thousand of them. Using the same speaking stone, she moved to her raptors, only one thousand pairs of wings, but they would be invaluable to fight the flying Hive.

Her mind dove into the fast-flowing stream of the speaking stones, heading north. She saw green and stopped to gather the nine thousand of the tank-like Pride and the thirty thousand of her human claimed waiting at the camp. Carrying all of them with her, Lily vaulted across mountains and valleys, her mind swimming across the miles of the continent to where Pale One and the twenty thousand warriors of the Pack were waiting in the flaxen-yellow hue of the Ocean of Grass.

Lily turned her mind, now nearly a hundred thousand strong, through the scorched red of Death Valley, up over the thin pink and rarefied air of the rocky mountains, and into the misty pearlescent throbbing of the westernmost speaking stone. Toshi was standing right next to it. He called out to her.

Lily, has the war begun?

Yes, Lily replied. She played the vibration of the redwood grove and jumped her army. *I'm here.*

"She's here," Toshi said, his eyes searching past the army at Bower City's gates and into the distant smudge that was the redwood grove.

"Obviously," Ivan remarked dryly. He looked down at the orderly ranks of disciplined soldiers. "She didn't bring enough."

"That's not Lily," Toshi said, frowning with confusion. "That's the other one. The Salem Witch. Mine is coming."

He craned his head to look up at the Hive as more of them streamed into the air from the city. The din of their wings rattled his bones. He saw Warrior Sisters rising up from the restricted zone. Toshi wondered whether the antidote had ever made it to his family. Whether it even worked.

"There," Ivan said, pointing to a figure being carried to the ramparts over the main gate. "That's Grace. They're building her pyre right there."

Toshi stared at Ivan. "They're really going to burn her?"

"Oh yes," Ivan replied as a sinister memory stole through him. "I hope that witch of yours is as strong as she seemed. I once saw Grace spend two whole days and nights on the pyre." He looked down at his hands and Toshi could have sworn he saw flames licking inside Ivan's eyes. "We chopped down every tree. Burnt all the switch grass. We even threw our clothes on the fire. And through it all she burned. Screaming. Laughing." When Ivan looked up again his eyes were sunken and haunted. "Grace lives for the pyre." He clapped Toshi on the shoulder, shaking himself. "I have serum to distribute and you have crossbows to steal." A thought occurred to him. "This would be a lot easier if we were stone kin."

Toshi was struck by the offer. "It would be an honor," he said.

When they touched each other's willstones Toshi was surprised

344

to find Grace was there at the forefront of Ivan's thoughts, but not Grace as they both knew her now. Toshi saw a backdrop of dusty mining towns, horse-drawn carriages, homesteaders in broad-brimmed hats and gingham prints, and Grace as a girl with long plaited hair, a buckskin dress, and beaded moccasins.

"That was a long time ago," Ivan said, drawing Toshi back to the here and now. "Come. We have a lot of work to do."

They went back downstairs, stopping in the room where Grace had learned to spirit walk in the hopes that they could help Red Leaf, but the shaman was gone. They continued on down to the lab where the forced calm had given way to pandemonium. Mala was nowhere to be found. The table she had been manning was tipped over, and vials were scattered all over the floor. People were pushing and shoving their way into the lab to grab handfuls of the serum and rush out. Toshi tripped over something and realized that he was stepping on a body.

Toshi pulled the inert woman out of the main flow of the mob and checked her pulse. There was a welt the size of goose egg on her neck. She was dead from a sting.

He looked out a window. Workers were swarming outside, coalescing into great clouds and descending on the most panicked people. When the cloud flew away and moved on to the next person, the dead body left behind would be covered in stings. One sting would be enough to kill a person in ten seconds, but the Workers were overreacting as much as the people were. Their hive was being invaded and they were turning on anything that was not them.

"Everyone, calm down," Ivan shouted, holding up his hands, but the mob was past listening.

"I need good climbers," Toshi shouted amid the rushing, grabbing confusion. Ivan called out two men by name.

"Avery! Michelson! Come with me," he ordered.

Two tall young men stopped trying to hold back the tide of people and came forward. Ivan had them gather up as many darts full of pesticide as they could carry and led them out the back way and through the twisting passages of the villa. There were no Workers indoors. They were all out on the streets, swarming.

They stopped at one of the many service storerooms. Ivan went to the dusty shelves littered with fishing poles, skis, tennis rackets and all other kinds of recreational equipment. He pulled down a large duffel bag. Inside were ropes and grappling hooks for climbing, which he distributed between them. Toshi, Avery, and Michelson looped the thin, strong rope over their shoulders and put the pesticide in the duffel bag.

"Toshi," Ivan called after them as they ran. Toshi stopped and looked back. "Good luck."

Toshi nodded. *You, too, old friend.*

When they hit the street, they saw that the situation had deteriorated further. Bodies lay here and there in the streets. Swarms of Workers were expanding and contracting in the air in a murmuration. They were chasing people indoors, and anyone left outside would be targeted.

Toshi's raiding party ran to the nearest watchtower. Storm clouds started forming into a wheel over the city and the sky turned an ominous shade of pewter. Grace was on her pyre, and her power was building. As the raiding party pounded down the streets Toshi felt a sharp sting on the back of his hand.

He started counting to ten.

Lily opened her eyes. She stood among the redwoods. Rowan was still clasping her hand.

Her army shifted out of the shadows of the ancient giants, their faces stark with awe. Jumping was a new experience for most of them,

346

and even for those who had done it before, the sight of the towering redwoods was enough to strike them dumb.

Tell them to calm down, Rowan said in mindspeak.

Lily did her best to explain, and to those claimed that couldn't understand, she did her best to comfort them.

Now. Tell them not to kill one another, Rowan added.

"Right," Lily breathed. She could feel all her claimed balking at being thrown together like this, and it wasn't just the ranch hands against the Outlanders anymore. The Pack hated the Pride. The Pride hated the raptors. The simians hated the humans. The insect Woven felt nothing, but everyone hated them. This wasn't an army. It was a melee waiting to happen.

What have I done?

Remind them why they're here, Rowan said in mindspeak. *Get them to focus on fighting the Hive.*

Lily felt a clamor rising in all of them. They would not accept this. The hatred between them went too deep.

"Wait," Lily whispered desperately to herself. She could feel control slipping away. Grumbling, shouts, and hisses rose up from the ranks. She could force them to work together. Control them. Bend them to her will. That would be the easiest way. That would be what Grace would do, maybe even what Lillian would do, too.

Lily was neither of those people, and she decided she never would be.

She ran to the highest point she could find—which happened to be the back of one of the raptors—and climbed up with a silent appeal to him to help her do this. She steadied herself against the raptor's enormous head and shouted what she only dared whisper before.

"Wait! Listen to me. You aren't enemies," she called. "Hear what I have to say before you all tear one another apart!"

"Listen," Rowan yelled.

"Listen!" Una echoed, backing him up.

Every face in the crowd turned to her. She looked out, taking it all in, searching for a place to start. Her claimed. They were all so different. They were together, but she still needed to find a way to unite them. She took a deep breath and began.

"I come from a world where people never know what it's like to be someone else. We can only imagine what it feels like to walk around in someone else's shoes. That's what we say, by the way—walk around in someone else's shoes—which is so small compared to what you can actually do here.

"In my world we don't know what it is to live a different life from the one we were given, to be a different race or gender, forget about being a different species. In my world we fear anyone who's different. We think those people are our enemies and that they want to take what's ours or destroy our way of life. We think like that because, well, what else are we supposed to think? We can't know someone else's mind like you can.

"Things should be so different here. But what do I see? The same division, the same fear, the same us-against-them mentality that I see back in my world. Walltop hates the Outlanders. Why? Because the city isn't large enough for everyone and Outlanders are always trying to sneak in illegally. Outlanders hate the Woven. Why? Because the Woven took their land. The Woven hate the humans. *Why?*" Lily paused, knowing this was the missing puzzle piece. "Because a human enslaved them and forced them to be killers. A human *created* them in order to tear this world apart.

"Your hatred isn't real. The things that divide you aren't real. They were created by greed. Someone has set you all against one another so she could profit. Someone has made it so you need walls—walls that divide you and make you weak so she can be stronger. This world has only one true enemy, and we can fight her. Here. Today. I brought you all together for this one purpose, but first you have to stop fighting one another. It's up to you. I'm not going to force you. The choice is yours."

Lily jumped down and rejoined Rowan on the ground. She felt the silence as deeply as she heard it. She waited. No one left. No fights started. Everyone just stood there, staring at her.

"What's going on?" she mumbled to Rowan.

"They're waiting for orders," he told her, eyes bright as he buried a laugh.

Lily panicked. "I have no idea what to do," she said.

"That's okay. I do."

Rowan turned. Tristan, Caleb, Una, and Breakfast were right behind him. Alaric and Pale One were right beside them. Rowan turned back around and pointed to a group of ranch hands on one side, and then at a bunch of wolves on the other.

"You start cutting down the trees, and you drag them into a pile," Rowan ordered. "Our witch needs a pyre." When no one moved, he started yelling. "Quickly! The Hive will be on us any minute now! Who has axes?"

Spurred into action, Woven and human alike started scurrying before Rowan's anger. He struck out into the disarrayed clusters of men, women, and Woven and started arranging them into groups.

As Rowan moved away from them, Lily felt a hand on her shoulder. She turned and saw Tristan.

"I need to talk to you," he said urgently, his eyes still following Rowan's back as he stalked away, barking orders.

"Now?" Lily asked, motioning to the utter chaos that was moments away from tumbling down upon her head.

"I've been trying to get you alone for weeks, but Rowan never leaves your side," Tristan said, dragging a hand through his hair.

"There's something I need to tell you. In case one of us doesn't make it. I need you to know something."

"What?" Lily asked, concerned, and recalling that every time Tristan had tried to speak with her alone lately, Rowan had appeared to interrupt and hurry them off in different directions.

"Rowan never meant to abandon the coven. He intended to go with us when we made the crossing. It wasn't his choice to stay behind." Tristan took a deep breath. "It was your Tristan's."

"What are you talking about?" Lily said, completely blindsided.

"When you woke up after being in the cage, do you remember how he didn't have a mark on him, but Caleb and I got the stuffing beat out of us when we tried to get your willstones from Rowan?" he asked. Lily nodded numbly. "Well, I cornered your Tristan and made him show me what happened. This is his memory."

. . . The three of us can hear Rowan making noises in his sleep. Caleb told me he has nightmares sometimes, but this is sad. He sounds like a child, whimpering and pleading. I wonder what he must have gone through as a kid to be like this, and I feel bad for the guy. Almost bad enough to stop this, but not quite.

I hang back and let the other Tristan and Caleb go rushing into Rowan's tent. Rowan barrels through the two of them quicker than I'd thought. He's terrifying, even without Lily's strength in him. Feral. I wince a little as he drops the other me. He starts to charge me and I back off, yelling.

"Whoa, take it easy! It's me."

His eyes clear and he seems to snap out of it. He runs his hands through his hair, looking at what he's unwittingly done to his stone kin.

"Didn't you tell them?" he asks me.

He already knows I didn't—if I had, they wouldn't have tried to jump him—but he can't accept it yet. It's hard to accept it when someone's set you up. He sits down heavily, his eyes skipping around, thinking.

"Why?" he asks.

I sit down next to him. I want to get this right so he understands. He's got to be the one to leave her or I don't stand a chance.

"Say I *did* tell them. Say I give them the whole story—that I was the one who told you in mindspeak to take her willstones away in that split second when Alaric was going to slit her throat. Then I tell them that you were going to break Lily out of her cage tonight while Alaric was away from camp, and we were all going to ride off into the frigging sunset together. What then?"

He looks at me, still not understanding.

"Do you know Lily at *all*?" I ask. "Because if you did, you'd know she'll never forgive either of us. If she ever finds out the truth, she's going to hate both of us for doing this to her, even if it was for her own good."

"No, she—" he starts to argue.

I cut him off. "Yes, she will. I've known Lily since kindergarten, and I've never seen her forgive anyone. Do you know I'm her only true friend in our world? That's because if someone picked on her for her red hair or her rashes or her weird mom, that person was never allowed to play with us again. She held a grudge against pretty much every person in our town. She pushed everyone away until I was the only person left in her life."

Uncertainty flashes in his eyes. There's only one nail left to drive into this coffin, and I hope it's enough.

"Now, what if Lily hates both of us?" I ask. "Who'll take care of her if she's sent us both away? Who's going to love her? She'll be alone, Rowan."

He drops his face into his hands. I don't know if he's crying or not, but I can't let that stop me. The guy had his chance with *his* Lillian and he blew it. He can't have mine. She was always supposed to be mine, since we were little kids. I feel bad for him, but getting Lily back is all that matters. I know I can make her happier than Rowan can. I know it.

He picks up his head. I don't see tears, but the hollowed-out look he gives me is even worse somehow. "Juliet says Lily wants to go west. You're going to need me. The coven's going to need me," he says. His voice is thin and lacking conviction.

"She won't want you there," I say.

"Still. I'll follow, just in case. She doesn't have to know."

And then he can swoop in and save everyone at the last minute. Be the hero. Win her love. What can I say to stop him? Maybe only the truth will work.

"Look, she's gotta hate someone for what we did. That's how she works. Let her hate you." I'm begging the guy now. "Give me a chance to make her happy. Stay away."

Finally he nods. He looks lost, like he just woke up in a room he doesn't recognize. I feel like shit about it, but at least she's mine . . .

The memory ended and Lily stood staring at Tristan. He looked ashamed but relieved for finally getting it off his chest.

"Why didn't you tell me before?" Lily asked, still too shocked to feel the hurt that some small part of her knew was coming eventually.

"For the same reason Rowan doesn't want me telling you now," Tristan said, seeming fed up with the whole thing. "Because your Tristan was dead and we didn't want to tarnish his memory. Because Rowan was convinced you'd still hate him anyway for not catching up with us in time to save him. Because you *don't* forgive and you never forget."

Lily couldn't look at him. She was too ashamed of herself. She blindly reached for Tristan's hand.

"Can you forgive me?" she asked. He made an uncertain sound

and she mustered the courage to glance up at him. "I'm sorry, Tristan. I'll try to change."

This wasn't the reaction he'd expected. "You're not angry?"

"No," she said. Lily squeezed his hand tightly and then let it go. "I have to find Rowan," she said, and ran into the throngs of people preparing for battle.

She felt her way to him, calling out in mindspeak, and quickening her pace until she was bumping into people as she passed. Everywhere she looked, scared people were girding themselves for war. Couples were embracing. Children were being separated from parents they might never see again. Friends were exchanging daggers and swearing oaths to look after the others' families if only one of them came back. Lily could hear it all as she ran past. Her claimed were whispering about their fears and their loves and their losses in her mind.

As she plowed on, seeing the surprised stares she was drawing, Lily finally figured out how he'd always been able to find her. She'd always know where he was because it was where she most wanted to be. Rowan was standing in a clearing surrounded by braves, distributing arms.

He spun around as she skidded to a stop a few feet from him.

"Rowan," she said.

Everyone dropped what they were doing to watch. Caleb, Tristan, Una, and Breakfast caught up with Lily a moment later and regarded her cautiously while she confronted Rowan.

"What happened?" he asked, his eyes worried, and the sword in his hand drooping by his side.

"Why didn't you tell me?" she asked, breathless.

"Tell you what?" he asked, and then confusion turned to understanding. His eyes flicked to Tristan. "You told her."

Lily strode forward, her cheeks red and her eyes shining with unshed tears. "How could you keep that from me? Especially after what Lillian did to *you*?" Her voice broke. Words like "hypocrisy" and "irony" floated around in her head. Instead she inarticulately blurted out, "It's like . . . the exact same thing only backward!"

She stormed right up to Rowan and he braced himself, like he thought Lily was going to hit him. Instead she threw herself into his arms and kissed him. After one stunned moment he dropped the weapon in his hand and lifted her up against his chest, holding her off the ground as he kissed her back.

"When this is over, you and I are going to sit down and tell each other every secret we're keeping from the other," Rowan said when he finally set her back down.

"Okay." She smiled up at him. "You go first," she said, winning a laugh from him.

"Ah, guys?" Una interrupted. "So glad you two worked it out, but we need a little more direction here. What's the plan?"

One quick squeeze that promised a proper reconciliation later, and Rowan released Lily.

"Tristan," he said, every inch the general again. "I want volunteers who can handle heights and who are good shots with a cross-bow to ride the raptors." He turned around and glared at the rabbit-like stares he was receiving from the ranks. "Step up! If you don't volunteer I'll hand you over to Una and she'll put you on the back of a lion." He grinned. "*If* the Pride doesn't decide to eat you first."

"You heard the man," Una repeated crisply as she clapped her hands, snapping the gawkers to attention. "Raptor riders with Tristan, Pride riders with me."

"Caleb. I need you to coordinate between Alaric and the Pack," Rowan said. "I'll introduce you to Alpha, the Pack's leader. Are you going to be okay fighting with the wolves?" Caleb nodded once. He didn't like his assignment, but he knew what was at stake. "They speak our language, you know. That's why I'm putting the Outlanders and the wolves together. I think we have more in common than you realize," Rowan told him. Caleb looked stunned by this for a moment and then he seemed to rethink it. Rowan turned to Breakfast. "And you—"

"Guard Lily while she's on the pyre," Breakfast finished for him. "This ain't my first rodeo."

"Exactly," Rowan said, and turned back to Lily, his demeanor softening. "Reach out to Lillian. Stay linked with her. The two of you are going to have to work as one for our armies to synchronize."

Lily called out to Lillian.

I'm here, Lily said. *My army is in the redwood grove.*

I'm climbing my pyre now. Keep your army hidden until I tell you to join us and then stay open to my call. You're going to have to jump your army out of the blast zone as soon as I tell you to.

Listen to me. You can't use the bomb, Lillian, and if you're counting on using it to save you in the battle you're going to die. Carrick—

Lily felt heat and pain as the fire rose around Lillian and their connection was severed as all of Lillian's concentration went into changing heat into force. Lily called her over and over, but Lillian didn't answer. She looked up at the swaying treetops, unsure if Lillian had understood her. Lillian's witch wind began to howl through the grove, whispering and moaning around the branches like ghosts summoned to the battlefield.

Lily looked around her, taking this one moment to be right where she was, right at that moment. Rowan was marshaling her army into shape. Men, woman, and Woven were running this way and that. Axes were being put to the trunks of the redwoods and every thump of the metal biting into the venerable wood was like a sin inside her heart. But this was war, and Lily knew that the trees were just the first of many to die this day.

Toshi, Lily called. *Where are you?*

She caught a glimpse of the streets blurring past as Toshi ran through Bower City.

I'm a bit busy at the moment, he replied. She could hear him counting in his head. He got to ten. *I'm not dead.* He seemed surprised by this.

Lily could feel sweat streaking down his back and the bubbling hysteria of a squashed laugh in his chest. He looked to his left and his right and she saw rough-looking men carrying rope on either side of him. Lily recognized them as hers by their willstones, and called each of them by name. *Avery. Michelson.*

We're trying to get crossbows from the Hive's lookout platforms so we can use the pesticide we developed, Toshi continued.

Does it work?

Don't know yet. But the antidote does.

They're still building my pyre, but I'll give you what power I can, she replied. *Where is the antidote?*

Ivan has it, Toshi replied.

Good. Let me know if you succeed with the pesticide, Lily told him. *I have an impossible task for you when you're done with that.*

Oh, good. My favorite.

Lily smiled to herself. She transmuted as much energy as she could spare and filled Toshi's, Avery's, and Michelson's willstones with force. She felt them revel in it and smiled. A wave of exhaustion hit her and she staggered to the side. Juliet caught her.

"You need to sit," Juliet said, leading Lily through the confusion and to a mossy rock.

"I just need salt," Lily said as she sat down. She looked over Juliet's shoulder and noticed that Alaric's painted guard had shadowed every step Juliet took.

"Alaric really meant it when he said you were going to stay out of the fight, didn't he?" Lily asked, gesturing to the guard.

"Yes." Juliet rolled her eyes. "I feel so useless, and so do they," she said, indicating her entourage.

Lily got an idea. "I need your help. I'm going to jump someone here, and he's going to have a whole bunch of antidote for the Workers' stings. Do you think they could help you distribute it? I'd need you to fan out and give it to as many as you can," Lily said.

"Definitely," Juliet said.

Lily reached out to Ivan in mindspeak and found him in his lab, frantically making more antidote and pesticide. She called his name softly.

Lily, he replied, surprised but polite as always. *Forgive me. I'm out of practice being someone's claimed.*

This is going to be a little strange for you, she told him in mindspeak. *But I need you to pick up as much antidote as you can carry.*

Ivan did as she asked and Lily jumped him to her. He appeared before her, his arms laden with bags full of vials.

"That was one of the most singular experiences I've ever had," he said with a quaver in his voice.

"Ivan, this is my sister, Juliet," Lily said, smiling. "She's going to help you distribute the antidote."

Ivan nodded at Juliet politely as he handed her what he carried. He then turned back to Lily. "Send me back to my lab," he asked. "I'll keep making it for as long as I can."

"Contact me when you've got more, and I'll jump you back here," Lily replied, and then sent him back to his lab.

Toshi looked up at the Warrior Sisters' platform, still wondering how he was supposed to get up there, when he felt a rush like he'd never experienced before. His body felt light, his head clear, and every sense was sharpened.

He heard Avery and Michelson groan. They felt it, too. The three of them met one another's eyes with small, secret smiles on their faces.

"So that's what all the fuss is about," Avery said, his smile breaking into a grin.

"I guess we'll die happy, then," Michelson added.

Toshi let out a shaky laugh and redirected their attention to the platform. It suddenly didn't seem difficult to climb at all. The three of them clambered up the bare scaffolding with ease. They didn't even need the rope.

The top of the platform was deserted. All the Warrior Sisters were at the perimeter. Toshi looked toward the tiny orange glow of Grace's pyre on top of the wall. Above her the Hive was swarming. A strange, circular cloudbank was forming in the darkening sky. It started to rotate over Grace's pyre, and then there was a pause in the mounting tension like the end of an inhale just before a scream. A single beam of light shot out of the pyre and into the sky.

The Hive was unleashed. They streamed over the wall and flew down upon the waiting army. A moment later, Toshi felt the ground shake and another beam of light pierced the sky from the direction of the battlefield. The Salem Witch answered Grace's call to battle.

"Here," called Michelson. Toshi went to him and saw crossbows hung neatly inside a wall box.

Toshi took down one of the crossbows, fitted a dart into the firing mechanism, and aimed over the side of the platform. Down below at street level, a swirling mass of Workers was flying past. Toshi shot the dart into the swarm. He heard a pop as the dart exploded in its center. Nothing happened.

"Damn," Avery said.

"What do we do now?" Michelson asked. "Do we go back to the lab?"

"Wait," Toshi said, holding up a hand.

The cloud of Workers seemed to be thinning, and a trail of dark specks was starting the litter the ground. Then all at once, the swarm fell out of the air, dead.

Toshi reached out to both Ivan and Lily. *It worked. The pesticide worked*, he told them.

Try to kill as many swarms inside the city as you can, Lily said. *The more you kill there, the less will be able to join the Warrior Sisters on the battlefield.*

We're on it, Toshi replied.

The raiding party stripped the box bare, tied the crossbows across their backs to climb down, and left them at the base of the tower before moving onto the next. Toshi passed Ivan an image of what they were doing so Ivan could send other rebels to gather the crossbows and start exterminating the Workers.

Toshi contacted Lily again. *What was that impossible task you were going to give me?*

I want you to go through the back door of the Hive and kill the Queen.

Ah. Toshi's insides liquefied.

You should be able to get to her easily. The Warrior Sisters are aboveground, fighting, Lily said, trying to give him confidence. She sent him images of how to get to the Queen.

"You two keep at this," Toshi said aloud as his team approached the next platform. "I'm going to need all the rope."

"Where are you going?" Michelson asked, taking the coil off his shoulders and passing it to Toshi.

Toshi didn't dare say it, he merely gestured to city center. "Our witch has given me an impossible task," he said.

He kept one crossbow for himself and took as many darts as he could. He left them to it and ran toward the Hearing Hall, pausing every chance he got to shoot down swarms of Workers.

The first wave of Warrior Sisters started flowing over the wall and raining down on Lillian's soldiers.

The sky over the battelfield darkened as the wheel of Lillian's storm clouds began to rotate above her. A ray of blindingly bright light shot up from Lillian's pyre into the center of the wheel, knocking everyone back with a pulse of energy.

Lily locked the iron-and-diamond cuffs around her wrists as she ran to her pyre. Rowan ran beside her, pulling her crown out of his satchel. When they got to the base he carried her up the uneven mountain of cut logs to the stake waiting at the top. Lily had never seen a pyre this high before.

"I have an ax crew stationed below with Breakfast to keep the fire well fed," Rowan told her hastily. He started threading the chains on the stake through the rings on Lily's cuffs. "Tristan will keep a squadron of raptors over you to repel any air attacks by the Warrior Sisters. Una will lead the Pride and the ranch hands on the left flank. Alaric, the Outlanders, and the Pack will be to the right. I'm leading the insect Woven straight up the middle."

"How will you lead them?" Lily asked. "The insects don't understand language."

"I've become stone kin with all the queens," Rowan said with a troubled look on his face. Lily stared at him, knowing how much it cost him to do that. "The point is," he continued, "they'd have to get through our entire army before they could get to you—"

Lily put her hands over Rowan's and made him look up at her. "I love you."

"And I love you." He placed the blackened crown on her head and kissed her hard, crushing her against him. "I'll be with you," he whispered, and then turned and climbed down.

Lily looked up. She could hear her chains, her breath, and the wind. High above her the tops of the redwoods rubbed up against the storm-dark sky. Thirty feet below, her army went about their frenetic last-minute arrangements for battle. Weapons were checked. Ranks were ordered. Strategies were concocted. Former enemies became stone kin to coordinate in battle. Only Lily stood alone. Waiting to burn.

She smelled it first—just a hint of smoke teased out from the pulpy smell of the wood, and then suddenly there was so much smoke she was choking on it. Her eyes streamed as she coughed and sputtered, her body bent double as she hung in her chains. The heat rose, and Lily knew three full seconds of terror.

Gift me, Rowan called out in mindspeak.

The heat began to build until Lily was shrieking. A hurricane wheel of her own began to form over the creaking redwoods until a boom sounded out and light shot up from Lily's smoke willstone.

It's nearly time, Lily, Lillian called. *When the Hive has committed all its forces to fighting my soldiers in the center, send yours out of the grove on all sides to surround us.*

I understand, Lily replied. Lily could feel Lillian's exultation in the throes of battle with her army, but her body was weak, and she was burning more than she should. *Lillian. There's something you need to know about the bomb.*

You can't convince me not to use it, Lillian replied.

I know. That's why I had Carrick dismantle it.

Lily felt Lillian's dismay, and then she Gifted her army and sent the screaming horde of men, women, and Woven onto the battlefield.

Toshi jerked to a halt when he heard the boom. He saw a third beam of light shoot into the bruised sky and knew that Lily's army had taken the field. Dread consumed him. They wouldn't last long if he didn't kill the Queen.

Toshi could feel echoes of agony and ecstasy from the rest of Lily's claimed as they hurled themselves into battle, and his feet turned on their own and started running. Feeling Lily's power in him, Toshi reached Hearing Hall in moments.

He ran through the forest of columns, a petrified echo of the redwoods surrounding Lily, and went to the door that opened into nothing. He tied the climbing ropes together and used them to ease himself down into the darkness. When he reached the end of his rope he let himself drop.

His magelight blazed out as he fell. When he finally hit the floor, he picked himself up and started running again.

Lily exulted.

She bounded across the field with her fearless Pride. She soared through the air with her fierce raptors. She swarmed across the ground with her frozen-souled insects. She led the charge with Rowan onto the field, thundering toward the struggling and dying Walltop soldiers, delirious with mad joy, and almost went back on her word. As Rowan tore into the leading edge of Warrior Sisters with his battalion of queens, Lily felt herself sliding toward taking all of him.

There was a part of him that wanted it, too. He wanted to know what it was to burn on the pyre. It was for this reason alone she resisted, even when he wouldn't have. She couldn't let Rowan burn.

Warrior Sisters cracked their cat-o-nine-tails whips, and when they couldn't use their whips they fought with their bare hands. Their movements were blindingly fast and brutal. They did not fight with punches and kicks, but rather they grabbed on to an opponent's limb and tried to rip it off or they'd fly up as high as they could, let go of their struggling victim, and let gravity do the killing for them. They attacked in concert with their Sisters, but they were as brutal with one another as they were with their victims. If one was losing a fight, the others did not waste their efforts on a lost cause. If one was winning, others joined her to end it quickly.

Workers swarmed, and they were felling Lillian's uninoculated soldiers by the dozens. Their swollen bodies hardly looked human, and the sight of them angered Lily. She contacted Tristan, who was engaged in an aerial battle with the Warrior Sisters.

Tristan—fly into the city, she ordered. *Gather rebels with crossbows. Shoot the swarms from raptorback.*

I'm supposed to stay over you and protect you, he argued.

Get that pesticide. Kill the swarms. My fire will protect me.

Lily wrapped her hands around her iron chains and held on as the logs beneath her turned to crumbling red coals. She called out to Breakfast for more wood and his team piled her pyre ever higher. She drew the heat into her crucible of a body and changed it faster and faster until all of her claimed were overflowing with power. Lily's army basked in her mounting strength, throwing themselves at the Warrior Sisters in frenzy, while Lillian's army began to falter.

Lillian! How can I help you?

I'm dying, Lily, and when I die it won't be quietly. You must take my claimed from me or they'll die with me.

I don't know how.

I'll give you everything I am. Everything but one part—the worst of me. That I'll take with me to my grave.

Lily's vision scoped out from her pyre, pulled up into the air, swirled over the battlefield, and spiraled down into Lillian's.

Clawing agony assaulted her. A thousand regrets rained down on her head. Every memory Lillian ever had, every mistake she ever made, every willstone she ever claimed, every love, and every hate she harbored in her heart transferred from Lillian to Lily in an instant.

All but one. Lillian kept Carrick for herself.

Watching as if from a great height, Lily saw Lillian lying atop her smoldering pyre, the fire nearly extinguished. Her skin was black with soot and streaked red with blood.

Come, Carrick. Carry me to our grave, Lillian called.

Toshi was lost.

He blundered through row after row of womb combs, his blood chilling at the thought of the horrors they unleashed. Desperate now, Toshi ran toward what he hoped was the back wall. His feet made a squelching sound and seemed to stick. He was standing in wax.

Relief over finding the hive quickly gave way to fear as he hurried down the ever-narrowing passageway. The smell of honey grew so strong it made him dizzy. He saw evidence that others had recently come this way in the wax. He followed the footprints left by Lily's coven to a bottleneck. He climbed through, his heart in his throat, and saw the Queen. She was writhing on her velvet throne, her body twisted and racked with pain.

Toshi hefted his crossbow, aiming it directly between her bulbous, rainbow eyes, and then lowered it. He forced himself to raise the muzzle of his weapon again. His hands shook as he watched her spasm and clutch at her pillow in mute agony. The healer in him wavered, and the one precious second he'd been granted passed him by.

Rough hands grabbed him and wrestled him to the floor, knocking his crossbow out of reach. Toshi saw male torsos under their insectoid heads. The drones had squat bodies that were thick and square as bricks. Bristling hairs stuck up from their shoulders and backs. As they tried to rip off his arms and legs, Toshi noticed their stunted wings would never fly.

He felt his limbs straining as they were pushed into unnatural positions, but they didn't break. Still full of Lily's power, Toshi fought back. He reached past the waving tubes in their mouths, grabbed ahold of their hairy, ovoid heads, and started wrenching them around. He rolled, and they rolled with him, pouncing on top of him in a pack and swarming over him.

The knot of them crashed through a wax wall and Toshi felt warm, sticky honey flowing over him. He jumped up to his feet, only to be knocked back again. More drones joined the fight as the sticky, bloody ball of them pushed through another wall. Toshi scrambled to get his feet under him and noticed that he was being pushed back and uphill, away from the Queen's chamber.

He threw himself against them, pushing and shoving and trying to make his way back as they formed a blockade to steadily inch him out of the hive. He dug in his feet, only to feel them sliding back in the wax. He killed one after another desperately, trying to get back to the Queen.

He tasted fresh air and felt earth under him as the pile rolled. The drones had evicted him from the hive.

Only two wheels of clouds darkened the sky. Only two beams of light pierced their centers. Tasting victory, the Hive surged forward, throwing themselves against their foes with reckless abandon.

Lily was torn. Half of her hung from her iron-and-diamond shackles. Half of her gasped for breath on a pile of ash.

Hang on, said one half of her to the other. *Survive this battle, and we can heal you. Toshi can save you.*

The part of her left in ashes spoke for the last time.

I have seen myself as many things. I have been the hero and I have been the villain. I may never be a hero again, but at least I can make my final act a heroic one.

I summon Carrick to me. He doesn't want to come, so I force him. He fights me, his limbs stiff, but my will is stronger. He picks me up in a gruesome parody of a bride and groom, and carries me into the redwood grove. He can feel how hot my skin is, and he knows what it means. He is not the first mechanic I've marched to his own death.

As we near the exit of the hive, we pass by a pile of drones fighting one of Lily's claimed. The one who can heal me. For a fleeting moment the thought of salvation shines a light in my dark mind. Toshi could cure me. Take all this pain away. I don't have to die, but the war would go on, and many others would die in my place.

I don't give Carrick the order to stop. We pass by my last chance at life and I grow hotter until my body bursts into flames. I smile. I choose this for all of them. I choose this for Rowan.

Carrick carries me into the mouth of the hive. Drones step up to stop us, but we have become a blowtorch that scares them away. Carrick would scream in agony if I would let him. But I won't.

Wax melts as we pass. The walls and ceilings drip and sizzle. We make our way to the Queen's chamber as the hive dissolves around us. Carrick carries me to the Queen and lays me down beside her. In death I will become the bomb that was denied me.

I think of Rowan. I'm grateful that my final thought is of love.

Time to die.

Half of Lily ended. The other half took refuge in her coven.

She saw Toshi. The fireball of Lillian's passing was heading right for him. It emerged from the hive and roared toward him. Lily jumped Toshi away before the fire could consume him.

She saw Rowan. He staggered, his heart skipping, when he heard the explosion. He knew Lillian was dead. He looked up into the sky and saw the Hive break ranks just when it was about to be victorious.

She saw Tristan. He wheeled his raptor and aimed his crossbow at a dark clump of Workers, but the tight swarm suddenly dispersed and flew off in every direction before he could fire.

She saw Una. Una felt her lion slow. She cut off one more Warrior Sister's head, and then turned to see what her lion was looking at. The enemy was running away.

She saw Caleb and Alpha. They stood back to back, fighting a ring of Warrior Sisters who surrounded them. Without warning, the Warrior Sisters dropped their whips and leapt into the sky.

She saw Leto. His left leg was broken. It stuck out awkwardly. He hauled himself up onto his right knee as he watched the retreat, unable to rejoice. Too many dead Walltop soldiers were scattered around him for this win to feel like victory.

She saw Breakfast. He swung his ax and blinked the sweat and soot from his eyes. He saw a flash overhead and paused to look up. The Hive was flying away.

Again, she saw Rowan. Alaric raced past him. He was running toward the main gate of Bower City—and to the pyre that was still ablaze on the ramparts.

Toshi dropped the arm he'd raised to cover his face against the oncoming fireball, and found himself on top of the Governor's Villa, standing next to the speaking stone.

He allowed himself one moment of utter confusion before he wrangled his wits back in order. *Ivan*, he thought, and raced down the stairs of the villa, through the maze of passages, and into the lab.

Toshi found Ivan, still furiously making pesticide as fast as he could, and pulled him away from the vats.

"It's over," Toshi told his old friend. "The Queen is dead."

Ivan's eyes drifted off to the side, the barest hint of a smile turning up the corners of his lips. His face suddenly darkened.

"Grace," he whispered. "Is she——?"

"Still on the pyre," Toshi answered before Ivan could finish asking. The two of them turned immediately and ran through the city to the wall.

Lily heard the hissing and tasted the wet smoke before she realized what was happening. Bucket after bucket of water was being shuttled to her and dumped over the last flames. Her pyre extinguished, Lily cut off the loop of power flowing between her and her claimed. She could hear voices all around as her claimed dug to get her out of the remnants of her colossal pyre.

Relief gushed through her, thick and sweet as honey, but a mountain of burnt and half-collapsed logs both surrounded and covered her.

"Hold on, Lily. I'm almost to you," Rowan said, his voice sounding muffled and far away.

"I'm here," she called out.

Water started dripping down through the collapsed tinder above her, black and greasy with charcoal. She heard the thunking of an ax as Rowan got closer and closer to her, and felt the half-joyful, half-frightened thrill thumping inside him.

It's over. We won, he kept whispering inside his mind, repeating it over and over, trying to convince himself it was true.

"There she is——I see her!" he shouted to the crew behind him. Lily saw Rowan throw aside his ax and start wrenching logs away with his hands.

Lily pulled her chains free from the crumbling stake, and reached up to him as he threw the last log aside and gathered her to him.

"We did it," he whispered, his voice breaking.

"We really did," she replied, smiling through tears as she clutched at him.

She couldn't seem to get close enough to him as they kissed and held each other. She pressed herself against him, laughing and crying and babbling all at once. They held each other in the center of the scorched pile while the rest of the timber crew cleared a path, wanting nothing but to stay exactly where they were.

Toshi and Ivan passed teams of rebels still combing the streets for swarms, their expressions cautiously hopeful that the battle was over. Bodies were already being collected and taken off the streets on stretchers. The injured were rushed to healers, who had set up triage centers every few blocks. Toshi noticed that not everyone getting help was a citizen. The restricted zone must have emptied into the city proper at some point during the battle, and Toshi held out hope that his family had made it across.

When they reached the wall they found that the stairs that zigzagged up to the top were cleared of the Warrior Sisters who usually guarded them. Toshi and Ivan took the stairs two at time. When they reached the top they heard voices. Someone had beaten them to Grace.

Grace's pyre steamed under her knees. She crouched atop the pile of doused logs, facing an Outlander with a fierce face. He threw the empty bucket he was holding aside and strode toward her.

"Grace Bendingtree. I am Alaric Windrider, sachem of the last tribe. I find you guilty of genocide," he declared.

Grace shifted on her knees, her shackles jingling softly. "Aren't I supposed to get a trial first?" she asked, smiling.

"No trial," he said. He pulled a knife out of his belt and her smiling face fell.

"Sachem? What are you going to do with that?" Toshi interrupted, edging his way forward uncertainly.

As Toshi frantically combed his mind for some kind of argument to present to Alaric, a small swarm of Warrior Sisters flew toward them and landed on the battlement. Alaric faced them, dropping into a fighting crouch and brandishing the long knife in his hand. Toshi felt Ivan push him back, protecting him, but the Warrior Sisters weren't looking at any of them. They went directly to Grace.

Grace looked at her former claimed uncertainly as they stalked toward her. "Wait," she said, holding out a tentative hand. "No—"

Before Ivan, Toshi, or Alaric could make a move, the Warrior Sisters snatched Grace up by her arms and legs, flew her past the edge, and let her go.

She screamed the whole way down. When she finally struck the ground and went still, the Warrior Sisters flew away.

"Grace is dead," Lily said as she and Rowan scrambled out from the extinguished pyre. Clouds of steam still rose around them, filling the air with fog. Fatigue was taking Lily over, and turning her legs to jelly.

"Alaric?" he asked. Lily shook her head and showed him what Toshi had just shown her.

"The Hive did it," he said, surprised.

"They had the most reason to hate her, I suppose," Lily replied. She narrowed her eyes at Rowan. "You knew Alaric ran up there to kill her, didn't you?" she asked.

"Yes." Rowan met Lily's eyes and held them. "And I was going to let him." Lily nodded, accepting it, and pulled his arm even tighter against her body. The subject was closed.

Rowan helped Lily out of the blackened crater, but she wouldn't let him carry her. No matter how much it hurt, she was going to walk away from this. As she minced through her claimed on her blackened feet, Lily passed Breakfast, still hefting his ax, his other arm draped over Una's shoulder. Una stood next to a lion, her hand resting casually on her new stone kin's back. Tristan grinned at Lily and Rowan and she grinned back. Beside Tristan, Caleb stood with Alpha. She noticed that they had exchanged knives and raised an eyebrow at him. Caleb shrugged to show he was as surprised as she was at this new alliance. Mary and Riley were there, scattered among the painted braves who still guarded Juliet. Lily even caught a glimpse of her mother, wandering among the stumps of the hacked-down trees. Samantha looked sad, as if she were mourning someone.

Lily leaned on Rowan's arm, limping her way across the battlefield. She met Leto in the middle.

"We took the field, Lady," he said, grimacing in pain from his broken leg.

"We did, Captain," Lily replied gravely, surveying the heavy losses Walltop had incurred.

"Stay where you are," Rowan told Leto. "We'll send a stretcher."

"There are few injured," Leto said, despite his condition. "The Warrior Sisters don't stop until either they're dead, or their opponent is."

"Thank you, Captain," Lily said.

"Lady," he replied, bowing awkwardly from his prone position as Lily passed.

Lily released Rowan's arm and walked across the battlefield on her own. She summoned healers to the battlefield to tend to the wounded. She called to them in mindspeak, and then jumped them directly to those who needed help.

Her feet, always the first to burn on the pyre, screamed at her with every step. Blood dripped down her hands and off the tips of her fingers from the raw skin under her jingling shackles. Her crown dug into her scalp, heavy and sharp, and she lifted her chin under its weight.

Lily stood in front of the gates of Bower City, her coven—both human and Woven—arrayed behind her. At her feet was the split corpse of the witch she had conquered.

"Open the gates!" Lily called out over Grace Bendingtree's dead body.

The heavy doors opened. Toshi stood on the other side with Alaric to his left, Ivan to his right, and Mala standing behind them. Mala's mouth was smiling but her eyes were glowering.

"The city is yours," Toshi said, relieved.

Lily walked through the gates and stumbled to her knees.

EPILOGUE

FORMER SPECIAL AGENT REBA SIMMS SWITCHED HER BAG of groceries to her left arm so she could reach her keys.

She let herself into her Dorchester apartment already knowing someone was in there. She'd always known when there was someone behind a wall or just around the corner. That ability to sense things she couldn't see or hear had saved her life more than once. Still, when she rounded into her kitchen, the gun she kept taped under the coffee table drawn and pointed in front of her, she was surprised to see who was waiting for her.

"Please, Agent Simms. There's no need for that," Lily Proctor said, gesturing casually to the gun.

She looked different. She was dressed in a spidery-black gown and her fiery-red curls were arranged carefully around what appeared to be a tiara made of some kind of twisted black metal. It was studded with white gems and Simms would bet anything they were real. Next to her sat Rowan Fall. He was dressed differently, more like a man than a teenager, in a crisp linen shirt and perfectly tailored jacket that hugged him with such devotion it appeared to be in love with him.

Not that Simms could blame it. There was something about his eyes and the way he looked into people, never just at them, that was embarrassingly alluring.

The extraordinary-looking pair of young people weren't holding hands, but the way they tilted ever so subtly toward each other made it clear that they didn't have to touch to feel the other. Even the air between them crackled with a kind of magnetism that had yet to be discovered by science, but that poets had been writing about since the dawn of time.

"We came here to offer you a position in a new city out west," Rowan said. Lily and Rowan looked at each other and shared a secret smile.

"Rowan and I have our hands full in Salem, but this new city needs some restructuring. It could use an honest and . . . ah . . . persistent woman like you." Lily frowned at the still-raised gun. "You know that doesn't work on me."

Simms lowered the gun a little, but she didn't put it away. "How did you get in here?" she asked. Probably the dumbest question out of the thousands that she had for Lily Proctor, but it was the first one that came out of her mouth.

"I'm a witch, Reba. And so are you," Lily replied.

Simms sat down at the kitchen table. She looked at her hands. They were thick, square things, not delicate like the soft, pale pair folded neatly in Lily's lap. They were hands that had gotten things done. Hard things. They were shaking now.

"I was always different," she said quietly. "Did I ever tell you that I used to get allergies?" She looked up at Lily, who shook her head once. "I did," Simms continued. "I got teased a lot for it, too. Or maybe it was just the other kids sensing something off about me."

Rowan waited to make sure Simms had finished before

continuing. "This place we want to take you is far. You won't be able to come back here."

"Carrick explained some of it to me," Simms said. Her mouth twisted around Carrick's name like it was a curse word. "He said I was better suited to your world."

"There's more to it than that," Lily said. "You've seen what I can do, and you're still searching for a way to repeat it. That was my mistake." Lily glanced down at her lap. "I had a teacher once—a shaman—who thought that the only way to fix a mistake he'd made was to send me back to my world, even after I'd seen his. But you can't unfire a bullet. You're a danger to this world now. You belong in ours." Lily frowned and looked at Rowan. "I think that's the first time I've ever agreed with Carrick," she said. The look they shared was more intimate than a kiss.

Simms couldn't help but stare. She'd never had that. Oh, she'd had men chase her for reasons neither of them could understand, but it had never worked out. There had always been something they'd wanted from her that she couldn't seem to give them. As the years passed it had been easier to not get involved. Better to live alone than go through the disappointment of not being enough and not getting enough back to ever feel satisfied.

"You won't be able to come back here, not unless Lily sends you," Rowan said clearly.

Simms snorted. "I have no husband, no kids, no family. I don't even have a job anymore after what happened with you. All I have is three appointments a week with a psychiatrist. And I actually look forward to them."

"You're not crazy," Lily said, her passion hushing her voice until it was barely above a whisper. "You're not sick. There's absolutely nothing wrong with you." Lily smiled at her. "You are *strong*, Reba.

Difficult to get along with," she added with a smile, "but all the best witches are."

Simms looked down at her hands again, and this time they were completely steady. "What would I have to do to go?" she asked.

Rowan stood and took a velvet jeweler's envelope out of the inner pocket of his jacket. "It will be difficult," he told her. "But only for a few moments."

"I can handle difficult," Simms replied confidently.

Rowan nodded, as if he expected as much, and opened the envelope to reveal a collection of lead-colored rocks.

"Just one more thing before we get started," Lily said. "You wouldn't happen to know where we could find that surfer, Miller, would you?"

ACKNOWLEDGMENTS

I'd like to thank Holly West and Jean Feiwel for their unswerving guidance and faith in this series. Working with you has been such a joy. To my stellar agent, Mollie Glick, I can only say wow. We did it while pregnant and breast-feeding and pumping. And on one memorable occasion we did it breast-feeding and pumping at the same time in a strange room with hospital equipment lying about because for some dumb reason we're still trapped in the dark ages when it comes to offering mothers a place to breast-feed their children. (But I digress.) Mollie, you make it look easy, and I'm in awe of you. A million thanks to Morgan Dubin, Elizabeth Fithian, Caitlin Sweeny, Mary Van Akin, Angus Killick, and everyone else at Macmillan for making this series happen. I also have to thank Elizabeth Nelson, Kaitlin Huwe, and Lillian Lopez for all their help with Pia while I frantically tried to finish this book while caring for a new baby. To Robyn Shwer and Stephanie Aoki—you kept me sane while wacky hormones did their best to turn me into a crazy person. And, of course, all my love to Albert and Pia.

THANK YOU FOR READING THIS
FEIWEL AND FRIENDS BOOK.

THE FRIENDS WHO MADE

WITCH'S PYRE

POSSIBLE ARE:

JEAN FEIWEL, *Publisher*

LIZ SZABLA, *Editor in Chief*

RICH DEAS, *Senior Creative Director*

HOLLY WEST, *Editor*

DAVE BARRETT, *Executive Managing Editor*

RAYMOND ERNESTO COLÓN, *Senior Production Manager*

ANNA ROBERTO, *Editor*

CHRISTINE BARCELLONA, *Associate Editor*

EMILY SETTLE, *Administrative Assistant*

ANNA POON, *Editorial Assistant*

Follow us on Facebook or visit us online at mackids.com.

OUR BOOKS ARE FRIENDS FOR LIFE.